Praise for *New York Times* bestselling author Kat Martin

"Fans of Martin's Raines of Wind Canyon trilogy are going to love meeting more of this testosterone-and-honor-laden family…"

—*RT Book Reviews* on *Against the Storm*

"Kat Martin is a fast gun when it comes to storytelling, and I love her books."

—*New York Times* bestselling author Linda Lael Miller

"Kat Martin is a very gifted writer who takes you from the beginning to the end in total suspense."

—*Fresh Fiction* on *Against the Wind*

Praise for *New York Times* bestselling author B.J. Daniels

"B.J. Daniels is at the top of her game…the perfect blend of hot romance and thrilling suspense."

—*New York Times* bestselling author Allison Brennan

"Daniels is truly an expert at Western romantic suspense."

—*RT Book Reviews*

Kat Martin is a *New York Times* bestselling author of more than fifty historical and contemporary romance novels. To date she has over fifteen million copies of her books in print in seventeen countries, including Sweden, France, Russia, Spain, Japan, Argentina, Poland and Greece. Kat and her husband, author L. J. Martin, live on their ranch outside Missoula, Montana, and spend winters at their beach house in California. Kat invites you to visit her website at katmartin.com.

B.J. Daniels is a *New York Times* and *USA TODAY* bestselling author. She wrote her first book after a career as an award-winning newspaper journalist and author of thirty-seven published short stories. She lives in Montana with her husband, Parker, and three springer spaniels. When not writing, she quilts, boats and plays tennis. Contact her at bjdaniels.com, on Facebook or on Twitter, @bjdanielsauthor.

New York Times Bestselling Author

KAT MARTIN

AGAINST THE STORM

HARLEQUIN® BESTSELLING AUTHOR COLLECTION

ISBN-13: 978-1-335-01632-4

Against the Storm

Copyright © 2018 by Harlequin Books S.A.

The publisher acknowledges the copyright holders of the individual works as follows:

Against the Storm
Copyright © 2011 by Kat Martin

Wanted Woman
Copyright © 2004 by Barbara Heinlein

Recycling programs
for this product may
not exist in your area.

HARLEQUIN®
™ www.Harlequin.com

Printed in U.S.A.

CONTENTS

Visit the Author Profile page
at Harlequin.com for more titles.

AGAINST THE STORM

Kat Martin

To my personal assistant and friend, Rita Michell,
for her many years of hard work and support.
And for making all the hard work fun.

Chapter One

Snow Dogs. Trace Rawlins sat at a table in back of the Texas Café thinking of his client and her white rapper husband, Bobby Jordane, the lead singer of the wildly successful rap music group, the Snow Dogs.

It seemed the perfect name for the mangy group, who sang about decadent society yet seemed to be the root of the problem. Only Bobby was married, his beautiful wife of the last three years was a creamy cocoa-skinned African American. Why she had ever married the guy, aside from his seven-figure bank account, Trace couldn't imagine.

Apparently, Shawna had come to the same conclusion, for she sat a few tables away next to her attorney, Evan Schofield, there for a meeting with Bobby.

Bobby Jordane was a wife beater par excellence, and he was extremely unhappy that Shawna had filed for divorce. But Schofield had managed to set up a meeting at a neutral location kept secret from the media, in the hope something could actually be accomplished.

The restaurant was old and narrow, with wooden floors and a long, varnished-wood lunch counter, a place for locals where a guy like Bobby wouldn't even be recognized. This time of day, the lunch crowd was gone and it was too early for dinner patrons. Only two other tables were occupied, one by an older man and his wife drinking chocolate shakes, another by two young women eating hamburgers. One of them was a foxy redhead Trace tried not to notice, but his gaze wandered back to her again and again.

Unfortunately, he seemed to have a penchant for trouble where redheads were concerned.

He returned his thoughts to the meeting at hand, which was supposed to include only Bobby and his attorney, Shawna and Evan Schofield, Trace's longtime friend.

But Bobby was a hothead, and Evan was no fool. He didn't trust Bobby, and neither did Trace. Everyone in Houston had read about the couple's fiery clashes and Bobby's out-of-control behavior, which recently had landed him in jail. Shawna had threatened to file a restraining order, and Evan had hired Trace, a private detective and the owner of Atlas Security, to keep a protective eye on his client.

The bell above the café door rang, flipping the little ruffled curtain above the glass. True to form, Bobby sauntered in without his attorney, just the other two obnoxious members of the Snow Dogs.

Clyde "The Mountain" Thibodaux hailed from New Orleans. Big, bald and tattooed, he was bare-chested beneath his leather vest. A small black goatee clung to his chin.

Lenny Finks, known to his fans as Lenny the Sphinx, was the nerd of the group. Skinny and homely, with kinky auburn hair, he was the talent behind the act, the guy who wrote the music, though Trace refused to call it that. Lenny was harmless, except for the viperous tongue he used to lash at the group's critics. He was a necessary component and the reason for the group's unbelievable success.

Bobby himself was as tall as Trace, about six-two, and as lean and solidly built. Having taken years of martial arts, Bobby thought he was a tough guy. Trace flicked a glance at the bruises on Shawna Jordane's beautiful face, clamped down on a surge of anger and wished he could show him ex-Ranger tough.

Instead, he tipped back his white straw cowboy hat, shifted in his chair and sipped his coffee, his gaze fixed on Bobby, who swaggered over to Shawna's table, his friends close behind.

"Hey, babe."

"Hello, Bobby." Her voice held the faint edge of fear.

Bobby turned a hard look on the man beside her. "So…*Evan*…you wanted me to come down here so we could have a little chat. Is that right?"

The lawyer, a slender man with sandy brown hair and intelligent eyes, sat up a little straighter in his chair. "I was hoping we might be able to make some progress in the matter of your divorce," he said.

Bobby shifted, his legs splayed in a belligerent stance. "You get my wife to file for divorce and you want me to come here so we can *talk?*" Reaching out, he grabbed Evan by his red-striped power tie and hauled him to his feet. Shawna screamed and Trace went into action.

Tossing Lenny out of the way like the skinny little runt he was, he reached out and grabbed hold of the back of Bobby's black, silver dragon T-shirt. Trace spun him around, waited an instant for Bobby to throw the first punch, then ducked and nailed him solidly in the jaw. Bobby went down like a sack of wheat, his head hitting the wooden floor with a melonlike thump that had his eyes rolling back in his head.

"You son of a bitch!" Clyde's blunt, meaty hands balled into fists as he lumbered forward, swinging a roundhouse punch meant to send a man to his knees. Trace ducked, turned a little and threw a straight-from-the-shoulder blow that sank four inches into the big man's stomach. Clyde grunted, doubled over, and Trace took him out with an uppercut to the chin.

Blood gushed from his nose and Clyde flew backward, knocking over a table and sending the surprised older couple scrambling out of the way. It was exactly the kind of thing Evan Schofield had hoped to prevent when he had hired Trace.

"Sorry, buddy."

Evan held up a hand. "Not your fault. I should have known this wouldn't work." He grinned. "Besides, it was worth it to see Bobby get what he had coming."

Shaking off the ache in his hand, Trace reached down and picked up his cowboy hat, settled it once more on his head. Lenny stood next to Bobby with his mouth gaping and his eyes wide. "Y-you shouldn't have done that."

"You don't think so?"

"Bobby...Bobby's gonna be really mad."

Trace chuckled softly. "If you're smart, you'll get him out of here before somebody calls the police. He doesn't need any more trouble."

Evan pulled out Shawna's chair. "Let's go."

She rose shakily to her feet and turned to Trace. "Thank you, Mr. Rawlins. You have no idea how good that made me feel."

A corner of his mouth edged up. "Oh, I think I do."

Shawna turned and started walking, but before she had reached the door, a camera flashed, capturing her retreat. Then the photographer turned toward the man moaning softly on the floor. The camera flashed again and again, taking photos of Bobby Jordane that would be wildly embarrassing to a guy with an ego as massive as his.

Trace inwardly cursed. The redhead. Just as he'd figured, they were nothing but trouble.

Striding toward her, he reached out and jerked the camera from her hands, turned it around and deleted the last series of digital photos.

"Hey! What do you think you're doing? You can't do that!"

"Nice camera," Trace said. Walking over to the lunch counter, he handed it to Betty Sparks, the owner of the café.

The sexy redhead raced along behind him. "Listen, whoever you are—that's my camera! You can't just—"

"I just did. And you can have it back as soon as they're gone." Trace tipped his hat to the redhead and her friend, a tall, svelte brunette a year or two older. "Have a nice afternoon, ladies."

Turning, he strolled out of the café.

* * *

"Did you see that? Oh, my God!" The brunette's attention followed the man who strode down the sidewalk outside the window. "Who was that gorgeous hunk?"

Maggie O'Connell's gaze jerked toward the window just as the tall, lanky cowboy in the white straw hat disappeared from view. "What are you talking about? That bastard just ruined my pictures. Bobby Jordane and his estranged wife? You know how much photos like that are worth?"

Maggie turned at the sound of a groan, saw the guy with the kinky hair—Lenny the Sphinx, his fans called him—help Bobby to his feet. Clyde the Mountain swayed upward until he was standing. Wordlessly, the small group staggered toward the door.

Maggie looked longingly at the lady who held her camera, but the older woman just shook her head.

Maggie sighed. She wouldn't be getting photos of Bobby Jordane sprawled on the old plank floor, beaten to a pulp. Not today.

"I hate to remind you, but you aren't the tabloid type," said her best friend, Roxanne De Mers. "You didn't come here to take pictures. You came for a late lunch with a friend. It just turned out to be a little more exciting than we planned."

Roxy swung back to the window, watching the rap stars as they made their way to the long white limo waiting out front. "I wonder who he was."

Maggie didn't have to ask who her friend was talking about. The cowboy was, at the very least, impressive. Tall and lean, with wide shoulders and slim hips, he had thick, dark hair neatly trimmed, golden-brown eyes and a set of biceps that were impossible to miss.

Still, she didn't appreciate his interference in her business. As the limo door closed, shutting the three men inside, she walked over to the counter to collect her camera, which the broad-hipped woman readily handed back to her.

"So who was he?" Maggie asked, nodding toward the window. "The Lone Ranger out there...what was his name?"

"You a reporter?"

"I'm a photographer. Mostly I do outdoor shots. I just saw an opportunity and took it—or tried to."

"Sorry it didn't pan out."

"Me, too. I can always use a little extra money."

"Name's Betty Sparks," the woman said. "Me and my husband, Bill, own this place."

"Nice to meet you, Betty. I'm Maggie O'Connell. You make a great burger."

"Thanks."

The woman, who was in her late fifties, with a cap of short, curly gray hair, tipped her head toward the door. "His name's Trace Rawlins. Owns Atlas Security. He's a private investigator."

Walking up beside Maggie, Roxanne sighed dramatically, a hand over her heart. "I think I'm in love."

"The redhead's got a better chance," Betty said. "Trace has a weakness for 'em."

"No, thanks. I don't do cowboys."

Betty chuckled. "If I was twenty years younger, I'd dye my hair."

Maggie laughed. "How much do we owe you?" She walked over to the purse hanging on the back of her wooden chair and started digging for her wallet.

"On the house," Betty said. "It's the least I can do."

Maggie smiled. "Thanks."

"You new in the neighborhood?"

She nodded. "I just bought one of those town houses they built a few blocks away. Vaulted ceiling upstairs. Good north light, great place to work, you know?"

"Welcome, then. Maybe we'll see you again."

"If it's always this much fun in here," Roxanne said, "I'm sure you will."

Betty just laughed.

Maggie put her Nikon back in its case and slung the straps of the camera bag and her purse over her shoulder. Roxanne tossed a couple bills on the table for a tip, and the two walked out the door.

"You know that trouble you been having?" Roxy said.

Maggie paused. "What about it?"

"That cowboy…he's in the security business and he's an investigator. He might be able to help you."

Maggie started to argue, to say she didn't need any help. Then she thought of the way Trace Rawlins had handled those three men. "I hope it doesn't come to something like that."

But it might and both of them knew it. For more than a month, someone had been following her, phoning her and hanging up, leaving messages on the windshield of her car. So far it hadn't been more than that, but it was frightening just the same.

When she got home, she was going to look up the number for Atlas Security.

And write it down beside Trace Rawlins's name.

Trace returned to the Atlas Security office on Times Street. He lived in a house in the University District not far away, a place with a yard for Rowdy, his black-and-white border collie, with big shady trees and an old-fashioned, covered front porch. When his dad died, Trace had inherited the house along with the business, a company his father had started when he first got out of the army.

Seth Rawlins had been a Ranger, a tough son of a bitch. Following in his footsteps, Trace had also enlisted and become a Ranger, figuring on a career in the military. Then six years ago, his dad had been killed in a car accident and Trace had come home to take over the business as he knew his father would have wished.

He slowed his dark green Jeep Grand Cherokee, pulled into the parking area in front of his office and turned off the engine. Recently, he had purchased the two-story brick structure—or rather, he and the bank owned it together until he paid off the mortgage. Which, since his profits were up and he was making double payments, he hoped wouldn't take too long.

In the years since he'd taken over his father's business, he had doubled the size of the company and opened a branch in Dallas. As a kid, with his dad gone much of the time, he had been raised on his grandfather's ranch, a place where hard work was expected of a man. Trace still owned the ranch, but it was leased out to a cattle company now. He only went out there once in a while, to check on the old house and the acreage he'd retained around it, but he always enjoyed the time he spent in the country.

He wiped his feet on the mat in front of the office door and stepped inside. The walls were painted dark green and the place was furnished simply, with oak desks for his staff and oak furniture in the waiting area.

Framed photos of cattle grazing in the pastures on the ranch hung on the walls.

He looked over to the reception area. "Hey, Annie, what's up?"

Seated behind her desk, his office manager, Annie Mayberry, glanced up from typing on her computer.

"You got a couple of calls, nothing too exciting." Annie was in her sixties, with frizzy gray hair dyed blond, and a rounded figure from the doughnuts she loved to eat in the morning.

"Maybe you could give me a hint," Trace drawled.

She pulled off her reading glasses. "You got a call from Evan Schofield. He says Bobby Jordane is threatening to sue you for assault. Evan says not to worry about it. Bobby couldn't stand for anyone to find out he got his—I'm quoting here—'ass whipped' the way he did."

Trace chuckled, but Annie's penciled eyebrows went up. "So you got in a fight with Bobby Jordane?" Disapproval rang in her voice. "I thought you'd outgrown that kind of thing." Annie had worked for his father before Trace had taken over. She had mothered Seth Rawlins, who had lost his wife when Trace was born, then mothered Trace, since he didn't have one.

"It wasn't exactly a fight. More like a discussion with fists. Mostly mine." Absently, he rubbed his bruised knuckles.

"You know you're getting way too old for that rough stuff."

"I'll keep that in mind." She was a small woman, but feisty. She didn't take guff from anyone, including him, and that was exactly the way he wanted it. "What else have you got?"

"The Special Olympics called looking for a donation. I phoned the bookkeeper, told her to send them a check."

"Good. What else?"

"Marvin's Boat Repair called. Joe says he's finished working on your engine. *Ranger's Lady*'s running like a top."

Trace nodded. "I think I'll go down to Kemah for the weekend." As often as he could manage, Trace made the forty-mile trip to where he docked his thirty-eight-foot sailboat. He loved being out on the water. There were times he wondered if being a SEAL wouldn't have been a better fit than being a Ranger. But then he wouldn't have met Dev Raines and Johnnie Riggs, two of his closest friends, and guys like Jake Cantrell.

"Jake called," Annie said as if she read his thoughts, which she seemed to have a knack for doing. "He's taking a job down in Mexico for a while. He'll be gone at least a couple of weeks, maybe more."

Jake had come to Houston with Trace after they'd finished a rescue mission with Dev and Johnnie that took them into Mexico. Cantrell, a former marine, mostly freelanced, hiring himself out as a bodyguard for executives who worked for big corporations. He had worked in the Middle East but specialized in South America. Jake did pretty much anything that wasn't illegal and paid him plenty of money.

"That it?"

Annie handed over three more messages. "One's a potential client. You'll need to call him back. And Hewitt Sommerset called." He was CEO of Sommerset Industries. "He wants to talk to you about that report you just finished."

Hewitt believed one of his employees was embezzling funds. The surveillance equipment Atlas installed had proved he was right.

"I'll call him right now."

"The third message is from Carly. If I were you, I'd lose that one."

He scowled, stared down at his ex-wife's name scrolled on the paper. "Anything important?"

"The usual. Said she just wanted to hear the sound of your voice."

Trace crumpled the note and tossed it into the trash can beside Annie's desk. For some strange reason he was a magnet for needy women. It was no surprise he had married one. He'd been divorced from Carly nearly four years, something the petite redhead had a way of forgetting.

Trace walked past Annie's desk into the main office area. Sol Greenway was working away at one of his three computers. At twenty-two, Sol was Atlas's youngest employee and a near genius when it came to electronics. Sol handled background security checks, security problems, information retrieval, online forensic services, and just about anything else that had to do with computers.

In the middle of the office, Ben Slocum and Alex Justice, both freelance investigators, sat behind their desks. Ben had his cell phone pressed against his ear. Alex was cleaning his Glock 9 mm.

"How'd it go with Arnold Peters?" Trace asked Alex.

"I took him the photos. His wife was seeing some oversexed football player. Peters took one look, broke down and cried like a baby."

"Why the hell do they hire us? They say they want

the truth, but what they really want is for us to tell them they're wrong and everything at home is just peachy."

Alex's grin cut a dimple into his cheek. "Far as I'm concerned, the best thing to do is stay single."

Trace thought of Carly and the trail of men she'd ushered in and out of his house while they were married. "You can say that again."

Continuing on, he went into his office and closed the door. He needed to return Hewitt's call. The investigation was over, but Trace liked the guy and knew Hewitt was taking the information hard. The embezzler was his son-in-law.

Trace had a few other calls to make, but he didn't personally handle as many cases as he used to. These days, he could pick and choose, and since the weekend was coming up, he would probably give anything new to Ben or Alex.

Trace imagined himself stretching out on the deck of the *Ranger's Lady* in the warm Texas sun, hands behind his head and catching a few rays.

He smiled.

Sounded like the perfect plan.

Chapter Two

Maggie O'Connell walked out of her newly purchased town house and headed for her red Ford Escape hybrid parked in front. She loved the car, which got over thirty miles to the gallon, loved the room in the back for the cameras, tripods, meters, lights and miscellaneous equipment she used in her work.

At twenty-eight, Maggie had achieved an amazing amount of success as a photographer. What had started as a hobby while she went to college as an art major on a partial scholarship had ended up a career.

Part of it was luck, Maggie admitted. After graduation from the University of Houston, she had managed to snag a part-time job as an assistant to Roger Weller, a renowned Texas photographer—work that gave her an invaluable education in the field and also time to shoot the outdoor scenes that had become her trademark.

Weller helped her get her first gallery exhibition, which was surprisingly well received. Several more shows followed and her clientele grew. Now her photos hung in some of the most prestigious galleries in Houston, Dallas and Austin.

Her mind on her upcoming show at the Twin Oaks Gallery and the photos she intended to shoot that afternoon, Maggie had almost reached her car when she jerked to a shuddering halt. Setting her camera bag at her feet, she reached a shaking hand toward the scrap of paper pinned beneath the windshield wiper. Very carefully pulling it free, she began to read the message.

My precious Maggie,
How long before our destinies are fulfilled? When will you understand that your fate is entwined with mine and I am the only one who can give you the peace you need?

Maggie glanced frantically around. Only two other cars were parked in front of the six recently completed town house units where she lived, a Toyota Camry and a Chevy Camaro. Both vehicles were empty. The breeze ruffled the leaves on the freshly planted shrubs in the flower beds out front, and a couple of teenagers rolled by on their bicycles. No one who looked like he might have left the note.

She stared down at the torn slip of rough brown paper, which matched the two others she had already received. She had hoped, after moving into the condo two weeks ago, that whoever had been leaving the creepy messages would stop.

She hoisted her camera bag over her shoulder, holding the note with just two fingers in case the man had left prints. She scanned the lot once more for anyone who seemed out of place, but no one was there.

Maggie hurried back inside her town house, the paper fluttering in her hand, her stomach a little queasy. Easing her camera bag to the floor, she closed the front door and leaned against it. After couple of steadying breaths, she opened her purse and dug out her cell phone and pulled up her best friend's name.

She hit the send button, and with every unanswered ring, her anxiety grew.

Roxanne finally picked up.

"Roxy? Rox, it's Maggie. I—I got another note. It was under the wiper blade on my car."

Her friend softly cursed. "Where are you?"

"I'm back inside my house. I looked around the parking lot. No one was there."

"Listen to me, Maggie. You need to take that note to the police. What was the name of that police lieutenant you talked to before?"

"Bryson. But he isn't going to help me. He doesn't believe me. That isn't going to change."

"It might. You have this note and the two you got before."

"I didn't keep the first one. I thought it was just a prank."

But it wasn't really a matter of having the notes as proof. It wasn't a matter of the police believing her. The cops were punishing her for a crime she had committed years ago.

A crime she was indeed guilty of committing.

"I won't go back there," she said. "I won't be humiliated that way again."

A long pause ensued. Roxanne was one of the few people who knew that as a teenager, Maggie had falsely accused the high school quarterback of rape.

At sixteen, she'd been stupid and irresponsible. The truth of it was she'd had sex that night with Josh Varner, though it certainly wasn't rape. She had encouraged the handsome football player, not fought him, but she'd been frightened of her dad's reaction when he found out.

"All right," Roxanne finally said, "if you won't go to the police, go see that private detective, the guy who runs Atlas Security."

"Who, Rawlins?"

"You have to do something to protect yourself, Maggie. You don't know how far this guy might be willing to go. Maybe Trace Rawlins can help."

Maggie didn't like it. The cowboy seemed cocky and far too self-assured. Worse yet, she didn't like the jolt of attraction she'd felt when he looked at her.

But she didn't like the snide remarks and sideways glances she had gotten at the police station, either.

Josh Varner was the son of a Houston police officer who was now a captain in the vice squad. Hoyt Varner had a score to settle for the unfair trouble she had caused his son years ago.

In a way Maggie didn't blame him.

"If you won't call him, I will," Roxanne said from the other end of the phone, jarring her back to the moment.

"All right, all right, I'll call."

"You want me to come over?"

"No, I'll be fine. I was just on my way to the grocery store, but I guess that can wait."

"Yeah, I guess it can."

Maggie ignored the sarcasm.

"Call me after you talk to him," Roxanne said.

"I will."

"Call him right now. Promise me."

"I said I would, didn't I?"

Roxanne signed off and Maggie hung up the phone. She glanced around the town house, which was still stacked with boxes she hadn't yet unpacked. Walking over to the breakfast bar separating the living room from the kitchen, she picked up the address book lying on the counter next to the phone and flipped it open.

On a yellow sticky note pressed inside the vinyl cover, she had printed the name Atlas Security. The address on Times Street was there, along with the company phone number and Trace Rawlins's name.

She stared at the yellow square of paper, then snatched it out of the address book. The office was in the University District, not that far away. Picking up the *People* magazine she had been reading while she drank her coffee that morning, she very carefully laid the note from her windshield inside the cover and closed it. With the yellow sticky note in hand, she grabbed her purse and headed back to her car.

As she crossed the lot, she scanned the area for anyone who might be watching, but whoever had left the note was gone. Maggie climbed into her little SUV and cranked the engine. As it began to purr, she shifted into gear and drove out of the lot, searching to the right and left, but seeing nothing out of the ordinary.

It didn't take long to find the brick building with the neatly printed Atlas Security sign on the front. Maggie parked the Escape, picked the magazine up off the passenger seat and got out of the car. She paused when she reached the front door.

Maybe Trace Rawlins wouldn't help her. Maybe just like everything else she had done in her life, she would have to find a way to handle this alone.

She drew in a shaky breath, thinking maybe this time money would solve the problem. Maybe—for a price—she could find someone willing to help.

Trace reached for his coffee mug and realized his coffee had grown cold. Seated in the chair behind his desk, he'd been going over some upgrades he wanted to install in the alarm system in the library at Rice University, one of the company's longtime clients. He looked up at the sound of Annie's voice.

"Someone here to see you," the older woman said. She tucked the yellow pencil in her hand above an ear. "Her name's Maggie O'Connell."

"O'Connell. Doesn't sound familiar. She say what she wanted?" He had been hoping to leave for home within the hour, pack up his gear and his dog and head for the shore.

"She didn't say, but you'd better watch out." Annie didn't bother to hide her grin. "She's a redhead."

He ignored a trickle of irritation. Annie knew his penchant for fiery-haired women and the trouble more than one of them had caused him over the years. And she didn't hesitate to goad him about it.

On the other hand… "Send her on in."

He stood up as the lady walked through the door. Five-four at most, slender yet curvy in all the right places. Once he got past the great body in snug jeans and a T-shirt with a Kodak ad on the front that read A Picture Is Worth a Thousand Words, he recognized her in a heartbeat.

The photographer he had clashed with three days ago in the Texas Café.

"Well, we meet again," he drawled. "I hope you aren't here because Betty wouldn't give you back your camera."

"Betty gave it back. She seemed like a very nice woman."

He thought of the scene at the café, the sizzling temper the redhead had unleashed when he had deleted her photos, and amusement touched his lips. "What can I do for you, Ms….O'Connell, was it?"

"That's right. After our little…disagreement, Betty mentioned you were a private investigator."

"That I am. You need something investigated?"

"Actually, I do."

He motioned for her to take a seat in one of the two dark brown leather chairs opposite his big oak desk, and sat back down himself. "Why don't you tell me how I can help you?"

She opened the *People* magazine he hadn't noticed she carried, being distracted by her nicely rounded breasts and shapely little behind. And there was all that glorious red hair.

With the magazine nestled in her lap, she opened the first page, then used the tips of her fingers to pick up a piece of brown paper that looked as if it had been torn from a grocery sack. Reaching over, she set it on his desk.

"Someone's been leaving notes like this on my car. This is the third one I've found. Whoever is doing it is beginning to scare me. I thought maybe I could hire you to find out who it is and make him stop."

Trace rose from his chair, leaned over and turned the

paper around to face him, being as careful as she had been. If there were fingerprints on the note, he didn't want to smudge them.

My precious Maggie,
How long before our destinies are fulfilled? When will you understand that your fate is entwined with mine and I am the only one who can give you the peace you need?

He didn't like the tone. He could understand why the lady might find the notes upsetting.

He sat back down in his chair. "You need to call the police, Ms. O'Connell. They'll make a report of the incidents and keep an eye out in your neighborhood for whoever may be leaving these."

"I've been to the police. It hasn't done any good. I want to know who this is and I want him to stop."

"And you think I can do that for you?"

"I saw the way you handled those three men. I imagine you could take care of this guy if you wanted to."

"I don't assault people for a living. That isn't my job. On the other hand, if my client is in danger, sometimes steps have to be taken."

She seemed to mull that over. "I guess what I'm saying is I'd like to hire you. Your receptionist told me what you charge, and that would be fine. If I'm your client and something happens, you would be obliged to protect me."

His gaze ran over her, the smooth skin and stubborn jaw, the big green, troubled eyes, the red hair curling softly around her shoulders.

He cleared his throat. "I'll need to see the other notes before I decide."

She bit her bottom lip. She wore peach-colored lipstick and her mouth was full and perfectly curved. He wasn't generally this taken with a woman, at least not at first glance. But there was something about her... He told himself it was just that damned red hair.

"Actually, I only have one."

"One?" he repeated, having lost track of the conversation.

"One of the other two notes. I threw the first one away. I thought it was a joke. I should have brought the second note with me. I wasn't thinking. I just wanted to get here, to talk to you, see if you could help."

She was worried, he could tell, maybe even a little frightened. She set her purse in her lap, then unconsciously twisted the strap one way and then another.

"As I said, I'd like to see the other note."

She rose from her chair. "I'll get it for you right now. My condo isn't that far away."

Trace stood as well. "I'd rather come with you. I can see where you live, take a look at the neighborhood, see where your car was parked when the notes were left."

"The first one was left on my car before I moved out of my apartment. It's about a mile or so away from where I live now. But I think that's a good idea."

She started for the door, but he caught her arm. "I'll drive. My car's right out front." He grabbed the white straw hat he had exchanged for his usual brown felt Stetson as the weather began to warm, and led her through the reception area. Opening the door, he waited while she walked outside.

"The Jeep Cherokee," he said, and one of her burnished eyebrows went up. "What? You were expecting a pickup?"

She shrugged, smiled. "You're a cowboy. I thought all you guys were pickup men."

He chuckled, thinking of the Joe Diffie song and wishing at the moment he owned one. "'Fraid I only drive one when I'm out at the ranch." He helped her into the vehicle and closed the door, rounded the hood and slid in behind the wheel.

She settled back and snapped her seat belt. "You have a ranch?"

"Technically, yes. The place belonged to my grandfather. My dad sold half when Granddad died and used the money to go into the security business. The land that's left is leased to a company that raises Black Angus beef. I kept the old ranch house and fifty acres around it. I pretty much grew up there as a kid. I stop by every once in a while just to keep an eye on things."

"The photos in your office...the rolling fields with the grazing cattle. Those were taken on the ranch?"

"Not by me, but yes. Gabe Raines, a friend of mine from Dallas, took them when we were out there together. I liked them so had them blown up and framed."

"They're very good."

"I'll tell him you said so." Gabriel Raines was Dev Raines's brother, one of his closest friends. They had worked together last year when Gabe was having trouble with an arsonist. Gabe was in construction. Taking pictures was just a hobby, but Gabe seemed to have a good eye.

They drove away from the office, leaving the small business district behind, moving along Kirby Street through a neighborhood of stately older homes and smaller, even older residences like the one in which he lived. Big sycamore trees overhung the streets, shading the asphalt. Manicured lawns climbed from the curb to the front of each house.

Heading south at Maggie's direction, they passed Holcomb Street, wound around a bit, eventually turned onto Broadmoor and into a six-unit town house development that looked very new. The units were nicely constructed, utilizing the land without destroying too many trees. The buildings, beige with redbrick trim, had a vaulted roofline, and each unit had its own brick chimney.

"That one's mine. The one on the end, unit A."

He pulled into a space Maggie indicated in front of a row of matching two-story dwellings. "This your usual parking spot?"

She nodded. "There's a guest space on the right. I keep my car in the garage at night."

They got out of the car and Maggie led him toward the door of her unit. He liked the way she moved, sexy and confident. He liked the way she looked, too, with that little spray of freckles across her forehead and the tip of her nose.

His groin tightened. His instincts were warning him to stay away from temptation, and Maggie O'Connell was certainly that. He would give the case to Alex or Ben, he told himself. As soon as he had a little more information.

She unlocked the door and Trace followed her in. "I'll get the note," Maggie said. "I'll be right back."

He watched her climb the stairs in the entry, admiring the firmness of the muscles in her hips and thighs.

The lady stayed in shape, it was clear. He liked that in a woman, since he believed in staying fit himself.

As she disappeared, he glanced around the condo, which was almost empty. Just a beige, floral-print sofa and matching chair in the living room, a maple coffee table and a couple brass lamps, one of them sitting on the floor. Cardboard boxes were stacked everywhere. There was a dining table in an area off the living room. She had a laptop set up there. Good to know she was computer literate.

Maggie returned with the note, carrying it gingerly but not as carefully. "I handled it when I first got it. Fingerprints never occurred to me until today." She walked to the breakfast counter and laid the note on the gold-flecked white granite top. Trace moved it a little so he could read the words.

Precious Maggie,
Such a delight you are. Soon you will come to
me. Soon you will understand we are meant to
be together.

There it was again, that odd, eerie tone. Trace couldn't put his finger on exactly what it meant, but he didn't like it. He placed the second note beside the first, compared the hand-printed letters. Bold. Well formed. No misspelled words.

Maggie looked up at him. "Will you help me?"
Give the case to Alex, a little voice said.

A muscle tightened in Trace's cheek. Alex Justice, with his good looks and dimples… Trace glanced down at Maggie and desire curled through him. Her eyes were on his, green and worried. A surge of protectiveness overrode his good sense.

So she was a redhead. So what? So what if he already felt a strong attraction to her? It didn't mean a thing. She could be in serious trouble and she needed his help.

"You have any idea who might have written these?" he asked.

Maggie shook her head. "I've tried to think. It doesn't sound like anyone I know."

"Educated. Forceful. Older, maybe. This is not some bum off the street."

"No, I don't think so, either."

"If I'm going to find this guy, you're going to have to help me. I'll need to know things about you. Things about your past, about your work. Some of it fairly personal. If you're willing to tell me what I need to know, I'll help you."

He watched the uncertainty move across her face. Unlike his ex-wife, talking about herself didn't seem to be high on Maggie's agenda.

"I'll tell you as much as I can," she said, which wasn't the answer he wanted. He guessed for now it would have to do.

"All right, Maggie O'Connell. If we're going to get this done, we might as well get to it."

Chapter Three

"Before we get started," Trace said, "I need to go out to my car. I'll be right back."

Maggie walked into the living room and sat down on the sofa in front of the empty brick hearth, waiting while he disappeared outside, then returned carrying a leather briefcase. He sat down in the floral-print chair at the end of the sofa, took off his cowboy hat and rested it on the padded arm. He was dressed in sharply creased jeans, a short-sleeved white Western shirt with pearl snaps, and a pair of freshly polished, plain brown cowboy boots.

His hair was a dark mink-brown, but in the sunlight streaming through the window, little streaks of gold wound through the ends. The man was broad-shouldered, lean and fit, but she had already discovered that during his run-in with Bobby Jordane in the Texas Café.

She had noticed the gold in Trace Rawlins's brown eyes, his straight nose and white teeth. Now she noticed the sexy, sensual curve of his mouth, and found herself staring more than once. He was a good-looking man. But that and the fact he knew how to use his fists were all she really knew about him.

After the way he had bullied her in the café, she wasn't even sure she liked him.

The brass latch on his briefcase clicked open and Trace took out a state-of-the-art recorder, a Montblanc pen and a yellow legal pad.

"Let's start with the present and work backward," he said, turning on the recorder. "You're a photographer. Is that a hobby or what you do for a living?"

She smiled. "I'm lucky. I'm not rich, but I make a very good living doing the work I love."

Trace glanced at the barren white walls of the town house.

"My pictures are all still in boxes," Maggie explained in answer to his silent question. "I'm working on a photo project that's been keeping me really busy. I'm unpacking a little at a time."

"What kind of project?"

"A coffee-table book. It's called *The Sea.* It's set around the ocean and the different kinds of things people do that involve the sea—jobs, recreation, that kind of thing."

His gaze sharpened with interest. When he looked at her with that direct way of his, her skin felt warm. "Why did you pick that subject?"

"I love the ocean. I do mostly outdoor photography.

I love shooting any kind of landscapes, but the sea has my heart."

His eyes gleamed and tiny lines appeared at the corners. She wondered if they were laugh lines or life lines, or just a reflection of the time he spent out-of-doors.

"I'd love to see some of your work," he said.

Maggie smiled. "I guess I'd better get busy and unpack those boxes."

They talked about her business a little more, about the people she dealt with in the galleries where her photos were displayed, and people she might have encountered during her shows.

"Do you keep a list of your clients?"

"As much as I can. I enter them into a file on my computer."

"Anyone in particular who's bought an extraordinary amount of your work?"

"Not that I can think of. I have clients who've purchased three or four pieces. That's not that uncommon." Maggie sighed. "As I said, the notes don't strike any sort of chord. I can't imagine I know this person."

"Maybe you don't. Starting tomorrow, I'm going to put a tail on you for a couple of days. It'll be me or a guy who works for me named Rex Westcott. I'll show you his picture, so if you happen to spot him, you'll know he's not the guy we're after. We'll keep tabs on you, watch for anyone who might be following you."

She felt a trickle of relief. "All right."

"Of course, that might not be the way he operates. Obviously, he knows where you live. He might know a whole lot more."

Maggie didn't like the sound of that. It was one of

the reasons she stayed away from social networking sites like Facebook and Twitter.

Trace asked her more questions about roommates at school, old boyfriends, someone she might have jilted.

"To tell you the truth, I don't date that often. I had a boyfriend when I went to college. We were pretty serious for a while, but it didn't work out."

"What was his name?"

"Michael Irving."

"Anyone else?"

She hated to mention David, since she had been the one at fault for the breakup, and she didn't want to cause him any more trouble.

"Maggie?"

She released a breath, determined to reveal as little as possible. "I went out with an attorney named David Lyons for a while. We lived together a couple of months."

"Bad breakup?"

His eyes were on hers. The man didn't miss a thing. "Pretty bad. It was my fault. I didn't mean to hurt him, but I did."

"When did it end?"

"First of April, two years ago."

"Where is he now?"

"I haven't seen him. I heard he was dating someone."

Trace stopped making notes and looked at her. There was something in those golden-brown eyes that seemed to see more than she wanted.

"What about now?" he asked. "Are you involved with anyone at the moment?"

Maggie shook her head. "I've been way too busy." She wondered if there might be something personal in the question. She wasn't sure how she felt about that. "And I really don't like the dating scene. I suppose eventually I'd like to meet someone, but not right now. I've got my career to think about. I'm happy the way I am."

He studied her as if he wasn't sure he believed her. She wondered if he was one of those men who thought every woman was desperate to find a husband. Or maybe exactly the opposite. That she was just another faithless female concerned with only herself.

"It'll take some time to check all this out," he said. "The thing is, you might know this person and not realize it. He—or she—could be using this odd style of writing so you won't figure out who it is."

She frowned. "You don't actually think this could be a woman?"

"Unless your sexual preferences go both ways, probably not."

She smiled. "I'm boringly heterosexual."

His eyes seemed to darken. Maggie felt a warm, unwelcome stirring in the pit of her stomach, and inwardly cursed her bad luck. An attraction to Trace Rawlins was the last thing she wanted.

"The handwriting looks masculine," Trace continued, "but there definitely are women stalkers. Jealousy over a past relationship with a man, or your success as a photographer. That kind of thing."

He kept asking questions, moving her backward in time. Thinking about the incident with Josh Varner, she began to grow more and more uneasy.

"Tell me about your family," Trace said, making notes now and again.

"My mom and dad divorced when I was four. Mom moved back to Florida where she was raised, remarried not long after and had another kid. I stayed here and lived with my dad."

"He still alive?"

"He passed away a couple of years ago."

"I lost mine a while back. I still miss him."

Maggie made no comment. Her dad had been demanding and a tough disciplinarian, but she had loved him and still missed him.

"How about high school? Anything stand out? Any old grudges that might blossom years later?"

She forced her gaze to remain on his face. No way was she telling him about Josh Varner. Josh didn't even live in Texas anymore. He had gone to UCLA on a scholarship and then taken a job in Seattle with Microsoft. She'd heard he made barrels of money.

And if he wrote her a message, it wouldn't sound anything like the words on the notes she had received.

"I, um, can't think of anything. Besides, if it was something from high school, why would the person wait all these years?"

Trace's pen stopped moving. "Usually something happens, an event of some kind. A stressor, it's called. A trigger that digs up old memories, sometimes twists them around in a weird direction."

She shook her head. "I really can't think of anything." At least nothing that had recently occurred. Still, she was glad he looked down just then to write another note. She had always been an unconvincing liar.

"It may well be that this guy has seen you somewhere but the two of you have never met. He could be fixated on you for no good reason other than the color of your hair, or that you look like someone he once knew."

A little chill ran through her. "I see."

Trace reached over and squeezed her hand. "Look, we're going to catch this guy. There are very tough laws against stalking."

She nodded. Just his light touch reassured her. Maybe this was a man she could count on, a man who could make things turn out all right.

They talked awhile longer, but he didn't bring up her past again. If something happened that involved her Great Shame, as she thought of it, she would tell him. If she did, she knew the look she would see on his face. At the moment, she just couldn't handle it.

Trace rose effortlessly from his chair, to tower over her on his long legs. "On the way back to the office, you can show me where you lived when you got the first note." He packed up his stuff, closed the briefcase, clamped on his cowboy hat. "I'd like to take the notes," he said, "check them for prints."

"All right."

Trace bagged the notes and she led him to the entry.

"You keep your doors and windows locked?"

"I'm pretty good about it."

His glance was hard and direct. "You be better than pretty good. You be damned good."

She didn't like his attitude. On the other hand, he was probably right. Even in a good neighborhood, the crime rate in Houston was high.

"I'll keep the doors locked."

"Good girl. Let's go."

She felt his hand at the small of her back, big and warm as he guided her out of the house toward his Jeep, then opened the door and helped her climb in. They cruised by her old apartment. He stopped in front and made a thorough perusal of the area, then turned the Jeep around and headed back toward his office.

"Anyone in your old apartment building who might be interested in you in some way?"

"There're only four units. A retired lady school-teacher lives in one. There's a single mother and her four-year-old son, and an older man in a wheelchair. The one I left is still vacant."

"Looks like we can rule out the apartment residents."

They reached his office and Trace walked her over to her car.

"Remember what I said about keeping your doors locked."

"I will."

As Maggie drove back to her town house, she couldn't help thinking that in going to a private investigator she had done the right thing.

She didn't like the attraction she felt, but it was only physical, nothing to really worry about. Trace was a handsome, incredibly masculine man, and she hadn't been involved with anyone in years.

And she felt better knowing she had someone to help her.

Even if she had to pay for it.

Trace sat in front of his computer, staring at Maggie O'Connell's webpage. The black background showed off a dozen photos of the Texas Hill Country, including the imported African game that roamed the grasslands, and a variety of magnificent sunsets that lured the viewer deeper into each scene.

On another page, there were shots of small towns and beaches along the coastline bordering the Gulf, and wonderful action photos of various power- and sailboats skimming over the water in Galveston Bay.

The colors were brilliant, the angles of the photos showed the subject to the very best advantage, and there was always something a little different, something intriguing about each picture. At the bottom of the page, information on the three galleries in Texas that carried limited-edition prints of Maggie's work was listed, and a contact email address.

Trace searched through the dozens of other sites that popped up on Google when he referenced her name, and the more he searched, the more frustrated he became.

Damn, his client wasn't just a good photographer, she was practically a celebrity. She was a well-known, well-respected artist whose work had been viewed by thousands of people.

And any one of them could be the person who was stalking her.

Trace leaned forward in his leather chair and punched the button on the recorder, listening again to his conversation with Maggie. When he finished, he reviewed the notes he had taken.

He went to work on her list of names, verifying what little information he had. Nothing turned up. Michael Irving and David Lyons both had webpages. Irving was a certified public accountant in Dallas. Lyons was a corporate lawyer in Houston with Holder Holder & Meeks.

It was after seven by the time Trace finished. The office was closed. Annie had left for the night and Alex and Ben were out working cases. Trace had decided to postpone his trip to the shore until next weekend, and had called Rex Westcott to start the tail on Maggie tomorrow morning. He had sent Rex's photo to the email address she had given him: photolady@baytown.com.

Photolady. Looking at some of her work, he realized she was far more than that. He might have smiled, except that he didn't like complications, and Maggie O'Connell was nothing but. Her life was complicated. The possibilities of who her stalker might be were endless.

And the unwanted attraction Trace felt for her only made matters worse.

He sighed as he rose from his chair, plucked his hat off the credenza behind his desk and prepared to leave. A knock on the front door caught his attention. He glanced at the clock, saw that another hour had passed and wondered who knew he would be there this late.

He settled his hat on his head and started for the front door, turned the lock and pulled it open.

"Good heavens, Trace," said a familiar female voice, "where on earth have you been?" Carly Benson Rawlins stormed past him into the office, whirled and set her hands on her hips. "Why didn't you return my calls? I needed you, Trace. Why didn't you call me back?"

"Good evening, Carly. Why don't you come on in?"

His sarcasm went unnoticed.

"How could you be so insensitive?" She was petite and voluptuous, with long, straight red hair that fell past her shoulders. She had the prettiest blue eyes he'd ever seen. He cursed as he watched them fill with tears. "H-how could you ignore me like that?"

"You aren't my wife anymore, Carly. I can ignore you whenever I want."

She sniffed, tilted her head back to look up at him.

"What if something had happened? What if I'd been in a car wreck or something?"

"Were you in a car wreck?"

"No, but I could have been. Did you see that newspaper article in the *Chronicle* this morning? That woman who drove down to the shore and never came back? Her parents are frantic. She was my age, Trace—twenty-nine years old and she just disappeared."

"I saw it. The police think maybe she took off with her boyfriend or something."

"Or maybe she was *murdered*." Carly shuddered with feigned revulsion. "A woman needs a man to look out for her." She smiled, her tears long forgotten, looped her arms around his neck and went up on her toes to look into his face. "You know I still love you, Trace. Sometimes I just need to know you're still there for me."

He took hold of her wrists and eased her back down on her feet. "Look, Carly. You aren't in any sort of danger and you need to get on with your life. That's what people do when they get divorced."

"I never wanted a divorce and you know it."

"No, but you wanted other men in your bed. That didn't work for me."

Her chin angled up. "You weren't there, Trace. You were working all the time."

"I was trying to build the business, trying to make a life for us. I'm sorry I couldn't keep you properly entertained."

"It was all your fault and you know it."

Maybe some of it was, but mostly he had just picked the wrong woman, as his friends had tried to warn him. Carly was wild and self-centered. She hadn't been ready to settle down when he'd married her. She wasn't ready now.

Still, he felt sorry for her. She wasn't happy. He wasn't sure she ever would be.

He turned her around and urged her gently toward the door. "We've been through all this before." *A thousand times,* he added silently. "Things just didn't work out, that's all. Go home, Carly. Entertain yourself with someone else."

She jerked to a halt at the door. "You're cruel, Trace. Cruel and heartless."

If anything, he was too soft when it came to women. Years ago, he had learned to control his temper. He had come to value his self-control. He'd been raised to treat a woman like a lady. He did his best to do just that.

"Good night, Carly," he said gently, then waited as she stormed out the door. Trace watched her drive her little silver BMW sports car down the alley out of sight, and wondered which of her many admirers had bought it for her.

He lifted his hat, raked back his hair, then settled the hat a little lower across his forehead. He had no idea why his ex-wife continued to plague him. They were never right for each other, never should have married. They might have been in lust at one time, but they were never in love.

That same kind of attraction to a good-looking redhead had hit him several other times in his life. None of those times had ended well.

Trace thought of Maggie O'Connell and warned himself not to go down that road again.

Chapter Four

It was pitch-black in her upstairs bedroom. Only the night sounds of crickets and cicadas intruded into the darkness of the high-ceilinged room. Maggie tossed and turned beneath the lightweight down comforter, unable to sleep with so much on her mind. She needed to get the photos completed for her coffee-table book. And she had a show coming up. She had most of the pictures ready, but could use a few more for the exhibit.

She sighed into the darkness. She had so much to do. Aside from her work, she needed to unpack, try to make the town house more of a home. There wasn't much furniture downstairs, and only a bed, two nightstands and a dresser in her bedroom, stuff she'd had for years.

She still had a few pieces to bring over from the apartment before the end of the month, when her lease was up, and some things she needed to buy, and of course her photos and some prized Ansel Adams pieces that needed to be hung on the walls. She wasn't much of a decorator but she could do better than the way it looked now.

She punched her pillow, turned onto her back and stared at the ceiling. Tomorrow was Saturday. She planned to drive down to Galveston, take some shots around the harbor. She needed to get up early. Which meant she had to get some sleep.

She closed her eyes, tried to clear her head.

That was when she heard it. The faint scraping of a chair against the ceramic tile floor in the kitchen. She listened, straining her ears. Was that the patio door sliding open? Was that a footstep she heard on the stairs? Her heart was pounding, thumping against her ribs. Her palms felt slick where she clenched the sheet. She thought of the notes she had received, wondered if the man who had written them was crazy enough to break into her home.

She listened again, trying to decide if she should call 911. The police would show up, she figured, even if they knew she was the caller. But as the seconds stretched into minutes, she realized the only sound she was hearing was the fear pumping through her veins.

When the noise didn't come again, she began to relax. She had imagined the intruder. There was no one in the house. As Trace had insisted, she had carefully locked the doors.

She glanced at the digital clock beside the bed: 2:15. She lay there in silence, her ears focused to catch any noise out of the ordinary, but she didn't hear anything more. The little button in the center of the bedroom doorknob was pushed. It wasn't much of a lock, but it gave her some sense of security. At least she would know if someone was trying to get in.

She watched the clock, the numbers slipping past. At two thirty-five, she rolled out of bed. No other sounds had reached her. Maybe she had fallen asleep for an instant and dreamed the entire incident. Things like that had happened to her before.

Still, she had to know.

Reaching for the blue fleece robe tossed over the foot of the bed, she slipped her arms inside and tied the sash around her waist. After years of living in the Texas heat, she slept in the nude, but she always kept the robe handy in case there was some sort of emergency, like a fire, or just someone arriving unexpectedly at her door.

She listened again for a moment, heard nothing and quietly turned the knob. Easing the door open, she waited. Just the ticking of the antique clock that she planned to hang on the wall in the living room but hadn't done yet. Sticking her head out in the hallway, she glanced both ways, but no lights were burning; nothing seemed out of the ordinary.

After tiptoeing down the hall, she slipped into her photo studio and grabbed a makeshift weapon—a unipod, the one-legged stand she sometimes used to steady her camera. She quietly retraced her steps with it clutched in both hands, and descended the stairs.

No movement. No sound. Maggie flipped on the light switch, illuminating the glass lamp hanging in the foyer, casting a bright glow partway into the living room.

Nothing.

The tension eased from her shoulders. She turned on the light in the kitchen, turned on a lamp in the living room, took a look around. She had imagined the entire episode—thank God.

It was the note. The notes were making her edgy and restless, sending her into a tailspin. She hoped Trace Rawlins would find the man who had been harassing her.

She moved through the house, making a brief inspection of the locks, finding them all secured. She turned off the brass lamp in the living room, then padded back to the kitchen. Her hand paused midway to the light switch as her eyes caught something sitting on the breakfast bar.

A cold chill swept through her. The only things there when she had gone to bed were the telephone, the old-fashioned answering machine she still used and the address book she kept beside them.

Her mouth went dry. She forced her feet to carry her to the counter. Her hand shook as she reached toward the small porcelain statuette sitting on top. It was no more than five inches high, a man in a black tuxedo dancing with a woman with upswept red hair wearing a long, flowing, pale green evening gown.

Maggie swallowed. Her gaze shot around the kitchen, but she had checked the rooms and the closets and found no one there. Picking up her address book with a shaking hand, she flicked it open. Trace Rawlins's business card rested just inside.

Frantically, she dialed the cell number printed on the card, terrified that the man who had left the statue might be hiding in the house and she just hadn't found him. With the phone pressed against her ear, she listened to the ringing on the other end of the line and prayed Trace Rawlins would answer.

* * *

The boat was running with the wind, *Ranger's Lady* skimming over the surface of the frothy blue ocean. The early-spring air felt fresh and cool against his skin. Gulls screeched and turned over the top of the mast, circling the boat in search of food.

Trace was smiling, enjoying the perfect day, when Faith Hill's sweet voice began to sing to him through his cell phone. In an instant, he was jolted awake, a habit from his days in the Rangers. His hand shot out and grabbed the phone off the bedside table, and he pressed it against his ear.

"Rawlins," he rasped in a sleepy voice.

"Trace, it's Maggie O'Connell."

"Maggie?" Worry slid through him. He rolled to the side of the bed, swung his long legs over the side. "Maggie, what is it?"

"Someone…someone was in my house tonight. He left…left something for me on the counter."

A chill ran down Trace's spine. "Have you called the police?"

"I—I called you instead."

His fingers tightened around the phone. "Are you sure he isn't still there?"

"I—I don't think so."

"Not good enough. Hang up and call 911. I'm on my way."

Trace hung up the phone, grabbed his jeans off the back of a chair and pulled them on without bothering with his briefs. After dragging a T-shirt over his head, he pulled on his boots and headed for the door. Sensing his urgency, Rowdy followed, but the dog was used to his master's odd hours and didn't make a fuss.

Trace's shoulder holster hung on the hat rack beside the back door. He used a Beretta 9 mm semiauto when he carried, which he hadn't needed to do lately. He slipped on the holster, snapped out the weapon and checked the load as he hurried outside toward his car.

It didn't take long to reach Maggie's town house. He was glad he had been there before. It was almost three in the morning, but the lights were on. As he strode up the walkway, he could see her through a small window over the sink in the kitchen, standing there in her bathrobe, her arms wrapped around herself as if she were cold.

No patrol car was in sight. Trace silently cursed the time it was taking them to get there. He knocked on the door. "Maggie? It's Trace."

She opened the door an instant later, her shoulders sagging with relief as he walked past her into the entry.

"Thank you for coming."

He glanced around. "I thought the cops would be here by now."

Her gaze strayed from his. "I, um, didn't call them."

Frustration tightened Trace's jaw. "Why the hell not?"

"You were on your way. I took another look around. I'm sure he's not here."

Trace shook his head. "Dammit, Maggie." Pulling the Beretta from its holster, he made a check of the rooms downstairs, the coat closet, the bedroom and bath. He made the same search upstairs, the master bedroom and bath, and the photo studio. Returning downstairs, he opened the door from the entry into the garage, flipped on the light and took the single step down.

Maggie's Ford Escape sat in the garage. The door

leading outside was locked. There was no sign of who-ever had come into the house.

"I checked the doors and windows," he told her as he returned to the kitchen. "They're all locked. No broken latches, nothing. Any idea how he got in?"

"I don't know."

"Show me what he left you."

She led him to the breakfast bar. "That." She pointed toward the item on the counter. "It's pretty innocuous, just a little porcelain statuette, but…"

"But it means something. At least to him."

Trace examined the dancing couple, carefully painted by hand. Using a paper towel, he lifted the piece to examine it more closely, noting that the bottom was uneven, as if it had been attached to something, and broken off.

He set the statuette back on the breakfast bar. "Does it mean anything to you?"

Maggie shook her head. "I've never seen anything like it. It looks a little like one of those things you put on top of a wedding cake."

"Yeah, but it isn't. Check the bottom." He showed her the uneven edges. "At one time, this was attached to something. Glued on, it looks like."

"I have no idea why anyone would leave that here," she said, her gaze still on the figurine. Her eyes were the same pale green as the woman's dress, her hair the same fiery red. The porcelain figure meant something, all right, and whatever it was, it wasn't good.

Trace glanced around the town house. "Your locks are a joke. Tomorrow I'll have my guys come over and install some decent ones, along with a security system."

"They're, uh, kind of expensive, aren't they?"

For the first time, he smiled. "You're a client. You get a special price. We'll just do the basics—the windows and doors, a couple motion detectors."

"I guess I don't have much choice."

He gently caught her shoulders, forcing her to look at him. "We need to call the police, Maggie. Someone broke into your home. This isn't the first problem you've had. You need to file a report, keep the cops in the loop."

She looked away, studied her slender feet, showing beneath the hem of the robe, the pale peach polish on her toenails. Trace's gaze followed hers and he found himself wondering how smooth her skin would feel, how responsive she would be if his hand moved up her thigh. He wondered what she was wearing beneath the robe, and felt himself harden inside his jeans.

Son of a bitch. He forced his attention back to her face, amazed that he had allowed his attraction to sidetrack his thoughts.

"What is it with you and the cops?" he asked. "You don't have a record, do you?"

Her eyes widened. "No, I... No, of course not."

But he thought that her face went a little pale. He pulled out his cell and dialed 911, and a few minutes later a white-and-blue patrol car rolled up. A Hispanic officer whose name tag read Gonzalez, and his slightly chubby, blond-haired partner, walked into the town house in response to the call.

The blond cop, Sandowski, searched the unit, while Gonzalez took Maggie's statement, which briefly recapped the events of the night.

"So that's it?" Gonzalez said, making a final note on

his pad as she finished. "You heard a noise and found the statue on the counter?"

"That's what happened, yes."

"Was anything stolen?"

"I don't think so. I haven't noticed anything missing."

He looked at Trace. "What about you? You got anything to add?"

Trace explained that he had come over after receiving Maggie's call. "She was clearly upset. She's been getting threatening messages left on her car, hang-up calls, that kind of thing."

Sandowski returned from his search just then. "I checked the doors and windows. No sign of forced entry. Are you sure your cleaning lady or a friend didn't leave the statue there? Maybe you just didn't notice it before you went to bed."

Maggie's pretty lips thinned. "It wasn't there."

Gonzalez wrote something on his notepad. "We'll take a look around outside before we leave. I suggest you check with friends, see if maybe one of them was playing a joke or something."

"It wasn't a joke," Maggie said tightly.

The officers headed for the door. It was obvious they believed she had just overlooked the presence of the porcelain figurine.

Maggie had said the cops weren't able to help her. Clearly, they weren't convinced the threat against her was real. First thing in the morning, Trace would take the figurine down to his office, do a check for prints on it and the notes she'd received.

"Will you be able to sleep?" he asked once the police were gone.

"Probably not." She raked soft red curls back from

her face. Sleep-tousled, they teased her cheeks and shoulders. His fingers itched to touch them.

"You need to get some rest," he said a little gruffly, thinking that under different circumstances he might have exactly the sleeping pill she needed. As it was, Maggie was his client, his responsibility. He had no intention of trying to seduce her.

He almost smiled. And he was pretty sure if he tried, his chances of success would be slim to none.

"I was planning to drive down to the shore tomorrow," she said, "take some shots for my book. Now...I don't know...."

"That might not be a bad idea," Trace said before he could stop himself. "Until you walked into my office, I was thinking of heading to Kemah for the weekend. I've got a boat docked there."

One of her burnished eyebrows went up. "A cowboy who rides a boat instead of a horse?"

He smiled. "That's me."

"Kemah's a charming little town. I've gotten some great pictures on the boardwalk."

"Maybe we could drive down together. My men will be working here all day, installing the security system and changing the locks. You could get away from all that for a while and I could get in a little sailing."

And he could take Rex's place, keep an eye out, see if anyone followed them down.

Maggie looked at him with a combination of weariness and suspicion.

"I'll drive," he offered. "You can sleep on the way."

"And you'll bring me back tomorrow night?"

A cautious lady. In her situation that was good. "Unless you decide you'd rather stay and sleep aboard," he couldn't resist adding.

She sliced him a sideways glance. "I'll let you know in the morning."

Trace just smiled. "In case you haven't noticed, it is morning, Maggie."

Chapter Five

As soon as he got home, Trace stretched out on the overstuffed sofa in his living room still wearing his jeans and boots. Rowdy curled up on the beige carpet next to the sofa, and both of them fell asleep. Trace slept like a rock till six, then made himself some coffee, loaded his gear in the back of the Jeep and drove down to the office.

There was a fingerprint kit in the back room. He dusted the notes for prints, but as he had figured, the rough brown paper yielded nothing.

He held more hope for the little porcelain statuette, but after careful examination and dusting, it appeared the figurine had been wiped clean. Which in itself revealed something about Maggie's stalker.

Whoever it was was careful. Very careful. No sign of forced entry. No footprints that Trace had seen. He would bet he could dust the whole condo and no prints would turn up. Since the town house had recently been for sale, it wouldn't have been difficult for the intruder to get a key. Trace would talk to the Realtors who'd handled the listing and sale, see what might come up.

His Jeep was loaded and ready. The office wasn't officially open on weekends, but Ben, Alex and Sol were usually in and out. Annie came in whenever she needed to play catch-up. The alarm system installers worked for JDT Security Systems, the company that handled all the Atlas jobs. Trace phoned Ed Wilcox and got the guys going on what would be an overtime job at Maggie's.

By nine he was finished and heading back to the town house. He wanted to interview the residents in the other five units, see if anyone had heard or seen anything last night.

As he drove toward Broadmoor, he found himself smiling. He was working, sort of, providing a protection detail for his client—not that he planned to charge her for a trip to the shore. But the better part of the bargain was the day he would be spending at sea, sailing with the pretty little redhead on his boat in Galveston Bay.

Maggie was surprised she had agreed to the trip. But as Trace had said, the security people would be working in the town house all day, and she really needed to take some more pictures. She wanted to finish the coffee-table book and if she got lucky, she could get a few more shots for her show at the Twin Oaks Gallery in a couple weeks.

After Trace left in the wee hours of the morning, Maggie had returned upstairs and managed to get a couple hours of sleep. But it wasn't nearly enough. As she dressed in a pair of cropped navy blue pants, a red-striped top and sandals, she yawned, feeling groggy and out of sorts. Coffee helped but not that much. At least the weather was good. Still cool, but no longer cold, the air not too humid.

Trace returned at ten, his Cherokee loaded with gear. "You ready?" he asked when she opened the door.

"Just about." She looked down at the black-and-white dog standing next to him on her doorstep.

"That's Rowdy," he said. "Rowdy, this is Maggie."

Her eyes widened when the animal barked.

"Hi, Rowdy," she said, because he seemed to demand a greeting. "It's very nice to meet you."

He barked again.

She bit back a laugh. "I just need to load my camera gear." She turned to collect the Nikon D3S sitting in its case in the entry. It was equipped with a fantastic Tamron 28-300 lens she had purchased a few weeks back. The new equipment had set her back nearly seven thousand dollars, but in her line of work, it was an essential investment.

Trace walked past her, gently elbowing her aside when she reached for the bag, and hoisted the strap over one of his wide shoulders.

"I'm used to carrying my own equipment," she said.

"I'm sure you are." But he kept on walking, hauling the stuff out to his Jeep and loading it into the backseat.

"I hope you aren't charging me extra for that," she grumbled as she carried her yellow canvas swim bag out to the car.

He grinned, a flash of white in a suntanned face so handsome it made her breath catch. An amazing face, she thought, with those hard, sculpted features and intense, whiskey-brown eyes, so warm and direct they sent a little quiver into her stomach.

"No extra charge," he said, sliding her tripod onto the seat. "Not today."

She watched the flex of those incredible biceps she had noticed at the Texas Café, and told herself there was nothing wrong with being physically attracted to a man. After all, she was a young, fully mature woman, though she rarely gave in to those sorts of urges.

"Oh, I almost forgot the sandwiches."

He smiled. "Sandwiches, huh? I like the way you think. I'm hungry already."

Maggie ran back inside and grabbed the small cooler she had filled with ham-and-cheese sandwiches on fresh rye bread, and a couple Diet Cokes. Mr. He-man probably drank the real thing, but today, diet would have to do.

Trace and Rowdy walked to the rear of the Jeep. "Load up," he said, and the dog hopped onto the tailgate, went inside and lay down on his bed. Trace left the rear window rolled partway down to let in fresh air, and the little dog seemed pleased.

"Rowdy looks very much at home back there," Maggie said as she climbed up in the passenger seat. "Do you always take him with you?"

"Most of the time. Rowdy loves to sail almost as much as I do."

"Smart dog."

"He's a border collie. They're bred to herd cattle and sheep, one of the smartest breeds."

"Where did you get him?"

"Gabe Raines—the guy who took the photos in my office? His brother owns a ranch in Wyoming. Rowdy was a pup from one of the litters up there."

Trace closed her door, then went around to the driver's side and slid behind the wheel. He wasn't wearing his cowboy hat today, just a white ball cap with an anchor on the front, plus jeans and a yellow knit shirt. No boots, either, just a pair of white canvas deck shoes that were clean but had seen plenty of wear.

The lack of sleep didn't seem to faze him. He looked every bit as good as he had the night before.

Not liking the train of her thoughts, Maggie sat up a little straighter. "I'd like to get a dog someday," she said, just to make conversation. "I had a cocker spaniel when I was a kid, but my mom took it with her when she went back to Florida. I keep thinking someday I'll get one, but right now I'm too busy."

Trace cast her a glance. "You said you were four when your mom and dad divorced. It must have been tough on you."

She felt the old familiar ache in her chest. "It was hard. My mother went on with her life and we barely stayed in touch. My dad did his best, but he had to make a living. He owned a small trucking company so he was gone from home a lot."

"Mine, too. My mom died when I was born. My dad was in the army, so my grandparents pretty much raised me."

"Out on the ranch," she said, remembering what he had told her.

"That's right."

When he didn't add more, she let the subject drop. Didn't sound as if either of them had had a fantastic childhood.

The Jeep rolled along the shady streets. From her town house, they drove through the University District onto the 59 Freeway, then took the 45 south toward the ocean. Kemah was one of a string of seaside communities that fronted Galveston Bay.

At the edge of the water, small weekend retreats that had been there for years sat next to sprawling, newly constructed mansions. Fine white sand surrounded them, lush vegetation and lots of palm and live oak trees.

Trace kept his boat—a sleek, white, low-hulled thirty-eight-footer—at the Kemah Marina, she discovered.

"What kind of boat is it?" Maggie asked. He climbed aboard, then reached down to take her hand and guide her up the steps and onto the deck. "Hunter Legend. Been a great boat to own."

It was immaculately clean inside, she saw as he gave her a quick tour, and nicely fitted out with blue canvas cushions and lots of teakwood kept highly polished. A dining area and a galley; two cabins and a head.

"So what do you think?"

"She's beautiful." *Ranger's Lady* was the name painted on the stern. "Name fits, too. Lone Ranger, right? That's the way I thought of you that day in the Texas Café."

Trace chuckled. "Not that kind of Ranger. U.S. Army. Kind of a tradition in our family."

"You were a Ranger?"

He nodded. "My dad, too. That was the reason he was gone so much."

"Where were you stationed?"

"South America, mostly. We were there but we weren't, if you know what I mean."

"I think I can figure it out." She cast him a glance. "I bet you've always been somewhat of a maverick."

Trace grinned. "Somewhat."

She looked away, not liking the flutter that grin caused in her stomach. "Mind if I take some shots?"

He glanced around. He had been doing that all day. Second nature, she imagined, for an investigator. And she was, after all, paying him to find a stalker.

"Go ahead," he said. "I'll get ready to cast off while you wander a little. Just don't go too far."

"No problem."

Trace went to work, and she watched his easy, economical movements. No wasted effort, just do the job and get it done. There was a certain grace there, too. She wondered what he'd look like on the back of a horse, and thought he would probably look as if he'd been born there.

Leaving him to his work, she climbed onto the dock and took some photos of the yachts in the marina. She wandered a bit, snapping a shot here and there: an old lady in a huge straw hat walking her little rust-colored Pekinese; two old men playing cards at a table next to the water; a little kid licking the biggest yellow-and-white rock candy sucker she had ever seen.

She returned to the *Ranger's Lady,* snapping photos along the way. When she reached the boat, she realized Trace must have been watching her the entire time she was gone. He was only doing his job, she reminded herself, nothing more. Which for reasons she couldn't explain, she found mildly annoying.

He helped her aboard, then went back to examining one of the lines that hoisted the sail.

He had stripped off his cotton knit shirt and jeans, leaving him bare chested in a pair of navy blue swim trunks. With his back to her, she couldn't help checking him out. His skin was a smooth golden-brown and rippling with muscle. His legs were long and corded. There wasn't an ounce of fat anywhere to be seen.

She couldn't resist a couple of shots of such a gorgeous man at work on his boat, but at the rhythmical click of the shutter, Trace turned. Broad, solidly muscled shoulders, a chest banded with sinew and lightly furred with dark hair, and a six-pack stomach…

She felt that funny lift again, only a little embarrassed to be caught staring. "I guess you really were a Ranger."

He just shrugged. "There were times being in condition meant the difference between life and death."

"You're not a Ranger now," she reminded him.

"Old habits die hard." He lowered a pair of wraparound sunglasses over those whiskey-brown eyes. "You ready?"

She looked at him standing there with his legs splayed, his gaze on the horizon, and had the oddest feeling he was as much a Ranger now as he ever had been. The breeze gusted just then, rattling the ship's rigging. The Gulf stretched in front of them, blue and beckoning.

"You bet I'm ready."

Trace tossed off the lines and Maggie settled herself on one of the blue canvas cushions. Rowdy took a place beside her. His ears perked up as the boat began to move, anticipation clear on his little doggy face. Trace manned the wheel and the boat eased away from the dock.

"You'll have to earn your keep, you know." He flicked her a glance. "I'll need you to bring up the fenders and tend the dock lines, maybe take a turn at the wheel. You'll have to remember to duck when we come about, and of course you'll need to watch for pirates."

She laughed, gave him a smart salute. "Aye, aye, Cap'n."

Trace grinned. They settled themselves for the trip, the hull slipping smoothly over the water until they reached the open ocean, then the wind picked up and the boat heeled over. The stiff breeze tugged at Maggie's curls, blowing them across her face, so she dragged the heavy red mane into a ponytail held in place with a small hair elastic.

"I've been sailing only a couple of times," she said. "I went out with a friend when I was in college."

"Michael Irving?" It was a casual question, yet she thought Trace had just morphed back into a detective.

"A friend in my art history class. Her dad owned a forty-two-foot Catalina."

"Nice boat."

"Beautiful. So is yours. You really take good care of her."

Trace seemed pleased. "I do my best." He leaned back in the seat behind the wheel, his dark glasses hiding his thoughts.

The sun beat down so warmly she decided it was time to shed her own clothes. "I'm going to change. It's just too nice a day not to get some sun."

"Help yourself."

She disappeared below and came up a few minutes later in a red-and-white-striped bikini. The suit wasn't exactly modest, but it wasn't over-the-top risqué, either. She wore a loose-fitting white gauze shirt over it, but that didn't hide much. Though she couldn't see his eyes behind the glasses, she could feel his very thorough inspection, burning like a laser.

"I guess you like to stay in shape, too," he said a little gruffly.

She did. Very much so. And she was way too glad he noticed. "I ride my stationary bike in the mornings. I lift a few weights to build bone strength, and I play racquetball whenever I get the chance."

"Is that so? We'll have to have a match sometime."

"You like to play?"

His gaze moved over her again. "Oh, yeah, I like to play." But his drawl had deepened and she was no longer sure he was talking about raquetball.

They fell into a comfortable silence, enjoying the wind and the sea, and the gulls darting back and forth at the stern. When they approached a group of sportsmen fishing for tarpon, Maggie grabbed her camera and went to work. One of the men had hooked up to a real monster, and just as she focused, the fish jumped spectacularly into the air. She caught the shot, snapping a series of photos in milliseconds.

She laughed joyously as the tarpon plunged back into the sea. "My God, did you see that?"

Trace lifted his ball cap and settled it back on his head, a habit she had noticed when he was wearing his cowboy hat. "I sure did. Looks like you got a couple of great photos there."

She replayed the digital images. "Oh, this makes my day."

"Just being out here makes mine."

Maggie agreed. It felt so good to be out on the water, the boat sliding over the surface. They ate the ham-and-cheese sandwiches she had brought, but ignored the Diet

Cokes. Instead, Trace cracked open a bottle of chilled chardonnay, poured it into two stemmed glasses, and they toasted the perfect day.

Relaxed, Maggie removed her cover-up, put on some sunscreen, stretched out on the cushions and let the warmth of the sun seep through her. With so little sleep last night, she must have dozed off. The sun had moved toward the horizon and Trace was turning the boat when she awakened.

"Time to go home," he said.

Maggie felt a twinge of disappointment. "I didn't mean to fall asleep."

"After last night, you needed the rest."

She inhaled a deep breath of the salty air. "It's been wonderful."

Trace seemed to share her mood. "Tomorrow's Sunday. We can spend the night if you want. Two staterooms down there. You wouldn't have to worry about your virtue."

She was surprised to discover she was tempted, but then sighed. She hardly knew Trace Rawlins, and it was never smart to get involved with someone who worked for you. "Thanks for the offer, but I need to get back."

"Not a problem." Wheeling the sailboat expertly through the opening into Clear Lake, he turned toward the marina and his slip at dock A. Easing the vessel neatly into its berth, he tossed a line over the side and pulled the boat in close, then tied it in place.

They'd been out of cell phone range when they were at sea, but now Trace's iPhone started ringing down in the galley, where he had left it so it wouldn't fall into the water.

He hit the ladder, reached out and grabbed the phone, pressing it against his ear as he returned to the deck.

"Rawlins." The caller talked for a while and the lines of Trace's face went hard. "How'd it happen?"

More conversation, then a muscle tightened in his jaw. "Neither do I. I'm on my way." Trace hung up the phone and began to pull his jeans on over his swimsuit. "Looks like spending the night wouldn't have worked for me, either."

"What's going on?"

"One of my clients turned up dead. The police think he killed himself. I don't."

Maggie slid her pants over her bikini bottoms and adjusted the gauzy cover-up, tying it up around her waist. "You're saying it was murder?"

"Could be."

She slipped on her sandals. "I guess finding a murderer tops catching a stalker."

Trace shook his head. "One has nothing to do with the other. By the time we get home, your alarm system will be installed. As far as the creep goes who's been bothering you, you hired me to do a job and that's what I intend to do."

"What about the murder?"

He gave her a hard-edged smile. "Ever heard of multitasking?"

Maggie didn't doubt he could handle both cases. One glance at the dark look on his face and she felt sorry for the guy who had murdered his client.

"Besides," Trace continued, "if Hewitt was murdered, I already know who did it."

Chapter Six

They were headed back to Houston. The perfect day at sea had ended far too quickly.

As he dodged in and out of the heavy traffic on Highway 45, Trace mentally replayed the phone conversation he'd had on the boat.

"Trace, it's Annie. You need to get back to town. That Sommerset case you just finished? Hewitt Sommerset turned up dead half an hour ago in his study. The police are calling it a suicide."

Trace's stomach had knotted. "How'd he die?"

"Gunshot wound to the head. His son doesn't believe he pulled the trigger."

He clenched his jaw. "Neither do I." Hewitt was a good man. Trace needed answers and he was determined to get them.

The car in front of him slowed and he slowed as well,

his mind drifting from Hewitt to the pretty redhead in the seat beside him. At least for a while, he had been able to keep Maggie's mind off her stalker. He wasn't sure how the man who had left the notes was keeping tabs on her, but there had been no sign of him on their way to the shore or at any time while they were there.

The figurine was another matter. Someone had broken into Maggie's house. There were no visible signs of entry, but the locks were paltry and there were ways to get in without leaving evidence. By now, the security alarm would be operational and the locks all replaced. Even so, the guy was a threat that had to be dealt with.

Trace had spoken to Rex Westcott and put him on notice to be ready for the stakeout tonight. Maggie was safe for the moment.

Trace thought of the day he had spent with her. He didn't have a problem mixing business with pleasure, not when it was a good way to do his job. He had let down his guard and relaxed more than he'd meant to, something he rarely did with a woman, but he liked Maggie O'Connell. She was smart and talented and vibrant. Along with that, she was sexy as hell.

He flicked a glance her way, caught a glimpse of soft lips and gorgeous red hair, and his groin tightened. He wanted to take her to bed, taste those pretty lips and lose himself in all those sweet curves.

It was a bad idea, he knew. Every time he got involved with a woman disaster struck.

This is different, he told himself. Nothing more than a physical attraction. He wouldn't let himself get in too deep.

Trace took a last glance at Maggie, told himself that time would settle the matter one way or the other and forced his thoughts back to the more immediate problem at hand.

The death of his former client, Hewitt Sommerset.

Trace's hands tightened around the steering wheel. The Saturday traffic along Route 45 had turned brutal. Maybe there was a wreck up ahead, roadwork, something. Whatever it was, his frustration was making him edgy and restless. He stepped on the brake for the hundredth time, bringing the Jeep to a halt behind the white Toyota pickup ahead of him.

He slammed a hand against the wheel. "Dammit! I need to talk to the police."

Maggie turned in her seat. "You're going to the crime scene?"

He nodded. "As soon as I drop you off, I'm heading for the Sommerset house."

Her gaze went to the dense trail of cars rolling slowly along the pavement ahead of them. "Where is it?"

"The Woodlands." Thirty miles north of Houston. "At this rate it'll be dark by the time I get there."

She studied the slow-moving traffic. "You're probably right. It'll be even later if you have to drop me off. Why don't you just take me with you? I've got a good book. I can wait in the car until you're finished. I can see this is important to you, and I really don't mind."

He started to say no, then paused. It wasn't as if there was a shoot-out in progress. The questions he wanted answered and the information he had to deliver wouldn't take that long. And with traffic the way it was, it would save him at least forty minutes.

"You sure?"

"Thanks to you I got some terrific material today. It's the least I can do."

Trace smiled, feeling a wave of relief. "Great." He wanted to be there for Jason and Emily. Hewitt's son and daughter were both good kids. It was his son-in-law, Parker Barrington, Emily's husband, who was the problem.

"So what's the story?" Maggie asked. "The police think it's suicide but you think it's murder. Why is that?"

He rarely talked about a case, but most of this would be in the news in a couple of days, anyway.

"A few weeks ago, the victim—Hewitt Sommerset—came to see me. He wanted to find out if his son-in-law was stealing money from the company."

"And you found out he was."

"Parker Barrington is chief financial officer of Sommerset Industries. At Hewitt's request, we installed a couple hidden cameras, put a live feed in his computer. We caught him doctoring the books, siphoning money off to an account in the Cayman Islands."

One of Maggie's wing-shaped eyebrows went up. "So his hands were definitely sticky."

"Definitely."

"You think Hewitt Sommerset confronted his son-in-law, who killed him to keep from being caught?"

"It's possible. Depending on what Hewitt told him, Parker may not have realized other people already knew."

The heavy traffic continued until they got a ways north of Houston, then the cars began to thin out. The Woodlands was a huge development of homes, shopping centers and offices, even a prestigious golf course. What made the area such a desirable place to live was that all those things were hidden among dense grooves of trees and beautifully cared-for landscaping.

Trace wound his way along the curving roadways lined with trees and shrubs, and turned onto a street with massive homes tucked away among the foliage on oversize lots. The Sommerset mansion sat at the end of a cul-de-sac. Two patrol cars were parked in front, along with Jason Sommerset's flashy silver Porsche. Emily drove a Mercedes, but it wasn't there. Trace wondered where her husband was.

He felt a jolt of hot, dark anger. Parker Barrington was in for a little surprise when he found out all the evidence condemning him was well documented. Hewitt was a decent, hardworking man who had built an empire though years of dedicated work. He didn't deserve to be killed by an ungrateful, thieving son-in-law.

"You look like you're going to explode."

Trace shoved the car into Park and turned off the engine. Under different circumstances he would have smiled at Maggie's words. Instead, he took a deep breath and reined in his temper.

"You're right. Hewitt was more than a client. He was a friend. Until I'm completely sure what happened, I don't want to jump to conclusions." He cracked open his door. "You all right here?"

"I'll be just fine."

"With any luck, I won't be gone long."

Maggie watched Trace stop to speak to one of the policemen, who let him into the house. It was quite a place, at least ten thousand square feet, and painted a pale, dusky rose. Done in the French style, it sported a mansard roof and arched doors and windows.

The mansion was grand and imposing, and she wondered if Hewitt Sommerset had been happy there. She knew a little about him, what she had seen on TV. He was a well-known figure in the Houston area, a self-made billionaire, a philanthropist who donated millions to charity. He'd been a dedicated husband and father, a man who had greatly mourned the death of his wife two years ago.

In the time since then, Hewitt had returned to work, immersing himself more deeply in the company than he had for a number of years. Maybe that was the reason he had uncovered his son-in-law's nefarious activities.

Maggie couldn't help feeling sorry for the daughter who had married such a dirtball. She smiled, thinking she would love to be a fly on the wall when Trace confronted him.

Hearing a soft whine from the back of the Jeep, Maggie got out of the car, went around to the rear and let Rowdy out for a quick pit stop. Several patrol cars were parked at the curb, and a number of officers wandered in and out of the house. Rowdy sniffed the base of a nearby tree, took care of business and returned to the Jeep.

"Load up," Maggie commanded, as Trace had done, and the dog jumped back up. Making himself comfortable in his bed, he rested his black-and-white muzzle against the cushion.

"Good boy." Maggie reached in to pet him, then shut the tailgate.

The light was fading but still good. The days were getting longer, the weather warmer. She glanced around, her photographer's eye kicking in. The sun was beginning to set, but at this time of day, the soft golden rays filtering down through branches of the gnarled old oaks brought out interesting details: the uneven texture of the bark, the faint curl of a newly budded leaf.

Maggie reached into the backseat and grabbed her camera. While she was waiting for Trace, maybe she could catch a few good shots.

Trace crossed the black-and-white marble-floored entry reminiscent of a French château, heading straight to Hewitt's study. He had been there in the late afternoon just a few days ago, bringing his employer the damning evidence that had been collected against Parker Barrington.

The study, a huge, walnut-paneled room with two-story ceilings and heavy brass chandeliers, swarmed with people now, the forensics squad hard at work poring over the scene. Hewitt's desk was in disarray and a large bloodstain remained where his body had been found slumped over the top.

"Trace!"

He recognized the youthful voice, turned to see Jason Sommerset walking toward him. He was twenty-four years old, golden-haired, handsome as sin and spoiled rotten. It was amazing he'd turned out to be such a nice kid.

"Jason. I'm so sorry. I liked your father very much."

His face was pale, his eyes red-rimmed. But he wasn't crying now, he was angry. "Dad didn't do it, Trace. He didn't kill himself."

"Take it easy—I don't think so, either. We talked just last week. He was looking forward to the trip the two of you were taking to the Bahamas."

"Someone killed him. They made it look like he pulled the trigger, but I know he didn't."

Trace settled a hand on the young man's shoulder.

"That's why I'm here. To find out the truth one way or another."

Jason took a steadying breath. "I knew you'd come. Dad trusted you and so do I."

Trace just nodded. Clearly, Hewitt hadn't told his son what they had found out about Emily's husband. Jason was smart and he seemed to have inherited his father's gift for sizing people up. Trace wondered if the boy would be all that surprised to discover his brother-in-law was a thief.

Someone called Jason's name, and with a nod of his head that indicated they would talk again, he walked off down the hall, leaving Trace to the task he had come for. Returning his attention to the study, he scanned the room for anything out of place, and spotted the familiar features of Detective Mark Sayers, a classmate of his at community college and a longtime friend.

Trace walked toward him. "Got a minute?"

His head came up and surprise lit his face. "Hey, Trace." A little shorter, a little beefier, Mark had light brown hair and hazel eyes. Except for the cheap suits he wore and his overall rumpled appearance, he was a good-looking guy.

"Under different circumstances I'd say it's good to see you," Mark said. "But your timing's not great. I guess you must have heard—Hewitt Sommerset is dead. Looks like he killed himself."

"I don't think that's likely."

One of Sayers's light brown eyebrows went up. "That right? I didn't know the two of you were friends."

"Business acquaintances, mostly. Grew into a little more than that over the years. You and I need to talk."

The detective's interest sharpened. "Okay." Turning,

he led Trace down a hall lined with expensive paintings in heavy gilded frames, and turned into one of the numerous parlors in the house, this one elegantly furnished with peach brocade sofas and dark green velvet drapes. There wasn't so much as a piece of fringe out of place on the Persian rugs that covered the polished oak floors.

"I guess you've talked to Hewitt's son, Jason," Trace said as Mark closed the door.

"We talked to him. His reaction isn't unexpected. No son wants to believe his father killed himself."

"When did it happen?"

"Last night. Hewitt was supposed to be out of town, but something must have come up. Apparently he keeps his study door closed when he's away. The body wasn't found until this afternoon."

"How was it done?"

"Thirty-eight caliber gunshot to the side of the head. The pistol is registered to Sommerset, who allegedly kept it in a drawer in his desk."

"But someone else could have pulled the trigger."

"There were no signs of a struggle."

"Maybe he was unconscious."

Sayers pondered that. "I suppose it's possible. There weren't any obvious wounds to suggest that."

"Maybe not. Doesn't mean it couldn't have been done some other way."

Sayers looked unconvinced. "Hewitt left a suicide note, Trace. We found it on his computer."

"Typed, then. Not handwritten."

"It's the twenty-first century, my friend. Nobody writes notes by hand anymore."

It was a good point, one Trace silently conceded.

Not that he believed for a minute that Hewitt had actually written it.

"You need to find out where Parker Barrington was last night."

Sayers's gaze narrowed. "Why is that?"

"Parker was embezzling funds from the company. And not small change, either. Millions, Mark. Siphoning the money off to an account in the Cayman Islands."

"Jesus. You got any proof?"

"All you need. Hewitt came to me with his suspicions. We set up surveillance in Parker's office. I took him the cold, hard evidence two days ago."

The detective's eyes widened. "Two days ago? You're not thinking Parker Barrington killed Sommerset to cover up the theft?"

"Unless you can convince me otherwise, that's exactly what I'm thinking."

Sayers glanced away, as if he wished he could look back to the time of the murder. "I'll need to see what you've got."

"I'll have it in your office first thing in the morning."

"And I thought this one was going to be easy."

Trace's mouth edged up. "When are they ever easy?"

Mark friend laid a hand on his shoulder, walked him out of the parlor and back down the hall. Trace flicked a last glance into the study as they passed, and continued toward the foyer, lit by a huge chandelier.

"Have you talked to the daughter?" Trace asked.

"She and Parker were here earlier. She was really shaken up. We let him take her home."

Trace made a mental note to go see her. Once the dirt on Parker was uncovered, Emily was going to need all the support she could get.

Sayers stepped out on the wide front porch and Trace followed.

"Besides murder and mayhem," his friend said, "anything new and exciting going on in your life?"

Trace thought of Maggie, spotted her at the edge of the yard, snapping photos of beautiful flame-colored tulips growing around the base of a huge oak tree. They were almost the color of her hair. He watched the way she moved, with a confidence and ease that marked her as a professional. Why that turned him on, he couldn't say.

"Not much," he answered, but as he looked at Maggie, he was thinking maybe that would change.

Sayers's gaze followed his toward the tree and he started to frown. "That isn't… Jesus, Trace, tell me the redhead isn't with you."

Trace dragged his gaze away, finding it harder than it should have been. "She's a client. A photographer. Name's Maggie O'Connell. Matter of fact, I was planning to talk to you about her."

"I know who the hell she is."

Trace didn't like the sound of that. "Want to tell me why?"

Sayers drew him away from the hum of officers and people walking in and out of the mansion. "I shouldn't say this. I could get in a shitload of trouble, but…"

"What is it?"

"She came to us claiming she had a stalker. Said she'd been getting hang-up phone calls, that kind of thing."

"That's right. Go on."

"Captain Varner got wind of it. Turns out Maggie O'Connell brought rape charges against his son, Josh, when she was in high school. Josh was arrested. He claimed he was innocent, claimed Maggie was a willing partner. They were both underage or it would have been far worse. As it was, Josh got kicked off the football team and everyone in his school basically shunned him. They called him a rapist and a pervert, stuff like that. It went on for more than a week—until the O'Connell girl admitted she had lied about the rape."

"Maybe she was telling the truth and she just got scared."

"The boy was completely cleared. They'd been seeing each other for weeks."

"Son of a bitch."

"She's one of those women, Trace. She wanted attention and she got it. The charges were dropped and the records were sealed because of their ages, but it still caused Josh and his family all kinds of trouble. And believe me, Maggie O'Connell is still on Varner's hit list."

"Which is why the police aren't willing to do much more than show up if she calls them."

Mark shot Maggie a hard glare. "It's no secret in the department what happened. Captain Varner doesn't believe any of that bullshit about a stalker, and neither does anyone else."

Trace clenched his jaw so hard it hurt. Mark was the kind of guy who would check the facts, find out the truth. The story about the phony rape accusation was undoubtedly true.

"She's a good-looking woman, Trace, but I wouldn't trust her. Don't let her get under your skin."

Trace reined in his temper, which was beginning to build. "Thanks for the heads-up, buddy."

"Hey, man, we're friends. And you've already had more than your share of trouble with women."

Trace thought of Carly, remembered the sick feeling in his stomach when he'd found out she was sleeping with half the men in Houston. She was a liar and a cheat. He hated a liar, no matter how beautiful she was.

He just nodded as he walked away.

Chapter Seven

Maggie was smiling as she stuffed her camera back in its case, nestled it in the backseat and closed the door, then climbed into the Jeep. "How did it go?"

"Remains to be seen."

"Did you tell them about the embezzling?"

"I told them." Trace didn't say more, and the way his jaw was clenched, Maggie didn't press him. He started the car, slammed it into gear and roared away, slinging her back against the seat. His hands gripped the wheel as if he wanted to tear it out of the vehicle. Whatever had happened, things hadn't gone well.

Maggie kept her mouth shut. Better to give him a little space. As they raced toward Houston, far faster than the speed limit, she considered trying again to start a conversation, but one look at Trace's hard profile and she changed her mind.

They rode back in silence, neither of them speaking all the way to her town house. By the time they arrived and Trace turned off the engine, Maggie couldn't take another minute.

"All right, what is it?" she asked. "If it's the murder, I'll understand. If it's something else, something I've said or done wrong…"

He turned in the seat. "You're a liar, Maggie. In my book, that's as wrong as it gets."

Her stomach twisted at the look on his face. "What are you talking about?"

Trace climbed out of the car, rounded the hood and jerked open her door. "As of right now, I no longer work for you. Find some other sucker to buy into your bullshit."

Her eyes widened. Her own anger surfaced. "What the hell is going on? The least you can do is explain."

Instead of a reply, he caught hold of her arm and hauled her out of the Jeep. He pulled a key from a pocket of his jeans and held it out to her.

"Your new locks are in. The installers left a key with me this morning. You'll find another inside. I'll get your bag and your camera gear."

She planted herself directly in front of him, jammed her hands on her hips. "I'm not going anywhere until you tell me what happened back there that turned you into a maniac."

He ground his teeth, looking as if he wanted to throttle her. "I told you what happened. You lied to me. If you try real hard, I imagine you can figure out which particular lie I might have found a little disturbing."

An icy chill ran through her. He'd been talking to the

police. They must have seen her, must have said something. They must have told him about her Great Shame.

Her hands dropped to her sides. She realized she was trembling. "Josh Varner, right?"

"That's right. Your old boyfriend. Now go unlock the door so I can carry your gear inside and be on my way."

Her heart was beating too fast, slamming against her ribs. She felt sick to her stomach. Not wanting to make a scene in front of the neighbors, she led him to the door of the town house, used the key he'd given her to open the door and stepped aside so he could carry her gear inside.

Wordlessly, he stalked past her into the hall, set her camera case and yellow swim bag on the floor. The muscles in his shoulders seemed to vibrate with tension. He was angry. Furious. And he had every right to be.

She took a deep breath. "Okay, I probably should have told you."

Trace whirled to face her, his dark eyes burning into her like twin laser beams. "Probably?"

"All right, I should have told you. I didn't because I was afraid you would act exactly the way you're acting now."

"I said I'd help you if you told me what I needed to know. You didn't think I needed to know you had an enemy in the police department? That you'd accused some poor kid of rape when he didn't do a goddamn thing but take what you offered?"

She hated the way Trace made it sound, though every word was true. In the past she would have cried, but those days were over.

Instead, she steeled herself, forced up her chin. "I was sixteen years old. My dad caught me coming in at two in the morning and I was scared to death. I was terrified of what he'd do if he knew the truth."

"Beat you?"

"No, but—"

"I'm done, Maggie. You lied to me before. There's no reason to believe you're telling me the truth right now."

She steadied herself, fought for control. "I was ashamed to tell you, all right? It's the worst thing I've ever done."

His hard look didn't soften. No more Mr. Nice Guy, she thought. The charming Southern gentleman was gone. In his place was the fierce Army Ranger he had been and clearly still was. Gold flecks glittered in his dark eyes, and the muscles tightened in his jaw.

"Goodbye, Maggie." He started to turn away, but she caught his arm.

"Trace, please. At least give me a chance to explain."

"You've already explained. We had a deal. You didn't keep your end of it. Now the deal is off."

"But…what about the stalker?"

His jaw tightened even more. "Call the police."

"They won't help and you know it."

"The locks are changed. Your alarm is in. I'll send over one of the guys from JDT to show you how to use it." His smile was harsh. "Though odds are you won't need it."

He no longer believed her. By his standards, she wasn't worthy of his trust.

"Thank you for that."

Trace made no reply. Without a backward glance, he turned and stormed out the door. Maggie forced herself not to run after him. She had her pride, didn't she? Sure, she should have told him about Josh, should have known he would find out sooner or later. But she had wrongly believed that if he did discover her secret, she could simply explain and Mr. Nice Guy Rawlins would understand.

Now she knew Trace Rawlins wasn't always the calm, controlled, soft-spoken guy she had believed. He was a man of fierce conviction and strong emotions.

As she watched his long strides carry him toward the Jeep, something stirred inside her. Some primal instinct that found such a hard, determined man even more attractive than the gentleman he had once seemed.

He jerked open the door and slid behind the wheel, and desire slipped through her. She watched him start the engine, put the car in reverse, then drive away. In moments, he was gone.

Maggie's insides felt heavy. It was ridiculous. She barely knew the man, and yet flickers of heat still tingled through her body, along with a need she had taught herself to ignore.

But she had always been a passionate woman. Passionate about life, about her work, about her family and friends. It shouldn't come as a surprise she would respond to a passionate man.

Maggie sighed, wishing things could have been different, grateful the relationship hadn't gone further than it had before it fell apart.

She turned to assess her surroundings. The town house had been left neat and tidy. Aside from a note and a business card belonging to JDT Security Systems lying on her breakfast bar, and a second set of keys, there was no evidence the installation crew had been there.

She walked over to the counter. The note read, "Installation complete. Trace can show you how to set the alarm."

Except that Trace was gone.

He would send a man over, he had said, and she knew that he would. He was reliable, steady. But he had a temper she hadn't expected. She would have liked to discover the man beneath his surface calm, test the fire he kept so carefully controlled and explore the attraction between them.

If things had worked out differently...

But things hadn't worked out, and that was the end of it.

Trace sat in his office Monday morning reading the newspaper. Except for his Saturday trip to the shore, he'd had a shitty weekend. Hewitt Sommerset was dead. Parker Barrington had very likely killed him. And Maggie O'Connell had turned out to be just another deceitful woman.

He folded the paper and set it on his desk. The headline stared up at him. Missing Woman Found. The article told of a teenage boy finding a woman's body washed up on a local beach. No positive identification had been made at the time the article was written, but the victim's clothing and hair led authorities to believe it was the young woman who had recently disappeared. An autopsy was scheduled to determine the cause of death.

Unconsciously, Trace glanced toward the door, expecting Carly to appear any minute demanding his protection. He wasn't in the mood for his ex-wife and her dramatics, or any other woman—at least not right now.

His thoughts returned to Maggie and the bitter disappointment he felt. She had lied about the false rape, about the police and probably about the stalker.

Worse yet, she had made Trace lose control.

It didn't happen often. Like honor and honesty, in his family, control was a valued commodity. His daddy had lost his temper only once, when Trace had lied to him about sneaking out to meet his friend Willie Johnson and drinking the pint of whiskey Willie had stolen from his mama's special medicinal supply. Trace had been ten years old and his father had used a hickory switch to show him the error of his ways.

Later, his dad had come to him and apologized, as if he were the one who had done something wrong.

"I lost my temper, son. A man can't afford to let that happen. Not ever."

And because Trace wanted to be the man his dad believed him to be, he made sure it never happened.

Well, almost never.

In the army, his nickname had been Ghost. It wasn't just because he had a talent for appearing and disappearing without being seen, a skill that often came in handy. It was also because of the way he remained in control, the way he always stayed calm no matter the situation. Calm and controlled, out of sight and out of mind, as quiet as a ghost.

But Maggie O'Connell had broken through his well-honed defenses. He had begun to trust her, begun to let down his guard.

She's one of those women, Mark Sayers had said. The kind who crave attention, the kind who'll do anything to get it. But she hadn't seemed that way. Which just proved what a piss-poor judge Trace was of women.

Worse yet, part of him worried that maybe Sayers

was wrong. Maybe there *was* a stalker. Maybe—at least about that—Maggie had been telling the truth.

Trace leaned back in his chair, refusing to continue dwelling on his brief relationship with another woman he couldn't trust. He glanced up at a knock at his office door, watched it swing open. Annie never waited for permission.

"Detective Sayers is here to see you. Wants to talk to you about the information you left for him."

Trace sat up in his chair. "Send him in."

Mark walked into the office and closed the door. As always, his light brown hair was neatly combed, while his J. C. Penney suit was slightly wrinkled.

"Parker's got an alibi," he said, cutting straight to the point. "His wife says he was home with her all evening."

"Bullshit." Trace came out of his chair. "She's covering for him. Emily's been a fool for Parker since the day she met him."

"We've still got the embezzlement charges. The D.A.'s on it. He's putting together a case. He doesn't want to move until he's got all his ducks in a row."

"I'll talk to Jason, tell him what's going on. I'll ask him to speak to his sister, see if he can get her to tell the truth."

"He doesn't know about the stolen money?"

"Not yet," Trace said. "But he's in line to take over the company. He's going to need to be told."

"Might not be a good idea," Mark said. "Word is the kid's pretty hotheaded. He might come to the same conclusion you did, and try to do something about it."

Trace thought of the son who had worshipped his powerful father. "You might be right."

"We're on this thing, Trace. If Parker killed Sommerset, he's going down for it."

He nodded. "The funeral is on Wednesday. Once it's over, things will settle down. I'll talk to Emily myself, pay my respects. I'll be sure not to mention that her no-good husband was stealing a fortune from her dad."

Mark chuckled. "Sounds good. Let me know how it goes."

Trace walked his friend through the office, out to the unmarked brown Chevy he was driving that perfectly matched his inexpensive brown suit.

"So what happened with the redhead?" Mark asked as he opened the car door.

"I wouldn't know. She's no longer my client."

"Wise move. I can tell you that as far as I know, she hasn't made any more 911 calls."

"That's good, I guess." But Maggie had always been reluctant to call the police. She didn't think they would help her, and pretty much, she was right.

Trace didn't like the way that made him feel.

"Like I said, keep me in the loop." Mark slid into the car and drove out of the lot, and Trace returned to his office. The kid, Sol Greenway, was working at his desk in the glass-windowed office next to Trace's, partly hidden behind a couple of forty-inch monitors. Trace was good at digging up information, but the kid was better. He could find out anything, legally or illegally. Trace was careful not to encourage him.

Most of the time.

The door was open, Trace walked in and Sol looked up at him. "Yeah, boss?"

"Think you can get into an old, sealed, juvenile arrest file?"

Sol grinned. He pushed his long, straight dark hair out of his eyes. "Sure. Just give me a name."

"Margaret O'Connell. I'll get you her address and phone number and whatever else I've got."

"Shouldn't take long." Sol cracked his knuckles, a habit Trace found mildly annoying, then replaced his fingers on the keyboard.

Silently cursing himself for giving in to his worry about Maggie, Trace turned and walked back out the door.

Chapter Eight

The days slipped past. As promised, a man with JDT
Security Systems arrived at her door within an hour
after Trace had brought her home from their trip to the
shore. Mr. Wilcox had carefully shown her how to set
the alarm, and had checked to see that everything was
working as it should.

"It's a wireless system," he explained. "Fairly basic,
but it's all most people ever need. If the alarm goes off
and you don't enter the proper codes to turn it off, the
system automatically calls the security company. From
there, the police are notified. You should be perfectly
safe as long as you remember to turn it on."

"Thank you, Mr. Wilcox."

"No problem."

So far there hadn't been.

And she had to admit she felt safer with the alarm

system in and dead bolts installed. Since nearly a week had passed and there hadn't been any more notes or hang-up calls, she was beginning to think she didn't need Mr. He-man Rawlins, after all.

The doorbell rang. It was Friday night. The weekend had finally arrived and Maggie had plans for the evening. She checked the peephole, smiled and opened the door.

Dressed in tight red leather pants and a red silk blouse that left her midriff bare, Roxanne sashayed through the door. "You ready, lamb chop?" With her black hair swept into a twist and soft tendrils curling beside her ears, Roxanne, at thirty, was a fox.

Maggie smiled. "I'm ready." Her own outfit was a little less flashy, a very short black skirt, gold silk halter top, gold jewelry and very high black-and-gold heels. "I'm overdue for a little fun."

They were going to Galaxy, an upscale nightclub that catered to the late-twenties through early-forties crowd. Maggie loved to dance. Anything from modern to ballroom, country to hip-hop. Anytime, anyplace, she was game. She was especially good at swing and ballroom dancing, since her dad had insisted she take cotillion.

Cotillion. The old-fashioned word made her smile. Because she didn't have a mother "to teach her certain things," her dad had signed her up on her twelfth birthday, and insisted she attend classes once a week.

Now she was glad she had.

"Grab your purse, girl. Let's rock and roll." Roxanne was always up for going out. She liked drinking martinis and socializing more than actually dancing, but it worked out fine just the same. And since Roxy was leaving for a couple weeks to visit friends in New York, this was kind of a farewell evening.

"Car's out front," Rox said. "I've got Alonzo driving tonight so we don't have to worry if we get a little tipsy."

Roxanne had more money than she could spend, a legacy of her daddy's oil fortune. Though she was two years older than Maggie, they had gone to the U of Houston together, Roxanne starting as a freshman after she had spent a couple years jet-setting around Europe.

They had met in art history class, the one subject Roxanne knew backward and forward, since she had seen a number of antiquities up close and personal in her travels and developed an appreciation. Aside from their common interest in art, for reasons neither of them completely understood, they had become fast friends and still were.

Roxanne's white Mercedes S550 sat in front of the condo, with Alonzo, her good-looking part-time driver, seated behind the wheel. She and Maggie climbed into the backseat and headed for Galaxy, which was over by the Galleria.

It didn't take long to get there. Alonzo opened the door for them, and as they made their way toward the entrance, the doorman recognized them and waved them to the front of the line.

"Thanks, honey," Roxanne said to the big black bouncer with the thick Southern accent.

He just grinned. "You two gals be good tonight. Don't y'all go gettin' them boys stirred up and fightin' over ya."

Maggie laughed at the backhanded compliment. "We'll be sure to mind our manners."

They stepped inside, onto the stainless-steel floor in

the entry, and were captured immediately by the heavy beat of the music. The place was slick and modern, with lots of brushed chrome and dark wood. Mauve and blue lighting gleamed beneath the bar and along the walls, and the ceiling glittered with tiny white lights that winked like stars. The stainless-steel dance floor was large and the DJ was really good at choosing songs, usually a combo of top forty and Latin, with a little disco and the occasional country song thrown in.

Since the crowd was her age or older and Maggie was a regular, she knew a number of people in the crowd. As she and Roxanne slid onto high, dark blue leather seats at the black granite bar, a face she hadn't seen in months was one of the first she recognized.

Roxy leaned toward her, raising her voice a little to be heard above the music and the crowd. "Isn't that your old flame, David, sitting over there?"

Since she had already spotted him, Maggie kept her gaze fixed straight ahead. "That's him."

"I thought he was dating someone."

"I thought so, too." But clearly, he was alone tonight. Their breakup two years ago hadn't been easy and Maggie felt a tightening in her stomach.

The bartender walked over just then, olive-skinned and handsome. "What can I get for you ladies?"

"Grey Goose martini, if you please, Enrique." Roxy had an amazing memory for the names of good-looking men. "Up, and very, very dry."

"I'll have a Cosmo," Maggie added, but one or two were her limit. She was basically a white-wine drinker, though occasionally the strong, fruity cocktail tasted good.

Roxanne leaned closer. "Don't look now, but I think he's coming over."

Maggie inwardly groaned. She told herself not to glance in David's direction, but her eyes went there just the same. He stopped in front of her, a tall man, very lean and perfectly groomed, with blond hair and pale blue eyes.

"It's good to see you, Maggie."

She smiled, tried to ignore the thread of guilt she felt for the way they had parted. "You're looking well, David."

"Thank you. You look beautiful. But then you always do." Very formal, always proper, that was David.

"You remember Roxanne?"

"Of course. Hello, Roxanne."

Roxy took a sip from her long-stemmed glass. "I'm surprised to see you here, David. You were never much for socializing."

David did corporate law for Holder Holder & Meeks. He was happiest behind his desk working on briefs, or researching case law. Just going out with another couple for dinner was a major undertaking for David. Which had been a problem for Maggie, since her job required she attend various gallery shows around the state, and meeting people was just good business. It was also something she enjoyed.

"Would you like to dance?" David asked her.

The DJ was playing a slow song. She didn't want to encourage him, but she didn't want to be rude, either. "All right." Slipping down from the bar stool, she let him guide her through the growing crowd onto the dance floor. When she stepped into his arms, they felt as comfortable as they had during the months they had lived together.

But Maggie had discovered that a comfortable relationship wasn't enough for her. She wanted more, wanted the heat and the passion, wanted the kind of enduring love that happened in romance novels.

Maybe she would never find it. But she was determined to try.

"I've missed you, Maggie."

She looked up at him, tried to smile. "I thought you were seeing someone, David."

"I was, but it didn't work out."

"I'm sorry to hear that."

"I thought… I asked around. You aren't seeing anyone, are you?"

Why Trace Rawlins's image popped into her head, she couldn't begin to say. The man didn't even like her. "Not at the moment."

"I was thinking…maybe we could go out sometime. We're both older, wiser. Maybe things would be different between us now."

Maggie bit back a sigh. "Nothing's different, David. I still care for you as a friend—but nothing beyond that. There's no point in going through all of that again." *All that* being the breakup David had taken so hard, the terrible guilt she felt for ever making him think they might have a future together, when deep down she'd known it would never work.

The song came to an end and he walked her back to her seat at the bar. "Thanks for the dance."

She managed to smile. "It was nice seeing you, David."

He leaned down and kissed her cheek. "Take care, Maggie." Then he turned and disappeared into the crowd.

Maggie released the breath she had been holding.

"How did that go?" Roxanne asked, arching one black eyebrow.

"Take a wild guess."

Roxy lifted her half-full martini glass. "So David and his girlfriend broke up and he's sniffing after you again."

"Yes, they broke up. And I hope he's not sniffing. I hope this was a one-time thing."

"I think the guy has masochistic tendencies. You've only told him a dozen times it's never going to work between you."

"I know, but even with his busy job, David is basically lonely. He's a really nice guy. He deserves to find a woman who truly loves him."

"You tried, kiddo. That's all anyone can do."

"I guess." But she should have followed her instincts, should have known from the start she was going to hurt him. He was a good man, but not the one she wanted.

Another guy walked up to them just then.

"This is a really great song. You wanna dance?" His name was Doug Winston, Maggie recalled. Early forties, attractive in a kind of too-slick way and carrying a few extra pounds around his middle. But he was a very good dancer. Which was all that mattered when she came to Galaxy.

"I'd love to."

Roxy lifted her glass in salute as Maggie headed once more for the dance floor. This time she was able to give herself up to the hot beat of the music, to relax and enjoy herself.

She deserved a night out.

She wouldn't think about anything else, she vowed, and flashed a bright smile as she and her partner moved around the floor.

It was a little after midnight when Trace drove into the two-car garage behind his house. He'd been out to a movie and dinner with Ben Slocum and Ben's current girlfriend, Rita DeStefani. Rita's cousin Haley was in town for a visit, a pretty little blonde Trace had met before. The trouble was that Haley was a talker, and most of what she said was about herself. He had gone as a favor to Ben—who now owed him big-time.

Rubbing the ache in the back of his neck, Trace climbed the back porch steps, pulled open the screen door and stepped inside the screened-in porch. He unlocked the door and walked into the kitchen, flipped on the light switch and punched in the alarm code, turning off the system. Rowdy raced up, tail wagging, and Trace reached down to scratch his ears.

"It's been a long night, buddy," he said, and he was damned glad to be home.

Rowdy whimpered as if he understood.

Then Trace's iPhone started to ring, and silently, he cursed. Nothing good ever happened at this time of night. He sighed as he pulled the phone out of the pocket of his tan slacks and pressed it against his ear. "Rawlins."

"Trace…? Trace, it's Maggie. Please…please don't hang up."

His fingers tightened around the shiny hunk of plastic. "I'm not going to hang up. Tell me what's happened."

"I went out tonight and when I—I came home…when I came back to the house, my phone message light was blinking. Nothing bad has happened, you know, not… not since the last time. So I didn't think anything about it, but this time it…it wasn't just a hang-up call. When I played the message…oh, God, Trace, this guy is really scaring me."

"Check your doors, make sure they're locked. I'll be there in ten minutes." Trace didn't consider not going. His instincts had been warning him from the start. And earlier in the week, Sol had dug into Maggie's sealed juvenile records. Reading the transcripts of what she had said when she had gone to the police to tell them the truth about the rape had moved him deeply.

I love my dad so much.... I didn't want to hurt him. (subject begins to cry) When he caught me sneaking into the house, he asked me what happened and I—I just couldn't...couldn't tell him the truth. Josh and I... we didn't mean for anything to happen, we just...somehow things just went too far. I started crying, and Dad asked me if Josh had forced me to have...have sex with him. I looked at him and I couldn't make myself say the truth, so I just nodded. I thought I could find a way to... to straighten things out in the morning. (subject continues to cry) Then I found out Dad had gone to the police and I—I was terrified for Josh. But I didn't know how to undo what...what I had already done.

Reading the transcript had left Trace with a sick feeling in his stomach. She was just a kid at the time, he realized. At sixteen, still innocent, a young girl trying to find her way. If it hadn't been for her dad going to the cops—which Maggie hadn't expected him to do—the boy would never have been arrested.

Maggie had been horrified and riddled with guilt. As bad as it was for Josh, it was also a terrible trauma for her.

Trace pulled the Jeep into a parking space in front of her condo and killed the engine. As he crossed the asphalt to the sidewalk, she opened the door and just stood waiting. Her face was pale, her chest rising and falling in rapid breaths. As he stepped onto the porch, Trace reached out and pulled her into his arms.

"You all right?" he asked softly against her ear.

Maggie clung to him. She was so upset she was shaking. No way was she faking it.

She nodded, held on an instant longer, then took a deep breath and turned away. "I-I'm okay. Thank you for coming. I know the way you feel and I—"

"I was wrong. I should have listened to what you had to say."

She swallowed, looked as if she wished he would hold her again, but instead moved farther away. "Come on in and I'll play the message."

Trace walked inside and closed the door. He set his hat on the coat tree and turned. For the first time, he got a really good look at her. Black miniskirt, gold satin top that left her back and shoulders bare, sexy high heels. Her pretty red hair was clipped up on the sides, but soft russet curls hung down past her shoulders.

His groin throbbed. He'd been out with a gorgeous blonde all evening. He suspected she'd wanted him to take her to bed, but he hadn't felt the slightest urge. Now, just looking at Maggie, he was already hard and aching to have her.

He released a slow breath. "Let's hear the message."

He followed her into the kitchen, trying not to look at her ass.

He spotted her landline phone and the small black box next to it with the blinking red light.

"It's a little old-fashioned, but I can see the light and know right away when someone has called."

He waited while she punched the play button, and the message began. At first there was a scratchy sound he didn't recognize. Then a song began: "I…saw…you…I knew you would be my one true love. I…saw…you…a vision so pure and sweet, my only true love…."

It sounded like an old vinyl record, a little scratchy, a little wobbly, but he knew the song, had heard it a dozen times over the years. Still, he couldn't quite place it.

The voice that followed, electronically distorted, sent a shiver down Trace's spine. "Mag-gie…my precious Mag-gie. Some-day soon you will awa-ken to me. You will come to me, my Mag-gie. Soon."

He hit the stop button, looked over at her face. The last of the color had drained away, making the freckles stand out on her nose.

"I know it's distorted, but is there any chance you recognize the voice?"

She only shook her head.

"How about the song? You know what it is?"

"I've heard it. It's been years. I can't remember where I know it from."

"I recognize it, too, but only vaguely. It won't be hard to find the name. The question is does it mean anything to you?"

She replied with a shaky breath, "Not a thing."

Trace reached out and hit the message button again, took note of the time of the call, 11:00 p.m. Then he replayed the message. He would have played it a third time if Maggie's face hadn't gone paler every time she heard it.

"You're all dressed up," he said, his gaze skimming over her sexy clothes. "Hot date?" He tried to keep his tone neutral. He had no hold on Maggie O'Connell, no say in what she did or didn't do. Still, he didn't like the idea of her seeing another man.

"Roxy and I went dancing. We went to Galaxy. I love to dance. We don't go that often, but when we do, that's where we usually go."

He knew the place, upscale and classy, catering to a mostly thirties crowd. "Anything unusual happen? Any of your partners say anything, do anything out of the ordinary?"

She hesitated an instant too long.

"Don't make the mistake you made before, Maggie. I need you to trust me. I need you to tell me the truth."

She took a shaky breath. "David Lyons was there. The guy I used to live with? We danced together, but only once, and he didn't say or do anything unusual. In fact, he was extremely polite."

"Why didn't you want to tell me?"

She glazed down at the toes of those very high heels, and Trace's gaze followed. Damn, she had the prettiest legs. Slender ankles and nice high arches. He forced his gaze back to her face.

"David didn't make that call," she said. "He just isn't the kind of guy to do something like that, and I don't want to cause him any trouble."

"You still in love with him?"

She shook her head. "I was never in love with David. That was the problem. I hurt him. I didn't mean to but I did. I don't want to do it again."

"You hurt Josh Varner—now you don't want to hurt David Lyons. Is that about it?"

She swallowed. "I guess maybe that's part of it. I just know David was really…upset when our relationship ended. He's a very nice man and he doesn't deserve more problems from me."

"I'll be sure to keep that in mind," Trace said drily.

But now that he was back on the case, which apparently he was, he was going to see it through. David Lyons was on his list of suspects. For Maggie's sake, Trace would give the guy the benefit of the doubt, but he wouldn't overlook him completely. Not until her stalker was found.

"Anything else?"

Pondering the question, she worried her lower lip. It was plump, damp and shiny, and the muscles across his stomach contracted. He wanted to set his mouth there, find out how sweet those full lips tasted. He wanted to do a lot more than that.

Damn. This wasn't good.

"I can't think of anything," she said. "At least not at the moment."

"There are a couple of things we can do. You've already reported the calls, the notes and the break-in to the police. So far, they haven't been much help. That leaves the phone company. First thing Monday, arrange to get caller ID. You might get lucky and we'll be able to track another call backward if one comes in. Or if the caller number is blocked, which it probably would be, you can figure it's him, let it ring and not pick up."

"All right."

"Also, there's a thing they can do called a trap. Once it's set up, the phone company can figure out where any harassing calls are coming from. The bad news is you'll have to be here when the call comes in, and you'll have to log the time and date. Once the phone company finds the caller's number, they give it to the police, who track it from there."

"What if the police won't do it?"

"I've got a friend in the department. It shouldn't be a

problem. The trouble is, if the guy was careful enough not to leave his fingerprints, he's probably smart enough to use a disposable phone. Even if we get a number, it might not lead us anywhere." There were a couple other alternatives, but the trap seemed to be the best option.

Maggie looked up at Trace. "I think we should try it, don't you?"

"Absolutely. I do a lot of work with the phone company. I'll talk to them, set things up."

He glanced at the clock. It was nearly 2:00 a.m. "Why don't you get some sleep? We can talk again in the morning."

"I'll try." She gave him a wobbly smile. "I feel better now that I've talked to you."

So did he, he realized. He hadn't been able to stop worrying since he'd left her last weekend. She might still be in danger, but now he was around to make sure she stayed safe.

He stifled a groan. That he cared so much did not sit well with him.

"Lock the dead bolt and activate the alarm. Call me when you get up in the morning."

Maggie walked him to the door. She paused for an instant and looked up at him. "Thanks for coming."

He reached out and gently cupped her cheek. "I won't let him hurt you, Maggie."

She managed to smile as his hand fell away. He wanted to reach for her again, ease her back into his arms. He wanted to kiss her, strip off her clothes and make love to her.

She's the last thing you need, he told himself, as he turned and walked out the door.

Chapter Nine

Maggie set the alarm, then climbed the stairs, trying not to think of Trace, and failing miserably. She was ridiculously attracted to him, more every time she was with him. And the heat in those golden-brown eyes said the feeling was mutual. The problem was, though apparently he was going to help her, Trace didn't really trust her.

Which was hardly the framework for any sort of relationship.

It's just about sex, she told herself. Just chemistry. Pheromones did strange things to people.

Maggie walked into her bedroom and flipped on the light switch. She changed out of her clothes, pulled on an oversize pink T-shirt she'd been given at a breast cancer fundraiser and climbed into bed. But sleep remained elusive.

Instead she stared at the ceiling, her mind going over the notes the stalker had left, and the eerie message on her phone.

Who was he?

Someone she had met at one of her shows? Who had purchased one of her photos? Or maybe it was someone she had been introduced to by friends. His words hinted that he knew her in some way. She went over the last few months, the places she had been, the gallery shows where her work had been shown and sold.

Nothing stood out. There'd been a few men who had expressed an interest in her personally, even a couple of guys who had asked her out, but none had pursued the matter once she'd turned them down.

She was exhausted by the time the sun began to creep over the horizon, tired enough that she finally drifted into an uneasy sleep.

It was after nine when a knock at her door jolted her eyes wide open. Grabbing the robe at the foot of her bed, she pulled it on and hurried downstairs.

Wondering if Trace might have returned, ignoring a little curl of hope that he had, she gazed through the peephole. Not Trace. Instead, a young woman with a baby in her arms stood on her front porch.

Shock jolted through her. *Oh, my God.* Maggie reached for the doorknob, her mind trying to process the sight on her doorstep.

"Hello, Maggie. Long time no see." Blonde and slender, her half sister had grown taller than her by at least six inches. With high cheekbones, delicate features and big, thick-lashed blue eyes, Ashley had matured into an incredibly beautiful young woman.

Maggie finally found her voice. "Why don't you come inside?"

Ashley stepped into the entry. The last time Maggie had seen her, she had been a gangly, rebellious teen. Maggie tried to calculate how long that had been.

"It's been six years, if you're counting."

They stood in the foyer, both of them uncomfortable, Maggie still trying to get her mind wrapped around the fact that the sister she barely knew was standing in her home. "That sounds about right. That would make you…"

"I just turned twenty-one."

Maggie forced a smile. "And you have a baby."

"That's right." Wrapped in a soft blue blanket, and no more than a few months old, the infant fussed. Ashley jiggled the child soothingly.

"Let's go into the living room so you can sit down." Maggie started in that direction, barely able to feel her legs moving beneath her. She was still in shock, still trying to grasp the notion of Ashley with a baby. And probably no husband. That was, after all, the modern thing to do.

The girl sat down on the overstuffed, beige floral sofa, cuddling the infant in her lap. Thank God, Maggie had mostly finished unpacking. At least the boxes were gone from the living room.

"Guess you're pretty surprised to see me," Ashley said.

She managed another smile. "You could say that." They had never been close. In fact, the few times Maggie had visited her mother in Florida, there had been a certain animosity between the two girls. At fifteen, Ashley had been wild and out of control, dabbling in drugs and drinking. Maggie, older and working to make a living, had not approved.

"So...what brings you to Houston?"

Ashley looked away, and for the first time Maggie realized she was nervous.

She smoothed the baby's fine dark hair and carefully kept her attention fixed on the child. "Six months ago, Mom kicked Dad out of the house. His business was going bankrupt and you know how much Mom hates problems."

Maggie knew, all right. A similar thing had happened to her own father. Tom O'Connell's small trucking company had been having financial problems. Money was tight and her mother couldn't handle it. So Celeste took off, leaving them high and dry, and returned home to Florida. As soon as the divorce was final, she'd married the first man who asked her, only to have it end in a quick divorce. A third marriage the following year had produced Ashley, and lasted, apparently, until a few months ago.

"I was six months pregnant when she gave him the boot. Dad was having his own problems. I didn't have anywhere else to go, so I stayed with Mom after he left. We fought all the time. After I had the baby, it got worse. Last week, I packed up my things and moved out. I thought...I was hoping you would help me."

Maggie just sat there. "Are you asking me for money?"

Ashley straightened and her chin angled up. "I was hoping you would help me get a job, you know? Find a place to live, figure things out." She stood up, the baby still tight in her arms. "It was stupid. We're not even really sisters." She started for the door, and the sight of her leaving, clutching the tiny baby so desperately in her arms, squeezed something tight in Maggie's chest.

"Wait!" She hurried after the girl, reached out and caught her arm. "We *are* sisters. We just don't know each other." She didn't let go. "Come back and sit down. We'll talk things out, see what we can do. It might take us a while, but we'll manage. You can start by telling me your baby's name."

Ashley gazed softly down at the infant she carried, and a tender smile curved her lips. "His name is Robert. After my dad. I call him Robbie."

They walked back into the living room and sat back down.

"Does Mom know you're here?"

"I told her I was leaving. At the time, I wasn't exactly sure where I was going."

"You'll need to call her or she'll be worried."

"I doubt it."

"Still…"

Ashley shrugged her slender shoulders. "If I stay, I'll call."

Maggie gazed at the infant. He looked like every other baby she'd ever seen, with chubby cheeks, big inquisitive eyes, a little pug nose. "What about…Robbie's father?"

Her sister sighed. "I was a fool. I thought I loved him and he loved me. But Zig didn't give a damn. All he cared about was sex."

"His name is Zig?"

"His name is Sigman Murdock. Kinda weird, huh? Zig hated his name so he called himself Ziggy—you know, from Zig-Zag, the rolling papers? Should have been a tip-off, huh? But Ziggy was charming and super good-looking. By the time I realized the kind of guy he really was, it was too late."

Ashley bent and kissed the top of the baby's head. "Mom and Dad wanted me to have an abortion, but I just…I couldn't do it, Maggie." She smoothed a finger over her child's cheek and his big blue eyes followed the movement. "Robbie's the best thing that's ever happened to me, and no matter what, I'll find a way to take care of him."

Maggie looked at her sister and felt a tug at her heart. "You don't have to go. We'll find a way through all of this."

They would manage somehow. She wasn't about to toss her out in the street.

Still, Maggie couldn't help thinking, *Dear God, how am I going to work with a baby in the house?*

She knew nothing about children. Almost nothing about the young woman who had come to her for help.

And there was the matter of the stalker. It was hardly fair to put Ashley and her baby in danger.

Maggie sighed. If she thought her life was complicated before, she hadn't imagined the problem that had just arrived on her doorstep.

At the first light of dawn, Trace headed for the office. He wanted to know the name of the song on Maggie's message machine. He wanted to read the rest of the lyrics. Maybe they would give him a clue to the stalker's identity.

It was early Saturday morning, not a scheduled workday, but security wasn't the kind of business that had set hours. He turned on the overhead lights, made a pot of coffee and carried a mug of the steaming brew into his glass-enclosed office.

It took a minute for the computer to boot up. As soon as it had, he typed the first line of the song on Google: "I…saw…you…I knew you would be my one true love."

To his amazement, the phrase popped right up. There were at least a dozen sites on the first page, along with the movie from which it had come.

"The Prince and the Maiden," Trace said aloud. "Jesus, that's eerie."

"What's eerie?"

He turned, to find Ben Slocum standing in the open doorway. "You owe me, brother," Trace said. "Last night was way above and beyond the call of duty."

Ben just laughed. "Does that mean you went home with Haley, or you didn't?" He was as tall as Trace, his features harder, his slightly crooked nose having once been broken. His eyes, an icy blue, drew women like a magnet. Rita DeStefani, the shapely model who was Ben's current flame, was just one among a long, ever-growing list.

"Are you kidding?" Trace grumbled. "I was damned glad to get rid of her. Next time, find somebody else to pawn her off on."

Ben smiled. "Shouldn't be too tough. She's a good-looking girl and she likes to party."

"You mean she's easy. I guess these days I'm looking for more than a quick piece of ass."

One of Ben's dark eyebrows went up. "That sounds interesting. Who is she?"

Trace frowned. "I didn't say there was anyone in particular."

"Maybe not, but I'm betting there is. I can see it in your face."

Trace refused to think of Maggie. He wasn't about to fall for another redhead. He had learned his lesson.

He hoped.

"What're you working on?" Ben asked.

"The O'Connell stalker case."

"Thought you said you were dropping that one for personal reasons."

"She got a call from him last night. Played a song for her on her message machine. We both kind of remembered it, but we couldn't think of the name." He pointed at the computer screen. "It's from *The Prince and the Maiden*."

Ben leaned over and stared at the website, elyrics, showing on the monitor. "*The Prince and the Maiden?* That old animated kid's movie? That's weird."

"Guy electronically distorted his voice. Scared the hell out of her." Trace clicked the play button on the YouTube link and the music floated into the room. Both men listened, then Trace clicked it off. "I got a bad feeling about this one."

Ben straightened away from the desk. "They're all lunatics. Let me know if I can help."

"Thanks, Ben."

Ben headed for his office and Trace turned back to the computer screen, reading the words of the song again and again. The lyrics were relatively short: "I… saw…you…I knew you would be my one true love. I… saw…you…a vision so pure and sweet, my only true love…." The brief song played out, finally came to an end, a beautiful love song that could mean just about anything.

Could be the guy knew her or had met her some-where, or as it said in the song, she was only a vision in his mind.

Trace clicked on a couple more links, discovered the film was first released in 1959. Which didn't mean much, either, since it had been released again and again over the years, and almost everyone had seen the movie at some point in their lives.

He pulled out his cell phone, brought up Maggie's number and punched the button. It took a while for her to answer and he wondered if she might still be sleeping. The image of her naked popped into his head, all that glorious red hair spread out on the pillow.

Maggie sounded a little breathless when she said hello.

"Maggie, it's Trace."

"Oh, hi. I meant to call but I…got sidetracked."

He thought of the ex-boyfriend she had danced with last night. "Mind if I stop by? I've found the song and I've got a few more questions."

"Well, ummm… Sure, come on over."

Ignoring the hesitation in her voice and trying not to think that a visit from the ex might be the cause, he printed the lyrics and shut down the computer. After he talked to her, he planned to hit the real estate office that had sold her the town house, speak to the agents involved in the transaction. First he wanted to know if the song or the movie rang any bells with her.

He waved to Ben, grabbed his hat off the rack beside the door and walked out. A few minutes later, he pulled up in front of the town house. As he neared the front door, he could hear conversation inside. It sounded female, but he couldn't make out what the women were saying.

He knocked and Maggie opened the door.

"Good morning. Come on in." She smiled at him and a rush of heat went straight through him. All morning, he'd been thinking about her, trying to forget the feel of her soft body pressed against him last night. Clearly, it hadn't worked, and he silently cursed.

He pulled off his hat, ran a hand through his hair. "You sleep okay?" he asked, then grimaced as the picture he'd imagined of her naked in bed popped into his mind.

"Not great." She stepped out of the way and he walked past her into the entry. "Before we get started," she said as she closed the door, "there's someone I'd like you to meet."

Trace pulled his thoughts back to business, and followed her into the living room. His gaze shot to the young woman on the sofa, a baby in her arms.

"Trace, this is my sister, Ashley Hastings. And her son, Robbie. Ashley, this is Trace Rawlins. He, um, he owns the company that installed my new alarm system."

Trace frowned. It wasn't a lie. After all, he was in the security business. It just wasn't entirely the truth.

"Nice to meet you," he said, but he was thinking that Maggie O'Connell kept more secrets than the CIA.

He focused his attention on the younger woman, a stunning blonde, tall and slender, with delicate features and a short cap of softly curling hair. She could have been a model for *Vogue* magazine.

"Mind if I steal your sister for a couple minutes?" Trace asked her. "There's a couple of minor items we need to discuss."

Ashley smiled. "Not at all. It's nice to meet you, Trace."

"You, too, Ashley."

"Why don't you go ahead and finish getting settled?" Maggie said to her. "I'm sure this won't take long. There's food in the fridge if you get hungry."

Trace set a hand at her back, guided her out to his Jeep, and they both climbed inside. He tossed his hat into the backseat but didn't start the engine. "Why is it I'm just finding out you've got a sister?"

Maggie's head snapped toward him. "I'm sure I mentioned her. I said my mom remarried down in Florida and had another child."

He grunted. "From the way you said it, I didn't expect her to be a grown woman."

"I haven't seen Ashley in years. This morning she showed up on my doorstep, babe in arms. I couldn't just send her away."

"No, I guess not. But it sure as hell complicates things."

"I know."

"I get the idea you haven't told her about your stalker."

"Not yet, but I will. I didn't want her to think I was just trying to get rid of her."

"Is that what you want?"

Maggie sighed. "Let's just say I've got enough trouble without adding more. I don't really know Ashley. I haven't seen her since she was fifteen."

"What else?" he pressed, sensing there was more.

"Fine. You're so high on the truth, here it is—I've always resented Ashley for being the daughter my mother loved. I wanted a mother so badly, but Mom barely knew I existed. I know it's silly, but that's the way I felt."

His mouth edged up. "You're both grown now."

Maggie released a slow breath. "I know. And she's got a newborn. She and my mother aren't speaking, which means I've got to help her. I can't just turn her away."

Trace made no reply. She was right, as far as he was concerned. The girl was family. That was enough. And she was Maggie's sister. Secretly, he had always wanted a brother. Maybe that was the reason he'd become so close to Dev and Johnnie, his buddies in the army. The men were more like brothers than just friends.

"Listen, Maggie, this morning I went on the internet and found that song you heard last night. It's from an old animated children's movie, *The Prince and the Maiden*."

Her green eyes widened. They were rimmed by lashes nearly as thick as her sister's. "You're kidding! I saw that film when I was a little girl."

"Anything you remember about it that might help us?"

She thought for several long moments. Then shook her head. "I loved the movie. I guess I was a romantic even before I knew what it meant. Aside from that, I can't think of a thing."

He handed her the computer printout. "These are the rest of the lyrics. Anything stand out? Any flash of memory that could mean something?"

Maggie read the words, which were mostly a repeat of the first two lines. She sighed and dropped the sheet onto her lap. "I have no idea what this guy is thinking, Trace, I swear."

He picked up the paper, folded it, unsnapped his shirt pocket and tucked it inside. "It's not your fault. The guy is obviously a nutcase. You don't think the way he does. Probably better you don't."

"So where do we go from here?"

"I need to speak to your real estate agent."

She cast him a hopeful glance. "Can I go with you? The office is only a few blocks away. I need to get out of the house for a while, try to get my head together about all of this."

He should probably say no. The more time he spent with her, the more he thought about taking her to bed. "I don't see why not." At least with him, she'd be safe.

"Let me go tell Ashley."

On the other hand, as much as he wanted her, she'd probably be safer if she just stayed home.

Chapter Ten

Maggie leaned back in the deep leather seat as Trace drove the Jeep away from the town house. The Garmin Real Estate office was a couple miles away, in a small shopping center on Bissonnet.

As they started toward the door, she felt Trace's hand at her back, guiding her up the walkway, and just that slight touch made her skin feel warm.

The office was mostly empty, she discovered as they walked inside, with just a few agents sitting at metal desks. Photos of homes for sale rested on pedestals in the front window, and sales licenses hung on the walls.

"Mike Jenkins was the listing agent for all six town house units," Maggie told Trace, pointing to a short, stocky man with thinning hair seated at the desk farthest away. "That's him over there."

Trace urged her in that direction. Mike stood up as

they approached and greeted them with a smile. "Hello, Maggie. It's nice to see you. I hope you're enjoying your new home."

"It's great, thanks. Mike, this is Trace Rawlins. He's an investigator. Recently, I had a break-in. Trace is hoping you can help me."

Mike turned to him. "I'm happy to do what I can."

"I need to know who had access to the key to Maggie's condo."

"No one lately. Not since the deal closed. Before that, we all did." He gestured to the entire office. "While the condo was for sale, the key was on the sales board. Agents just sign it out when they need it."

"Then you have a record of who might have used it."

"That's right. We put the property sign-out sheet in the file after the sale closes." He walked to the back of the office and pulled open a drawer from a row of metal files along the wall. Withdrawing a manila folder, he closed the drawer and returned.

Mike opened the file, took out a sheet of paper and handed it to Trace. "This is a list of anyone who checked out a key."

"Are these all salespeople?"

"Well, yes, and pest control, cleaning people, the guy who did the home inspection."

A muscle jerked in Trace's cheek. "So pretty much anyone on this list could have made a copy."

"Well, I guess so, yes. But we're all professionals here. We've never had a problem."

"At least that you know of. You might want to consider rekeying a home after you've sold it."

"Absolutely. We always advise our buyers to do exactly that."

Trace turned a hard look on Maggie and a guilty flush rose in her cheeks. "Mike said I should rekey. I just never got around to it."

The Realtor's chubby face broke into a smile. "We look after our clients in every way we can."

"Anyone show an interest in the place after you'd shown it to Maggie?"

"There couldn't have been many," she interjected. "I made an offer just a few days after I first saw it, and the offer was accepted."

"That's right. Once the property went into escrow, it was taken off the market." Mike took the sign-out sheet from Trace's hand, looked down at the names and dates. "I showed Maggie the condo on Friday, the first of March." He opened the transaction file, thumbed through a couple pages. "We made the offer on Monday, the fourth, and the property went into escrow later that same day."

Mike glanced back down at the list. "Jim Brewer signed out a key on March 3, the Sunday before we made the offer. That would have been after Maggie had been there. Jim held an open house."

"I'll need to talk to him," Trace said. "Any idea when he might be in?"

"He's sitting another open house, at 2255 Woodale. It's just off Braeswood. You can find him there."

"All right, that's it then." Trace offered a hand and the agent shook it. "Thanks, Mike."

"Let me know if there's anything else I can do."

Trace urged Maggie back toward the door and she let him guide her out to the Jeep.

"I guess we're going to an open house," she said.

She found Trace's eyes in the mirror. She thought

he might say no, but instead he started the engine. "I guess we are," he said.

Maggie thought of the dozens of people who had been in the town house, people who could have made a key. It seemed impossible to find out if one of them had become her stalker.

"Why would this guy, my stalker, go to an open house? How would he even know I was interested in buying the place?"

"I'm not sure he did. But he got inside fairly easily, so either he had a key or he knew the layout, or both. Maybe he was following you the day Mike showed it to you. If he was, maybe he heard you say you planned to buy it, and he wanted to see where you would be living. Maybe he just went to the open house because you'd been in the condo and he wanted to be in a place you had been."

Maggie felt a chill. "I can't…can't believe he'd be that obsessed."

Trace flashed her a sideways glance. "You can't?"

She thought of the notes, of the eerie song left on her answering machine last night, and her insides tightened. How dangerous was this man? Just how frightened should she be?

And what about Ashley and little Robbie?

A sign appeared on the road: Open House, with an arrow pointing the direction.

"It's up ahead." Trace followed a trail of signs to an older, white, ranch-style home shaded by a cluster of big, leafy trees.

They walked inside and a thirty-something agent with short sandy hair and hazel eyes started over to greet them. He was wearing a suit and tie and a wide white smile.

"Mike Jenkins sent us," Trace said. "We aren't here to see the house, just to ask you a couple of questions."

The smile slipped away. "Oh?"

"I'm Maggie O'Connell. I bought one of the town houses your company had listed on Broadmoor. You held an open house on my unit the Sunday before I made the offer."

"I remember the place. You got a good buy."

"I like to think so."

Trace tipped his head toward the guest book lying open on the table in the entry. "Did you keep a guest register that day?"

"I did. That's the way we pick up clients."

"Lots of people show up that day?"

"No, just a few."

"Did everyone sign?"

"I think so." He walked over to the book and flipped the pages back to an earlier date. "Here it is…2818 Broadmoor, unit A. Only two couples came in that day." He glanced up, frowned. "Wait, that's not right. There was a man…he said he wasn't really a buyer, at least not yet. He just wanted to take a look around, get an idea of values for when he was ready to purchase. Since the condo was empty, I let him wander a bit. He didn't stay very long."

"What'd he look like?" Trace asked.

"Big guy. Forties. Heavyset. A touch of silver in his hair. Nothing that really made him stand out. I only remember him because he didn't want to sign."

"Dark hair?"

"Yeah, but with silver running through it. He looked

kind of distinguished. I figured he had some money. That's one of the reasons I let him wander."

Trace looked at Maggie. "Ring any bells?"

She shook her head. "A client, maybe. Someone who bought one of my pictures. No one specifically I can think of."

Trace turned back to the Realtor. "Thanks. We appreciate your help."

"Anytime."

They walked out of the house, heading for the car.

"You think the man Jim saw at the open house was him?" Maggie asked as they climbed into the Jeep.

"No way to tell, at least not yet. But it's something." Trace slid in behind the wheel. "If we get another lead that points to a guy who fits the same description, we'll know we have something."

"If it's him, it isn't David. He's younger than that, slim and blond, and he has blue eyes."

Trace grunted. "Sounds like a real pretty boy."

Maggie bit back a smile. "I guess you could say that." She looked at Trace from beneath her lashes. "You're kind of pretty yourself."

He laughed, white teeth flashing in a face so ruggedly handsome it made David look like a sissy. Trace turned to gaze at her and silence fell between them. He reached out and settled a hand on her cheek, and she could feel his working-man calluses, feel the strength. Leaning over, he very softly kissed her, just the lightest brush of lips before his mouth settled firmly over hers.

Maggie's pulse roared. Her breathing quickened and damp heat poured through her. Trace kept kissing her, soft moist kisses that made her toes curl inside her sneakers and need tighten like a fist in her belly. The kiss deepened, turned erotic. A soft moan escaped. He tasted like heaven. Like cinnamon and coffee and hot, sexy male.

God, she wanted this man. She wasn't sure what she wanted to happen after the sex, but she had never felt this kind of desire before, this strong an attraction, and she wanted to find out where it might lead.

By the time Trace ended the kiss, she had forgotten where they were, forgotten everything but the aching want clawing through her body.

When he settled his tall frame back against the seat, he was breathing as hard as she.

"I was afraid of that," he said, sounding almost angry.

"Afraid of what?" She couldn't concentrate. All she could think of was how much she wanted him to kiss her again.

"Afraid you'd taste as sweet as you do, and I'd want you even more than I already did."

Heat rushed into her cheeks. As much as she wanted him, she wasn't the kind of woman who jumped into bed with a man. She needed to know what she was getting into, needed to think this through before she did something stupid, the way she had with David.

A shuddering breath whispered out. She worked to slow her breathing, determined to force things back on a safer track. "So, um, how do we find another lead?"

He leaned down and cranked the key, and the engine roared to life. "We hope he calls after we set up the trap on your phone."

Maggie studied Trace's profile, tried not to think of that mind-blowing kiss. She was wildly attracted to him. But she didn't need any more trouble in her life, and it was clear this man was a handful. "You don't look optimistic."

He shrugged his broad shoulders. "There's a chance. But like I said, this guy doesn't seem the type to make that kind of mistake. He probably used a disposable phone."

"Like the ones you buy at the supermarket?"

"Right." Trace pulled the Jeep out into the street. "I'm putting Rex Westcott on your place tonight. He's good. You won't see him. Neither will your stalker if he shows up."

Her senses went on alert. "You think he might?"

Trace didn't bother to answer. The man had been there before. "You need to tell your sister."

Maggie moistened her lips, which suddenly felt dry. "I'll tell her when I get home."

Trace drove Maggie back to her town house. He was still hard inside his jeans. One lousy kiss. Dammit, he'd known better. He had rotten luck with women, especially redheads. But his willpower was nil where Maggie was concerned.

"Where are you going from here?" she asked, which put his big head back in charge, thank God.

"I need to talk to Emily Barrington. I called her this morning, told her I wanted to stop by early this afternoon."

"Hewitt's daughter?"

"That's right."

"So you're still working on the murder."

"There's still no proof there was one. I need to find out if Parker Barrington really was home with his wife the night her father died."

"Is that what Emily says?"

"That's what she says."

"So the case is ongoing."

"The D.A.'s building an embezzlement case against Parker. In the meantime, I'm doing some digging on my own." Trace turned the Jeep onto Broadmoor. Maggie's condo was just down the block. "I want you to keep me advised of your movements. I don't want this guy getting you alone somewhere, okay?"

She stiffened. "I've got to work, Trace. I need to take some more photos, finish getting others framed and ready for the show. I've got a black-tie opening on Friday at the Twin Oaks Gallery. It's a very big deal for me."

"It that so? Unless we catch this guy, you'll be bringing a date to the party."

"A date? I'm not bringing a date, I'll be working."

"Maybe I should have said *bodyguard*."

Her russet eyebrows shot up. "You?"

"That's right."

She eyed him as if she were trying to decide if he'd come up to scratch. "You'd have to wear a tuxedo."

The corner of his mouth quirked. "I think I can handle it."

"Yeah?"

"Yeah."

Maggie didn't say more and he wondered if she was comparing him to Pretty-boy Lyons. She'd said she wasn't in love with the guy. Carly never loved any of the men she slept with but it didn't keep her out of their beds.

"I don't suppose you'd take me with you to see Emily?" Maggie asked. "I could wait outside in the car."

Trace grinned. "Which is it? The sister or the baby?"

"Both. I don't know Ashley, and I don't know anything at all about babies."

He chuckled. "Come on, Maggie. I never took you for a coward."

She laughed. "Just shows you how little you know about me."

His humor slowly faded. All too true. He knew very little about her, and he was a rotten judge of women. Maggie seemed different, but he could damn well be wrong.

He let her off in front of her town house. The look of dread on her face softened his mood. "You'll be fine," he assured her.

"Thanks for the ride," Maggie said darkly. Squaring her shoulders, she marched up the sidewalk as if she were facing a firing squad.

From Maggie's, Trace drove across town to an area off the Allen Parkway. It was an elegant, prestigious neighborhood, with some of the most expensive homes in Houston. Parker Barrington's house looked like a Southern plantation, sparkling white, with two massive Corinthian columns out front and a balcony that wrapped around the second floor.

When Trace rang the bell beside the big double doors, a short, thin, dark-haired man in a black suit and white shirt opened the door. *The butler.* The pretension was Parker all the way.

Trace wondered how the man was going to adjust to the eight-by-eight cell he'd be sharing with some big bruiser, and almost smiled.

"Trace Rawlins," he said. "I'm here to see Mrs. Barrington. I believe she's expecting me."

"Why, yes, Mr. Rawlins. Please come in." The butler reached for the hat in Trace's hand, which he surrendered. "Mrs. Barrington asked that you wait for her in the long gallery. I'll let her know you're here."

"Thank you."

The long gallery overlooked a huge, manicured yard studded with tall, leafy trees. Clusters of yellow crocus, pink petunias and purple and yellow pansies bloomed along the walkways.

He sat down on a rose velvet chair next to a matching sofa that looked out at the grounds through small paned windows. He had met Emily a number of times over the years, but had never been to her house before. She hadn't seemed the type to be quite so enamored of society, nor her tastes quite so lavish. But the house fit Parker like an expensive leather glove.

He looked up at the portraits hanging on the wall, gilt-framed paintings of various family members. Hewitt and Caroline Sommerset, Emily's parents, were prominently displayed. He assumed the perfectly groomed blond couple in the picture to the left belonged to Parker.

In beige slacks and an embroidered blue silk blouse, Emily walked into the gallery a few minutes later. She had short dark hair cut in a stylish bob, the same blue eyes as Jason and her brother's fair complexion. Trace rose as she entered, her hands extended in greeting.

"Good morning, Trace. Thank you for stopping by."

He took her hands, gave them a gentle squeeze, leaned down and kissed her cheek. "I came to express my condolences, Emily. I admired your father very much. And I liked him."

Her eyes misted. "He was…my father was a very great man. I still can't believe he's gone."

"Hewitt was larger than life. I figured he'd live to be a hundred."

Emily glanced out the window, her gaze fixed on a bird that landed in a small marble fountain. "I still don't understand why he killed himself."

It was the opening Trace needed. "Are you certain he did?"

She sank down on the velvet sofa and Trace returned to his chair across from her.

"I can't figure out why he would. He seemed happy. He and Jason were planning a trip to the Bahamas. I thought he was really looking forward to it."

"I think he was."

She met Trace's gaze. "Jason believes he was murdered. That's why you're here, isn't it? You think so, too."

Trace steeled himself. "Yes, Emily, I do. I think someone shot him and made it look like he pulled the trigger."

"Is that…is that even possible?"

"It isn't easy but it can be done."

She clasped her hands in her lap. "Then that must be what happened. I don't think Dad would kill himself."

"There were circumstances, Emily. Before it happened, your father asked me to check into some…accounting problems that he had turned up. Do you know anything about that?"

She frowned. "No, why would I?"

"Because Parker was involved."

"Parker? You…you aren't implying…"

Trace made no comment.

"You're wrong, Trace. Parker wouldn't steal from my father. He…he wouldn't do something like that."

"I didn't mention stealing, Em. I think maybe your

instincts have been telling you that something was wrong, and because you love Parker you don't want to face the truth."

She rose from the sofa, her spine stiff and her face pale. "I think...think you should leave now."

Trace stood up, too. "Was Parker home with you the night your father died, Emily? Or was he out well past midnight? Past the time that your father was killed?"

She swayed on her feet, seemed to shrink inside herself. "Oh, God. He wouldn't do it, Trace. He couldn't—could he?"

"You need to tell the police the truth, Em. You need to let them sort it out."

She swallowed, wiped at the tears rolling down her cheeks. "H-he wasn't home with me that night. H-he came in late. When I asked him where he'd been, he said he was downstairs in the library. We both...both knew he wasn't. I had looked for him there." She straightened, seemed to find some inner strength. "Find out what happened, Trace. Find out if my husband...if Parker murdered my father."

"I've got to tell the police, Emily. They need to know so they can continue their investigation."

She nodded, sank back down on the sofa. "Tell them. Find out the truth."

"You can't mention this to Parker. Not yet."

Tight lines formed around her mouth. "That won't be a problem. He's hardly ever home."

"Take care of yourself, Emily." Turning, Trace strode back to the entry, took the hat the butler held out to him and left the house.

The first call he made was to Mark Sayers.

Chapter Eleven

"So there you have it," Maggie said, finishing what she had finally gotten around to telling her sister. "I've got some creep stalking me, and staying here puts you and little Robbie in danger."

Ashley gently jiggled the baby in her lap, making him smile. "And Trace Rawlins is the man you hired to find this guy."

"That's about it. I should have told you when you first got here, but it just seemed like too much to handle all at once."

The infant wrapped his tiny fingers around Ashley's thumb and made a little cooing sound. A soft smile curved Ashley's lips, then she looked up. "Did you mean what you said about helping me and Robbie?"

"Of course I did. It was kind of a shock, seeing you

out on my porch like that. But I meant it. We're sisters. I'll do everything I can to help you."

Ashley sat up a little straighter on the sofa. "Then we're staying. You've got this Rawlins guy working on the problem—he's a major hunk, by the way. If you're paying him, he's not going to let anything happen to you, right?"

"That's what he says." She ignored the "hunk" comment, though she certainly agreed. "The problem is we don't know what this guy might do next. Until we catch him, anything could happen."

Ashley shrugged. "I ran away from home when I was in high school. Mom probably never told you that."

Maggie shook her head. "No, she didn't. But we don't talk very often, and when we do, all she ever says is everything's fine."

"I lived on the street for a while. I wasn't a prostitute or anything, but I slept in the open and I bummed around with some pretty strange people. I made friends with a couple of girls who turned tricks, and they talked about guys who like to be spanked and stuff. There are some real weirdos out there. I learned real fast to stay away from certain kinds of men."

Maggie's heart squeezed to think of the young girl who had been out there alone, struggling to find her way. "I'm sorry you felt you had to do that. I'm glad you went back home."

"I figured out pretty fast that Mom and Dad weren't all that bad. I mean, they fought all the time and mostly ignored me, but at least I had a decent place to live. I went back to high school and graduated before I took off again."

Maggie watched the baby's eyes drift closed. At three

months old, he slept most of the time. He was so tiny and sweet. "Where did you go after high school?"

"I got my own apartment and took a job in a cocktail lounge. Pay wasn't good but the tips made up for it. Unfortunately, that's where I met Ziggy."

"Robbie's dad," Maggie said darkly, disliking the guy more every time she heard his name.

"Yeah. Like I said, Zig was really good-looking, you know? All the waitresses were hot for him, but I was the one he wanted. I guess that made me feel important. I let him move into my apartment for a while and even paid his bills." Her lips tightened. "One thing about Ziggy—he taught me how to take care of myself. If the creep who's been bothering you comes around, he'll get more than he bargained for."

Maggie grinned. It was beginning to seem there was a lot more to her sister than just a rebellious nature and a penchant for getting into trouble.

"Trace's people changed the locks and installed an alarm system. We should be safe enough inside the house."

"I'd like to stay, Maggie, if you'll let me."

Maggie reached over and caught her sister's hand. "I'd love for you both to stay."

Ashley's eyes glistened. "Thanks. Want to hold him? He's ready for his nap so he won't wiggle around too much."

Maggie swallowed and stood up. "I've never held a baby. I really don't know how."

"It's easy." Fussing with the blanket, Ashley gently settled her son in Maggie's arms. "Just make sure you keep his head supported."

She did as Ashley instructed, nestling the baby

against her shoulder, feeling the warmth of his tiny body seeping into her. Something softened inside her, made her heart swell.

"Are you nursing him?" she asked.

Ashley shook her head. "I wanted to, but I couldn't make enough milk. The doctor said Robbie wasn't getting the nutrients he needed, so I stopped. He's doing a lot better now."

Maggie gazed down at the infant in her arms. "He seems really happy."

Her sister smiled. "He almost never cries. He's such a good baby."

Maggie moved a little, gently swaying, watching as the baby's big blue eyes slowly began to close. "I'm an aunt," she said, feeling a ridiculous smile spread over her face. "It feels kind of funny." She looked at Ashley. "And kind of wonderful, too."

The girl wiped a tear from her cheek. "I wanted Mom to love him. But she hated Ziggy so much she couldn't get past it."

"Well, I love him already," Maggie said. "And we're going to make sure Robbie has everything he needs."

Ashley's shoulders seemed to relax, as if some of her burden had been lightened. "Thanks, Maggie." Her lips firmed. "And in the meantime, we're going to help Trace catch the creep who's been harassing you."

Maggie gazed down at the tiny baby in her arms and worry filtered through her. What if something happened? She only hoped that in letting Ashley stay she was doing the right thing.

Trace called Mark Sayers about the conversation he'd had with Emily, then arranged for Rex Westcott to handle surveillance on Maggie's town house that night. He knew Westcott was completely reliable, that he would be watching for anyone hanging around the condo, and he wouldn't be spotted.

Still Trace worried. There was something about Maggie's stalker that had his instincts on alert, something that warned there was more going on here than it seemed. The guy might just be a loony, like most of them. Or he might be extremely dangerous, as Trace's gut continued to insist.

And now there was a young girl with a baby in the house.

Of course, the stalker's obsession was with Maggie. He wouldn't be interested in the girl, but there was always the risk of collateral damage. Trace didn't want Maggie's sister and her baby caught in the crossfire.

After a restless night, Trace drove to the office Sunday morning. The sun wasn't quite up, but it was already warm. In another month it would be full-blown summer.

Trace brewed a pot of strong coffee, filled his mug and sat down at his desk. He returned to Maggie's list of names and continued digging, looking for anything interesting he might find on the internet.

A little after eight, Rex Westcott walked in. He was not quite six feet tall, late thirties, slim with medium brown hair and intelligent hazel eyes. A slight limp from an old army wound caused a subtle hesitation in his gait.

Trace left his office and walked out to greet him. "Everything go all right?"

Rex yawned. "A little too all right. It's such a quiet neighborhood I had a helluva time staying awake."

"Coffee?" Trace asked with a smile.

"I'd kill for a cup."

The men walked back to the kitchen area and Trace poured a mug for Rex. "No sign of the guy, then?"

"No, and I looked pretty hard for any indication he'd been there the nights before. No cigarette butts, footprints in the flower beds, broken shrubbery, nothing."

"We'll try it again tonight. After that, we'll wait and see."

Rex finished his coffee in a few big gulps. "That'll keep me awake long enough to drive home. I'll get some sleep and be ready to go out again."

"Sounds good."

Rex left the office, and a few minutes later, Alex Justice walked in. He sniffed the air and flashed a grin that cut a dimple into his cheek. "Coffee! Thank God."

"Long night?"

"Early morning. I'm working that security breach on the Consolidated Boatyard. I need to get down there, take another look around."

"No rest for the weary."

"You got that right."

Alex stayed only long enough to check his phone messages, his email and whatever might have landed on his desk, then he was gone.

Trace called Maggie, relayed Rex's boring night, went back to his digging, came up with nothing, then went home. What he really wanted to do was see Maggie.

Which was exactly the reason he didn't.

Monday went much the same, except that the hum of people working in the office eased his nerves. That and hearing from Rex that again Sunday night he had seen no sign of Maggie's stalker. Trace had spoken to the phone company and they'd set up the trap, which would be operational beginning tomorrow. He needed to speak to Maggie, remind her that if the stalker phoned or she got any more hang-up calls, she needed to write down the time and date. Until that happened, all they could do was wait.

Trace checked the clock, decided that with a baby in residence, it was probably too early to call. Since he had plenty to do just running the business, he figured today would be a good time to play catch-up, so he settled in to work.

At ten o'clock he phoned the town house. Ashley answered.

"Hi, Ashley, this is Trace. I need to speak to Maggie."

"She isn't here, Trace. She said she had some work to do for her book. She took off about fifteen minutes ago."

He clamped down on a thread of anger. Dammit, he'd told her to check in with him before she left the house. "You know where she went?"

"Down to the shore. She wasn't sure where she was going to wind up. Wherever the shots looked promising, she said."

His temper began to heat. He remembered the young woman in the newspaper who had recently disappeared. Her body had washed up on the beach, and he had heard on the news that the police believed she had been murdered.

"I'll try her cell," Trace said, thinking of Maggie's stalker and worrying the same kind of thing could happen to her. "If she calls, tell her to phone me right away. Tell her I need to talk to her."

"Okay."

Ashley hung up and Trace clenched his jaw. What the hell was Maggie thinking to go off on her own that way? He worked hard at staying calm, but Maggie had a way of stirring him up. He told himself it was just that damned red hair, but he knew it was more than that. Knew he was beginning to care way too much.

He dialed her cell number but the call went straight to her voice mail.

Worry tangled with anger. He wanted to strangle her. Dammit, he thought he'd been clear. He didn't want her out there where the guy might be able to get her alone.

He stood up and went for more coffee, though he'd already had more than his share.

Where was she?

Dammit to hell and gone.

For the first time in days, Maggie felt free. She'd awakened early, rode her stationary bike and worked out a little with her free weights, then showered and dressed for the day. She had left the house half an hour ago, just as Ashley was getting up to feed the baby. Late enough that Maggie figured her watchdog, Rex something-or-other, had already gone home.

There'd been no sign of her stalker again last night. She was sure he hadn't appeared, or Trace would have called. Or more likely, his watchdog would have called the police and had him arrested.

Still, the guy was out there somewhere, and just because he hadn't been at her house last night didn't mean he couldn't be waiting for her to leave this morning. With that in mind, she had backed her little Ford Escape out of the garage with an eye on her surroundings, passing Ashley's battered old baby-blue Chevy parked in the unit A guest space.

As Maggie rolled out onto the street and drove toward the freeway, she memorized the color and model of each car behind her, even noted some of their license plate numbers to see if they continued to travel the same route she did.

The farther she drove out of town, the easier it was to keep track. By the time she was cruising Highway 45 twenty miles out of Houston, none of the cars she had seen earlier were anywhere behind her.

She was absolutely sure she wasn't being followed, which gave her a great sense of relief.

Galveston was her destination. A lot of reconstruction was still going on after the damage done by Hurricane Ike a few years back. Sometimes the men and machinery working against the backdrop of the sea made dramatic photos.

She prowled Galveston Harbor, then headed for the beach, stopping here and there for any sort of interesting shot. School was still in session. It was Monday, so the beaches were relatively empty. Always fascinated by the contrast between white sand and blue sea, she snapped a few shots, one she particularly liked of the beach patrol practicing their rescue procedures for the upcoming summer season.

When her stomach began to growl, she pulled into a parking lot in front of a little thatch-roofed restaurant called the Lunch Shack. Delicious aromas wafting through the order window drew her in that direction, and she snapped a couple shots of the Asian chef in his tall white hat working over the grill.

She ordered crispy, deep-fried fish and chips, blow-

ing her calorie count for the next several days. As she
licked the last bite of tartar sauce off her fingers fifteen
minutes later, her cell phone started to ring.

Trace had been calling, but she hadn't picked up. She
knew he was going to read her the riot act, but she'd
simply had to get away. Ashley had called to tell her he
was looking for her, and Maggie had promised to call
him on her way back to the city.

She dug the cell out of her purse to see if he was calling again, recognized Roxanne's number and answered.

"Hey, stranger," Roxy said. She was still visiting
friends in New York, a couple she had met in Rome
and a gay friend she knew from Carnevale in Venice.
"I've been meaning to call, but time just slipped away.
I figured you'd let me know if anything happened, but
I've still been worried."

Plenty had happened, but she didn't want to get into
all that now. "Well, my sister showed up. That was a
big surprise. She has a baby."

"Your sister? Ashley? The teenager who lives in
Florida?"

"She isn't a teen anymore. She's moved in with me
for a while. It's a long story. You can meet her when
you get home."

"Well, that's certainly news. What about the stalker?"

"Oh. Trace is back on the case. We talked, got things
straightened out."

"Talked, huh? That's all you did?"

"For the moment." She told Roxy about the break-in
and the figurine, and generally filled her in.

"Listen, I'll come back early if you need me."

"I'm fine, really. I've got an alarm system now and
Trace seems to know what he's doing."

"I'm here for you, you know. If something happens, you call me."

Maggie smiled. She could always count on Roxanne. "I will, I promise. Enjoy the rest of your trip."

Roxy laughed. "Are you kidding? I'm practically a fixture on Fifth Avenue. I do love New York."

Maggie grinned as she ended the call. Feeling better after the conversation, she wandered a bit with her camera, took a couple of seascapes she thought might have potential. She was smiling when she returned to her car.

The smile slid away at the sight of the brown scrap of paper stuck beneath the windshield wiper. The lunch she'd just eaten went sour and nausea rolled through her stomach. Her heart was pounding. Her hand shook as she reached for the note, carefully pulled it from under the rubber blade.

Beloved Maggie. It is almost time for us to meet. Not yet, but soon. Soon, my dear, dear Maggie.

Sweet God, how had he found her? She'd been so careful, so sure she hadn't been followed. She glanced wildly around the Lunch Shack parking lot, but saw only a brown-and-black dog sniffing for garbage and a Hispanic couple with two young children walking toward the food order window.

Her Nikon D3S hung from a strap around her neck. Lifting the camera with trembling hands, she fought to steady the big 28-300 Tamron lens, and began clicking shots of each car parked in the area, including the license plates. The effort was probably futile—undoubtedly, the man had left the note and driven away, as he had done before—but maybe not.

Maybe he was still somewhere nearby, watching her, waiting for her to leave. Her skin prickled. She told herself maybe this time she would get lucky and get a photo of his tag.

As soon as she finished shooting, she slipped the strap off her neck and packed the camera away, climbed into the little SUV and dug her cell phone out of her purse. She brought up Trace's number, then realized she had used the last of her battery power talking to Roxanne.

"Dammit…" Tossing the phone onto the seat beside her, she started the engine. Trace had very specifically told her not to go out without letting him know, but she was used to being on her own and there was only so much time she could spend indoors. She wondered if he would lose his precious self-control and let his temper show.

She might have smiled if the situation had been different. She would enjoy another glimpse of the man beneath the iron control, the hot-tempered male he worked so hard to hide.

But as she pulled onto Highway 45, she wasn't thinking of the angry man she'd be facing when she got back to the city. Instead, all the way back to Houston, she kept glancing in the mirror, searching for the man who was ruining her life.

Chapter Twelve

Cursing beneath his breath, Trace hung up the phone in his office. Maggie hadn't called, and she wasn't answering her cell phone. Ashley had spoken to her, given her his message, but still Maggie hadn't bothered to call.

Shoving back his chair, he got up from his desk and paced to the front of the office to stare out the window, as he had done a dozen times already today.

"You're gonna wear out the carpet," Annie said, peering at him over the top of the little half-glasses perched on the end of her nose.

"Dammit, the woman is nothing but trouble."

"According to you, they all are."

He shot a dark glance her way but the receptionist ignored it.

"She's a photographer, right?" Annie shifted in the chair behind her desk. "She's got a show coming up. That's what you said. The woman has work to do."

"Yeah, well, this guy is a real weirdo. So far we have no idea who he is or what he might be capable of doing."

"Then I guess you're convinced he's real."

"What?" Trace turned to face her.

"It wasn't that long ago you dropped the case because you thought she was making the whole thing up."

"That's not exactly the way it was. I thought she wasn't being completely honest with me, and she wasn't."

Annie scoffed. "Women are allowed to keep a few secrets, honey. It's a rule."

His mouth edged up but he refused to smile. "I'll be in my office, doing my damnedest to work." He started in that direction, trying to get his mind off Maggie, who was probably enjoying the day while he stewed and fretted.

"If I remember, she was driving a little red SUV the day she came to the office to hire you."

He stopped and turned. "That's right. Why?"

"She just pulled into the lot."

Trace felt a sweep of relief. Striding to the door, he took a calming breath as he stepped outside and spotted Maggie getting out of her car, looking sexy as hell with her fiery hair a little windblown and her cheeks slightly flushed. He tried not to remember the way she tasted, tried not to think of that kiss, willed himself not to get hard.

But as she approached him, the look on her face sent his worry spiking up again.

"Dammit, where the hell have you been? I've been calling your cell for hours."

"I needed to take some pictures. I thought maybe Galveston. I drove down this morning." She was wearing jeans and sneakers and a simple white shirt. How that outfit could possibly arouse him, he couldn't imagine, but it did.

He drew on his self-control. "That where you went?"

She nodded.

"Why didn't you answer your phone?"

"I know I should have. But I knew you'd be mad. I needed to get out of the house. I had work to do, so that's what I did." She held out a piece of rough brown paper. "Unfortunately, I found this on my windshield after I stopped for lunch."

Trace's stomach knotted. "Dammit, Maggie." He took the note from her hand, read the words and softly cursed. "Did you get a look at him?"

"No, but I took pictures of all the cars parked in the area, including their license numbers."

"Good thinking. Maybe something will turn up."

"The thing is, I was really careful, Trace. I watched every car behind me until I was miles out of town. If he followed me, I should have seen him. I don't know how I could have missed him."

"It isn't always that easy to spot a tail."

"I just…I'm telling you, I was careful. I can't figure out how he did it."

Maggie was no fool. If she had been that observant… An alarm went off in his head. "Stay here, I'll be right back."

He headed inside, went into the equipment room and picked up a handheld bug detector, which was small, but one of the best on the market. Returning to the parking lot, he went over the car front to back. As he neared the trunk, the red light began to flash, and he heard the warning sound of the beeper.

Cursing softly, he reached beneath the rear bumper and pulled off a little round circle of plastic with a shiny metal center.

He held it up. "This is how he found you—GPS tracking device."

"He bugged my car?" Maggie gasped. "Oh, my God!"

Trace looked at the piece of plastic in his hand. "Pretty sophisticated. It's motion sensitive. Only goes on when the car is moving. Saves the battery." He dropped the bug in his pocket. "This guy's not your usual nutcase, Maggie. This joker's got a brain. We need to check your house."

Her head jerked up. "My house? Oh, God, you don't...don't think he's put something like this in my condo?"

"If he had a key, he could have hidden a microphone somewhere inside before you moved in. Or on the day he went to the open house—assuming that was him."

"He...he couldn't have hidden a camera, could he? I mean, I would have noticed—wouldn't I?"

Trace didn't want to think about the bastard taking lewd pictures of Maggie. "Depends on the size of the device and how well it's hidden."

She shivered. "He could have been watching me for weeks."

Trace made no reply. They wouldn't know until they searched the condo. "I'll get my gear and follow you back to your house."

Maggie nodded, but her face was pale.

Trace returned to the equipment room for an even more powerful detector, one that could pick up video as well as GPS, audio and phone transmitters. Maggie was waiting in her car when he climbed into the Jeep, and they pulled out of the lot together.

At the condo, Ashley opened the door. "You're supposed to call Trace," she said. "He sounded pretty pissed."

Maggie flashed a sugary smile at him over her shoulder. "Trace is a man of iron control. He never gets pissed. Do you, Trace?"

He grunted as he carried his equipment into the house. "If anyone can make it happen, darlin', it's you."

Maggie smiled as if that somehow pleased her.

Women. He would never figure them out.

Maggie sat nervously on the sofa next to Ashley as Trace made his way methodically through the house with the equipment he had brought, a little silver box the size of a laptop computer. Terrified of what her stalker might have seen, she insisted he start upstairs.

"Nothing in your bedroom or bath," he called down to her. "No cameras, no listening devices."

She felt a rush of relief. "Thank God."

"I can't believe this," Ashley muttered. "Bugging your car? The guy's got some nerve." Dressed in a pair of khaki shorts that showed a long stretch of leg, and a pink midriff top, her short curls a little messy, she glowed with a vibrancy that had been missing when she had first arrived. Maggie felt good about that.

Trace checked the upstairs hall, began to scan her studio. When she heard the beeping sound, Maggie's stomach clenched. Jumping up from the sofa, she rushed for the stairs.

"Where is it?"

"Top of the closet door. With the door shut it's almost invisible. Even with it open, the thing is really hard to see." Trace showed her the tiny camera, then dragged a plastic bag out of the hip pocket of his jeans and slid the device inside.

"You think he could have left prints?" Maggie asked.

"I doubt it. But it's always worth a look." He headed downstairs, swept the guest bedroom using earbuds to hear the beeping, since the baby was asleep, then the guest bathroom and powder room. Finding nothing, he headed into the living room, and finally checked the kitchen.

He was almost finished when the beeping began again. Maggie's stomach sank. "Where?"

"Behind the decorative trim over the sink." He pointed upward. "Lens looks out through the ornamental holes in the design."

Maggie walked over to where Trace was pulling down the second tiny camera. "Why would he put them in the studio and kitchen instead of the bedroom?"

Trace slid the camera into the bag, his dark brows drawing together. He shook his head. "I don't think he wanted to interfere with your privacy. His notes sound old-fashioned, almost gallant. 'Dearest Maggie. Precious Maggie.' The song he played comes from *The Prince and The Maiden,* which is set during a more chivalrous time. Maybe that's the way he thinks of himself."

"Like some knight in shining armor?" She rolled her eyes. "Give me a break."

"Could be."

"That's creepy," Ashley said as she walked into the kitchen.

Trace's jaw hardened. "Yeah."

A sharp knock sounded at the door and a jolt of

adrenaline shot through Maggie. She set a hand over her pounding heart and started for the entry, but Trace was already there. He looked through the keyhole, then pulled open the door.

"Jason. What the hell are you doing here?"

The man who walked in was over six feet tall, young and blond and extremely good-looking.

"You went to Emily's," he said hotly. "She wouldn't tell me what you wanted, but she's totally freaked out. I want to know what the hell you said to her."

Trace closed the door. "You need to take it easy."

"I'm not taking it easy. My father is dead. I don't believe he killed himself. I don't think you do, either. I want to know what the hell is going on."

Trace released a slow breath. "You're right. You deserve to know the truth. I should have followed my gut and told you last week. If you'll calm down, we can talk about it right now."

Maggie sensed that some of the fight went out of him. For the first time he seemed to realize the scene he was causing in someone else's home.

"Sorry," he said.

Trace turned. "Maggie, this is Jason Sommerset, Hewitt's son. Jason, this is Maggie O'Connell and her sister, Ashley."

Jason nodded at Maggie. "Nice to meet you." He was dressed in perfectly tailored tan slacks, a short-sleeved burgundy sweater and a pair of expensive Italian loafers. He turned to Ashley and opened his mouth to greet her, but no words came out. She was just that pretty.

"Nice to meet you, Jason," she said with a smile, which gave him time to find his voice.

"You, too, Ashley."

"How'd you know where to find me?" Trace asked.

"Annie told me. I kind of pressured her into it."

Trace chuckled. "Nobody pressures Annie. She probably figured you had a right to know what was happening." He tipped his head toward the door. "We can talk outside." He spoke to Maggie. "Excuse us a minute, will you?"

"The patio's nice and private. There are chairs out there. I'll bring you a glass of iced tea."

Jason was still staring at Ashley. They had the same crystal-blue eyes, which at the moment were locked together as if they were in combat and the first to look away would lose the war.

Trace clamped the younger man on the shoulder. "Come on, son. I should have listened to my instincts and told you the truth from the start."

Trace's words broke the spell and Jason's gaze swung back to him. "It's about damned time," he said.

The men walked out to the patio through the sliding glass door in the living room, and Ashley's gaze followed.

"So who is he?" she asked with an elaborate show of nonchalance that spoke louder than words.

"Jason's father was the late Hewitt Sommerset, founder of Sommerset Industries."

"Jason said something about his father…that he didn't believe he killed himself. Does Trace think he was murdered?"

"That's what he's trying to find out."

Through the glass door, they watched as Trace and Jason sat down around the umbrella table Maggie had purchased after moving into the house.

"Good-looking guy, huh?" Maggie said, keeping an eye on her sister.

Ashley shrugged. "I know all about good-looking men. Most of them aren't worth the powder to blow them up."

Maggie laughed. "There have to be a few good ones out there." Her gaze went to Trace, sitting on her patio as if he belonged there. If he was half the man he seemed, he was definitely a white-hat guy.

"I guess so," Ashley said halfheartedly.

"Jason seems nice enough."

"They all do," she said drily.

Maggie didn't pursue the topic. Clearly, her sister's experience with "Ziggy" was enough to sour her on men. At least for the moment.

Walking into the kitchen, Maggie took out two glasses and filled them with ice. She leaned into the fridge for a pitcher of tea, filled the glasses and set them on a tray. As she started for the patio, she noticed Ashley looking through the glass doors at Jason.

More than once, she saw Jason glancing back.

Jason fisted a hand on the patio table. "You're telling me that my brother-in-law—my sister's husband—may have murdered my father."

"We don't know that. We know he was embezzling money. We know he was stashing it away in an offshore account. We know there's a chance your father confronted him. The rest is only conjecture."

"Parker was out that night, not home like he said. Emily told you that."

"That's what she said."

Jason shot up from the chair. "That bastard killed my father. I know it."

Trace stood up across from him. "You don't know anything—not for sure. And until you do, you have to hang on to that temper of yours. If you don't, you'll only make things worse."

"I'll kill him, I swear it."

"That's just great. You'll go to jail for the rest of your life—exactly what your dad would have wanted. That attitude of yours is the reason I didn't tell you in the first place."

Jason sank back down in his chair. His head tipped forward and he ran his fingers through the golden hair at his temples. Finally, he straightened. "I guess you're right."

"You guess?"

"Okay, you're right."

"That's more like it. If you're going to be the head of the family—and run Sommerset Industries—you're going to have to man up, make some tough decisions. This is one of them."

The sliding door opened just then and Maggie walked out carrying a pitcher and glasses. The sun flashed on her fiery hair and the muscles across Trace's belly clenched. She put the tray on the table and set a glass of tea in front of each of them.

"Thank you," Jason said.

She smiled. "It looked like it was getting a little heated out here."

Jason flushed at the innuendo. Trace figured the heat he was feeling had nothing to do with the weather and everything to do with how badly he wanted to take the woman in front of him to bed. She turned and went back inside, and he watched the way her jeans cupped her sweet little ass. For an instant, he wished he could turn himself into a piece of denim.

"So what do we do?" Jason asked, forcing Trace's thoughts in a safer direction.

"We've done our homework. The police are all over this. They want Parker nearly as much as you do."

"Not even close."

"Maybe not, but the result is the same. Parker winds up in prison for the rest of his life."

Jason gritted his teeth. "He deserves to fry."

"Yes, he does, but maybe this is better." Trace's smile was grim. "You ever think what a nice little play toy Parker will be for some big roughneck bastard inside those walls? Parker's cushy days are over."

Jason's smile looked equally grim. "I guess maybe I could live with that."

"That's better. That's the attitude your dad would expect from you." Trace took a sip of his tea, tasted the sweetness, felt the chill slide through him. He flicked a glance toward the door, wishing the drink could cool his blood.

Jason's gaze followed his. "The redhead…she your girlfriend?"

"My client," Trace said.

"She's hot."

Trace took another cooling sip. "Yeah."

"What's the, um, story on the blonde?"

He'd been waiting for the question. The attraction between Jason and Ashley had hummed clear across the room. "I don't know too much about her. She's Maggie's half sister. Had it rough, I guess. But seems to have gotten herself pretty well squared away now. She has a baby."

Jason's head came up. "A baby? She's just a kid."

"She's old enough, only a few years younger than you. Maggie says she recently turned twenty-one."

Jason took a drink of his tea. "So she's married."

Trace shook his head. "Nope."

"Where's the kid's dad?"

"Blew her off, I guess. Or maybe she blew him off. He was kind of a no-good, I think. Makes you appreciate the father you had."

Jason looked back at the house, to where Ashley stood near the sliding glass door. She was as beautiful as Jason was handsome, Trace noted.

"When all this is over, maybe... Would you mind if I asked her out?"

"Up to you. Just be careful. Ashley doesn't deserve to be hurt any more than she has been already."

The younger man nodded.

Sensing their conversation had come to an end, Maggie appeared at the door, slid it open and stepped out on the patio. She turned and smiled, and Trace felt as if he'd been sucker punched. He cast a glance at Jason, wondered if the kid's momentary loss of speech when he'd met Ashley meant he'd felt the same thing.

Whatever it was that the two women shared seemed to run in the family.

Trace found no prints on the bug or the video cameras. He hadn't expected he would. On Tuesday, a crew installed surveillance cameras at the front and back of Maggie's town house.

Trace also called Mark Sayers to tell him about the

cameras hidden in Maggie's condo and the GPS tracking device on her car.

"She's not making this stuff up," Trace told the detective. "Whatever she might have done as a kid, this is no joke. Maggie's got a serious problem."

"Yeah, well, sounds like you might have one, too. You'd better be careful, buddy. You don't exactly have a sterling record where women are concerned—especially redheads."

Trace clenched his jaw. "Just do your job, Sayers. Make sure the department knows what the hell is going on."

"She needs to file a report."

"She's already filed a report. I'll be happy to file another one if that's what it takes."

"Okay, okay, take it easy. I'll put out the word."

"Thanks." Trace hung up the phone and sat there thinking about the department and Hoyt Varner, wondering how far the captain was willing to go to get revenge for his son after all these years. Far enough to put Maggie's life in danger? The guy was a police officer. Trace had trouble convincing himself he would go that far.

At least the trap was up and working. He didn't have much faith in it, especially not after seeing the sophisticated equipment the stalker had installed in the house and car. Still, maybe the guy would call, and they would get lucky and be able to trace it back to the point of origin.

The week slid past. There weren't any new incidents and nothing showed up on the outside video cams. Trace's biggest worry was Maggie's upcoming gallery show.

The Friday night opening, which was also a benefit for a local children's shelter, had been featured in the newspapers and on TV, a very exclusive, invitation-only preview of Maggie's latest work. That much publicity could mean trouble.

It also gave them the best opportunity they'd had so far of catching the stalker.

Surveillance equipment didn't come cheap, especially not the quality that had been used on Maggie's car and in the apartment. That meant the guy had money. At five hundred dollars a ticket, the average Joe wouldn't be at the gallery opening. But the stalker could likely afford it.

The only possible description of the stalker they had came from the Realtor, Jim Brewer: big, in his forties, distinguished-looking, with silver-streaked dark hair. Unfortunately, that description fit a lot of men.

Trace would be watching, ready for any sort of trouble. But the guy was smart and he wouldn't want to give himself away. There was a good chance he wouldn't show up and the evening would go off as smoothly as planned.

If that was the case…

Trace thought of the weekend ahead. He wanted Maggie O'Connell. He was tired of playing the gentleman.

Unless work interfered, on Friday night he intended to do a helluva lot more than just be her escort.

Chapter Thirteen

The weather changed later in the week, turning overcast and cloudy. By Friday evening, big black thunderclouds hung over the city, the harbinger of a heavy spring storm.

Maggie thought there might be fewer people at the opening, but maybe not. Since the ticket proceeds were going to the Weyman's Children's Shelter, publicity for the show had been overwhelming. It had become a who's-who-in-society event.

Wearing a long, slender, emerald-sequined gown with narrow rhinestone straps, Maggie paced from the living room to the front door and back.

Ashley sat on the sofa watching the Food Network, to which she seemed addicted. Nestled in her lap, the baby made soft little sucking noises as his mama gave him his bottle.

Ashley grinned at the show on TV. "Isn't she great?"

"Who?" Distracted as she waited for Trace, Maggie looked over at the screen.

"Giada De Laurentiis. Not only is she beautiful, but she's a really terrific cook." Her dream, Ashley had confessed, was to work in one of the nicer restaurants in town. Eventually, she hoped to attend one of the exclusive culinary schools in Houston and become a chef.

"She certainly has a following," Maggie said, thinking that Ashley had chosen a fine ambition. And since she loved to experiment with new recipes, Maggie was reaping the reward. Which meant she needed to get out on the racquetball court and burn a few calories.

She checked her watch, made another quick trip to the powder room to check her lipstick, then returned to the living room and began to pace again.

"Don't you know you're supposed to keep a man waiting?" Ashley said from the sofa. "You're at least fifteen minutes early."

"I know, I know. I'm a little nervous about the show."

"Oh, and here I thought it was because that hot cowboy of yours was going to be your date."

Maggie cast her a glare. "He's not my cowboy, he's my bodyguard. That was made perfectly clear."

"Okay, but if you don't come home tonight, I'm not going to panic, okay? I'll set the security alarm when you leave, and if the creep calls, I'll write down the time and date."

Maggie thought of the night she had found the porcelain figurine on the counter, and worry filtered through her. "You've got my cell number. If something happens—"

"I've got it. Stop worrying."

Maggie walked into the kitchen. She didn't feel quite right about leaving Ashley and the baby alone. But the alarm was working, and half of Houston knew she would be at the opening. If the guy was truly obsessed with her, surely he would show up there.

Maggie hoped so. She hoped she would be able to figure out who he was, get him to stop his harassment and get her life back in order.

She looked out the window over the kitchen sink. "Oh, my God, he's here." But she wasn't exactly sure the long white stretch limo that pulled up in front of the condo wasn't there for someone else. Not until the driver opened the rear door, and Trace set a hand on the crown of his hat, ducked his head and stepped out.

A gold box glittered in his hand as he walked toward the town house, and Maggie hurried to let him in. Her heart was pounding. It was ridiculous, but she couldn't stop a little thrill of anticipation.

"Don't act so eager," Ashley called out from the living room. "You're supposed to play hard to get."

Maggie grinned. "I am hard to get, but thanks for the advice." She took a deep breath and pulled open the door the instant Trace knocked, stepping back as he walked in.

Except for his crisp white shirt, he was dressed all in black: black Western tuxedo, black ostrich cowboy boots, black felt hat with a silver concho band. He looked like the Marlboro man on the way to a White House dinner, and he looked delicious.

A little curl of heat settled low in her stomach. "A limo? You didn't have to do that." But she loved that he had been so thoughtful.

"You're the star tonight. You ought to get star treatment." He handed her the gold box. When she lifted the lid, a gorgeous purple-throated, white-ruffled orchid nestled in gold-flecked tissue.

"It's beautiful," she said a little breathlessly.

"So are you." Those whiskey-brown eyes slid over her, moving from the loose red curls on her shoulders, pulled up on one side to show off her diamond earrings, to the soft cleavage the dress exposed, all the way to the rhinestones on her strappy high heels. "You're gonna knock 'em dead tonight, darlin'."

A rush of pleasure poured through her. Trace took out the corsage and slipped it on her wrist, and unexpected moisture stung her eyes.

"I never got to go to the prom," she said. After the incident with Josh, she'd been forced to hide out at home. Then she had moved to another school and none of the boys had asked the new girl to go. She smiled softly. "I feel like a prom queen tonight."

Something moved across his features, something hot and fierce. He understood, she realized, and her heart squeezed a little.

"Night's just gettin' started, darlin'." The words and the smoldering look in his hot, dark eyes made her breath catch.

"Have a good time, kiddies," Ashley called out from the living room. "I promise I won't wait up."

"Smart-ass," Maggie called back with a smile, and Trace laughed.

"You remembered to put my cell number in your phone, didn't you?" Trace asked Ashley.

"I've got both your numbers in my phone. Just go!"

His hand settled at Maggie's waist, guiding her toward the door, then outside to the car. Dressed in full chauffeur apparel including a jaunty little short-brimmed cap, the tall, slim, very efficient looking driver held open the door.

Maggie slid into the car, sinking into the deep red leather seat, and Trace slid in beside her. Tiny white lights lit the interior, which was partitioned off from the front. A silver ice bucket in the mahogany bar on one side held a bottle of Dom Pérignon.

"You thought of everything," she said, properly impressed.

"I guess we'll see." Trace's eyes touched hers as the car eased out of the parking lot. Reaching for the bottle, he unwired and popped the cork, poured the bubbling liquid into a crystal flute and handed it over, then poured one for himself. "I'm on duty, so this is all I'll have for now."

"Same here. I need to be at my best tonight."

"Honey, there's no doubt of that." He lifted his glass. "To the most successful opening you've ever had."

Raising hers, she silently added, *and to catching the maniac who is destroying my life.* She clinked her glass against Trace's, praying her stalker would be there. Hoping he would say or do something that would give him away.

"Your sister seems to be settling in okay," Trace said, resting his broad shoulders back against the seat.

"She wants to be a chef." Maggie smiled. "She's already a darned good cook."

"Sounds promising."

"I really like her. She's funny and smart. She's a great mother. She really loves that baby."

"How about you?" He took a sip of his champagne. "You like kids?"

Maggie shrugged, felt the slight friction of the rhinestone straps against her bare shoulders. "I've never had time to really consider having a family. Being a successful photographer meant everything to me. Making that happen took up most of my time."

"And now?"

"Now I have time to consider what's really important to me." She studied him from beneath her lashes. "How about you?"

He didn't answer right away, just took another sip of champagne. "I got married, planned to have kids. It didn't work out."

She could tell it was a touchy subject, but she was curious. "That was then. How about now?"

Beneath the brim of his dressy, black felt hat, his eyes cut toward the window. "I've still got a bad taste in my mouth."

Maggie didn't press for more. She wasn't looking for a long-term relationship. Apparently neither was he. She told herself a no-strings affair was exactly what she wanted. That things might just work out. It could be good for both of them. Couldn't it?

It didn't take nearly long enough for the limo to turn onto Westheimer Road and pull into the line of cars arriving at the Twin Oaks Gallery. A red carpet stretched from the curb to the etched-glass front door, and valets parked the vehicles that pulled up to the curb.

A slew of reporters, both newspaper and local TV, took photos of the glamorous attendees making their way up the velvet-roped walkway.

Not exactly the Academy Awards, but an event like this was a first for Maggie and she was excited, and more than a little nervous. It occurred to her that she was glad Trace was with her, bodyguard or not. He had a way of steadying her, keeping her calm.

Well, at least until she looked at him. Then her mind shot off in the direction of sex, and she had to rein in her thoughts.

"We're almost there," he said, sitting forward in the seat to peer outside. Just ahead of them, a shiny red Ferrari and two big black SUVs with dark tinted windows pulled up to the curb.

"The Ferrari…that's Matthew Bergman," she said. "His father's a big patron of the arts and a well-known philanthropist. Matthew's a photography buff."

"I've done some work for the father," Trace said, causing Maggie to speculate on the endless number of business contacts he seemed to have. It occurred to her that Trace was a very well respected man.

The first SUV pulled up to the curb. "That's Senator Logan and his wife." Maggie watched as a man with silver hair stepped out of the car, followed by an attractive woman in a long, beaded, burgundy gown. "The second car is probably his aide, Richard Meyers, and his publicity spokesman, Duncan Ross. Now that Logan's running for governor, he rarely travels without an entourage."

It was their turn next. The limo rolled to a stop and one of a swarm of red-vested valets opened the door. "Welcome to the Twin Oaks Gallery," the young man said.

"Here we go," said Trace, and Maggie took a steadying breath. As she slid out of the limo, camera lights came on and several microphones appeared in front of her.

"This is quite an event, Ms. O'Connell." A short,

slightly overweight reporter leaned toward her. "The proceeds from the tickets go to charity. Have you done this kind of thing before?"

"I've donated photos to help raise money for various nonprofit organizations, but nothing like this. The Weyman's Children's Shelter is a very good cause. When they approached me with the idea of combining the benefit with the gallery opening, I was happy to agree."

"Who's your escort?" one of the female reporters asked. Her gaze swept over Trace as if he were a juicy piece of meat, and her red lips curved in a smile of female awareness.

"Just a friend," Trace replied, before Maggie could answer. Not that it would stay secret for long.

They walked up the red carpet and went into the gallery, which was beginning to fill with guests. Soft music played in the background while waiters in short white jackets hurried by with flutes of champagne on silver trays.

Standing just inside the door, Faye Langston, the owner of the gallery, spotted Maggie and approached, a glass of champagne in her hand. She was tall and svelt, with heavy dark hair cut in a straight style that framed her face. Her nose was too long, which made her striking instead of beautiful.

Faye bent and kissed Maggie's cheek. "We sold every ticket," she said proudly. "The shelter will come out with a nice bit of money. Now all we have to do is sell some of your work."

Maggie hoped they would. Faye and Maggie were both donating a percentage of their profits to the shelter, which they hoped would help increase sales.

"Faye, this is Trace Rawlins. He owns Atlas Security. Trace, this is Faye Langston, the owner of the gallery."

"A pleasure to meet you, Ms. Langston," Trace said, removing his black felt hat. One of the waiters appeared out of nowhere to take it, and Trace ran a hand through his thick dark hair, which settled neatly in place. Maggie felt an urge to reach over and do the same.

Faye smiled up at him. "It's nice to meet you, Trace, and I hope you'll call me Faye." A slow, knowing smile curved her lips. "I'm sure you'll take good care of our guest of honor tonight."

Trace's dark gaze drifted over Maggie. "That's my plan," he drawled, with such an undercurrent of heat, Maggie's stomach contracted.

"Oh, look, there's Senator Logan…." Faye waved and smiled. "If you two will excuse me…" With a wink at Maggie, she silently slipped away.

Now that Maggie was actually there, she was beginning to relax. Dozens of her photos hung on the walls around her, each framed in a way that best displayed the work. Color and light, background and subject matter all came into play.

She had chosen the frames herself, and Faye had hired a calligrapher to make the delicate signs below each picture that included the title Maggie had selected, the date and place the photo had been taken. Each shot was limited to a certain number of prints that could be made and sold—an edition of twenty-five for this particular show—and each framed photo was personally signed. Looking at them now, she felt pleased and proud of the job she had done.

"You take beautiful pictures, Maggie," Trace said, his gaze fixed on a shot of the harbor during an approaching storm, a piece she had titled *Ferocity*. The shadowy light of day was fading as a seething wall of vicious black clouds rolled ominously toward shore. In the distance, a tiny sailboat raced frantically against time and weather to reach the safety of the harbor before the storm swept it away. "There's something special about each one, something that makes it unique."

Maggie smiled, appreciating the compliment a little more because it came from him. "I remember that day very well. The scene was so compelling I had to stop and take the shot, but at the same time it was frightening. I was afraid for the little boat. I stayed to watch until I was sure it reached the harbor."

Trace cast her an assessing glance, but made no comment. People began to approach her, the crowd growing, surrounding her, wanting a piece of her time.

"I'm gonna wander a little," Trace said, giving her room to do what she was there for. Be the celebrity of the evening. And help Faye sell her work.

"Hello, Trace. It's good to see you."

He turned at the sound of a female voice. "Mrs. Logan. It's always a pleasure." At fifty, Teresa Logan was beginning to show the strain of life as a senator's wife. Fine lines marked the corners of her eyes and settled around her mouth. Her blond hair had begun to thin. There had been a time when she had been as beautiful as her daughter.

Cassidy appeared just then, looked up at him and smiled. "Hello, Trace." They had dated the summer after Cassidy's graduation from high school. She had just turned eighteen, a feisty little auburn-haired girl with big, innocent blue eyes. Trace had just finished two years at community college.

Cassidy was married to a prominent surgeon now, her hair now blond and swept up in a sophisticated style.

"It's good to see you, Cassidy."

"It's certainly been a while." She smiled. "I hope you're doing well?"

"Business is good. Life is good. How about you?"

Before she could answer, her father, the senator, appeared at her side. "Trace. It's good to see you." Reasonably tall, with a solid build, and at sixty still setting women's hearts aflutter, Senator Logan was all smiles tonight, though when Trace had been dating his daughter, the man had done everything in his power to end the relationship.

He needn't have worried. It was never serious between them. Cassidy had bigger fish to fry and Trace had been set on a career in the army. Still, they had liked each other, which was enough to worry a man with the kind of political ambitions Garrett Logan had, even back then.

"Trace, this is my aide, Richard Meyers." Slenderly built, Meyers was dressed in expensive clothes and gold aviator-style glasses. He was vain, Trace guessed, with plenty of ambition.

"And this is my media coordinator, Duncan Ross, and his wife, Elaine." Duncan was a balding man in his forties, with sincerity stamped all over his face. Elaine was short and plump and looked like a well-dressed housewife, which only added to her husband's credibility.

"Nice to meet you," Trace said.

"Trace is an old friend of Cassidy's."

Cassidy rolled her pretty blue eyes. "Not that old, Daddy, please."

The senator laughed. His expensive black tuxedo fit him perfectly, the ideal contrast to his leonine mane of silver hair. "Trace and Cassidy dated for a few weeks one summer."

"We were just friends," Trace said. "At the time, her father was terrified his little girl was going to run off and marry some cowboy with horse manure on his boots. But Cassidy was a lot smarter than that."

Everyone laughed.

"Trace joined the Rangers and I went off to college," Cassidy explained. "That's where I met Jonathan."

Trace smiled and shrugged. "And the rest, as they say, is history."

"I'm sorry Jonathan couldn't be here tonight," Cassidy said. "I would have liked for you to meet him."

"I'd have liked that, too."

They chatted for a while. Trace had never been a fan of Garrett Logan or his politics; in the last election, he had voted for the other candidate. But Logan was a smooth talker with the good looks and style that won voter confidence. Now, tired of the D.C. scene, he was running for governor. Odds were he'd win that, too.

The conversation waned and Trace excused himself. He started toward Maggie, who had never been completely out of his sight, and saw that she was still in conversation with a group of admirers. He flashed her a glance, caught one in return and began to make his way around the room. He was looking for anyone who fit the description the Realtor had given them, or anyone who seemed to be taking more than a casual interest in Maggie.

There were only a few big men in the right age bracket, with salt-and-pepper hair. Trace made a point of introducing himself to each one and getting his name, but none pushed any of his hot buttons. Though there was always a chance something would turn up when he plugged their identities into the computer.

On the other hand, there seemed to be an endless number of men who took a more than casual interest in Maggie.

One was there now, good-looking, late thirties, dark hair and blue eyes. He had managed to separate her from the other guests vying for her attention. Trace felt a shot of adrenaline that tested his careful control. He told himself it wasn't jealousy, and headed in Maggie's direction.

Chapter Fourteen

Maggie noticed Trace bearing down on her, and darted a glance around, expecting to see the stalker. Then she realized he was glaring at Roger, and relaxed. The photography instructor was hardly a threat. He was the man responsible for a good deal of her success.

"Trace, I'm glad you're here. I'd like you to meet Roger Weller. I told you about him. I worked for Roger when I was in college. He was my mentor and I owe him a great deal."

Roger gave her a lazy smile. "And I've been trying to collect for years." His gaze ran over her, leaving no doubt as to what he meant. "So far it hasn't worked."

Maggie felt Trace stiffen beside her. "Is that so?"

"Roger and I are just friends," she said firmly. "He doesn't even live in Houston anymore, he lives in L.A." She cast Roger a warning glance. He had always seemed to want more from their relationship than Maggie was willing to give, but he had never really pressed her. "I was his assistant. Roger taught me everything I know about photography."

"I would have taught you a whole lot more, honey, if you'd just given me the chance," he teased.

"Roger, please." She looked up at Trace, saw his jaw clench. "He's kidding. We've always had a very professional relationship."

"That's right. Maggie didn't believe in mixing business with pleasure."

Trace pinned him with a glare. "Too bad for you, I guess."

"It's nice seeing you, Roger," Maggie said, taking hold of Trace's arm. "Now, if you'll excuse us, I'm afraid I need to mingle."

"I'm in town for a while before I head back," Roger told her. "Maybe we can have lunch."

Maggie tried not to look at Trace, knew the temper she would see in his eyes if she did. Clearly, his disposition wasn't nearly as calm as he liked to think.

She managed to smile. "I'm awfully busy, but maybe we can work something out."

Roger's mouth faintly curved.

Maggie turned and led Trace away before his testosterone got the best of him.

"Maybe you can work something out?" he said darkly.

"I was just trying to be polite. Besides, it isn't as if we're involved. You're here as my bodyguard, nothing more. It really isn't any of your business."

"Oh, we're involved. As soon as we get out of here, I'm going to show you exactly how involved we are."

Maggie's breath stalled. When she looked into those

hot brown eyes, her heart skipped several beats. "You...
you what?"

"One more word about *Roger* and I'll haul you into
the back room and show you right now."

Maggie's eyes widened. Dear God, he meant it! She
could tell by the way his teeth were clenched, by the
muscle that worked in his jaw. He was jealous, and more
than a little aroused.

"We...we can't leave—not yet."

Trace took the words exactly as she meant them. She
wasn't going to stop him. She wanted him to kiss her,
touch her, make love to her.

Beneath his tuxedo jacket, his broad shoulders relaxed. "That's all right, darlin'. We've got all night."

Her pulse started racing even faster than it was
before. And now that she knew his intensions, knew
what was going to happen after they left the gallery,
she didn't want to waste any more time than she had to.

The hours seemed to drag after that. Champagne
flowed and trays of sumptuous hors d'oeuvres were
devoured, refilled and greedily consumed again. More
guests arrived. The police chief, Charley Benton, a stout
man with a receding hairline, stopped by. Maggie spotted him talking to Senator Logan, their heads bent close
together, Benton laughing at something the senator said.
The newspapers had mentioned their close relationship and that Benton was backing the senator's bid for
governor.

"You're selling a lot of pieces," Trace said as a
framed photo titled *Taste the Wind* was tagged with a
red sticker to indicate it was sold. It showed a deserted
stretch of shore, palm trees bent like ballet dancers,

their fronds moving gracefully to the wind's relentless song.

A framed O'Connell photograph, depending on its size, went for as much as twenty-seven hundred dollars. Of course, there were a lot of expenses, and the gallery took a hefty share of the profit.

Trace's attention turned to the photograph beside it. "I'm partial to this one, *Harbor Sunset*. Makes me want to go sailing."

Maggie had taken the picture at dusk, a snapshot down a long row of gleaming white powerboats docked in the Blue Fin Marina near Seabrook. People, just small specks in the photo, sat on their decks sipping icy drinks, mesmerized by the sunset casting soft, red-gold light over the bay. "Someone else must have liked it, too," Trace added.

Maggie smiled at the Sold sticker. "I guess your champagne toast worked. This was definitely the most successful show I've ever had."

His gaze sharpened. "Was? Past tense? Does that mean you're ready to leave?"

His dark eyes glinted. She read the heat, the promise. "Yes…" was all she said.

Trace made a brief call on his cell, and a few minutes later the limousine appeared in the alley behind the gallery. Just as Maggie had done several times during the evening, he checked his phone to be sure no message had come from Ashley. Then he waited as Maggie said a quick goodbye to Faye Langston and disappeared quietly out the back door.

He took off his tuxedo jacket and tossed it onto the seat,

then helped her in and climbed in beside her. They both leaned back with a sigh. "You did good, kid," Trace said.

Maggie grinned. "I did, didn't I?"

She turned toward him, removed his hat and set it up in the rear window behind the seat, then ran a hand through his hair, setting the heavy dark strands back into proper position. "I've been wanting to do that all evening."

"That so? Well, this is what I've been wanting to do." Catching her chin, he tilted her head back and settled his mouth over hers. Soft, moist lips. Warm, sweet breath. Instantly, he went hard.

"Damn, I want you," he said between nibbling kisses, slow, easy ones that had them both breathing faster. His control slipped a little as her lips parted and his tongue slid in to taste her. Maggie kissed him back and the kisses he'd meant only as a prelude deepened, turned hot and fierce. His insides tightened and his groin throbbed.

One of the rhinestone straps on her gown slipped off her shoulder. Trace pressed his mouth against her bare skin, inhaled the floral scent of her perfume. Maggie made a soft little sigh as he slid the second strap off, eased the gown down to her waist, leaving her breasts exposed. Her nipples were big and pink and pretty. He took one into his mouth, suckled, tasted, felt it harden against his tongue, and heard himself groan.

"Trace…" she whispered, arching upward, urging him to take more of her. Her breasts were full and tilted slightly upward. Her skin was pale and as soft as the petals of a rose. He took what he wanted, took his fill, and reveled in her sweet little mews of pleasure.

He wanted more.

He told himself he couldn't take her, not here. Not in the backseat of a car. But his hands gripped the hem of her sequined gown and shoved it up to her waist. She was wearing a tiny black lace scrap of a thong. He pushed it aside and his gaze fell on the tangle of ruby curls between her legs. The elastic snapped in his fingers as if it wished to do his bidding, and he eased her thighs apart and began to stroke her.

She was wet and slick and he ached to be inside her. Lust clouded his senses, a red haze that blinded him and urged him on. He could hardly breathe, hardly think.

"I need you," he said, kissing her again, plundering her mouth, inhaling her scent. His hands found her breasts, teased, caressed them. "I don't want to stop."

"Don't…don't stop, Trace, please."

Insanity took over, destroying his resolve. All he knew was heat and driving need. When he felt her unbuttoning his pleated white shirt, felt her fingers gliding over the muscles of his chest, he hardened to the point of pain. When she tugged the shirt from the waistband of his slacks, began to work his zipper, he nearly came.

"Maggie…God…"

"I want you, Trace. I can't wait any longer."

He knew better. Tried to fight for control. He had planned to take her back to his house, seduce her slowly, properly. Instead, he stroked her, felt her tremble, heard her moan. He didn't remember opening the condom, sheathing himself. He just felt the swift, hot burst of pleasure as he thrust himself deeply inside.

He tried to slow down, give her time to adjust, but when she moved beneath him, when she whispered his name with a sob, he completely lost control.

Long strokes claimed her. Deep, hard, penetrating

strokes made her his. He wanted more. He took her and took her, made her come and then come again before he allowed himself to take his pleasure.

His pulse still thundered as he slowly spiraled down. Beneath his hand, the beating of her heart matched his own. He had told the driver to take his time, and thank God, the man had listened. It wasn't until Trace heard the deep male voice over the intercom telling him they had almost reached their destination that his thoughts began to focus and he realized what he had done.

Silently cursing, he eased himself from the soft warmth beneath him, got rid of the condom he barely remembered putting on.

"Dammit, I didn't mean for that to happen."

She adjusted her position on the seat, pulled her skirt down and the narrow rhinestone straps back into place. She looked up at him, and in the glow from the tiny white lights illuminating the interior, he saw her smile.

"That was some ride, cowboy."

Heat rose at the back of his neck. "I was planning a more subtle seduction."

Maggie reached out and cupped his cheek. "Were you?"

He turned his head, kissed her palm. "Don't think for a minute we're done here. I'm not through with you, lady. Not by a long shot."

She smiled as if that had been her plan all along. "Ashley said she wouldn't wait up."

His mouth faintly curved. "I'd kiss you again, but if I do, I'm afraid of what the driver might see when he opens the door."

Maggie laughed.

They climbed out of the car and he led her up the

walk. He turned off the alarm, then lifted her into his arms and carried her inside. He heard his high-tech doggy door squeak, knew Rowdy had trotted into the kitchen from the backyard. Trace kept walking. Inside the master bedroom, he closed the door.

It was getting late but he wasn't the least bit tired. He was taking Maggie O'Connell to bed, and sleep was the last thing on his mind.

The storm had politely waited to break until they'd reached the safety of Trace's house. Maggie lay snuggled against him, his solid length and hard-muscled body a comfort as lightning flashed and thunder rumbled outside the bedroom window. Inside, she lay warm and content in his big king-size bed, beneath the soft breeze of a ceiling fan, and a lightweight down comforter.

They had made love twice since he had taken her to bed. The first time was the slow seduction he had promised, a melding of mouths and bodies, the soft give-and-take of a leisurely joining. The second time was more fierce, more demanding. Her cowboy had a sexual appetite as strong as she had suspected. He liked making love and he wasn't shy about taking what he wanted.

But his loving wasn't one-sided. Trace gave as much as he demanded.

As she curled against him in the darkness, one of his hard arms draped over her waist, she listened to the sound of his breathing, mixed with the heavy rumble of rain on the roof and the fierce sighs of the wind outside the window.

She thought of the pleasure he had given her, deeper, more consuming than anything she had experienced before. She thought of the way he had kissed her, caressed her, and a thread of desire curled through her.

Nestled spoon fashion against him, she felt his body begin to stir, felt the heavy length of his building erection. She could hardly believe it. Surely he couldn't want her again so soon.

"I can feel your heartbeat," he whispered against her ear. "I know what you're thinking." He bit down on the lobe. "I'm thinking it, too."

He moved a little, prepared himself. Maggie moaned as he entered her, began the rhythmical movements that aroused her, made her ache with yearning. He was big and hard, his strokes long and deep, quickening her blood and overwhelming her senses. Her body contracted around him, gloved him, milked him as he rode her. Pleasure rolled through her, dense and fierce, deep and drugging. Her climax hit hard, sucked her in and wouldn't let go. Her body was beginning to attune itself to his, to anticipate, to crave his invasion, relish it.

Trace groaned as he followed her to release, held her as she waited for her heartbeat to slow. Seconds ticked past. His muscles relaxed. His breathing went deeper and she knew he had settled back into sleep.

Maggie closed her eyes, weary and spent and wonderfully sated. But she didn't fall sleep. Instead, she listened to the heavy fall of rain and the wind whistling through the trees, her mind spinning back through the weeks since that day at the Texas Café. She had convinced herself what she felt for Trace was merely physical. He was really a hot guy and she was wildly attracted to him. That kind of desire was new to her and she wanted to experiment, find out what it was all about.

In college, she'd been attracted to Michael Irving's

intelligence. Sex had been sort of a personal challenge, something to do to overcome the trauma after her night with Josh Varner. She'd met David Lyons and been attracted to his steady nature, his comfortable companionship. But she had needs, she had discovered during the time she had been with him. Sex was usually more her idea than his and never truly satisfying.

What she felt for Trace was different. Deeper, more alluring. Worrisome.

She didn't know what she wanted from him aside from more of his mind-boggling, incredible lovemaking.

She told herself that was enough.

Chapter Fifteen

Maggie watched Trace step out of the shower, rubbing his hair with a fluffy white towel, another riding low on his hips. With those long legs, impressive pecs, six-pack abs and wide shoulders, he was gorgeous.

"I'll be dressed in a minute," he said.

"Okay, but I get to watch."

He just smiled and began to search through his underwear drawer. She'd already had coffee and fresh-baked Pillsbury orange-frosted breakfast rolls, courtesy of her host. He had let her shower first, and she was dressed and ready, wearing a pair of gray, lightweight drawstring sweatpants and a black T-shirt with a gold eagle on the front with the words Ranger Up printed underneath.

As bad as she looked, it beat the heck out of arriving home in a long green evening gown.

While Trace pulled on a pair of jeans, she used the

rubber band on the newspaper she'd found in the kitchen to pull her hair back in a ponytail. All the while, she watched him, enjoying the play of muscle, the movement of crisp dark hair on his chest, the gleam of smooth suntanned skin.

"Keep looking at me that way and we aren't getting out of here for at least another hour."

Maggie laughed but her stomach dipped. After last night and this morning, sex should be the last thing on her mind.

"Okay, I'm going. I need another cup of coffee, anyway."

She made her way back to the kitchen, which was homey for a guy's, kind of a 1950s retro look with a chrome, Formica-topped table and red vinyl chairs, and red-and-white-checked curtains at the windows. The appliances, top of the line, were white. So were the cabinets and countertops.

Trace had given her a tour that morning. Three bedrooms, two baths and a powder room he had added himself. There was a dining room with a mahogany Duncan Phyfe table and six matching chairs.

"It belonged to my grandmother," he'd explained. "My dad and mom used it before I was born. I ended up with it. I guess I kind of like the way things were back then, you know? A quieter time and all. So I kept the stuff Dad had, and just worked around it, made it more my own."

One of the bedrooms had been converted into an office, with equipment as modern as money could buy: an iMac, a laptop, a printer that copied, faxed and scanned. A row of built-in mahogany file cabinets ran along one wall, and his matching desk was wide and fairly neat.

In the living room, a big flat-screen TV, at least fifty inches, was hidden away in a built-in mahogany cabinet so it didn't dominate the room. The sofa and chairs were burgundy, overstuffed and comfortable, the beige carpet a high-quality deep pile. Some nicely framed artwork hung on the walls, mostly Texas landscapes done in an impressionist style.

He'd done a good job. It was the kind of place a man would want to come home to. Or a place a young couple might raise a family. He'd told her he had wanted that once.

"I guess we'd better get going," he said as he walked into the living room. Along with his usual blue jeans he had on a light blue knit shirt and a pair of brown Rockports.

No hat today. Trace was a man of many facets. Maggie was coming to like each one.

A thought that got her moving. She didn't want to like him *too* much.

"I'm supposed to be at the gallery by noon," she said. "Faye and I plan to go over the sales, see which pieces were sold and have to be replaced. I need to get them reprinted, matted and framed. I only do them one at a time. Less chance of being damaged."

"There's something I'm going to ask you to do."

She looked up at him. "What's that?"

"Get me a list of your clients, people who've purchased your photos. You have one, right?"

"I do. But if you count the sales off the internet, you're talking about a lot of people."

"We don't have a choice. I'm running out of airspeed and altitude here. We can limit the time frame, go back just a couple of years. We're looking for collectors, people who purchased, say…at least three pieces."

"All right. It'll take me a little while to get the list into some kind of workable order. And some of my clients buy through art brokers. It'll take longer to run those names down."

"Do the best you can."

"Okay."

"I've got to stop by my office, check on a couple of things. It's right on the way to your house and it won't take a minute."

"That isn't a problem," Maggie said.

A few minutes later, Trace pulled the Jeep into the lot and turned off the engine. "You can come in if you want. Doesn't look like anyone's around."

She glanced down at her borrowed clothes. No way was she going anywhere but home. "That's okay, I'll just wait for you here."

He nodded, climbed out and disappeared inside the building. He had been gone only a few minutes when a sassy little silver BMW convertible pulled into the parking lot. Maggie watched as a petite redhead slid out from behind the wheel. She wore snug designer jeans, a crop top and high-heeled sandals. With her endless curves, brilliant blue eyes and straight, silky red hair, she wasn't just pretty, she was beautiful.

The office door opened just then and Trace walked out. An instant later, the gorgeous redhead threw herself into his arms.

Trace inwardly groaned as he spotted Carly sashaying toward him, hips swinging, a smile on her perfectly made-up face.

"Good morning, sugar." Before he realized her intent, Carly arms went around his neck and she kissed him full on the mouth. "Don't you look handsome today?"

He caught her wrists and set her back down on her feet, his gaze shooting to the Jeep, where Maggie watched from the passenger seat.

Carly reached up and undid a top button on his shirt. "There, that's better. Mustn't hide all those pretty muscles."

Trace refastened the button. "I've got a friend with me, Carly. Is there something you need?"

"My, aren't we in a testy mood?" She turned and looked over at his Jeep. "Who is she? Do I know her?"

"No. Look, I've got to go. What is it you want?"

"I just happened to be driving by. I saw your car and thought maybe you'd buy me breakfast."

"I ate breakfast hours ago. You were probably still asleep." He glanced over at her little sports car. *Or maybe not.* "I thought you were seeing someone. I'm sure he wouldn't be too happy to know you were hanging around your ex-husband."

"I don't think of you as an ex, sugar. And who cares what Howard thinks? It's not like we're living together or anything."

"That's his car, isn't it?"

She gave him a kitty-cat smile. "It's *my* car. Howard bought it for me."

"I've gotta go, Carly. Take care of yourself." Trace started walking. He must have been completely insane to marry her. Jesus, what was he thinking? With his little head, obviously, instead of his big one.

He opened the door of the Jeep, climbed in and cranked the engine.

"Old friend?" Maggie asked. He didn't miss the sharp edge to her voice.

"My ex-wife."

Her eyes widened. "*That's* your ex-wife?"

"I would have introduced you, but Carly isn't someone you really want to meet."

Maggie sat up a little straighter. "She didn't look like an ex-someone. Looked more like a present-tense someone to me."

He turned, cast Maggie a look. "If you knew her, you'd understand. Once Carly gets her hooks into you, she doesn't let go. I've been trying to get rid of her for the last four years. So far it hasn't worked."

"How often do you sleep with her?"

The wheel jerked. Trace stepped on the brake, slowed the car and pulled over to the curb. "I don't sleep with Carly. Half the men in Houston have been in her bed, but in the past four years, not me."

Some of the fight went out of Maggie. "Look, it's none of my business. Last night was just a lark for both of us, anyway."

A muscle ticked in his cheek. "A lark? That's all it was to you?"

She shrugged.

"That's bullshit, Maggie. It was more than a lark and you know it." His temper was heating. Damn, the woman knew how to fire him up. He leaned over, caught her face between his hands and crushed his mouth down over hers. It was a hard, dominating, possessive kiss that told her exactly how he felt.

When he let her go, Maggie blinked up at him.

"It wasn't a lark," he said.

She swallowed.

"Say it."

"All right, it wasn't a lark. I'm not sure exactly what it was, but it wasn't that. Not to me."

He felt himself relax. "I don't know where this is going, Maggie. Apparently you don't, either. But we're going to find out. Okay?"

She just nodded. "Okay."

Trace put the car in gear, eased into traffic and drove on. All the while he was thinking that Maggie O'Connell was nothing at all like Carly.

Or at least he didn't think so.

As soon as Maggie got home, she dashed upstairs to change out of her borrowed clothes. Ashley was waiting in the entry when she came back down.

"Everything okay last night?" Maggie asked. "I didn't get a call, so I figured nothing happened."

"Nothing happened." Her sister flashed her a knowing grin. "Have fun last night?"

She felt the pull of a smile. "Actually, it was pretty amazing. At least until his ex-wife showed up this morning."

Ashley's grin faded. "He's still seeing her?"

"Says he isn't. The thing is, Carly's a redhead, just like me."

"So…?"

"So the first time I met him, the woman at the café said Trace had a thing for redheads. Maybe that's the only reason he's interested in me. Maybe he has some kind of hang-up about it or something."

"If you were a blonde and he had a blonde ex-wife, you wouldn't think anything about it."

That was true and it made her feel better. And Carly

didn't really look that much like her. Carly was shorter, curvier. Even her hair was a lighter, more coppery shade of red. She was prettier, but there was nothing Maggie could do about that.

"Maybe you're right." She glanced toward the guest bedroom. "Robbie down for his nap?"

Ashley nodded. "Listen, I need to talk to you."

Maggie started walking toward the kitchen. "Okay, so talk." Ashley fell in beside her. "I need some tea," Maggie said. "Want a glass?"

"That'd be great."

She leaned into the fridge and took out the pitcher of sweet tea she usually kept there.

"There's leftover pot roast with a burgundy demi-glaze sauce left over from supper last night."

"Wow. Sounds good." Maggie had been eating like royalty since her sister arrived, a perk she hadn't expected. "But I've got to get down to the gallery. Save me enough for a sandwich when I get home."

Maggie filled a couple glasses with ice and poured the tea, handing Ashley a glass and filling one for herself. "So what's up?"

"I don't exactly know how to say this. It's not that I'm ungrateful or anything, but I've been living here, sponging off you for a couple of weeks now. It's time I got a job. I need to make some money to take care of my son."

Maggie took a sip of tea, giving herself time to think. The truth was she was beginning to like having her sister and little Robbie around. "You don't have to worry about that. I've got plenty of room."

"That isn't the point. I spoke to Mrs. Epstein. She says she hasn't met you yet, but she's your neighbor in the unit next door. I saw her out working on her patio and we got to talking through the fence. She's really nice and she loves kids, especially babies. Her husband died four years ago. Her son and daughter are grown and married, and she even has a couple of grandkids. I think she'd be great to watch Robbie while I'm working."

"I hate to point this out, but you don't have a job."

"I know, but it's time I started looking. I'm a really good cook, Maggie. Not a chef yet, but good enough to work the lunch shift or something at a restaurant. That way I'd be home most of the time, and Mrs. Epstein could take care of Robbie while I was on the job."

It sounded logical. If the situation were reversed, Maggie wouldn't want to be dependent on a relative to take care of her and her child.

"All right, why don't we do this? I'll ask around, ask Trace to ask around, see if we can find something without you having to knock on doors."

"That'd be great, and I can keep watching the paper, see if there's anyplace that needs cooking help."

"Okay, then. Looks like we've got a plan." On impulse Maggie reached over and hugged her. "I'm glad you came here."

Ashley hugged her back. "So am I." They sat down at the breakfast counter and Ashley sipped her tea. "I know you didn't feel that way when I first showed up at your door."

Maggie shrugged. Denying it wouldn't help anything. "We didn't really know each other. And the truth is, I was always jealous of you. I guess you probably figured that out."

"Jealous? Why would you be jealous of *me?*"

"Because Mom loved you. She barely knew I existed."

"Are you kidding? Mom bragged about you all the time. The people at her bridge club used to watch for stories about you in magazines. They'd cut them out and give 'em to her."

Something eased in the area around Maggie's heart. "Really?"

"I was nothing compared to you. I was a total loser. That's hard on a kid, you know."

Maggie's throat tightened. "You weren't a loser. You were smart and beautiful. You had a lot of friends."

"Would-be friends. Not worth spit when it came down to it."

Back then, Maggie hadn't realized what a difficult time her sister was having. "It was different for me. I always missed having a mother, but at least I had a dad who loved me." Even after her Great Shame, he had forgiven her, stuck by her.

"In their own way, Mom and Dad loved me," Ashley said. "But they fought all the time and they mostly ignored me. In a way, you were the lucky one."

Maybe she was. Maggie had never considered that before. She reached out and caught hold of Ashley's hand. "You know what I figured out?"

"What?"

"I like you, Ashley Hastings. I really do."

Her sister laughed. "And besides that, I'm a really good cook."

Chapter Sixteen

Maggie started working on the client list for Trace. She kept both email and snail mail addresses as a means of promoting her shows and the release of her new photo collections. It was all on computer, which was a major help. She went back two years, looking for anyone who had purchased two or more pieces, but the list was too long and unwieldy. She narrowed it to three purchases, then to four.

Each effort took a while. Eventually she checked her watch, saw that she needed to leave in order to make her appointment at the gallery and closed down the machine.

When Maggie arrived, Faye was busy with customers picking up framed photographs they had purchased at the gala.

"The walls are practically empty," she said, beaming as she met Maggie by her car. "What a terrific show."

Maggie made a mental note to get the new buyer information from Faye to add to her client list. Then she leaned into the back of her Escape and pulled out the first of five pieces from an earlier show she planned to put on display until she'd had time to print and frame more pictures for the new collection.

"Here, let me help you." Faye reached for another of the 24 x 36 photos, which were bubble-wrapped for protection.

"I can do this," Maggie said. "You're hardly dressed for it." The gallery owner wore a tailored blue skirt with a light blue silk blouse and low-heeled sandals.

"I'm fine," Faye said. "Faster if we both carry them in."

Working together, they got them inside and unwrapped. "I hope you can get the replacements done fairly soon. I'll have to hang something else until I get them. I'd like to have them up no later than week after next."

"That shouldn't be a problem." She would have to get in touch with the company that did the prints, but Fine Art Photo Imaging had always been prompt. The framing was another matter, but she worked closely with Frontier Framing and because she gave them a lot of business, her jobs got top priority.

For the next half hour, Maggie worked with Faye, climbing ladders and carefully hanging photos in the empty spaces left by those that had sold, adding some other photographers' pieces Faye had in the other room, then adjusting the spotlights to show off each work to its best advantage.

"The opening was such a success the Weyman people have already been calling to set up a date for a benefit next year," the gallery owner said as she climbed down a ladder. "I hope you'll be able to do it again."

"I don't see why not."

She smiled. "Your pieces really made the show a hit. People loved what they saw. There's such a poignancy about your work. You've got a wonderful talent, Maggie, for catching exactly the right shot at exactly the right moment."

"Thanks, Faye."

The dark-haired woman reached up and adjusted a smaller photo along the wall. "So…what about the cowboy? Half the women at the opening were swooning over him."

And I was one of them, Maggie thought. *The one who wound up in his bed.* The notion didn't sit as well as it might have.

"Actually, he was here as my bodyguard."

One of Faye's dark eyebrows went up. "Do tell."

Maggie filled her in on the stalker and the notes and phone calls she had received. "I thought maybe it was one of my clients. I was hoping he might show up last night, but I don't think he was here, and neither does Trace."

"Is there anything I can do to help?"

"Just keep an eye out. We have a description of someone who could be him, but no way to know for sure. A big guy in his forties, with silver-streaked dark hair. If someone fitting that description, or anyone else comes in wanting an unusual amount of information about me, let me know."

"Don't worry, I will. I hope you catch the sick bastard."

"So do I."

"In the meantime, bring me those photos as soon as you can. I can't sell them if I don't have them."

Maggie smiled, enjoying the momentary high from her success. Like everything in life, she knew it could end in a heartbeat.

"Magnificent photograph." Richard Meyers stepped back to admire the framed picture *Harbor Sunset* he had been instructed to purchase last night and pick up this morning. *Harbor Sunset* was an amazing shot of the Blue Fin Marina awash in the red-orange light of a flaming sunset. "Too bad it'll have to be destroyed."

Garrett Logan stared down at the picture on the table in his study. "You had just better hope we get our hands on that…what is it? The negative, but they don't call them that now."

"Memory card. We've got to get rid of everything Maggie might have photographed that day. That means we need to get hold of the card she used in her digital camera." Richard walked over to the wet bar in the corner, poured the last half of a can of Diet Pepsi into his frosty glass. "I talked to Faye Langston last night. Maggie prints and frames each picture one at a time. She works out of the studio in her home. If we move on this, we should be able to make the entire collection disappear before it becomes a problem."

Garrett looked down at the information card that had come with the purchase, the words elegantly drawn in calligraphy. The date of the photo was April 20.

His stomach clenched. "It's already a problem." He raked a hand through his thick silver hair. "Of all the bad luck."

Picking up the magnifying glass he had been using

to examine the shot, Garrett leaned over to study the photo again. The names of the expensive white yachts lined up along dock B weren't apparent until he looked through the glass. Once he did, there was no doubt that the plush, fifty-one-foot Navigator, *Capitol Expense,* was his personal yacht. There was also no doubt he was the man sitting at the table on deck.

And the woman across from him...

He felt a wave of nausea. Thank God for Richard. He could count on him to handle this problem the way he did everything else. The man had become indispensable. Which worried Garrett a little, since he knew that was exactly Meyers's plan.

"Once we get rid of the memory card," his aide said, "there'll be no proof the two of you ever met. This'll all go away."

Annoyance filtered through the senator. Richard had a way of making everything sound so easy. "That's all well and good, but how, exactly, do you intend to make that happen?"

"I'm not quite sure yet. We'll need to do a little digging, find out everything we can about Maggie O'Connell—where she lives, where she works. We'll figure out where to find the card and get rid of it."

Garrett felt a trickle of his old self-confidence returning. Getting information out of people was his long suit.

"I heard a little gossip last night," Richard continued. "Just a whisper, but apparently, Maggie's been having some problems. Claims some guy has been stalking her, even broke into her house. I thought maybe you could use your connections with the police department, see what's really going on. Might be something that could work to our advantage."

Garrett started nodding, his confidence growing. "I'll handle it. I'll get on it right away. I'll let you know what I find out."

Richard smiled. "Perfect."

Trace adjusted his phone against his ear. "Thanks for letting me know," he said to Mark Sayers, the man on the other end of the line.

"Hey, no problem. We appreciate your help on this."

Trace hung up and leaned back in his chair, a smile of satisfaction on his face. On Monday afternoon, Parker Barrington had been arrested for embezzling funds from Sommerset Industries. Since the money ran into the tens of millions, the D.A. was able to convince the court that Parker was a flight risk, and the judge refused to set bail. At least the bastard was in jail. Which was a damned good start, but still not enough.

After Emily had amended her statement, refuting Parker's alibi for the night of Hewitt's murder, the police had gone back and done a more in-depth autopsy on the body. The results were not yet in but were due any day. Trace hoped the coroner would find something that would prove the shot that had killed him was not self-inflicted.

The office was humming, Annie working away up front. Through the glass wall in his office, he could see Alex Justice leaning back in the chair behind his desk, his feet propped up, his cell phone pressed against his ear. Ben was staring at his computer screen as if it held infinite secrets, working the keyboard and mouse. Rex had come and gone. He'd been making daily stops at Maggie's, picking up video cards from the wireless cameras aimed at her front and back doors, looking for anyone who might have approached the town house aside from neighbors and the kids playing in front. No one seemed out of place or looked suspicious.

Trace got up and walked into the office next door. Sol looked up from the computer screen, sat back and pulled off his horn-rimmed glasses.

"What's up, boss?"

"I've got some names I need you to run. I want to know if any of these guys have a connection to Maggie O'Connell."

Sol rubbed the bridge of his nose. "You think one of them might be her stalker?"

"They fit a possible description, but I talked to them at her opening on Friday night and I didn't get any vibes. Doesn't mean something can't turn up." He set the brief list down on Sol's desk. "And while you're at it, take another look at the first list of names I gave you. Go a little deeper, see if we might have missed something."

They had both done a search of the personal acquaintances Maggie had listed for Trace that first day. So far neither of them had come up with anything.

Maybe the third time would be the charm.

"I'll give it a shot," Sol said, which meant he might have to cross a legal line or two, but both of them would pretend he hadn't. Turning back to the computer screen, he started pounding away on the keyboard, and Trace returned to his office.

Roger Weller's name was on Maggie's original list, but sometimes the most interesting information couldn't be found on the net.

Last night Trace had phoned Johnnie Riggs, a good friend and ex-Ranger buddy who lived in L.A. Riggs made a living by digging up information—the kind people wanted to keep hidden. Mostly he worked nights, hanging around bars and nightclubs, talking to people on the street, working his contacts. If you wanted to know about someone in Southern California, Johnnie Riggs was your go-to guy.

Trace hadn't connected with Riggs last night, but he had left a message. When the phone on his desk started to ring, he wasn't surprised to hear his friend's husky voice on the other end of the line.

"Hey, man, glad you called," Johnnie said. "I was beginning to think you'd cocked up your toes."

Trace chuckled. "Still alive and kickin'. Hard at work, just like you. I need you to do a little digging."

"Yeah? Got a name?"

"Roger Weller. He's a celebrity of sorts, fairly famous photographer. My client used to work for him. Says he taught her everything she knows."

"That right?" Johnnie said, a suggestive note in his voice.

"According to her, not that kind of everything. She's fairly well known in the business herself. From what her photographs sell for, she makes more than a decent living, and Weller's a far bigger name."

"So the guy's got bucks."

"I did a preliminary search on the net. He's got a house in Laguna Beach. Owns his own gallery there."

"Not a cheap place to live."

"I want to know his off-the-record story, not just what the magazines say about how talented he is. And I want to know if he had more than a mentor-student relationship with Maggie O'Connell."

"That your client?"

"That's her."

"Redhead?"

Trace felt a trickle of annoyance. "As a matter of fact."

Johnnie chuckled.

"She's got a stalker, Hambone." It was Johnnie's Ranger name, well deserved since the man could eat his weight in food and never gain an ounce of fat. "This guy put cameras in her house, bugged her car. He isn't kidding around."

"Not good."

"No, it isn't. Let me know what you find out."

"Will do. I'll get back to you soon as I have something." Johnnie hung up the phone and so did Trace.

He needed to know about Weller, but it bothered him to be checking up on Maggie. He wanted to trust her. For the most part, he did.

But marrying Carly proved he couldn't trust his instincts with women. He needed to be sure Maggie was telling him the truth.

Ashley swung her racquet at the ball, slamming a return her sister missed, and scoring the final point in the game. It was over at last—thank God—since after having the baby, she was way out of condition.

"That was fun," Maggie said, walking toward her.

Ashley took the towel she handed her, wiped her face and neck. Both of them were perspiring and panting. Mrs. Epstein, the next-door neighbor, was watching Robbie while they played. Ashley looked down at her cheap, pink-and-silver plastic wristwatch. Robbie had been sleeping when they'd dropped him off, but he was probably awake by now.

She bent at the waist, bracing her hands on her knees

and sucked in a final deep breath. The pounding of balls in the neighboring courts echoed around them. "I am so out of shape." Which was why her sister had won the first two games, then let her win the third.

"Give yourself a break," Maggie said. "You just had a baby."

Ashley straightened, blew out a breath. "I haven't played in ages."

"I try to play a couple of times a week. I don't always manage."

Ashley grinned. "It felt really great, even if you did let me win."

Her sister laughed. "Next time you'll beat me fair and square."

Ashley glanced back down at her watch. "We've been gone almost two hours."

Maggie walked over to the bench against the wall and began to stuff her gear into a blue-and-white gym bag. "I know you're nervous. It's the first time you've ever left Robbie with someone else. I'm a little nervous myself."

"We should get back." Ashley handed her the racquet she had borrowed, and they headed for the door. All the way to the town house, she worried, which she guessed all new mothers did. But when they knocked on Mrs. Epstein's door and the older woman pulled it open, everything seemed to be fine.

Doris was giving the baby the bottle Ashley had prepared before they left the house, and he was making those joyful little sucking sounds that meant he was happy.

"How's he doing?" Ashley asked.

"Just great." With short, slightly wavy, iron-gray

hair, Mrs. Epstein was robust though a little stoop-shouldered, and she always seemed to be smiling. "He's a lovely little boy. Such a pleasure to watch."

"Looks like he's had enough," Maggie said, when the bottle was almost empty and Robbie no longer seemed interested.

The baby grinned and waved his chubby little arms as Mrs. Epstein handed the bottle to Maggie and the baby to Ashley. Robbie gurgled a laugh. Obviously he and Mrs. Epstein were getting along just fine.

"Well, we'd better get going," Ashley said.

"Keep track of your hours," Maggie told the older woman. "We'll write you a check once a week if that's okay with you."

Their neighbor straightened the paisley blouse she wore belted over a pair of navy pants, and gave them one of her warm, grandmotherly smiles. "Why, yes, dear, that's just fine."

"Thanks, Mrs. Epstein," Ashley said, hoping she would find a job soon so that she could pay the woman's meager wages herself instead of relying on her sister.

The baby's eyes began to drift closed. Inside the town house, Ashley went into the bedroom and put him down in the crib Maggie had bought for him. Ashley smiled as his little mouth parted in sleep.

The phone rang in the kitchen just then and she turned and started back out the door. So far there hadn't been any more calls from the stalker, but every time the phone rang, both she and her sister jumped.

Maggie walked to the breakfast bar and picked up the receiver. She listened for a moment, smiled and looked over as Ashley approached down the hall. "It's for you," she said.

"Is it Mom? She and Dad are the only ones who know I'm here."

Her sister just grinned and handed her the phone. "Hello?"

"Ashley? This is Jason Sommerset. We met the day I came over to your house to talk to Trace."

As if she could forget Mr. Tall, Blond and Handsome. "I remember. Hello, Jason."

"Listen, I was thinking… Things are starting to smooth out a little for me. I was wondering if you would like to have dinner sometime."

Dinner? She hadn't dated since she had dumped Ziggy—or he had dumped her, depending on how you looked at it. "I'm a mother," she blurted dumbly, as if that meant she couldn't have supper with a man. "I have a baby, Jason."

"I know. Trace told me. I like kids. I don't see what that has to do with our having supper."

She scrambled, searched her brain, trying to think of an excuse. She wasn't ready to date. Was she? "Babies take a lot of time. It would be hard to get away."

"But not impossible," he said.

She drew a steadying breath. "Well, um, how would you feel about coming to dinner over here?" She looked to Maggie for approval and saw her sister nodding vigorously.

"Are you sure it wouldn't be too much trouble?" Jason asked.

"I love to cook. It wouldn't be any trouble at all."

She could hear the smile in his voice. "That'd be great. I'd love a home-cooked meal. What night?"

Ashley turned, mouthed, "What night?"

"How about tomorrow?" Maggie mouthed back.

No way, she thought, needing time to work up her courage. "How about Wednesday?" Maggie kept nodding. "Around seven?"

"That works for me. Anything I can bring?"

Just your gorgeous self, Ashley thought. "Maybe a bottle of wine."

"That's a given," he said. "I'll see you Wednesday night."

The call ended and Ashley set the receiver back in its cradle. "I've got a date," she said, still feeling shell-shocked. "With Jason Sommerset. He knows I have a baby."

Maggie ran over and hugged her. "Trace says he's a really nice guy."

Some of Ashley's excitement slipped away. "They all seem really nice in the beginning." Turning, she walked back to the bedroom to check on her little boy.

Maggie worked on her client list, but her concentration was wearing thin when the phone rang downstairs. Ashley had taken the baby and driven her old blue Chevy down to the library. She needed to find a cookbook—Italian, something special to make for Jason. Recipes off the internet just weren't the same, she said.

Wondering if it might be Trace, Maggie hurried to the breakfast bar, smiling as she picked up the phone. The sound of music floated over the line and her stomach instantly knotted.

"I…saw…you…I knew you would be my one true love. I…saw…you…a vision so pure and sweet, my only true love.…"

Her heart was thrumming. Her palms grew damp

as she checked the time of the call on the kitchen clock and jotted it down on the pad beside the phone. *Hang up,* she told herself as the song continued to play. *You have the information they need to track the call.* But her fingers refused to obey.

Then he began to speak. "My dear…dear Mag-gie…" The same electronically distorted voice, the same eerie chill racing down her spine. "I've missed see-ing you, Mag-gie. I've missed watch-ing you…. Soon, my prec-i-ous dar-ling. Soon it will be time for us to be together."

Fear coursed through her. "You bastard! Leave me alone!" She slammed down the receiver, getting a vicious thrill at the thought of the noise ringing in his ear. She was breathing hard, her whole body shaking. She hadn't seen Trace since the morning after the gallery show when he had brought her home. He had called several times, but after their night of lovemaking, both of them seemed to need a breather, time to sort things out.

Earlier, he had phoned to tell her he was checking on the men at the opening who fit the description of the stalker. So far nothing of interest had turned up.

She dialed his cell number with a shaky hand, and Trace answered on the second ring.

"Maggie," he said, recognizing her caller ID.

"He phoned again, Trace. It was…it was just like before."

"Where's Ashley?"

"At the library."

"Check your doors. I'll be right there."

He didn't have to come over. He could have gotten the time of the call, dialed the phone company from his cell and started them working on whatever it took to implement the trap.

But she was glad he was coming. She wanted to see him. Needed to see him.

A few minutes later he banged on the door. Maggie opened it, saw the handsomest cowboy she'd ever encountered and walked straight into his arms.

Trace held her tightly. "You're shaking." He ran a hand through her hair, smoothing it back from her face. "That bastard. I swear when I get my hands on him…"

He didn't say more. Didn't need to. She could think of a dozen things *she'd* like to do if she ever got her hands on him.

Trace caught her shoulders, eased her back to look at her. "You okay?"

She nodded, released a shaky breath. "I'm okay." She smiled. "Better now that you're here." She went over to the breakfast bar, hit the button on the recorder they had set up to catch the calls. Trace followed. Pulling his hat off, he set it on the counter.

The recording began. The song played as it had before. The distorted voice came on: "I've missed see-ing you, Mag-gie. I've missed watch-ing you.…"

"Jesus," Trace said when the call came to an end. "He's missed seeing you." The creep's video cameras were gone. The GPS gone from her car. "I'll just bet he has."

Trace reached for the phone, dialed the phone company, a special number set up as part of the trap. He gave them the information they needed, then hung up.

"They'll call us right back. If they get a location, I'll phone the cops, have them meet me there."

He and Maggie waited anxiously. Fifteen minutes

later, the phone rang and Trace picked it up. He listened, started shaking his head. He hung up and turned to face her.

"It was worth a try," he said, his features grim. "Call came from a cell phone. Disposable, with no way to track the owner or the address it came from. Just as I figured."

Maggie closed her eyes as despair settled over her. She fought an overwhelming urge to cry.

Trace eased her back into his arms. "We're gonna get this guy. Everything's gonna be all right."

She nodded, though she wasn't completely convinced.

"Since the trap didn't work, you'll need to change your phone number."

Maggie started shaking her head. "No way. I work out of my house, Trace. This is my business number. It's on my website, on my business cards. I'm not changing it. I'm not letting that creep control my life."

Trace blew out a slow breath. "If you feel that strongly, at least hang up when you realize it's him. Your calls are all being recorded. There's no reason to let him upset you."

Maggie nodded. Trace was right. There was no reason to let this guy have that kind of power over her. "All right, I'll hang up. I should have done it tonight."

"Good girl. I know how hard this is for you."

"I don't suppose you've come up with anything useful."

Trace shook his head. "Nothing's turned up on the outside cameras. I don't think he was one of the men at your show. So far he's covered his bases, but sooner or later he's going to make a mistake."

"I hope so."

"They always do. In the meantime, you need to play it safe, keep doing what you have been. If you leave the house, you need to take somebody with you."

Maggie's shoulders tightened. "I have to work, Trace. I have lots of things to do."

"This guy could be a serious threat, Maggie. And he's not going to be patient much longer."

She walked to the kitchen sink and stared out the window. Just the empty street, a lone streetlamp and a cluster of trees on the opposite side of the road… She wondered if the man might be somewhere out in the darkness right now. Watching. Waiting.

She turned back to Trace. "Maybe you're right. Maybe he's getting impatient. If he is, maybe we can force the issue, set some other kind of trap. He's after me. Let him come and get me."

Trace ran a hand through his hair. "I've considered it. I don't like it. I don't like the idea of using you as bait. I was hoping we could find a better way."

"Well, so far nothing's worked, and I'm tired of feeling like a prisoner in my own home."

He left the counter and walked up beside her at the window. For a moment, his gaze traveled from the lighted front porch into the darkness across the road.

"What about your client list? How's that coming along?"

"I'm working on it, but so far nothing stands out. No one's bought an extravagant number of photos, at least not that I've found so far." Maggie looked up at him. "I want this over, Trace. We've got to do something to catch this guy."

Trace's glance went back out the window. For several

long moments he said nothing, then murmured, "We took the GPS off your car, so he can't track you from a distance. That means if he wants to see you, he has to follow you. Maybe we *can* draw him out."

Excitement replaced Maggie's despair. She liked the idea—more than liked it. She wanted this to end.

"I'll plan a trip. Go down to the shore like I always do. Last time, he bugged my car to find me. He can't do that now, but if I let it be known I'm going—tell Faye down at the gallery, mention it at the photo processing shop I use—maybe he'll find out and come after me."

"It might work. He's been keeping pretty good tabs on you somehow."

"For all we know he could be out there right now. Maybe he'll be watching that morning when I drive away."

Trace's jaw went hard. "If he follows you, we'll be ready."

They laid out a plan, a photography expedition to Kemah. They both knew the area, and *Ranger's Lady* was docked there, which would give them a base of operations.

"I'll have a couple of my guys in place before you get there. They'll know what to look for. He shows up, we'll have him."

They decided to make the trip next Friday. There would be less people milling around than on the weekend, fewer folks to worry about if things went south.

"Waiting is good," Trace said. "Give him a little time to cool his heels, get anxious, maybe a little careless."

Maggie's excitement built. "You really think it might work?"

"I think there's a chance."

She relaxed for the first time that evening. Trace reached for her, captured her face between his palms. His hands felt warm against her skin, then his lips brushed lightly over hers, settled, melded, and soft heat expanded inside her.

"God, I've missed you." He kissed her softly again. "Now that I've had a taste of you, I want you more than ever."

Her pulse kicked up. He was a strong man and virile. She could feel the control he used to hold himself back, and it made her want him more. Maggie gave herself up to a series of soft, seductive kisses that melted her insides and turned her whole body hot and liquid. Deep, wet, openmouthed kisses. Long, heart-stopping kisses that seemed to have no end. Dear Lord, the man could kiss.

Sliding her arms around his neck, she pressed herself more fully against him, felt the thick ridge of his sex, hard beneath the fly of his jeans. He cupped her bottom, lifted her against him, let her feel his need.

"Damn, I want you." Another deep kiss and he turned his attention to her breasts, palmed them, teased her nipples through her light cotton T-shirt. He caught the hem and drew it off over her head. She wasn't wearing a bra and those whiskey-brown eyes darkened.

"So pretty," he said, running a finger around the tip of one breast, bending to take the fullness into his mouth. Maggie's legs went weak. She made a little mewling sound as he lifted her into his arms and turned toward the stairs. There was purpose in those dark eyes, and remembering the last time he had made love to her, her body began to throb in half a dozen places.

He took the first stair, then another. At the rattle of a key in the lock, he jerked to a halt.

"Ashley!" Maggie said. "Oh, my God."

Trace set her on her feet, and she raced back down the stairs, grabbed her T-shirt and pulled it on just as the door swung open.

Her sister set the baby carrier down on the ceramic tile floor. "I found just the thing! Jason is going to love it." Then she spotted Trace and the excitement in her face changed to an expression of concern. "Did something happen while I was away?"

"I got another call," Maggie explained, casting a look at Trace, her body still thrumming with desire for him.

"We're going to catch him," he declared. "It's only a matter of time. Until then, you keep an eye on your sister, okay?"

"I will, don't worry," Ashley replied.

Trace's gaze locked with Maggie's and his look said he wanted to take her home with him, finish what they had started. "Probably not a good idea to leave your sister here alone tonight—not after telling the SOB to bugger off. You never know how some of these jokers will respond."

He was right, of course. She couldn't leave Ash and the baby, not tonight. Still, she was aching for more of those hot, wet kisses, more of his amazing lovemaking, and the smoldering look he gave her said he felt the same.

"I'm as close as my phone. If anything happens— anything—you call me. And the police. I talked to Detective Sayers. He's put them on notice this isn't a drill. They'll come if you need them."

"All right."

Ashley carted the baby carrier down the hall to their bedroom and Maggie walked Trace to the door.

"Best laid plans and all that," he said, settling his hat on his head.

She just shrugged.

"I hear Jason's coming over for dinner. Kid called to tell me. Kind of thinks of me as Ashley's protector, I guess. He promised to be on his best behavior."

"Good for him."

"You'll want to leave the lovebirds alone, so why don't I make dinner for you at my place that night?"

One of her eyebrows went up. "You can cook more than Pillsbury breakfast rolls?"

He grinned. "Quite a bit more." His gaze ran over her, as hot and sexy as before. "You might want to bring your toothbrush."

Her stomach contracted. Maggie smiled. "Sounds like a plan."

Chapter Seventeen

Richard Meyers stood in the darkness behind the abandoned warehouse. Though it was well after midnight, the temperature was warm, the air damp and heavy. Only a sliver of moon lit the black sky. The property around the old metal building was littered with trash and rusty pieces of iron. A rat scurried into an overturned garbage can, and Richard shivered against an edge of fear.

A place like this was the last spot he would have chosen. He didn't know the man who had set up the meet, just a voice at the end of a telephone line, someone who knew the right people—for the right price.

Yesterday, Senator Logan had spoken to a contact in the police department, who had talked to a friend, a captain in the vice squad named Varner. Varner knew all about Maggie O'Connell and her possible stalker.

He'd had a run-in with the woman years ago. The senator had gotten all the lurid details of the false rape charges and the fact that Varner had a long-standing grudge against Maggie.

According to Logan, at first the captain had believed Maggie's 911 calls were nothing but a publicity stunt. Lately, he had come to believe that "some kook," as Varner had put it, was obsessed with her. After the trouble she had caused his son, Varner figured it was poetic justice.

As far as Richard was concerned, the important point was that Maggie O'Connell had an enemy. If that enemy happened to break into her home and destroy her studio, well, one just never knew what a creep like that was capable of.

A noise in the darkness drew his attention. Footsteps crunching on gravel. A shadowy figure in a long coat with the collar turned up, and a narrow-brimmed fedora, appeared around the corner of the warehouse.

Right out of a spy movie. Richard bit back a laugh. He wondered how badly the guy was sweating inside the coat.

"You bring the money?" the man asked as he approached.

"I brought it," Richard said. "Half tonight. The rest when the job is finished."

The stranger nodded. In the darkness, with his hat brim in the way, it was impossible to see his face.

"There's a security alarm in the house," Richard told him. Another little tidbit the senator had uncovered. The man was a genius at getting people to spit out whatever he wanted to know. "Can you get past it?"

The man chuckled, a raw sound in the darkness.

"Unless the place is protected like Fort Knox, it won't be a problem."

"There may be surveillance cameras outside."

"I'll find 'em, take 'em out."

"The residence is a town house. There's another property attached, to one side. They said you could do the job without destroying the neighboring condos. We don't want anyone getting hurt."

"I can't make promises, but there are ways to handle it. I'll do the best I can."

Logan had been adamant. But the senator was Richard's meal ticket and unless the problem was taken care of, both of them were in serious trouble. He wasn't about to let all his years of hard work go down the drain. Besides, there were certain risks in everything.

"The woman's sister is in the house. She's got a baby."

"I'll keep that in mind." But he didn't sound particularly concerned. "Now, do you want this done or not?"

Richard drew in a slow breath. He was already in so deep he had no real choice. "Go ahead and do it." Reaching into his pocket, he handed over an envelope containing fifteen thousand dollars.

"I'll be in touch," the man said, stuffing the envelope inside the pocket of this of his coat. Turning, he walked back around the corner of the warehouse.

Richard watched until he disappeared. Only then did he realize he was sweating as much as the man in the trench coat.

Trace got a phone call from Johnnie Riggs on Wednesday morning. He was sitting behind his desk, trying not to think of Maggie and the dinner he was cooking for her that night, trying not to get carried away as he imagined all the ways he meant to have her.

The phone call saved him, but just barely.

"Hey, buddy, how's it hangin'?"

Trace almost laughed. If his friend only knew. Johnnie's image appeared in his head, six feet of solid muscle, thick dark hair and dark eyes, a five o'clock shadow that was there by ten in the morning. "Hey, Hambone. Hangin' in there. Whatcha got?"

"I got a line on your guy Weller. Interesting stuff."

"Yeah, like what?"

"Like the fact he's in the closet. So deep not even his friends know the truth. He pretends to be a player. Likes the image of being a lady's man, likes the attention from all the women. And it keeps him from having to explain why he isn't married, isn't involved with a particular female. Fact is the guy prowls the gay bars down in the district, picks up male prostitutes, gets his rocks off, then goes back to his straight life as a hotshot photographer. Sex with a woman doesn't interest him. Looks like your lady was telling you the truth."

"My client, you mean."

"She's a redhead. Six to one, you're sleeping with her."

Annoyance filtered through him. Johnnie knew him too well. "As I recall, you've got a penchant for blondes."

Johnnie chuckled. "Point taken. Anything else you need?"

"Not at the moment. Send Annie your bill."

"Hope the info helps."

"Helps my peace of mind," Trace said and hung up. He'd needed to know about Weller, he told himself. He was just being thorough. And though he felt a little guilty for doubting Maggie's word, he also felt relieved to know she'd been telling him the truth.

He was smiling, thinking of the night ahead, when the phone rang again. This time it was Mark Sayers.

"Coroner's report just came in," the detective said. "Thought you'd want to know."

"Tell me." Trace picked up a pencil, wrote the words *Coroner's Report* on the pad next to the phone.

"They found a needle mark in Sommerset's neck. Missed it the first time because they figured him for a suicide. The puncture convinced them to look in a different direction, and guess what they found?"

"Tranquilizer of some kind."

"That's right. Ketamine. It's used in darts to sedate animals—deer, bear, dogs, monkeys, a lot of different stuff. You can get it from a veterinarian or over the internet."

Trace's fingers tightened around the pencil. "What do you bet Parker's computer turns up an internet search for animal tranqs?"

"Department's on it as we speak."

"If they find it, you'll nail the prick." He penciled *ketamine* on his scratch pad, a reminder to look it up. "You told Jason yet?"

"No, but he'll get an official call sometime this afternoon."

Trace grunted. "Good thing good ol' Parker's in custody."

Mark chuckled. "Might just be. But near as I can tell, Jason's a good, solid kid. He'll handle it."

Trace could almost see the fury in Jason's eyes. He'd handle it because he had to, but he wasn't going to take the news well.

The call came to an end and Trace leaned back in his chair. Parker had been so cocksure he could get away clean.

It wasn't going to happen.

Hewitt deserved justice. It was beginning to look like he was going to get it.

"I got a job!" Ashley burst into the condo and began to dance around, holding a brown paper bag of groceries as if it were her imaginary partner. "I start Friday night!" She shuffled her feet, twirled dramatically as Maggie descended the last few stairs.

"You got a job?"

Ashley grinned. "Yup!"

"I think I missed something," Maggie said. "Maybe you'd better start at the beginning." For the last couple hours she'd been upstairs going through her photography files, sorting memory cards, getting ready to take the pertinent ones to the photo imaging shop to have the pictures reprinted. As soon as they were ready, she would deliver them to Frontier Framing, get them matted and framed, then get them to the gallery.

Ashley carried the groceries into the kitchen and set them on the counter. "There was this ad in the paper, you know? I've been reading the Help Wanteds every morning. The job's only for a couple of weeks while Eddie—that's the cook—looks after his mom, but it's working in a restaurant and I have to start somewhere."

Maggie began to smile. "Congratulations. That's wonderful, Ash. So where exactly is it you'll be working?"

"The Texas Café." She began pulling groceries out of the bag, the ingredients she needed to cook supper for Jason Sommerset. Maggie had a hunch it had taken the last of the meager savings Ashley had brought with her from Florida.

"I'll be working for a woman named Betty Sparks. I told her I was living in Houston with my sister, Maggie O'Connell, and she said she knew you."

Maggie thought of Trace's fight in the café with Bobby Jordane, and inwardly winced at her shabby attempt to grab a paparazzi-style photo. "We met a few weeks back."

"She asked me if you were dating a guy named Trace Rawlins, and I said it looked that way, and she laughed."

Maggie felt a trickle of irritation. "I'm sure she did." But Maggie had a hard time seeing the humor. Betty had warned her Trace had a weakness for redheads. Apparently, she was just another one of them.

The thought did not sit well. She told herself her interest in Trace was also strictly physical, and managed a halfhearted smile.

"So you got a job at the Texas Café, and…?"

"And I start Friday night. I really liked Betty and I think she liked me. She said as long as I could cook, she'd teach me the rest of what I needed to know. I'm really excited about it."

"That's great. I'm so happy for you." Maggie shot a quick glance at the groceries spread out on the counter. "I take it Robbie's at Mrs. Epstein's?"

"I took him over a little early, since I had to go to the job interview, and cooking this stuff isn't easy. I really need to concentrate."

"You seem excited about seeing Jason."

Ashley pulled the cellophane off a package of cut-up chicken, set it in the sink and turned on the water. "I'm not sure. I'm kind of nervous. I know he's out of my league. There's only one thing he could possibly want from me. I don't know why I said yes."

Maggie rounded the breakfast bar and walked into the kitchen. "That is so not true. You're beautiful and you're smart. You have goals and you're willing to work hard to reach them. You have a lot more to offer a man than just your body."

Ashley looked up and her features softened. "That's really a nice thing to say. Thanks, sis."

She drew her into a hug. "I mean it. Jason's lucky to get a shot."

Ashley shook her head. "He isn't getting a shot. He's getting dinner. That's all."

Maggie smiled. "He's getting your wonderful company for the evening. That's worth a heckuva lot."

Her sister grinned. "He's getting chicken cacciatore with prosciutto tortellini gratinato. And lemon mousse with raspberries for dessert. That really is worth a lot."

Both of them laughed.

"So what about you?" Ashley asked as she began retrieving various pots and pans for the meal she was preparing. "You're going over to Trace's, right? Are you guys getting serious?"

Maggie scoffed. "Are you kidding? We hardly know each other. We're strictly in lust."

"I'd say you know each other pretty well. He always seems to be there when you need him. That's more than you can say for most men."

She pondered that, and how Trace had a way of making her feel safe and protected. "Not most men," she corrected, "but a lot." She smiled. "I never thought I'd have the hots for a cowboy, but I have to admit I do."

"But it isn't anything serious," Ashley said with a hint of amusement.

She shrugged. "I like him. I think he likes me. In bed, he's amazing."

Ashley had started to reach for a bowl, but stopped and turned.

"What is it?" Maggie asked.

"I've never felt that way about sex. You know, having the hots for a guy? Ziggy…well, he wasn't my first, but there were only a couple others, and none of them were amazing."

Maggie reached up and looped a curl of her sister's hair behind an ear. "You're young. You've got lots of time. You can wait until just the right man comes along."

"Is Trace the right man for *you?*"

Maggie ignored a funny little quiver in her middle. "When it comes to sex, he sure is." Grinning, she turned and headed back upstairs.

Her grin slowly faded. She just hoped her attraction to Trace didn't go a whole lot deeper than she wanted to admit.

Chapter Eighteen

Everything was ready. The dining table was set with the white linen cloth Ashley had purchased at Bed Bath & Beyond when she discovered Maggie didn't have one. She had also purchased four place settings of white porcelain dishes, the kind the chefs used on TV. Thankfully, Maggie had decent flatware and a set of expensive crystal wineglasses.

"I saw them and I just had to have them," her sister had said with a smile and a shrug. "I have no idea why, but wine always tastes better in a pretty, long-stemmed glass."

Which, oddly enough, seemed true. Jason was bringing the wine, so the rest of Ashley's money went to buying the actual food. Except for the small bouquet of mixed spring flowers she had bought at the grocery store and arranged in a clear glass vase she had found beneath the kitchen sink.

Supper was simmering on the stove, the chicken, tomatoes and spices bubbling in the skillet. The pasta was finished and covered to keep warm, the arugula salad crisp and chilled, just waiting for her to add her special oil-and-vinegar dressing. The lemon mousse was in the fridge.

She turned at the knock on the door, took a moment to catch her breath and slow her pounding heart. She smoothed the long skirt of the white piqué, sleeveless summer dress she was wearing with a pair of strappy silver sandals, and headed for the door.

When she opened it, Jason Sommerset stood before her. For several seconds she just stared. He looked like a movie star, only more masculine, and for an instant she considered just closing the door and pretending she wasn't there.

"Can I come in?" he asked, a smile of amusement on his lips.

"Oh, yes, of course. I just…I haven't dated in a really long time and… Well, to tell you the truth, I was never any good at it."

His smile widened. "Then we'll pretend this isn't a date, just two friends getting to know each other."

She felt a little of her tension ease, returned the smile. "Okay."

Jason handed her the bouquet she had only just noticed. She took it with a trembling hand. "Pink roses. They're gorgeous, Jason. Thank you."

"You're welcome." He walked past her into the house and set the bottles of wine he had brought on the kitchen counter. "I didn't know if you liked red or white so I brought both."

"Either is great with me, although red would probably go better with dinner."

She carried the flowers to the breakfast bar. They were neatly arranged in a pretty pink vase, so she wouldn't have to stop cooking to take care of them. She had never been given roses before. It made her feel feminine and kind of soft inside. She wondered if he had chosen them especially for her or if roses were what he usually brought a woman.

He turned toward the stove, sniffed the air. "Oh, boy, that smells delicious."

She grinned. "Chicken cacciatore with prosciutto tortellini gratinato. Lemon mousse with raspberries for dessert."

His blond eyebrows went up. "I guess you really do like to cook."

"I really do. Eventually, I'm hoping to get into a culinary school. I want to be a chef."

"Wow, I'm impressed."

"Too soon yet to be impressed, but maybe someday…"

"Definitely. You'll do it. I can see the determination in your eyes."

Something warmed inside her. He was taking her seriously, something few of the men she'd known had ever done. They talked while he opened the bottle of red, a French wine—a Rothschild Bordeaux, the label said, expensive she was sure. Ashley got the pair of Maggie's good glasses she had put on the table, and he poured wine into each.

"Where's your little guy tonight?" Jason asked, handing her one of the glasses.

"He's staying with the lady next door, Mrs. Epstein. Robbie really likes her. So do I."

"That's great. You know you didn't have to get a sitter. I wouldn't have minded if he had been here with us."

Ashley glanced at him, a little surprised. Ziggy had no patience with kids. Even if he'd stuck around, he would have been a terrible father.

The delicious aroma of simmering chicken, tomatoes and herbs filled the air. Jason lifted his glass. "To new friends."

She lifted her own. "New friends." They clinked the glasses together and each took a sip. She was no wine connoisseur, but it really tasted good.

"I like it," she said. "I don't know much about wine but I need to learn if I want to be a proper chef."

"I could teach you the basics," Jason offered. "For instance, this is a French Bordeaux. That means it's from the Bordeaux region. The date, 1999, is the year it was released for sale."

He told her a little about the white wine he had brought, which was a California chardonnay from the Napa Valley. "The truth is, almost all the modern French wines come from California stock. The original vines were destroyed by the Phylloxera virus in the early 1900s. Healthy vine stock had to be imported back to Europe."

Ashley smiled at the interesting little tidbit. It was nice to talk to someone who treated her as if she had a brain. "That's cool. I had no idea. I bet the French do their best to keep it a secret."

"I'm sure they do."

She smiled again. "You know they're starting to make wine in Texas. I don't know if it's any good."

He grinned. "Hey, if it's from Texas, it's got to be good, right?"

She laughed. So Jason thought like a true Texan, not just some jet-set rich boy. He continued to surprise her. She liked that about him.

"Are you hungry yet?" she asked. "The chicken looks like it's ready."

"Oh, yeah." He helped her carry the chilled salad plates from the fridge to the dining table, returned and retrieved their wine, while Ashley dished up the supper she had prepared, plating it prettily as she had seen chefs do on TV.

Jason held her chair as she sat down, then took his seat across the rectangular table.

"Everything looks great," he said, surveying the colorful spring bouquet and the elegant place settings she had taken such care to arrange. "You've done a beautiful job, Ashley. I feel like I'm eating in a gourmet restaurant."

She felt a rush of pride. "I hope the food is up to your expectations."

Jason surveyed the steaming plate in front of him, a hungry look in his eyes. He decided to try the salad. "This is really good. What's that spice in the dressing? I don't quite recognize it."

"Curry powder. It just gives the oil and vinegar and other spices a little extra zing."

Jason lifted his glass, then set it back down without taking a sip. Instead, his eyes remained on her face. "I almost called today and canceled our dinner. I got some bad news earlier. I wasn't sure I would be very good company."

She had noticed he seemed slightly distracted. "What happened?"

"You know my dad died. I mentioned it when I was here before, and it was in all the papers."

She nodded. "I saw it on TV. After you left the day you were here, Trace told us you didn't believe it was suicide, and neither did he."

Jason swallowed, the muscles in his suntanned throat going up and down. "The coroner's report came in today. They found small amounts of a drug in my dad's system. Something called ketamine, a tranquilizer they use to sedate animals. That bastard married to my sister drugged him and murdered him and made it look like he killed himself."

Ashley's heart went out to Jason. Believing a trusted member of the family was responsible made his father's death even more painful. "Are you sure he's the one who did it?"

"He was stealing company money. He did it, all right. If he wasn't in jail, I swear, I'd kill him." Jason glanced away, his jaw tight. When he looked at her again, he seemed so haggard, so defeated, that Ashley reached out and put her hand over his where it rested on the table.

"I don't think your father would want that, Jason, not for the son he loved. He would want justice. That's something you can make sure he gets."

She caught a quick flash of moisture in Jason's eyes, then it was gone. He turned his hand over, laced his fingers with hers.

"That's what Trace said. No matter how long it takes, I'll make sure my dad gets the justice he deserves, and Parker Barrington spends the rest of his life in prison."

He didn't let go of her hand, just gave it a gentle squeeze. "I'm really glad I came. You're not like the other girls I know. I think you really care about people. Most of them only care about how they look and how much money I spend on them."

Ashley eased her hand from his, then missed the warmth. "I'm glad you came, too." She smiled. "And I have a feeling my chicken cacciatore is going to make you feel even better."

Jason laughed, and she thought it sounded a little lighter than it had before.

"I haven't had a home-cooked meal in ages. Even when my mom was still alive and we had a chef, we mostly ate catch as catch can."

Ashley could hardly image a life like that.

"But next time it's my treat," he insisted. "If you still don't want to go out, we'll go to the store together and I'll buy the groceries."

Ashley looked at Jason and soft heat curled in the pit of her stomach. It wasn't lust. It was scarier than that. Jason wanted to see her again. They had more in common than she had believed.

She hadn't thought past tonight, but she wanted to see him, too.

Now she just hoped he liked the chicken cacciatore.

Trace opened the door and stepped back, welcoming Maggie into his house. He was dressed in dark blue jeans and a crisp white shirt, his black boots polished to a sheen. His hat was missing, his dark hair neatly combed, and he looked gorgeous.

A little thrill of excitement slipped through her. He was so damned sexy, so damned male.

"You look good enough to eat," he drawled, his golden-brown eyes going over the yellow sundress she wore. It was printed with miniature peach daisies that matched her lipstick, and his gaze settled on her mouth.

Bending his head, he kissed her, a brief melding of lips as he led her into the house and closed the door.

His mouth found hers again, long enough to stir the heat beginning to curl low in her stomach.

"Peaches," he whispered, the flavor of her lipstick. "Darlin', you taste as good as you look." He moved closer, sank his fingers into her hair and tipped her head back, holding her in place as he ravished her lips.

She could taste his desire for her, thick and strong, feel the heat of his skin, the mounting tension in his body.

He started to pull away, save making love for later, but her heart was pounding, her insides quivering. Going up on her toes, she slid her arms around his neck and pulled his mouth down for another kiss. It turned deep and erotic and left no doubt as to what she wanted. When she opened for him, his tongue slid inside to tangle with hers, and arousal trembled through her. She heard Trace groan, and his whole body tightened.

"If we don't stop now," he whispered, kissing the side of her neck, "we aren't going to make it through supper."

Maggie made a soft little purring sound, let her head fall back as he rained kisses over her neck and shoulders.

"You started this, cowboy. Now food is the last thing on my mind."

He growled low in his throat and captured her mouth in another burning kiss. She hadn't expected the evening to go quite this way, but at the feel of all those hard muscles pressing against her and the heavy, demanding length of his erection, all she could think of was making love. She wanted more of his burning kisses, wanted him to touch her, do the things he had done the last time they had been intimate.

His mouth claimed hers as he backed her up against the living room wall—thank God, the curtains were closed—slipped down the straps of her sundress and peeled off the top.

For several long moments he just stood there, his gaze hot and fierce as he drank her in. Then he bent and took the fullness of her breast into his mouth, and Maggie swayed against him. Her nipples were diamond hard, and beneath the fly of his jeans, so was he. She clung to his neck, slid her fingers into the hair at his nape, marveling at the silky texture. She arched her back, giving him better access to her breasts, and he didn't waste time accepting her invitation.

Her stomach contracted. She loved the feel of his mouth against her skin, the rasp of his strong white teeth on her nipple. Maggie closed her eyes as he shoved her skirt up above her waist and reached for her, skimmed a hand over the flat spot beneath her naval. She was wearing only a pair of white thong panties. She gasped as he caught hold of the narrow strap between her legs and ripped it away, tossing the scrap of white satin over his shoulder.

"I'll buy you some new ones," he murmured, his mouth coming down over hers again.

Maggie whimpered as heat scorched through her. She caught the front of his white Western shirt and jerked it open, the snaps popping as she bared his chest and ran her hands over the bands of muscle, which bunched wherever she touched.

Heat scorched through her, so strong her legs felt weak. Trace kissed her again, long and hot and deep.

Her hands shook as she unfastened his silver buckle, then tugged his zipper down.

"I want you," she whispered. "You make me crazy."

His jaw clenched as if he was in pain. "Jesus God, lady."

She was in a fog of lust when he found her center and began to stroke her. Heat and pleasure rolled through her, need and sweet desire. She held on as he lifted her, wrapped her legs around his waist, freed himself and drove deep inside her.

Maggie moaned. He was big and hard, and every time he moved, pleasure swept through her. He took her with long, heavy thrusts that had her trembling, making little mewling sounds in her throat. She tightened around him, knew she was going to come.

With a wild, keening cry, she spoke his name and collapsed against his shoulder. When she looked up at him, she caught the gleam of male satisfaction in his eyes.

"Better hang on, darlin'. We aren't done yet."

Oh, my God. Maggie's eyes widened as he started all over again, slowing his rhythm as he regained control, giving her time to catch fire again.

They came together in a blaze of heat and passion like nothing she had experienced before, the pleasure so deep and sweetly erotic she felt the sting of tears.

Trace held her for several long moments, then kissed her softly. "You okay?"

She just smiled and nodded.

He carried her into the bedroom and set her on her feet in front of the bathroom door. "You probably need a minute."

She looked into those fierce brown eyes. "What is it about you?"

He chuckled. "I don't know, but I'd better go check on dinner before we decide to do a little more research on the subject." His gaze raked her in a way that meant he was ready all over again. "Unless you want to skip dinner altogether."

Maggie grinned. "Tempting." More than tempting. "But suddenly I discover I'm starving. I'll be right out." She gave him a last seductive smile, darted into the bathroom, closed the door and leaned against it, feeling boneless and pleasantly sated.

Until tonight, she hadn't realized what a hussy she was.

Maggie grinned.

Trace released a slow breath. He couldn't remember a woman who turned him on the way Maggie did. He drove her crazy? The woman was driving him completely insane.

For an instant while they were making love he'd felt a rush of lust so fierce he'd thought he was going to lose it. *Not gonna happen,* he'd told himself, determined that pleasuring Maggie was more important that pleasuring himself. At least for the moment.

He smiled as he walked into the kitchen. His willpower had paid off a thousand times over. Damn, he liked making love to her.

Trace heard her moving around in the bathroom and his smile slipped away. There was no doubt the sex was great. Better than great. But after Carly, he wasn't ready for a serious relationship. When he'd discovered the truth about his marriage, discovered what a fool he had been, he had sunk to an all-time low.

He was never really in love with Carly, and yet it had taken him months to get past his doubts and regain some of his old self-confidence. He didn't want to go through anything like that again.

Maggie came wandering in, interrupting his thoughts. She'd done a nice job of putting herself back together, but there was no way to hide it. She looked like a woman well loved.

He wanted to turn off the stove and carry her back to bed.

The night is young, he consoled himself, thinking of all the ways he meant to have her.

"What's for supper?" She sniffed the air as she poured herself a glass of white wine. "Something sure smells good."

"Spaghetti and meatballs, salad and French bread. That okay with you?"

"You bet." She lifted her glass. "Want one?"

"Does a jackrabbit like to run?"

She laughed, poured more wine and handed it to him. She stood close enough that he could smell her perfume, and his body stirred. Maggie went up on her toes and kissed him full on the lips, and his erection returned.

"Food and then sex," she said. "Sounds good to me."

Trace kissed her back. When Maggie moaned into his mouth and her nipples went hard, his decision was made. *Sex and then food.*

Maggie didn't protest when he carried her into the bedroom again.

Chapter Nineteen

Maggie woke up at two in the morning. She'd always had a reliable mental alarm clock and it served her well tonight. She needed to get home. Jason would be gone by now and she didn't want Ashley staying in the town house by herself. It was too soon after her telephone run-in with the stalker. What if the creep tried to break into the house?

She looked over at Trace, who was sleeping on his stomach, the sheet riding low on his hips. Lord, the man was gorgeous. A wide back ridged with muscle, smooth, suntanned skin and a tight little round behind... He attracted her as no man ever had, satisfied her as no man ever had, and yet she felt something deeper than just sexual desire.

Something she refused to think about with so much going on in her life.

Instead, she quietly put her now-wrinkled sundress

back on and headed for the door. She left a note on the pad by the phone, wrote "Enjoyed the meal and everything that went with it—not necessarily in that order" and headed out to her car. She couldn't lock the house up tight without a key, but pushed the button on the doorknob so no one could just walk in.

Her car was parked in front. She drove the little red SUV toward home and had almost reached the turn onto Broadmoor Street when her cell phone rang. She smiled as she recognized Trace's number.

"Hey, cowboy."

"I thought you were staying for breakfast," he growled. "I had a lot more plans for you."

She laughed, felt a little quiver of desire, which was ridiculous, considering. "I was worried about Ashley. I didn't want her there by— Oh, my God!"

"What is it?"

Maggie made a strangled sound into the phone.

"Maggie! For chrissake, what is it?"

"The house…the house is on fire!" Her throat closed up. "Oh, God, Trace, it's on fire!" She tossed the phone down on the passenger seat and stepped on the gas, fishtailed around the corner and shot down the street.

Orange and yellow flames roared into the air through the roof of the town house. Smoke billowed in thick, gray plumes into the ink-black sky. Her heart was hammering, trying to pound its way through her ribs. Her throat was as dry as the timbers going up in flames.

The first fire truck was already there, and another careened around the corner right behind her. Maggie jerked the wheel, forcing the car to the opposite side of the road and jumped out without closing the door. Her pulse was racing; tears blurred her vision.

Dear God, Ashley and Robbie! She started running across the street, heading straight for the front door, but stumbled and nearly fell when a fireman stepped in her way, blocking her path.

"You can't go in there, miss."

"That's my house! My sister's in there—my sister and her baby!"

The fireman's big gloved hands settled firmly on her shoulders. "They're okay," he said gently. "They're safe. They're right over there." He tipped his head toward the street, angling his wide-brimmed helmet in that direction.

Maggie's heart squeezed. She sagged in relief. Drawing in a shaky breath, she brushed the tears from her cheeks, changed course and hurried toward the slender figure huddled in a blanket on the curb, little Robbie tight in her arms.

"Ashley! Ashley, oh, God, are you all right?"

Her sister stood up, holding on to the baby, and Maggie wrapped her arms around them both. She was shaking all over, her legs weak with leftover fear and relief.

"We're okay," Ashley said. "We're both okay."

Maggie's throat clogged with tears and she started crying. "I shouldn't have let you stay with me. I was afraid something would happen. If you and Robbie had been hurt or—or…" She swallowed, unable to complete the awful thought.

"We're all right, Maggie, truly. This wasn't your fault."

She looked over at the row of town houses. None of the other units were burning. So far the firemen had been able to keep the blaze contained to her house alone. All the other owners seemed to have been evacuated, and small groups milled around in the darkness, watching the firefighters battle the fire. Mrs. Epstein sat on a lawn chair someone had been thoughtful enough to provide, and was talking to some of the neighbors.

Maggie watched the flames leaping into the air, the dense streams of water shooting toward the roof from three different hoses, the wall of smoke slowly changing from black to white, and her throat clogged even more.

A noise caught her attention. She turned at the sound of boots ringing on asphalt, and spotted the tall, familiar male figure. *Trace.*

"Maggie!" He strode toward her, his hat missing, his hair still rumpled from sleep. His eyes were dark and filled with concern, his forehead lined with worry. His glance went from her to the fire. Then he spotted Ashley and Robbie, and some of the tension drained from his features. "Everybody get out okay?"

Maggie nodded. "Everyone's all right." She started crying again, shifted so that Trace wouldn't see. She felt his hands settle gently on her shoulders. He turned her toward him, drew her into his arms and just held on.

"It's okay," he said softly. "Your sister and the baby are safe. The other residents got out okay. Everything's going to be all right."

A little sob escaped. "This is my fault." She swallowed past the lump in her throat. "I shouldn't have made him mad. Oh, God, Trace."

His arms tightened around her. "This wasn't your fault. None of this is your fault." He eased her a little away, brushed a light kiss over her lips. "You scared the holy bejeezus out of me, darlin'."

The soft drawl rolled over her like a warm caress. She knew she had frightened him, and the worry in his eyes made her heart twist. She sniffed, accepted the handkerchief he pulled out of the back pocket of his jeans and blew her nose.

"I shouldn't have gone to your house tonight. I should have stayed home."

"I don't think that would have pleased your sister and Jason very much, and it wouldn't have changed anything anyway." He turned his attention to Ashley, who stared at the fire as if she were in a trance. "Tell me what happened, honey."

Ashley turned to look at him. Beneath the blanket, she was wearing her shortie, pink flowered robe, and her feet were bare. "I don't exactly know. After Jason left, I went over to Mrs. Epstein's to pick up Robbie. I brought him home and put him in his crib and we went to bed. I was sleeping pretty hard until something woke me up. I don't know exactly what it was, some kind of noise, I guess. I got up to check things out, and when I reached the kitchen, I saw this bright yellow glow over the yard. I didn't realize the house was on fire until one of the neighbors started banging on the door."

She took a shaky breath. "I grabbed Robbie, my purse and the diaper bag, and ran out of the house. People were streaming out of the other condos. Someone had already called the fire department."

"The fire started upstairs?" Trace asked.

Ashley nodded. "In Maggie's studio, I think. The door was closed and I didn't see any flames until I got outside. Then I saw the whole roof on the back side of the town house was on fire."

Maggie looked at the flames chewing through the space where all her pictures were stored. Weeks of work, hours of effort. Her computer destroyed, along with the files that held all her photographic memory cards, as well as the list of buyers she had been compiling. Her stomach rolled with a combination of nausea and anger.

"He destroyed my studio," she said, fighting not to cry again. "He was mad because I hung up on him."

"I'm so sorry, darlin'. All your hard work gone because some lunatic wants you and can't have you." Trace gazed back at the town house, which was mostly smoking now, though flames still burned in part of the upper story.

Maggie followed his gaze. "Do you think maybe the security cameras might have picked up something?"

"There's a chance. Stay here. I'll be right back." He crossed the small grassy area in front of the condo and walked up to one of the firemen, the one who appeared to be in charge. They spoke for a while. Trace pointed toward the camera mounted under the eaves beside the front door. The man replied, Trace nodded, then turned and started walking back in Maggie's direction.

"The arson squad's already here," he said. "See that red Suburban? They'll be doing some preliminary work tonight, asking questions, taking pictures. They'll come back tomorrow after the debris cools down, bring the dogs in maybe, examine the interior. They'll be able to tell us how the fire started and whether or not it was arson."

"*He* did this. You know he did."

"Whoever did this knew a lot about electronics. We installed a good system. He had to be damned good to get inside without setting it off."

"He put cameras in my house. He knew enough to do that."

"This would be a whole lot harder."

"Could you get in?"

He frowned. "Yeah."

"I guess he could, too."

Trace's jaw hardened.

"So what about the video cameras?" Maggie asked.

"If they're intact, the arson guys will take a look at them, let us know if they find anything." He pinned her with a hard, dark glance. "You're not gonna like this, but you and your sister are coming home with me. You'll stay there until we get all of this figured out."

"Why? So he can burn your house down, too?"

"Trust me, he won't get into my place. Protection is my business. The only way he gets inside is if I invite him in."

Maggie didn't argue. She would rather have checked her weary little family into a motel, but clearly, the stalker was dangerous.

Maybe he figured if he couldn't have her, he might as well kill her.

Early-morning sunlight streamed in through the kitchen windows. The weather was heating up. Ninety degrees predicted, and the humidity wouldn't be any fun, either.

Trace poured himself a cup of coffee and carried it over to the kitchen table. Rowdy trotted up beside him, dropped down on the floor next to his chair and rested his muzzle on Trace's boot.

"Well, boy, we've got company, like it or not."

Rowdy's ears perked up and Trace chuckled. "What was I thinking? Of course you'd like it. Two pretty females lavishing you with attention." He set his cup on the red Formica tabletop next to the *Houston Chronicle* he'd carried in off the front porch. On a lark, or maybe in a moment of nostalgia, he'd remodeled the kitchen to look like the 1950s kitchen his grandmother had in the old farmhouse out on the ranch. White and red and chrome. He still liked coming home to it.

He flicked his gaze to the hallway off the living room that led to the bedrooms. His unwilling house-guests were asleep in one of them, exhausted after the fire last night.

Leaning back, Trace combed his fingers through his hair. Maggie felt responsible for the fire, but it wasn't her fault. If anyone was responsible, he was. She was paying him to protect her. He had failed.

Trace blew out a frustrated breath. He needed to talk to Anthony Ramirez, captain of the Arson Investigation Bureau. Tony was a straight shooter, and he and Trace had worked together before. Tony could confirm what Trace's gut had already told him—that the fire had been purposely set.

In return, he needed to bring Ramirez up to speed on the threats against Maggie and what little he had found out about her stalker. Until he talked to Ramirez, he couldn't be sure it was arson, but his instincts, bolstered by his brief conversation with a couple of the fire boys last night, were saying chances were nearly a hundred percent.

He had underestimated this guy at every turn. The last thing he'd expected the bastard to do was set Maggie's house on fire. The guy was obsessed with her. In some sick fashion, in love with her. Even if he'd been pissed, angry enough after the phone call to do her physical harm, a guy like that would want a face-to-face confrontation. He'd want to get her alone, have her all to himself when he meted out whatever punishment he believed she deserved.

Hell, she wasn't even there last night—which, since he had to have gone inside to start the blaze, he must have known. He had set the fire anyway, putting Ashley and her baby at risk.

Trace sipped his coffee, trying to get inside the guy's head. Trying to make sense of things. Coming up with a big fat zero.

Again.

Talking to Ramirez came first and foremost, but he also needed to talk to Mark Sayers. The cops had shown up last night and taken a preliminary statement. Mark wasn't officially involved in the case, but he was a friend and a detective, and Trace wanted him kept in the loop.

He glanced at his watch, saw it was still too early for Sayers to be at the station, looked back down the hall to the guest room door. He had a dozen things to do, but didn't want to leave without making sure Maggie knew how to operate his alarm system. He wasn't taking any more chances.

He got up and poured himself another cup of coffee. As much as he wanted to leave, he didn't want to wake her. She was exhausted and worried. She'd been terrified last night and he didn't blame her.

He'd been damned terrified himself.

With her cell line open and connected to his, he could hear her crying as she'd raced like a madwoman toward the fire that threatened her family.

Maybe it was realizing how much she cared about them.

Maybe it was realizing how much he had come to care for her.

Whatever it was, his stomach had been churning as he struggled to drag on his clothes, shove his feet into a worn pair of boots and get the hell on the road. His heart had thundered as he'd raced to the condo. All the way there, all he could think of was Maggie.

He wanted her safe. He wanted her out of danger.

Hell, he just plain wanted her.

And he was beginning to realize he wanted her for a lot more than just sex.

The thought scared the hell out of him.

A memory stirred, of Maggie and their heated lovemaking last night, and his blood headed south in arousal.

The worst possible punishment he could inflict on himself was having Maggie O'Connell sleeping in his house—and not sleeping in his bed.

Chapter Twenty

A knock sounded at the door and Trace rose to answer it. Rowdy padded along beside him as he crossed the foyer and looked through the peephole, to find Mark Sayers standing beneath the wide, overhanging porch roof.

"I was just getting ready to call you," Trace said. "Come on in." He stepped back and Sayers walked into the living room, his light brown hair neatly combed, his cheap suit already rumpled.

"Listen, I heard what happened last night. Unofficial word is arson. I guess I owe you an apology. Looks like Maggie's troubles are bigger than I thought."

"Apology accepted. But I'm still gonna need your help."

"Hey, I'm a cop. It's my job to protect and serve. I don't want to see anybody get hurt. Just tell me what you need."

"You want a cup of coffee?"

"Love one."

Trace led the detective into the kitchen, took down a a mug and filled it with the steaming, dark Colombian brew.

"Thanks," Sayers said, accepting the cup. "So what's your take on the fire?"

"Well, that's the thing." Trace led him over to the kitchen table and both men sat down. Rowdy returned to his place on the floor at Trace's feet. "This guy's a whack job, for sure. That being said, I still can't get a handle on him. Maggie wasn't even home last night. Her younger sister and her baby were there."

"Jesus."

"This creep gets past the alarm system and gets into the house, so he has to know Maggie wasn't there. But he lights the place up, anyway. It doesn't add up."

"He wanted to punish her, maybe, for something he believes she's done."

"She hung up on him a few days ago," Trace said. "Maybe he was mad enough to kill her sister to punish her, but in my book it just doesn't wash."

"You never can tell, I guess, but it woulda been a major overreaction."

"From the notes he's left, he's got some kind of sick infatuation with Maggie. Killing her little sister and her infant child would hardly endear him to her."

Sayers started frowning. He looked at Trace over the rim of his coffee mug. "You aren't thinking this might be just a coincidence? Some lunatic firebug torches her place and the police and everyone else jump to the conclusion the stalker's to blame?"

Trace shrugged. He hadn't put the thought into words, but it had been lurking at the back of his mind.

"I don't buy it," Mark said.

"I'm not much on coincidence, either. We'll know more after the arson guys finish their job. Tony Ramirez is a good man. He'll find the dots and string them together."

"You'd installed security on her place, if I remember."

Trace nodded. "And cameras front and back. He bypassed the alarm system as if it wasn't there. No word yet on the cameras, but odds are he took them out."

"You think her stalker is capable of that? You said he bugged her car, set up video surveillance inside the house."

"Like I said, I'll know more after I talk to Ramirez."

Sayers rose from his chair. "Let's meet again after. I'm not supposed to be involved in this case—so I'm not. Got it?"

"I got it. Thanks for coming by, Mark."

Just then the bedroom door swung open and Maggie walked out. She was wearing the bathrobe he'd loaned her, red hair in a sexy tangle around her shoulders. Trace felt that punch in the gut he'd felt before.

"I hope I'm not interrupting. I didn't know anyone else was here," she murmured.

"Maggie, this is Detective Mark Sayers. He was just leaving."

"I'm sorry about the fire," Mark said. "We're gonna catch this guy. A man like that is a danger not only to you and your family but to everyone in the community."

"Yes, he is. And I appreciate any help you can give us."

Trace followed Sayers to the door and closed it behind him. He was halfway back to the kitchen when a second, more frantic pounding started on his door.

"I think I'm living in Grand Central Station," he grumbled, returning to the door, this time spotting Jason Sommerset on the porch.

"Did you hear about the fire?" Jason strode past him into the living room. "I saw it on the news this morning. Maggie's town house burned up last night. I can't find Maggie, or Ashley and Robbie. I'm worried sick. Do you know where they are?"

"Take it easy, kid. Both women are here and so is the baby. Everyone's fine."

The tension left Jason's shoulders.

"Hello, Jason," Maggie called out from the kitchen, wagging her fingers in his direction. Trace noticed his traitorous dog curled at her feet. "Ashley's still sleeping. It was a very long night."

"I was really worried," Jason said. "I'm glad everyone's okay."

Just then the door down the hall swung open and Ashley wandered out into the living room, rubbing her short, messy blond curls. She was wearing the pink flowered robe she'd had on last night and was barefoot, her long legs exposed to way above the knees. She spotted Jason and froze like a deer in the headlights.

"Jason…"

He strode toward her, reached out and took both her hands in his. "Are you all right? What about the baby? I was scared to death when I saw what happened on the news."

Ashley swallowed and her eyes welled. She'd been the strong one last night. Now she crumpled. "I was so scared," she said, and Jason pulled her into his arms.

"You should have called me. I would have come."

"We hardly...hardly know each other."

He tipped her chin up. "We're friends, aren't we?"

Ashley gave him a watery smile. "I guess we are."

"You bet we are. And I've already got a place figured out for you and your family to stay."

"What?"

Jason turned to Trace. "A friend of mine is in Europe. As soon as I saw the news, I called him." A faint smile touched his lips. "Lucky for him it wasn't the middle of the night in France."

"Go on," Trace said.

"Jimmy owns a condo over in the Galleria. It's not far from my place. I told him what happened and he said Ashley, Maggie and the baby could stay at his house until he got home. He said he'd be gone at least another four weeks."

Trace started shaking his head. "That's not gonna happen. Maggie's the target. Ashley and Robbie wouldn't be safe. Just think about what happened last night."

Maggie came forward, her borrowed terry cloth robe trailing on the floor behind her five-foot-four-inch frame. He hid a smile. Damn, she looked delicious.

"Trace is right," Maggie said. "Ashley needs to be as far away from me as possible."

Jason's clear blue gaze swung back to the younger girl. "Then you and Robbie can stay. The place has security guards 24/7. We'll let them know what happened, make sure they keep an extra-sharp eye out for trouble."

"Maybe she should just stay here," Maggie said, her big green eyes going to Trace.

"I'm not the one who's in danger," Ashley said. "The

guy wasn't after me. He set the fire in Maggie's studio. He was mad at her. He wanted to hurt her. I just happened to be in the way."

"He could have killed you," Trace said softly.

Ashley shrugged. "That's the way crazy people are. They don't think about the consequences."

She had a point. And he agreed she would probably be safer somewhere away from her sister.

"I'd keep an eye on her," Jason promised, looking at Ashley as if she already belonged to him. "If she needs anything, all she'll have to do is call."

Damn, the kid had it bad. Trace almost felt sorry for him. "Let's see what the arson squad has to say. They might have information that will help us decide what to do."

"I'm not giving up my job." Ashley's slender hands slammed down on her hips, making the flowered robe creep higher. Jason looked as if he were going to swallow his tongue. Man, the kid was in trouble.

"You won't have to quit your job," Trace promised. "We'll work all of this out." Somehow.

Though, at the moment, he had no idea how he was going to make that happen.

Maggie showered and put on the same wrinkled sundress she had been wearing the night before, all the clothes she had left in the world. The dress smelled like smoke and dredged up memories of flames and fear she would rather forget.

She thought of the fire and hoped the downstairs area of the town house had fared better than the upstairs, and that her sister's clothes could be washed and cleaned. That what little Ashley owned hadn't been destroyed by the water and smoke. But there was no way the fire department was letting them back in the house today, not with smoldering debris and hot, charred wood still making it too dangerous to go inside.

Fortunately, in the University District there were a number of clothing stores. Deciding Mrs. Epstein needed a day or two to recover, Trace called his receptionist. Annie volunteered to babysit for a couple hours, time enough for an emergency shopping trip to nearby Rice Village. Maggie had met Annie at the office and Trace trusted her completely. Though Ashley worried about leaving the baby with someone new, Maggie was sure, once she met the lady, her concern would be assuaged.

Jason insisted on accompanying them. With their nerves still on edge after the fire, both women agreed. Of course he would have to drive Maggie's car, since his flashy silver Porsche wasn't big enough for all of them.

While they waited for Annie, Ashley changed into a pair of Trace's lightweight sweatpants and an olive-drab T-shirt, then sat down in the living room next to Jason to give little Robbie his bottle.

Trace reached out and caught hold of Maggie's hand, and she let him lead her into the kitchen. While she seated herself at the table, he poured her a mug of freshly brewed coffee, poured one for himself, then sat across from her. She couldn't miss the concern in his face.

"What is it, Trace? You're making me nervous."

"It's nothing like that. It's just that we've talked about the fire, but not about your work and what losing it must mean to you. It looks like your studio is gone, your pictures all destroyed. You'll have to start completely over. I just want you to know how sorry I am."

Maggie reached out and caught his hand. There was something about those strong hands that always made her feel safe. And she knew how talented they could be.

"I was frantic last night…terrified for my sister and Robbie. And I was furious about what that bastard did to me and my family. But my pictures weren't destroyed."

Trace frowned. "I thought you kept your memory cards in the studio. They weren't there?"

"They were there. For the past few days, I'd been making changes in my filing system. I was just about finished. The thing is, a year or so ago I decided to store all my work online. There's a service called Photodrive. It's a commercial file storage website designed especially for professional photographers. Once I finish a collection, I put every picture I've taken on the site, just in case something like this ever happened—though believe me, I never thought it actually would."

"My company uses online storage, too. At least for some things."

"Not everything?"

Trace chuckled. "I'm a little too paranoid for that. If you'd see some of these computer geeks at work you'd know that a guy with the right skills can get into almost anything. Hell, I'm pretty damned good myself."

"Ah…yet another hidden talent."

His mouth faintly curved. "I guess you could say that." He took a sip of his coffee. "So you're telling me you still have the original files."

"That's right. Everything's on Photodrive. All I have to do is retrieve the photos I sold at the opening, get them reprinted and framed, to replace the ones that were purchased, and I'm back in business."

His dark eyebrows drew together. "Besides you, who else knows you still have those pictures?"

"No one. Why?"

"No reason…at least nothing I can put my finger on. Just one of those funny hunches you get after you've been doing this as long as I have. I want you to hold off on reprinting the photos for a while. Don't tell anyone you still have them. Your friend Faye Langston, over at the gallery, isn't going to like it, but, hey, you had a fire, right? What can you do?"

"She isn't expecting me to have them until next week."

"Great. By then I'll have talked to Tony Ramirez. He's head of the arson investigation. I want to hear what he has to say before we make our next move."

"All right." She needed to get started. It took time to get the photos ready to sell, but she trusted Trace's judgment. And it would set her back only a few more days.

"My client list is also stored on Photodrive," Maggie said. "I'll have to start all over sorting them, and get the new buyers' names from Faye, but at least it wasn't all destroyed."

"That's great news. In the meantime, I guess you and your sister are going shopping."

Maggie grinned. "With Jason Sommerset acting as bodyguard."

Trace smiled, shook his head. "The kid's in big trouble."

"Nice trouble, though, wouldn't you say?"

Trace looked at her with those hot, golden-brown eyes. "I think I'm in the same kind of trouble."

Maggie laughed. "I think maybe I am, too."

"You realize if Ash and Robbie move to the Galleria, you'll be staying here with me."

Heat crept into her cheeks. "I'd probably be a lot safer."

"You also realize you won't be sleeping in the guest room."

Her pulse picked up. "No?" With his Western shirt open at the throat, his skin darkly tanned, she wanted to press her mouth there, just breathe him in.

"So you may not be as safe as you think."

She wished she could kiss him. "Maybe not. Then again, I've always believed in living dangerously."

Trace's gaze ran over her and his mouth curved in a slow, sexy smile. "Looks like I do, too."

Trace left the women with Jason. The kid was used to the good life, but he was also an athlete who excelled at tennis, had been captain of his college swim team and had learned how to handle himself. Trace chuckled as he remembered the story Hewitt had told him, how Jason had come home from high school wanting to learn to box. His mother had cried and begged her husband to forbid it. Being the ultimate negotiator, Hewitt had convinced their son to try martial arts instead. Jason discovered he had a knack for it.

He could defend himself if the need arose, and he stayed in shape. Jason could take care of the women, or at least knew what to do if they ran into trouble.

In the meantime, Trace had put in a call to Tony Ramirez, who had agreed to meet him at the Atlas office. He was waiting when Tony walked in. He wasn't a big man, but strong as a bull, with powerful shoulders and arms. He had short black hair and a Roman nose. And he was smart, which was why he was good at his job.

"Good to see you, Tony." The men shook hands and Trace led him back to his glass-enclosed office. "You want a cup of coffee or a Coke?"

"I just had lunch. I'm fine."

Trace closed the door and both men sat down. "I appreciate your stopping by. What can you tell me so far?"

Tony opened the file he carried, though Trace knew he kept most of the information in his head. "As you already know, the good news is no one was hurt. The bad news is it was definitely arson. The guy disabled the wireless alarm before he went in—probably used some kind of sophisticated software. Same with the cameras."

"I was afraid of that." Recently, Trace had used the same technique in Mexico on a rescue mission he had undertaken with his friends Dev Raines, Johnnie Riggs and Jake Cantrell. The high-tech gear had gotten them inside a fortified compound and into the sprawling mansion where a missing little girl was being held. Unfortunately, they'd had to shoot their way out.

"The perp went in through the sliding glass door," Ramirez was saying. "Started the fire in the studio. Multiple points of origin. Gasoline used as the accelerant. He opened the windows for ventilation. He really knew what he was doing. The whole damn room went up all at once."

"Definitely a pro."

Tony nodded. "He's a professional, all right, and way better than most. And here's the kicker. From the looks of it, the fire couldn't have been burning more than a few minutes when the 911 call came in. The station's just a couple of blocks away, but by the time the first truck arrived, the caller was already gone. The way it looks, there's a good chance the caller is the guy who set the fire."

"He wanted the fire boys to get there. He wanted the studio to burn, but not the whole house. He wasn't after the woman and her baby."

"I think he went out of his way to keep people from getting hurt, or setting the other apartments on fire. The way the blaze was constructed, it was meant to flash inward, taking out the room but not immediately burning into the unit next door. It would have, sooner rather than later. And with fire, there's always a chance something will go wrong. There's no safe way to commit arson."

"So there was the risk of loss of life, but the odds were in his favor."

"That's about it. Like I said, this guy's really good at what he does."

Trace leaned back in his chair. "Doesn't read like Maggie's stalker. What are the odds some nut job who has the hots for her is also a high-dollar torch?"

"Could be her nut job put up the money."

Trace pondered that. "Could be, but I don't see it."

"So what then? Someone with a grudge against Maggie?"

"I've been working that angle. So far it's led nowhere. A lot of people know about the stalker. Police, friends, people we've questioned. Maybe somebody wanted to jump on the bandwagon. Destroy her work and let the stalker take the blame."

"I hear she's pretty successful. Maybe someone doesn't like the competition."

"Maybe."

Tony stood up and Trace did, too. "Thanks, Tony. I appreciate the information."

"Hey, we're both on the same side." Ramirez stuck out a meaty hand and Trace shook it. "Take care of Ms. O'Connell. This may not be over yet."

Trace clenched his jaw. It wasn't over. But he was determined it would be. And soon.

Their arms loaded with bags and boxes, Maggie and Ashley returned to Trace's house late in the afternoon. Carrying another load of packages, Jason walked them to the door, and Trace pulled it open.

He smiled. "Welcome home."

Maggie's eyes widened at the sight of him cradling little Robbie against his broad chest.

"What in the world…"

"Annie had some things to do at the office. I was heading home so we swapped places."

Maggie looked at Ashley, Ashley looked at her and both burst out laughing.

One of Trace's eyebrows went up. "What? You didn't think I could change a diaper?" His mouth quirked. "I managed to figure it out."

Dropping her package, Ashley reached for the baby, and Trace gently handed him over. "Thanks, Trace," she exclaimed. "You've really been terrific."

"Not a problem."

Maggie gazed up at her tough Texas cowboy, thought of the way he'd looked standing there with a tiny baby in his arms and felt a tug at her heart. She had never met any man like him.

Jason cleared his throat, making his presence known.

"So what about Ashley using my friend's apartment?" he asked hopefully.

"I think it's a good idea," Trace said. "Until we know what's going on, Ashley and Robbie are safer staying somewhere Maggie isn't."

Jason grinned ear to ear. He turned to Ashley, who held her son in the crook of her arm. "I've got access to the key. I can help you move in whenever you're ready."

"The sooner the better," Trace said.

"I'm working tomorrow night." Ashley smoothed a hand over the sleeping baby's head. "I called Mrs. Epstein. She says her house is still a little smoky, but the fire department says it's safe. She's all set to take care of Robbie. I guess there's no reason for me to stay here." She held up one of the shopping bags, jiggled it and grinned. "Besides, I'm already packed."

Trace chuckled. "You and Maggie should be able to get back in the town house in a day or two. Maggie can give you a call when we get the word."

"Great."

The women searched through the bags, separating the items they had purchased, the baby clothes, pairs of shoes, slacks, blouses, jeans and T-shirts. Then Jason carried Ashley's share out to his car and returned for her and Robbie.

Maggie hugged her sister goodbye. Swept by a sudden sense of loss, she felt tears burn behind her eyes. "Call me or I'll call you. We need to keep in touch."

"I'll call, I promise."

Another quick hug, then Ashley and Robbie were gone. Jason closed the door and followed them across the porch.

Maggie felt a wave of sadness. Everything seemed

topsy-turvy, weirdly upside down. Her house was destroyed, her sister once more living out of a suitcase. She felt like sitting down and having a good, long cry.

She sensed Trace's presence behind her. His arm slid around her waist, drawing her against him. "She'll be all right. Jason's a good kid. He'll make sure she's got everything she needs."

Maggie turned, managed a smile. "I like him. I know Ash does, too."

Trace ran a finger along her jaw. "It's gonna be all right."

She nodded, but in her heart, she didn't really believe it.

"Come to bed with me," Trace said softly. "I promise to make you forget all this, at least for a while."

Her throat ached. She needed him and somehow he knew. Instead of a reply, she stood on tiptoe and kissed him. Trace kissed her back, lifted her in his arms and carried her into the bedroom.

True to his word, at least for a while, he made her forget.

Chapter Twenty-One

Richard Meyers stood in the shadows beneath the bridge. With the moon hidden beneath a layer of heavy black clouds, the darkness felt as thick as the humid air. Night sounds intruded: the rustle of leaves, a rodent scurrying through the dirt along the creek bed, the sighing of the wind through the branches of the trees.

He was a few miles out of the city on a two-lane road to nowhere, exactly the place the phone call he'd received had instructed him to be. Richard didn't mind the inconvenience. The job he had commissioned had been completed exactly as planned. The man he had hired was worth every penny.

He spotted the shadowy figure approaching out of the darkness. Same long trench coat with the collar turned up, same narrow-brimmed fedora pulled low across the face. Last time, Richard had fought not to laugh at the ridiculous costume. Tonight he felt like grinning in sheer relief.

"You got the money?" the man asked in a voice that sounded slightly rusty.

Richard handed him the envelope, the second installment of their arrangement, fifteen thousand more in hundred-dollar bills. Thirty thousand was a hefty sum, but he'd wanted to hire the best. Apparently, he had.

The man stuffed the envelope into the inside pocket of the trench coat. "Looks like our business is finished."

"Yes. Thank you." He couldn't believe he was thanking someone for committing arson. But since that night at the marina, everything in his life had changed.

The man made no reply, just turned and walked away, the bottom of his trench coat flapping as he headed into the night and disappeared into a copse of trees along the road.

It was over. They were safe. For the first time in weeks, he could look forward again, instead of backward.

Richard breathed a long sigh of relief.

Maggie heard the knock and hurried to the door. Trace's security system was activated. He had shown her how to use it and assured her that once it was set, no one would be able to get inside the house undetected. She wasn't expecting a visitor. Trace was working at his office. She and Rowdy were the only ones at home.

The dog stood beside her, his ears perked up, black-and-white head tilted toward the sound of someone on the porch. Only a little uneasy, she peered through the peephole and let out a little whoop of glee.

Punching in the alarm code, she hurriedly opened

the door. "Roxanne! I can't believe you're here! Good Lord, when I called this morning, I didn't expect you to get on a plane and fly home!"

The tall, statuesque brunette walked into the living room and drew Maggie into a hug. "Are you kidding? You didn't think I'd want to come back when I found out someone was trying to murder my best friend?"

Maggie sighed. "I don't think he was trying to kill me," she said, leading Roxy toward the kitchen. "I wasn't even there that night." She had called Roxanne in New York that morning. After everything that had happened, she found herself desperately in need of a friend.

"I hung up on him," she continued. "I guess it made him mad and he wanted to punish me."

"Punish you? You haven't done anything wrong! I hope they find the prick and somebody shoots him."

Maggie laughed. "I'm sorry you felt like you had to come back, but I'm really glad you're here."

Roxy smiled. "Me, too." She rolled those haughty blue eyes and fluffed the smooth dark hair curled under at her shoulders. "Besides, I was getting bored. How much shopping can one woman do?"

Maggie grinned, feeling better than she had in days. "Trace is down at his office. How about a glass of iced tea?"

Her friend scoffed. "I'd rather have a martini, darling, but at this hour, I suppose iced tea will have to do." While she sat down at the Formica-topped kitchen table, Maggie filled two glasses with ice and added sweet tea she took from the fridge. Then she carried the glasses over and settled across from her.

"I think it's time you told me what's going on," Rox

said. She glanced around Trace's tidy, masculine home. "Looks like a lot has changed since I left."

Maggie took a sip of tea. "I guess you could say that. I've got a family I didn't expect, the second floor of my house is a smoking pile of rubble and whoever did it is still out there somewhere." They had talked on the phone, but now she went into detail, bringing her friend up to date on the stalker, her sister and the baby, Jason Sommerset, and the fire.

"You aren't talking about *the* Jason Sommerset, son of the late Hewitt Sommerset?"

"One and the same," Maggie said. "Jason's a friend of Trace's. He's taken Ashley under his protection. My sister is beautiful, Rox. And she's really sweet. Jason seems to have a terrible crush on her."

"Well, she could certainly do worse than the heir to Sommerset Industries."

"It's funny. I don't think my sister cares how much money Jason has. She's had some bad times. The baby's father was a real loser. She just wants someone who will treat her well."

Maggie went on to tell Roxanne about the apartment Jason had arranged for Ash and Robbie till things got back to normal. "Ashley called when she got there, all excited. I guess the apartment's a real showplace. She says it has marble floors, an entertainment room the size of a small theater and gold nozzles in the bathrooms— of which there are many. It's a nice treat for her."

And Ashley having a place to stay would give Maggie time to work things out. Rebuilding the town house was going to take weeks, maybe longer. She needed to find somewhere else for them to live until it was finished, but she couldn't even do that until they caught the stalker.

"Jason Sommerset has all the money in the world," Roxanne said, "but as far as I know he's stayed out of trouble. No drunk driving, no rehab, nothing like that."

"He seems really great. I'm not sure how Ashley feels about him. I guess time will tell."

"I guess it will." Roxanne sipped her tea and grimaced, clearly wishing it was alcoholic. "You've done a great job of telling me everything, darling, but you managed to leave one small thing out."

"What's that?"

"The cowboy. You're living in his house. You aren't going to tell me nothing's going on between you."

Maggie's face went warm. "We're, um, involved, I guess you could say. Mostly it's just physical."

Roxanne eyed her assessingly. "Really?"

"Well, mostly. You said yourself the guy was a major hunk."

"So I did and so he is, but doing the dirty just for the sake of it isn't your usual style. Are you sure there isn't more to it?"

Maggie drew a circle in the frosty wetness on her glass. "I hope not. I mean, getting seriously involved with someone is the last thing I want."

"Sometimes things just happen."

"I suppose. Trace is pretty amazing. To tell you the truth, I'm doing my best not to fall in love with him."

Roxanne cocked a dark eyebrow. "Where's the fun in that, darling? Falling in love is what life's all about."

"Maybe. But sometimes there are other considerations."

"Such as...?"

"Such as…what if I'm like my mother, Rox? Celeste's a runner, you know? Whenever things go wrong, she just up and leaves. She ran from my dad, ran from her second husband. Now she's run off and left Ashley's father. So far, that's what I've always done. I run whenever things get too involved. I'm afraid of what'll happen if I ever let myself truly fall in love."

Roxanne reached over and caught her hand. "I'm not the person to be giving you advice. I've been in love more times than I can count—which means I've never really been in love at all. But I believe if Mr. Right comes along, somehow you'll know. And you won't have any desire to run away from him."

Maggie made no reply. She had a history of hurting the men she cared about. First Josh, then Michael, then David. She didn't want Trace to be another casualty of her changeable affections.

On the other hand, Trace's sexual history included a failed marriage and a string of redheads he cast aside like worn-out boots.

She didn't want to suffer that fate, either.

"For the moment, we're just enjoying each other," she finally said.

"And he's keeping you safe."

"That's right." But her heart was definitely at risk. There wasn't the least amount of safety in falling in love with Trace Rawlins.

Roxanne stood up. "I guess I'd better get going. I'm beat and have lots of unpacking to do. If you need a place to stay, just let me know."

"Thanks, Rox."

"I expect to hear from you every couple of days. If

you don't call, I'll be calling you. Just remember, I'm here if you need me."

Maggie walked her to the door and the women hugged.

"Take care of yourself, darling. Keep in touch."

Maggie managed to smile. "I will." But she was thinking of what Roxanne and Ashley both had said, and trying to convince herself Trace wasn't Mr. Right.

Ashley showed up early for work Friday night. The Texas Café was already full, customers laughing and talking in their pink vinyl booths, couples sitting at scarred wooden tables. Platters of spaghetti, burgers and fries, and homemade pie and ice cream slid out through the service window behind the long food service counter lined with pink vinyl stools.

On the way to the café, she had dropped the baby off at Mrs. Epstein's, whose house smelled a little like smoked sausage, but had suffered no real damage and was slowly airing out. Though her battered old Chevy sat in the underground garage of her borrowed apartment, Jason had insisted on driving her to work. He had dropped her off in front of the café with a promise to return at the end of her shift.

Ashley thought of him as she worked over the grill next to Betty Sparks, the gray-haired woman who owned the restaurant. Betty was instructing her on how to broil the perfect burger. Ashley was eager to learn.

"You have to start with good meat," Betty said. "That's the secret. Good meat cooked just right—not too done, not too rare. Then a good, sturdy sesame seed bun. Got to have the seeds to make it right."

She was learning to make chili, and how to deep-fry

fish and chips. She could make gourmet meals, but was learning the basics of how to cook for a crowd, how to handle the pressure and make everything come off the grill at the right time.

"I gotta check on things out front," Betty said, wiping her hands on a dishrag. "Don't worry, you're doin' just fine."

Ashley nodded. Filling in for the regular cook while he was taking care of his sick mother, she was only a little nervous at being left on her own. It was hot and moist in the kitchen, with steam coming off the steam tables, smoke off the grill, but she loved being there, loved that she was turning her life around, working toward her goals, making a future for herself and little Robbie.

An order for chicken fried steak came in. Betty had shown her how to use the café's premade flour mix to coat the meat patty. Ashley smiled when it came out of the pan perfectly golden-brown. A ladle of thick white, country sausage gravy went on top, a ladle of buttery corn, and she slid the plate through the service window for one of the waitresses to pick up.

She turned the stainless-steel wheel to check the next order, made a pair of creamy chocolate shakes, then returned to the grill for two more medium-rare burgers.

It was almost the end of her shift when the bell above the door rang and a new customer walked in. Ashley started at the sight of the thin, exotically handsome man with high cheekbones and thick black hair pulled back in a queue at the nape of his neck and tied with a leather thong. He wore black jeans and a leather vest with nothing underneath but a string of silver beads.

He looked like a rock star and she knew him instantly as the man who had fathered her baby.

Ziggy.

There he was, a vision out of her past who had stepped into the new life she was building. She wanted to wring his neck.

She leaned through the service window behind the front counter and spoke to Betty. "Would it be okay if I took a quick break? I've got a problem I need to deal with."

"Why, sure, honey." Betty's sharp eyes went to Ziggy, who sauntered over to the counter and sat down on one of the round, padded stools. "I'll take over until you get finished."

Ashley untied the strings of her white cotton apron and drew it off over her head, then walked out of the kitchen, heading toward the man at the counter.

Ziggy stood up as she approached. "Hey, babe." His black eyes raked her. "You're lookin' fine. Never know you just had a kid."

"That was three months ago, Ziggy. What the fuck are you doing here?" She winced as she slipped into her old self and said a word she hadn't used in months.

"What do mean, sweetheart? I came to see *you*—and our son, of course."

"Bullshit, Ziggy. How did you find me?"

"I talked to Tommy. Megan said you called and told her about your new job."

Megan Wiseman had been her closest friend in Florida. They hadn't talked in weeks, but the day Ashley had gotten her job at the café, she'd been so excited she had called her. Now she realized her mistake. Megan's boyfriend, Tommy Jensen, was a good friend of Ziggy's.

"So is that it?" she said. "You found out I was working, so you came here to hit me up for money?"

He clamped his hands dramatically over his heart. "You wound me, babe. I was just worried about you, that's all."

"I'm fine, Ziggy. I'm working—as you can see—and I'm doing just great. Now go away and leave me alone."

"You don't mean that, sweetheart." He reached out and cupped her cheek. Ashley knocked his hand away. "I'm your child's father," he said. "And you know how much I've always loved you."

"The only person you love is yourself, Ziggy. That's the way it was. The way it always will be. Now get out of here. Get out of my life before I do something I'll regret."

A familiar blond head appeared over Ziggy's shoulder. He was taller by a couple of inches and, in a completely opposite way, even better looking. And unlike her ex-boyfriend's arrival, just seeing him made Ashley's heart swell.

"You heard the lady," Jason said. "I'd advise you to leave. Now."

Ziggy turned. "Who the hell are you?"

"I'm a friend. And I'm asking you to leave. If you don't go on your own, I'll make sure you do."

Ashley couldn't believe her eyes. Jason was defending her. And from the look on his face and the way he was standing with his legs splayed and his weight on the balls of his feet, he was capable of doing exactly what he'd threatened.

Ziggy must have realized it wasn't a bluff. He took a step backward, putting some distance between them.

"Fine. You want her, you can have her. Her and that squalling brat she's got."

Jason's jaw hardened. The restaurant fell silent. He took a menacing step toward Ziggy, who turned and started rapidly walking toward the door. He gripped the handle and pulled it open, ringing the bell, then flashed a last look Ashley's way and stalked out into the night. The door closed with a whoosh behind him.

Ashley's eyes burned. She couldn't tear her gaze away from Jason.

People returned to their meals and conversations, laughing as if nothing had happened. In the Texas Café, maybe nothing had.

Betty appeared beside her. "You okay?"

Ashley swallowed. "I'm okay."

"It's gettin' near closing time. Why don't you and your fella go ahead and go on home?"

"But you said you wanted to show me how to close up tonight."

"You'll be workin' tomorrow. I'll show you then."

Ashley's chest tightened. She was making friends here, people she could trust. People willing to help her.

Betty smiled and sauntered away, and Ashley turned back to Jason. "Thank you. No one's ever been willing to fight for me before."

He reached out and touched her cheek. "I'll fight for you, Ashley. Anytime you need."

Her eyes filled. Jason had a way of cutting through her defenses. "Take me home, will you please?"

He just nodded. He waited for her to collect her purse, then led her outside. When they reached his vehicle, he paused beside the powerful sports car.

"You don't have to be afraid, Ashley. I won't let him hurt you."

Color washed into her cheeks. "I wish you hadn't seen him. Now you know how stupid I was to get mixed up with a jerk like that." She shook her head. "I feel so different now. I feel a thousand years older."

"You aren't the same person anymore. You're a mother now and that changes everything."

She looked into his handsome face. "Yes, it does."

Jason bent his head and very gently kissed her. It was the softest, sweetest kiss she had ever known.

"Let's go get Robbie."

Ashley nodded. Her throat felt tight.

Jason opened the passenger door, his gaze sweeping over the cramped interior of the Porsche.

"Looks like I'm going to need a bigger car," he muttered as he waited for her to slide into the seat.

Ashley couldn't tell if he was talking to her or himself.

Either way, it made her smile.

Chapter Twenty-Two

Wishing he could spend Saturday morning in bed with Maggie, Trace showered and dressed to go to work. When he walked into the living room, he spotted her pacing the floor and grumbling, glossy red curls flying at every turn.

She whirled to face him. "So...you're going off to work, but I'm just supposed to stay here."

"I've got some things I need to do," he said simply. He had a business to run, people who depended on him, and he wasn't going to find Maggie's stalker by staying in bed—an idea he infinitely preferred.

"I can't stay locked up this way much longer, Trace." Dressed in jeans that cupped her pretty little behind and a T-shirt that fit nicely over her luscious breasts, she looked good enough to eat. His mind raced back to the bedroom. With Herculean effort, he reined himself in.

Maggie stopped pacing and stood in front of him. "I have a job, just like you and everyone else. Besides, I'm used to being outdoors shooting. I've got to get out of the house, Trace."

He shook his head. "Not by yourself. It isn't safe and you know it."

Maggie blew out a breath. "We need to catch this guy. What about the trap we'd planned to set? Can't we go ahead and do it?"

He sighed. "We need to do something, that's for damned sure." He had told her about his meeting with Tony Ramirez, told her the guy who had lit up her condo was likely a professional torch. He hadn't mentioned his theory that there was a good chance more was going on than just some loony who was obsessed with her.

He still wasn't ready to break that little bit of bad news.

"It'll take me a while to get the word out," Maggie was saying. "But the fire might work in our favor. The story was all over the local TV news. I know Sally Grimshaw over at KGEO. I'm a local girl and fairly well known. I think I could get her to interview me about the destruction of my studio and what my plans are for the future."

It wasn't a bad idea. As long as Maggie didn't give out any personal details, just kept to the information they wanted the stalker to know. If they could catch him, at least one of Maggie's problems would be solved.

And the truth was, Trace might be wrong, and her stalker actually could be the one responsible. Hell, maybe the nutcase *had* hired a torch to burn up Maggie's studio. Crazy people were just that—crazy. There was no way to predict exactly what one of them might do.

"So what do you think?" she asked, pulling his thoughts back to the moment. "During the interview, I could mention how eager I am to get back to work. I could say I'm planning a trip down to Kemah to do some shooting this weekend. We could set it up the same as we planned before."

"It might work," he finally said. "Long as we have time to get ready. I need to talk to Ben and Alex. I want them there if the guy shows up." So far Trace had managed to keep his two friends away from Maggie. He'd been oddly reluctant to introduce her to a couple guys who looked as good as they did, and had half the women in Houston falling at their feet.

But he'd talked about their competence, told her how lucky he was to have them working for Atlas, even in a freelance capacity as they did.

Maggie looked up at him and smiled. "Okay, then. While you're at the office, I'll make a list, see what I can do from my end to start things rolling."

"All right, but let's work out the details before you make any calls."

"Okay." He could read her excitement. Her face was glowing, her green eyes bright. After her arrival at his house, she had commandeered his laptop, and for the past few days had been keeping herself busy by working on her client list, sorting names and looking for anyone with what seemed an inordinate interest in her pictures. So far, she hadn't found anyone.

Aside from that, she'd been answering sympathetic emails from friends and clients who had seen the story about the fire, talking to the insurance company about payment for the damage and trying to find a contractor to get started on the major job of rebuilding the town house.

But Maggie wasn't used to sitting home, and her frustration was evident.

"I've got quite a bit to do," he said. "I won't be home before supper. We can go out or I can pick something up and bring it back."

Maggie walked toward him, draped her arms around his neck. "Why don't I cook us something? I looked in the freezer. You've got a package of pork chops. I usually marinate them in a little teriyaki."

His mouth watered. "I thought you couldn't cook."

"Unlike my sister, my skills are fairly limited. But I can manage teriyaki pork chops and salad."

"Sounds great." And staying home with Maggie sounded a helluva lot better than going out to some restaurant and wishing he was home making love to her. "Try not to get cabin fever, and I'll see you tonight."

She gave him a soft, openmouthed kiss that made it hard for him to turn and walk away.

Hell, it just made him hard.

He chuckled to himself. His sex life had never been better. By now he should be ready for a change, but he was far from bored with the perky little redhead. In truth, he couldn't get enough of her. Sooner or later that would end, he was sure. As long as he didn't let his emotions get too deeply involved, he'd be okay.

Trace vowed not to let that happen.

Trace thought of Maggie all afternoon as he worked behind his desk. It was difficult to concentrate on the invoices Annie had asked him to review, to sign payroll checks or take care of the myriad other little details he had put off doing all week.

And another problem had arisen.

According to Detective Sayers, there was a chance Parker Barrington could get out of jail.

Emily Barrington had recanted her story, telling the police that she had been angry at her husband and co-erced into saying he had come home late the night of the murder. According to her, the coercer, unfortunately, was Trace.

Parker's fancy lawyers were making hay with the tale of the repentant wife who had said those things only because her husband had been ignoring her. The attorneys also insisted that someone had tampered with Parker's computer, using it to go online to look up infor-mation on tranquilizing drugs, inferring it was Jason, who would have had access to the machine.

Jason was going to go off the deep end when he found out.

Fortunately, there was still the not-so-small matter of the money Parker had stolen. The prosecutor was still convinced he was a flight risk, and so far the judge agreed. Trace just hoped Parker's expensive attorneys didn't come up with some new tap dance that would buy him a get-out-of-jail-free card.

Trace was convinced if the man did get out, he would be gone. And he wouldn't be taking his adoring little wife, Emily, with him.

A light knock sounded at his office door and Trace looked up from his computer screen. Through the glass, he saw Sol Greenway's lanky figure and waved him into the room.

"I saw you come in a little earlier," Trace said, having noticed his youngest employee sauntering into the office next to his a little over an hour ago. "What's up?"

"I came in to dig up some info for Alex, but one of the names on your list kept nagging me." Sol sprawled in the chair beside the desk and shoved his horn-rimmed glasses up on his nose. "I hate to admit I missed this before—not once but twice. I don't know why I went back to look at the guy again…something about the timing, I guess. Until today, I didn't make the connection."

Trace leaned over to take the paper Sol held. "What's this?"

"David Lyons was hospitalized a week after Maggie O'Connell moved out of his house. It was supposed to be some kind of kitchen accident. He cut himself while he was cooking. Stuff like that happens all the time, but it just kept bugging me. I think it was the date, you know, being so close to her leaving. Anyway, I went back into his hospital files—" Sol broke off as if he had already said too much about his hacking technique, and shook his head. "You don't want to know."

"No, I don't. Just tell me what you found."

"Lyons tried to commit suicide. He was distraught over losing his girlfriend. Slit his wrists. Came real close to dying."

Trace let the news sink in. David Lyons had been so crazy-in-love with Maggie that when she left him, he had tried to kill himself.

Which meant maybe he was just plain crazy.

"It was buried real deep. Lyons went to a lot of trouble to keep it secret. Three days after it happened, I found a big anonymous contribution to the hospital wing they were building at the time. I can probably go in and find out who it came from, but…"

"But your guess is it came from Lyons."

"Him or his parents. His family's loaded. An emotional problem like that could have affected his career."

But Maggie must have known. She had cared about the guy. Obviously in some way still did. She would have gone to see him the minute she'd heard he was in the hospital. Maggie had known and yet she hadn't told him. In fact, she'd gone out of her way to keep him from finding out.

Anger began to simmer inside him. He wanted to trust her. He'd been letting down his guard more and more. Maggie's silence felt like a betrayal of the very worst sort.

His jaw ached from clenching it so hard. "Anything else?"

"I'll keep digging if you want."

"Oh, yeah. That's exactly what I want. Maybe Lyons still has the hots for her. Maybe his obsession is mixed with some kind of weird need for revenge."

Sol nodded, stood up from his chair. "I'll see what I can find."

"Call my cell if you come up with anything."

Sol left Trace's office, went into his own and sat down behind his computer screens. Trace grabbed his hat and tugged it over his forehead, picked up his briefcase and left the office. Outside, the Saturday evening traffic was beginning to build. He'd been looking forward to going home.

The muscles in his neck tightened. In hiding the truth about Lyons, Maggie had lied to him again. Trace had known better than to trust her. He wanted her out of his house, out of his life. But there was no place safe for her to go.

Worse than that, part of him wanted her to stay.

By the time he turned into the alley behind his house, he had worked himself into a simmering rage. He tried for his usual calm, but couldn't seem to find it. He couldn't wait to confront her. She would just give him more bullshit, he knew. And yet, deep down, he wanted her to convince him she hadn't meant to deceive him.

He parked the Jeep in the garage on the alley and strode up the walkway to the back porch. Maggie turned off the alarm, opened the door and smiled as he walked into the kitchen.

"Hey, cowboy." She caught the brim of his hat, lifted it off and hung it on the rack beside the door. "I was beginning to think you'd forgotten our date." She was wearing a sexy little black dress that barely covered her ass, dangling silver earrings and silver bracelets that jangled whenever she moved.

The sound made his groin tighten. "I didn't know it was a date," he said darkly.

"It's always a date on the rare occasion I'm cooking."

He followed her into the dining room, saw that she had set the table with his grandmother's china and silver. The candles were lit and there was an arrangement of pink carnations and pretty white daisies in the center of the table.

It made him yearn for the things he'd once wanted, a home, a wife who loved him, kids one day.

It made the anger he was feeling bubble up inside him, twisting his stomach into a knot. He tried to clamp down on his emotions, but when she turned and slid her arms around his neck, when she rose up on her toes and kissed him, something inside him snapped.

He could feel every soft curve, the fullness of her

breasts and the hardening of her nipples. "I guess we did have a date," he growled, and kissed her with an angry fire he could barely contain. His heart was pounding, his blood surging hot and fast.

Maggie deepened the kiss, sliding her tongue over his, sucking his lower lip into her mouth. Her fingers moved over the front of his shirt. She popped the snaps and ran her palms over the muscles across his chest. He was close to losing control, worried he might, but Maggie didn't seem to care.

"I guess you missed me," she whispered into his mouth, pressing herself against his rock-hard erection. He was throbbing with every heartbeat, infused with a furious heat that ached to be released.

"Oh, I missed you," he drawled, kissing her deeply as he peeled the narrow black straps of her dress off her shoulders, tugged the bodice down and filled his hands with her luscious breasts. They were plump and enticing, and he lowered his head and tasted them, circled her nipples with his tongue.

Maggie moaned. He could feel her trembling, could sense her arousal. She wanted him and, damn, he wanted her.

He drove his hands into her silky red hair, holding her immobile as he plundered her lips. Maggie had closed all the drapes in the living room, and a pair of candles burned on the coffee table in front of the sofa.

He thought of her deception, thought of David Lyons and how far she had gone to protect him, and his anger swelled. He shoved her short black dress up over her hips, kissed her deeply, felt the tiny triangle of satin that covered her sex, slid it aside and stroked her.

She was wet and ready, breathing hard, pressing herself against his hand, urging his fingers deeper.

Trace obliged, stroking her nearly to climax, then turning her toward the sofa, bending her over the padded arm. She parted her legs, giving him access as he opened his fly, found her softness and positioned himself.

He took her in a single deep thrust, paused for a moment to regain control. Then he was moving, plunging deeply, taking what he wanted, telling himself he was punishing her for deceiving him. But he was only punishing himself.

With every thrust, his desire for her strengthened. With each of her soft little cries, his need for her swelled. He gripped her hips, drove himself deeper, faster, harder.

He wanted Maggie O'Connell.

But as they reached the peak together and she cried out his name, he realized he wanted more from her than just her beautiful body.

He wanted her trust.

And maybe even her heart.

It scared him to death.

"You're angry," Maggie said as she returned from the bathroom, her tousled hair combed and her short black dress once more in place. "I knew it when you walked through the door."

She could feel his dark eyes on her, following her movements as she continued toward him. God, he looked good. The line of his jaw wasn't as hard as it had been, and the muscles across his shoulders were no longer tied in knots. And yet she could still sense the tension running through his body.

"I was angry," he admitted. "I still am. But I would have stopped if you'd wanted."

"I know that." She paused in front of him. "I didn't want you to stop. You're a different lover when you're angry. You set your passions free. I like it."

His jaw tightened once more. "Damn it, Maggie."

"Tell me why you're so upset."

Trace blew out a breath. He wandered over to the dining table, picked up one of the pretty silver forks beside a flowered porcelain plate, then set it back down and looked at her. "You lied to me again."

She frowned. "I don't think so. I told you I wouldn't do that and I meant it."

"I found out about David Lyons."

A little tremor of unease moved through her. "I told you about David. I told you we lived together for a couple of months."

Intense brown eyes fixed on her face. She felt the impact as if he'd touched her. "You didn't tell me he tried to kill himself."

Her stomach clenched. She should have known Trace would find out. Digging up information was what he did for a living, what she had hired him to do. But she'd felt she owed a certain amount of loyalty to a man who had loved her so much.

"David was ashamed of what he tried to do. I didn't think telling you was important enough to override the pain it was bound to cause him."

Trace straightened, seemed even taller. "Someone is angry enough to burn your house down with your sister and her baby inside, and you didn't think it was important enough to tell me?" His temper was rising again. She wondered if maybe they'd end up having another round of hot, steamy sex.

"David isn't the stalker."

Trace strode toward her, reached out and caught her shoulders. "You can't know that. Not for sure. The man is obviously unstable. Maybe something happened recently that sent him off the deep end. I need to talk to him. I need to be sure he's not our guy."

Trace was right, she knew. She should have told him in the first place. Certainly after the fire, she shouldn't have hesitated. She was just so sure it wasn't David.

"All right, you can talk to him, but I'm going with you."

"Fine, but we need to do it now."

"Now? Right now? It's Saturday night. He's probably out on a date."

"Call him. If he'll meet us, we'll put supper on hold and eat when we get back."

"I'm telling you it isn't him. He wouldn't know the first thing about planting bugs and setting houses on fire."

"Maybe not, but he's got plenty of money—enough to pay somebody to do those things. If he did, then we can't know what he'll do next—or when."

A shudder ran through her.

"We need to eliminate Lyons as a suspect. Once we do, we can move forward, look in other directions."

She studied Trace's face, which was now closed up, hiding whatever he was thinking. "There's something you aren't telling me."

He hesitated, took a breath and slowly released it. "Look, odds are it was the stalker who paid someone to set your place on fire. The problem is the arsonist went in specifically to take out your studio."

"Because he was mad at me for hanging up on him."

"It's possible." Trace's eyes shifted away for an instant.

"But you don't think so." And suddenly it was clear. "You're thinking the fire might have been set for some other reason altogether, something that has nothing to do with my stalker."

His expression gentled. "It's something we need to consider."

Maggie started frowning, mulling over the prospect. "If it's true, who would go to that much trouble just to destroy my work?" She glanced up. "Someone who is jealous of my success?"

Trace's gaze held steady. "Or someone who wanted to get rid of something that was in one of your pictures." He waited a moment for the thought to sink in. "Your memory cards were in the studio. No one but you knew your work is also stored in Photodrive. Whoever set the fire was a high-dollar professional. Someone paid him a pretty penny to do a specific job."

"Which means if you're right, it must have been really important to get rid of my photos."

"We need to talk to Lyons. Afterward, if we're convinced it wasn't him, that he didn't hire someone to set fire to your studio for some sick kind of revenge, then we need to broaden our thinking."

Maggie sank down on the sofa, feeling slightly ill. "Oh, my God."

"Look, let's not get ahead of ourselves. At the moment, I'm working on the theory that David Lyons hired a guy to burn up your house just to cause you grief. He could afford it, and if he blamed you for driving him to the point of suicide, he might think he had good reason. Call Lyons. We'll see where it leads."

But as Maggie got up to retrieve her cell phone, she was thinking two things: that she had lost a little of Trace's trust tonight, something she discovered she wanted very badly.

And that he might be right, and her problems had just doubled.

Chapter Twenty-Three

David was kind enough to invite them to the apartment he had leased after the breakup. Number 7 Riverway was an exclusive, twenty-story building along Buffalo Bayou just west of the 610 Loop.

He answered the door, his blond hair neatly combed, his khaki slacks and polo shirt perfectly pressed, his eyes warm in greeting as Maggie came through the door. Trace walked in behind her.

"Thank you for agreeing to see us," she said. She glanced around the apartment, which was luxurious, ultramodern, done in dark brown and white, with brown marble floors and twelve-foot ceilings. Its Spartan design perfectly fit David's orderly persona, Maggie thought, though she preferred a cozier, less formal atmosphere. It was just one of a dozen reasons they had never really suited.

"I saw the fire on the morning news," he said. "I meant to call you, make sure you were all right."

"As it turned out, no one was hurt." She turned, inviting Trace into the conversation. "David, I'd like you to meet Trace Rawlins. He's a private investigator. He's looking into the fire and some other problems I've been having lately."

David's pale blue eyes ran over the man who stood at her side. They were about the same height, but David had a lanky build instead of Trace's solid, V-shaped body. They were perfect opposites—night and day.

"It's nice to meet you," David said. "Why don't we go into the living room? Would either of you like something to drink?"

"No, thanks," Trace said. Maybe David didn't notice the way he was sizing him up, the slight tension in his jaw, but Maggie did.

"We're fine, thank you," she said. "Trace has some questions he'd like to ask. We're hoping it will help the investigation."

"Of course." David led them into the living room with its high ceilings, brown marble fireplace and high-tech, built-in entertainment center. Intricate glass sculptures decorated the shelves and sat on the chrome coffee table in front of a plush brown sofa and matching chairs.

"At the moment we're just collecting information," Trace said. "We need to know where you were the night of May 13."

David frowned. "I was out to dinner with friends. Why?"

"That's the night someone set fire to Maggie's condo."

David straightened. "And you think I had something to do with that?"

"Someone was angry enough to destroy her studio. Her work was the target. After what happened between you, maybe you wanted some kind of revenge."

David's gaze darted to Maggie. His expression closed up as he looked back at Trace. "I'm afraid I don't know what you mean."

Maggie felt a rush of guilt. "He knows our relationship ended badly, David. He knows about your suicide attempt."

"You told him about that?"

"It happened," Trace said, interrupting before she could defend herself. "That's what matters. And your breakup with Maggie was the cause. The question is how far are you willing to go to make her pay for what happened?"

David slid onto the edge of his seat. "You're insane. I'd never do anything to hurt Maggie. I loved her." He turned in her direction. "Part of me always will."

Her heart squeezed. She had known how David felt before they had moved in together, known he was deeply in love with her and that she would never love him that same way. She hadn't meant to hurt him, but she had.

"You don't believe I set the fire, do you, Maggie? I told you I was out with friends that night, and I can prove it. Even if I couldn't, surely you don't believe I'm capable of something like that."

Maggie walked over to his chair, knelt down next to the arm. She reached over and gave his hand a gentle squeeze. "I don't believe you were responsible, David. I never did. I just… Trace needed to be sure." She rose, and so did the two men.

"The fire was set by a professional," Trace said. "Someone highly paid to destroy Maggie's work." He glanced around the fabulously expensive apartment. "You've got the kind of money it takes to do something like that."

"I had nothing to do with the fire. I've only seen Maggie once in two years—the night she went dancing at Galaxy. Now if you don't leave, I'm going to call the police."

"Maybe that's a good idea," Trace said darkly.

David sighed, made another attempt to explain. "Look, that night at the club…Maggie reminded me it would never work between us. Deep down, I knew she was right. It isn't her fault we're so different. It isn't her fault she never really loved me. It's just the way life is. I've accepted it. And I'd never do anything to hurt her."

Some of the tension went out of Trace's shoulders. He gave David a last perusal, then slowly nodded. "I appreciate your honesty. And your cooperation. Whatever we've discussed goes no further than this room."

David swallowed. "Thank you."

He walked them to the door. "So the two of you… Are the two of you…?"

Maggie tried to smile. "Trace is just—"

"Yes," he said firmly.

David smiled sadly. "I'm glad she's got someone looking out for her. Take care of yourself, Maggie."

Her eyes welled. "Goodbye, David. And thank you."

She walked out into the hallway. Trace followed, closing the apartment door behind them. She turned, lifted her chin. "So now are you convinced?"

"My job requires that I trust my instincts. I needed to see him, talk to him. It was clear he didn't know someone had been paid to set the fire. He's still half in love with you, but he isn't obsessed, he's just lonely.

He isn't your stalker. And he didn't pay someone to destroy your house."

"That's what I told you."

The corner of Trace's mouth edged up. "I guess you've got pretty good instincts yourself."

Mollified a little, she let him guide her to the elevator. Moments later they crossed the parking garage to the Jeep.

"So now we set our trap?" she asked as he held the door while she climbed inside.

"Yeah. Now we set our trap. And just to be on the safe side, we take a look at your latest photos. See if there's anything in one of them that might have convinced someone to pay big bucks and risk killing somebody so that no one would see them."

Standing on the huge front porch in the soft yellow lamplight, Jason banged on the front door of the big white-columned mansion so hard his fist began to ache. Billings, the butler, in his usual black suit and white shirt, pulled open the door.

"Why, Mr. Jason. It's good to see you. Please, come in."

Though Jason liked the little man with the dark hair and ready smile, he found his brother-in-law's pomposity in hiring a butler ridiculous. "I need to see my sister. Will you tell her I'm here?"

It was almost nine o'clock. He'd told himself to wait until morning, but his anger kept building until he just couldn't stand it any longer.

"I'll tell her," the little man said. "Why don't you wait for her in the blue room?"

"Thank you, Carl." It was Billings's first name, though neither Parker nor Emily used it.

The butler led him down the hall to the drawing room and disappeared, leaving Jason to pace the pale blue carpet beneath a pair of crystal chandeliers. The house was overblown and far too fussy for Jason's taste, with velvet sofas and gilded chairs, and porcelain figurines on rosewood tables.

The house he'd grown up in had been extravagant, but more subtle and in far better taste. This was done to suit Parker, not his sister. Emily had never had the courage to say no to her husband—which was the reason Jason was there.

Appearing in the open doorway, Emily floated toward him in a pair of loose-fitting black pants and a flowing, pink silk blouse, her short, dark hair gleaming in the lamplight. Even at this hour her makeup was flawless, but underneath, her features looked pale and strained.

He took a calming breath, reminded himself of the stress she was under.

"Jason. It's wonderful to see you." She stretched up on her toes and kissed his cheek.

"I know it's late, sis. This couldn't wait. We need to talk."

She flicked a glance at the butler, who hovered in the doorway. "Shall I have Billings bring us some tea?"

Jason clenched his teeth, fighting to rein in his temper. "I'm fine."

Billings took his cue and closed the tall, wood-paneled doors.

"Why don't we sit down?" Emily took a seat on the blue velvet sofa while Jason sat down across from her.

"I got a phone call today," he began. "The police tell

me you changed your story about what happened the night Dad was murdered."

Emily glanced away. "I didn't exactly change it. I just…clarified things a bit."

His control slipped a notch. "You lied, you mean. Parker didn't come home until well after midnight and you know it. What's going on with you, Emily? How can you sit back and help a man like Parker get away with murdering our father?"

Emily's spine stiffened. "Parker didn't do it. He says someone is trying to frame him. He insists he's innocent. As his wife, it's my duty to believe him."

"Do you also believe he didn't steal millions of dollars from the company? That he didn't stash the money in a half-dozen offshore accounts? Your name isn't on any of those accounts, Em. Parker never meant for you to go with him when he left the country."

She swallowed, kept her eyes on Jason's face, though he could see the effort it cost her. "I know he took the money. He was tired of working for a pittance of what he was worth."

Jason shot out of his chair. "Those are his words you're spouting, Em, not yours. The man is a thief and a murderer. Dad let him keep his job only because of you! Parker doesn't care about you, Emily. He never did. He married you for your money. He stole from all of us and he killed our father! How can you be such a fool?"

Emily started crying. "He says he's innocent."

Jason walked over and sat down beside her, slipped an arm around her shoulders. "I know you love him. You've loved him since the first time you saw him. Parker's handsome and charming. He pretended to be exactly the man you wanted. But it was all an act, Em, and by now you know it. You deserve a man worth ten times what he is, a man who will love you as much as you love him. A man who would never do anything to hurt you or your family."

Emily started sobbing, and Jason drew her gently into his arms. "You've got to tell the truth, sis. No half-truths, no more believing what you want to believe instead of what you know in your heart is true."

"I still love him, Jason. I love him so much."

"But you loved Dad, too. Remember how he always said no matter how old you got, you'd always be his little girl?"

She trembled. "I remember. I miss him so."

"Dad deserves justice. You know that, Em. Do what is right for our father. Do what is right for yourself."

She took a shaky breath and wiped the tears from her cheeks with the tip of her finger. "I know you're right. I've tried to tell myself the things you're saying aren't true, but I know they are. Parker doesn't love me. He never did." She shook her head. "I know I have to give him up, but I don't know how I'm going to get along without him."

Jason squeezed her hand. "I'll help you, sis. I promise." He smiled at her warmly. "I never understood how you could be so blindly in love with Parker, but for the first time in my life, I'm beginning to see. I've met someone, sis."

She looked up at him and a sad smile curved her lips. "You've always had girlfriends, Jason. As many as you wanted."

"Ashley's different. She's sweet and she's smart. She works hard and she has goals."

"You're a Sommerset. Maybe her goal is to marry

you and have anything she wants. Look what happened to me."

"I don't think Ashley gives a damn about my money. As far as marriage goes, I think she'd rather be a chef than a wife." He grinned. "I'm hoping if I take it nice and slow, I might be able to change that."

Emily studied his face. "I've never seen you this way."

"I've never felt this way. She has a son, sis. The cutest little boy. I want you to meet them."

Tears filled Emily's eyes. "Parker said he wanted children, but he never thought the time was right."

"Tell the truth, Em. Let Parker get what he deserves. If you do, I truly believe you'll find the kind of happiness *you* deserve."

The tears in Emily's eyes slipped onto her cheeks. She nodded. Jason rose and so did his sister, wiping away her tears as she walked him out to the foyer.

"I'll pick you up first thing in the morning," he said. "We'll go see the D.A. together. Changing your story back and forth doesn't exactly help their case, but at least this will straighten things out."

"All right."

"You're doing the right thing, sis."

Emily managed a wobbly smile as Jason bent and kissed her cheek. He left the house, a quick check of his watch telling him it was almost time to pick Ashley up after her shift. She was already becoming part of his life, and though he knew he should take things slow, make sure what was happening between them was real, deep down he was certain it was.

Jason smiled as he turned the key, firing the Porche's powerful engine, and reminded himself to start looking for another car.

Chapter Twenty-Four

Morning sunlight poured through the kitchen window, warming the house. It wouldn't be long before the air conditioner kicked on.

Rowdy barked, alerting Maggie to the chiming of her cell phone. She patted his head, ruffled his fur, walked over and plucked her phone off the kitchen table. Though hearing from her mother was rare, she recognized the caller ID and pressed the device against her ear.

"Hello, Mom."

"Maggie—thank God you answered. I've been so worried. I ran into Megan Wiseman, one of Ashley's girlfriends, at the grocery store, and she told me that no-good Ziggy is in Houston. Can you believe it? Ashley hasn't started seeing him again, has she? Dear God, that girl hasn't got a lick of sense."

Maggie's fingers tightened around the phone. "Ashley isn't seeing Ziggy, Mom. She's way past a jerk like that."

"Well, you don't know her. She's weak where that man is concerned. Look what he's done to her already—left her with a baby to raise and no father to help support it. If it weren't for your help, I don't know what would have happened to that girl."

Maggie clamped down on her temper. She and her mother had never gotten along. Why was it she always seemed to forget that? "Ashley's doing just fine on her own. She's got a job, Mom. Next week she's applying for admission to the culinary arts program at the art institute. She's hoping to get a loan for the tuition and I think she'll get it."

Silence fell. "You mean she's going to stay in Texas? She isn't coming back home?"

"She needs her independence, Mother. As I said, she's making her own way, and she's feeling really good about it."

"Well…"

"I'll tell her you called, Mom. I'll tell her you were worried about her."

"You just make sure she doesn't get tied up again with that good-for-nothing Ziggy."

Maggie fought for control. "Don't worry about it, Mom. Listen, I've got someone here," she lied. "It was really nice talking to you."

"Tell her to call me, will you?"

"I'll tell her." And Ashley would probably call. She didn't get along with their mother any better than Maggie did, but she wanted to change her life, do what was right. "Bye, Mom." Maggie ended the call.

"Who was that?" Trace asked as he wandered up beside her.

"My mother." She waved a hand. "Don't ask."

"From the look on your face, I don't think I need to."

"I've got to call Ashley, let her know Mom was worried about her."

"Was she?"

Maggie sighed. "In her own way, I suppose."

He walked to the counter and poured himself a cup of coffee. "When you're done, we need to figure a few things out."

She looked down at the short terry robe she was wearing, one of her recent purchases. "Can I shower first?"

Trace already had. His eyes darkened and his mouth took on a sensual curve. "I was waiting for you earlier, hoping you'd join me."

She wished she had, would have if the phone hadn't started ringing. "Next time," she promised with a mischievous grin. They had slept late and made love and slept a little longer. It was Sunday. It was okay to loaf a little.

She glanced at Trace and felt the same warm stirring she always felt when she looked at him. Dressed in jeans and a yellow short-sleeved shirt, freshly shaved, with his hair still damp, he gave her a look that said he had sex on his mind—which should be impossible after the night they had shared.

He'd started toward her, his intention clear, when a soft knock sounded at the door. With a last heated glance, he walked over and peered through the peephole. After a moment's hesitation, he lifted the latch and pulled the door open.

"Trace! Oh, thank heavens you're home!" His gorgeous ex-wife burst into the living room. Maggie ignored an unwelcome stab of jealousy.

"I've got company, Carly. What do you want?"

The redhead glanced toward Maggie, who fought the urge to run for the bathroom. She knew how she looked: still dressed in her short robe, her hair sleep-tangled, no makeup and her legs bare way above the knee.

Trace appeared resigned. "Carly, meet Maggie O'Connell."

"Hello, Carly," Maggie said, forcing a smile she hoped didn't seem like a sneer.

The other woman's full lips thinned. She made no reply, just returned her attention to Trace. "She was the one at your office."

"That's right. Now what do you want?"

"Howard and I broke up. He got mad over some silly notion about me and the pool boy, and now he won't pay my rent." She flicked a warning glance at Maggie, clearly wanting to speak to Trace in private.

"If you two will excuse me, I need to take a shower," Maggie said, glad for the chance to escape.

Angry for no good reason and embarrassed for some equally nebulous one, she walked into the bedroom and closed the door. After drawing a calming breath she dialed her sister's number, taking a moment to fill her in on the conversation with their mother, but giving an edited version. Maggie's cell rang just as she finished. It was Roxanne.

"It's me, darling. How are you?"

"Roxanne—I've been meaning to call, but it's just been so crazy. I'm all right. No more fires, no more notes on my car. Of course, I'm a virtual prisoner, but aside from that—"

Roxanne laughed.

"I don't suppose you can sneak out to go clubbing?"

"God, I wish." She hadn't been dancing since the night they had gone to Galaxy. With so much happening, Maggie felt guilty even thinking how much she'd like to go. "Listen, I've got to run. At the moment Trace's ex-wife is standing in the living room, and I haven't even taken a shower."

"I thought he wasn't seeing her anymore."

"He isn't. Or I'm pretty sure he isn't."

"Then get rid of her and take your shower with the Marlboro man."

Maggie laughed. "Good idea. Talk to you later."

As she headed for the bathroom, Maggie's humor faded. Maybe she was wrong and Trace was still in love with Carly. Maybe even seeing her on occasion. The woman was standing in his living room, wasn't she? That had to mean something.

Maggie turned the water on hot and high, hoping to distract her thoughts from the pair in the other room.

It didn't work.

Dear God, she had it bad.

"So you and Howard broke up," Trace said. "What's that have to do with me?"

Carly ignored the question. Her blue eyes traveled to the bedroom door. "Are you serious about her?"

He wasn't sure how to answer. He was attracted to Maggie, more than attracted. Sexually, she turned him on more than any woman he had ever met. Last night, he'd been jealous of her relationship with David Lyons.

He'd been possessive as he never was with a woman—not even his former wife.

Yet something was missing. After being married to Carly, he had serious trust issues. Just looking at her reminded him of the pain he had suffered when he had discovered the trail of men who had been in her bed. Maggie's constant evasions made trusting her almost impossible, and without that, he didn't see a future for them.

"She's my client," he said, avoiding the issue, hoping Carly would let the subject drop.

Her gaze slid once more toward the bedroom. "Looks to me like she's a lot more than just a client."

Trace's jaw tightened. "We're seeing each other, all right? Now tell me what you want."

Carly moved closer. She rested her palms on his chest and gazed up at him. The top of her head didn't reach his shoulder. "I was hoping you would loan me some money. Just a little, enough to cover my rent."

Trace took hold of her wrists and eased her away. "What about the alimony I pay you? It's more than enough to pay your rent and whatever else you need."

"Well, something came up. I'm a little short this month."

He didn't have to ask what that something was—either an expensive trip with one of her friends or a shopping excursion. "How short are you?"

"A couple thousand would do."

"You want me to give you two thousand dollars," he said darkly.

"I told you it's a loan."

"Yeah, right. Okay, I'll give you the money. But don't

ask me again. We're done, Carly. We have been for years. I'm not your husband. We aren't even friends."

"Don't say that!"

Ignoring her, he strode into the bedroom, where he kept his checkbook in the top dresser drawer. Trace took it out and wrote a check for two thousand dollars.

Just as he turned to leave, Maggie opened the bathroom door wearing only a fluffy white towel. Her glorious red hair curled around her face. The tops of her breasts rose enticingly, and her pale skin was moist and glistening. Little droplets of water beaded on her legs and he wanted to lick them off. He was hard, itching to pull away the towel and kiss all that bare skin.

"Don't bother getting dressed," he said gruffly. "I'll be right back."

Maggie opened her mouth, but he didn't give her the chance to argue. Returning to the living room, he handed the check to Carly and hurried her toward the door.

"Remember what I said. We're done, Carly. Don't come to me again."

She pouted as she stuffed the check into her purse and he urged her out of the house.

Closing the door, he strode back to the bedroom. But when he walked in, Maggie was no longer naked. She was dressed in jeans and a T-shirt. He didn't try to hide his disappointment.

"What did she want?" Maggie asked, her arms crossed defensively over her chest.

"It's always something. Money this time."

She tossed back her hair, moving all those damp red curls. His fingers itched.

"You must still care for her if you keep giving her what she wants."

"I feel sorry for her. Her life is a mess. Until she finds some way to change, it's going to stay a mess."

"And you're going to keep letting her jerk your chain."

He shook his head, his eyes on her face. "No. That's finished as of today."

"Why today?"

"Because you're here and you're important to me. Carly isn't. Not anymore. I told her it was finished and I meant it."

Maggie eyed him a moment, assessing his words, deciding whether or not to believe him. She moved closer, looked him in the face. "Are you sure?"

Trace slid his hand into her silky hair and dragged her head back, claiming her mouth in a hard, possessive kiss.

"Damned sure," he said against the side of her neck. "I want you, not Carly."

When he kissed her again, Maggie didn't fight him. He might have doubts about their relationship, but this was one area in which they seemed to be in perfect agreement.

It wasn't long before both of them were naked and back in his bed.

Trace played bodyguard all week. Tony Ramirez called to let him know it was safe for the women to go back inside the town house. Mrs. Epstein looked after Robbie while the sisters poked and dug through the waterlogged, blackened interior.

Jason insisted on accompanying them, and when

Ashley found her few worldly possessions mostly destroyed, Trace was glad the kid was there.

"Oh, no." Ashley sloshed through puddles of water to reach a soggy little brown teddy bear. One of its eyes was missing and the stuffing was coming out the seams in several places. The bear was in bad shape to begin with, but the fire hoses had finished the job.

"It's Brownie," she said. Hugging the bear to her chest, she started to cry. "I know it's silly, but I've had him since I was a little girl."

Jason walked up behind her, turned her into his arms. "It's okay, honey. You've got all those memories locked up in here." He smoothed a hand over her curls, then tipped her chin up so she would look at him. "Nothing can ever take those away from you."

Ashley clung to him and Jason held her until Trace found himself looking away, his own eyes a little misty. When he glanced at Maggie, his chest tightened. Hell, she was crying, too.

Damned women, he thought. But he didn't really blame them. Trace eased Maggie into his arms. "It's all right, darlin'. It's mostly just stuff. Stuff can be replaced."

"I know." She didn't move out of his arms, and he thought how right it felt to have her there.

Maggie finally took a breath and eased away, gazed wistfully up the staircase.

"It isn't safe to go up there," Trace said, reading her mind. "The second floor's pretty much destroyed and totally unstable. But we can poke around a little more down here if you want."

She nodded. He and Jason both wore rubber boots, and the kid had bought a pair each for Ashley and Maggie. The downstairs was intact except for the horrific water and smoke damage.

They tromped past the soggy sofa and chairs and went into the bedroom. Ashley was cheered a little when she discovered most of the clothes in her closet had survived the fire and just needed a good washing.

Trace followed Maggie down the hall to the linen closet. She reached up to a shelf overhead and took down a cardboard box.

"What is it?" he asked.

"Family pictures. Mostly me and my dad. There's a few old ones of Mom and Dad before she left, some baby pictures of me. Some photos of me and my college friends." Maggie hugged the box against her. "I was praying they wouldn't be destroyed."

"I guess your prayer was answered."

She looked into his face. "My prayer was answered when I saw Ashley sitting on the curb that night, holding little Robbie in her arms."

Trace knew exactly what she meant. He'd never felt such a rush of relief as the moment he had found them all safe.

"Have you hired someone to fix this place?" Ashley asked, sloshing toward her sister.

"I've been talking to a guy named Will Jacobs. He was recommended by a friend of Trace's in Dallas."

"Gabe Raines. He's a developer," Trace explained. "He says Will is one of the best. He's honest and he won't charge an arm and a leg."

"When's he going to start?"

"First of next week," Maggie said. "Will says it's at least a two-month job."

Ashley surveyed the water creeping into the wallboard, making it swell, the wet drapes sagging from their rods. "You know, sis, this place could have used a little decorating, anyway."

Maggie looked at her sister, thought of the odd pieces of junk she'd used to furnish the town house. She surveyed the destruction around them, the puddles of grimy water, the soggy furniture that would all need to be replaced. A giggle escaped, turning into full-blown laughter.

Ashley laughed, too. Trace chuckled and pretty soon all of them were laughing.

Maggie wiped her eyes. "I guess you noticed I'm not much of an interior designer."

Ashley grinned. "I kinda couldn't miss it. When you get the place remodeled, I'll help you. I'm pretty good at that kind of stuff."

"I bet you are, and that'd be great."

Trace tried for a smile, but his thoughts had returned to Maggie and her stalker.

To the fire that could have been lethal—and what might happen next.

Chapter Twenty-Five

The buzz of activity filled the white-walled interior of the Twin Oaks Gallery as Trace escorted Maggie inside. It was time to start moving forward with their plan to lure the stalker into the trap they were setting.

Trace had spoken to Ben and Alex, and both had agreed to help. On Friday, the men would arrive in Kemah before daybreak to stake the place out. *Ranger's Lady* would serve as headquarters for the operation.

"There's Faye," Maggie said, starting in the owner's direction. Trace was surprised to see spotlights shining on walls that were mostly bare.

"What's going on?" Maggie asked as the swanky brunette walked up to greet them.

Faye smiled. "I've been meaning to call. After the TV news broke the story of the fire, a rush of people poured in to look at your work. They were curious, I guess. People liked what they saw. The rest of your photos practically flew out the door." She laughed. "You just can't buy advertising like that."

Maggie glanced around at the empty spaces. "I guess not."

Two burly young men were busily hanging pictures, nicely framed black-and-white photographic portraits of interesting faces.

"Who's the artist?" Trace asked.

"Those belong to a guy named Zeke Meadows. I'm filling in with his work until Maggie can get me more pictures."

"I'm heading down to Kemah on Friday," Maggie said, spinning the story they had planned. "I'm starting to shoot again. I just need a little more time."

The brunette rolled her long-lashed blue eyes. "I guess there isn't any choice, but I can't sell—"

"What you don't have," Maggie finished for her. "Let my clients know I'm back to work starting Friday. Tell anyone who might be interested."

Faye cast Maggie a suspicious glance. She knew about the stalker, and the woman was clearly no fool. She turned to Trace. "So let me get this straight. You want people to know where Maggie's going to be this Friday."

"That's right."

"But you'll be there to make sure she's all right."

Trace smiled. "You can leave that part out."

Faye relaxed and returned his smile. "You got it, cowboy."

They talked a little while longer. Faye was upset that the fire had destroyed Maggie's latest collection, but as she had promised, Maggie kept silent about her Photodrive storage. She did a bang-up job of convincing Faye not to do anything until they could work things out.

Which pleased Trace in one way, but reminded him how good she was at lying by omission.

Trace told himself she'd done exactly what he wanted. The trap would give them the stalker, and the stalker would be the guy responsible for the fire.

He wished he believed it.

On Wednesday morning, Maggie did a TV interview with Sally Grimshaw of KGEO TV in front of her burned-out condo. Again, she talked about her Friday morning trip to the shore.

"So you're going back to work," Sally said once they'd gotten started. She was blonde and petite, very attractive and extremely dedicated to her job as a journalist.

"That's right."

"I'm sure your fans will be delighted to hear it."

Maggie adjusted the mic pinned to the lapel of her pale blue silk blouse, which like all her clothes was a recent acquisition. "I certainly hope so."

"The fire was reported to be arson. Do you have any idea who might have set it?"

The question threw her. For a moment she wasn't sure how to respond. She glanced at Trace, who was standing nearby, then decided to roll with it.

"I've been having trouble with a stalker. Phone calls, notes on my car, that kind of thing. He's seems the mostly likely suspect."

"I see. Have the police made any progress in finding him?"

Maggie flashed a phony smile into the camera. "I'm sure they're doing their best."

They talked a few minutes about her upcoming trip to the shore, then the cameraman turned off the bright white light and the interview was over. The piece aired on the morning news, was shown again at noon and repeated at five and eleven.

Word was out. Maggie hoped her stalker was still as interested in her movements as he had been before. If he showed up in Kemah—and she prayed he did—they would be ready.

There was just one last thing.

Trace wanted her to meet the rest of the team. He wanted her to be able to recognize the men in case there was trouble.

Alex Justice and Ben Slocum arrived at his house on Thursday night right after supper. Both in their early thirties, both over six feet tall, they were almost equally handsome. Alex, with his dark blond hair, blue eyes and dimples, had a lighter personality, charming and jovial, and yet she sensed an inner core of steel.

"It's a pleasure to meet you, Maggie," he said as he sauntered into the living room. No Texas drawl; instead there was a hint of refinement in his voice.

"You, as well, Alex. Trace has spoken very highly of you."

Alex grinned. "I'm amazed he mentioned me at all."

"Alex was in the air force," Trace added, tossing his friend a warning glance.

"Fighter jockey." Alex ignored him. "I hope Trace's been taking good care of you. The way he's kept you locked up, we figured we might have to stage a jailbreak."

She laughed, wondering if Trace really had purposely kept her away from his two gorgeous friends.

Maggie turned to the more somber of the pair, a man with dark hair, ice-blue eyes and unforgiving features. "I gather you served with Trace in the army."

"Rangers. Yes, ma'am." The drawl was back, not as slow and sexy as Trace's but with a slightly harder edge. Another Texan, she was sure.

Maggie smiled. "Looks like I should be safe enough with the three of you there to protect me. I just hope this works so I can get a place of my own and my life back to normal."

Both men glanced at Trace, but he made no comment. Once this was over, she would be moving out of his house, living again on her own. There was no commitment between them, no talk of the future. Both of them expected the arrangement to end.

Maggie told herself it was exactly what she wanted. They would still see each other, but they would be able to live their own lives. The thought made her stomach clench into a knot.

"Alex and Ben will be in place by the time you get to Kemah," Trace said. "You won't see them. But you can be sure they'll see you. I'll come in behind you. You'll be wearing a mic and an earbud so we'll be able to communicate. If you see someone you recognize, or something seems out of place, just sing out."

She nodded. "All right."

"This guy shows up," Ben said, "his ass is ours."

"Count on it," Alex agreed.

"I spoke to the county sheriff's office," Trace added. "They've been in touch with Houston P.D. and alerted their deputies. We'll have backup if we need it."

The men nodded. They finished the beers they were drinking while a few more items were discussed. The meeting ended on a determined note and the pair left the house. The sound of their footsteps crossing the porch faded away, then silence filled the living room.

Trace turned to Maggie, tipped her chin up and captured her lips in a soft, sexy kiss.

"Let's go to bed, darlin'," he said gruffly. "Forget all this for a while." The familiar heat was in his eyes, but there was something more. She recognized it as worry. He didn't like using her for bait.

But time had proved to be their enemy.

They didn't have any other choice.

Chapter Twenty-Six

Maggie ignored the butterflies in her stomach. A heat wave had settled over the city. The day was hot and clammy, the dense, humid air sticking to her skin. She prayed her stalker had seen her TV interview or heard through the grapevine via Faye that Maggie would be driving to Kemah this morning.

She wondered if he knew where she had been staying since the fire, wondered if he had kept track of her somehow. She wondered if maybe he had seen her drive away from Trace's that morning, and a shudder of apprehension slipped down her spine.

She checked her rearview mirror. As she drove her little SUV down Highway 45, Trace followed somewhere in the traffic behind her. He was driving Alex's BMW in case the stalker had seen him in the Jeep. Alex and Ben were already in place. They would be watching for her arrival. None of the men were taking any chances, but she still she felt very alone.

The trip seemed to take forever, the road stretching endlessly ahead of her. Her neck ached from constantly looking in the mirror, or searching the cars ahead or beside her. Finally, the 518 exit to Kemah appeared and Maggie sighed with relief. She pulled onto the road that wound its way east toward Kemah and Galveston Bay. She didn't see Alex's silver-blue Beemer, but she knew Trace was back there.

She reached up and adjusted the seashell necklace she wore, which contained a tiny microphone. The men could hear whatever she said. She was also wearing an earbud, easily hidden by her heavy hair.

"I'm on the 518," she said, just to hear the sound of Trace's voice in return.

"Good girl. I'm a ways back, but I've got your GPS location." He had affixed a bug to her bumper just in case something went wrong and he needed to find her.

"Roger that," she said with a grin, beginning to get into the part.

She heard his deep chuckle, and warmth curled through her. It was amazing how sexually attuned she was to him. He was an amazing lover, intuitive in the things she liked, at times able to bring her to orgasm with only a touch. It was getting more and more difficult to imagine sleeping without him.

Maggie shoved the thought away. At the moment, she didn't have time to think of her sex life or her nebulous future. She needed to focus on the task ahead.

Winding through the traffic, she finally reached the 146 and found her way into the parking lot in front of the Kemah boardwalk. The plan was to start there, taking shots in the area, then wander over to the boardwalk marina, where *Ranger's Lady* was docked.

She turned off the engine and rounded the Escape to the back. Opening the hatch, she grabbed her camera bag, pulled out her Nikon D3S, which had been in the back of her car the night of the fire, thank God, not in her studio.

She took her time getting ready, pulling on a yellow sun visor that matched her blouse, dusting off her white capri pants, lifting the strap of her camera over her head, attaching the Tamron lens.

If someone had followed or was already there watching for her arrival, she wanted to make it easy for him to find her.

She glanced around, looking for Alex or Ben, thinking maybe she would spot Trace, but saw no one. She ignored a moment of uneasiness and reminded herself the men were professionals. If they didn't want to be seen, they wouldn't be.

Sucking in a deep breath, she squinted, finding the sun bright even though she was wearing sunglasses and the visor. Then she pasted on a smile and started forward.

"I'm heading toward the entrance," she said into the mic.

"We've got you," Trace said into her earbud.

She meandered toward the red-white-and-blue arch, taking shots of kids and their parents, trying to look as if she was really interested and not just there as bait for a trap. She wandered awhile longer, careful to stay out in the open, making it easy to be seen.

A commotion to her left drew her attention. A man darted out of nowhere and ran toward her, and her heart jerked. Skinny black jeans, black T-shirt, long black hair tied back in a queue. He was lean-muscled and handsome. He was on a beeline course, headed her way, and she had never seen him before.

"There's a guy on your right moving toward you." Trace's voice held a note of tension.

"I see him."

"You're definitely his target."

"I don't know him, but—"

"I've got him," Alex said.

"On his twenty," said Ben.

The guy kept coming. He was young and nothing like she had expected.

"Hold your positions," Trace commanded. "Something doesn't feel right."

The man in black closed the distance between them. "Maggie? Maggie O'Connell?" He stopped right in front of her, his voice carrying into the mic.

"Yes? Do I know you?"

"I'm a friend of your sister's. Ziggy Murdock? I'm sure she told you about me."

The tightness in Maggie's shoulders relaxed. He wasn't her stalker, just Ashley's jerk of an ex-boyfriend. "I know who you are."

"Stand down." Trace's deep command came through loud and clear.

"I saw you on TV," Ziggy continued. "I thought if I could talk to you, maybe you could help me fix things with your sister."

Maggie glanced around at the tourists and locals, none of whom looked threatening. "I'm shooting, Ziggy. And even if I had time, I wouldn't help you. Ashley's life is on a different course now. She's over you and that's the way it's going to stay."

"Hey, she's got my kid, you know. That gives me some rights."

"Yes, it does. And I'm sure once she gets settled and you get your own life in order, Ashley will be willing to make some sort of arrangement, if you're really interested in seeing your son. Until then, as I said, I'm busy."

She brushed past him, kept walking. Ziggy followed, coming up beside her.

"You know what? You two bitches are just alike."

Maggie smiled. "I'll take that as a compliment."

"Yeah, well, fuck you." Ziggy turned and stomped away, his long, thin legs carrying him off.

Trace chuckled into the earbud. "Guess he made a long drive for nothing."

Maggie grinned.

"Nice work, ma'am." It was Slocum's hard Texas drawl.

"Thanks," she murmured.

Maggie trolled for another hour, meandering past the Saltgrass Steak House, circling the carousel, strolling beneath the Ferris wheel, taking photos along the boardwalk out into the bay. She took dozens of shots, but none were particularly good. Her mind wasn't on work. It was on catching a stalker.

A string of musical chimes threw her for an instant— a text message coming in on her cell phone. Maggie dug frantically through her purse, pulled out the phone and read the text marching across the bottom of the screen.

I didn't set the fire. I would never hurt you, Maggie.

Her insides turned to ice. She glanced frantically around, but no one was looking her way, or seemed the least bit interested. With trembling fingers, she reached for the necklace, adjusted the mic.

"I got a text," she said, facing away from the patrons on the boardwalk toward the open water, so no one could see her lips moving. "I-it's from him. He says he didn't set the fire. He says he would never hurt me." She took a deep breath. "Do you think he's here?"

"Could have come from anyplace," Trace's voice replied. "Forward the message and start walking. Keep your eyes open."

Maggie sent the message on to Trace. She knew he would try to find out where the text had come from. She steeled herself, forced herself to start again, to move at a leisurely pace.

The morning heated and the sun turned brutal, the humidity creeping higher and higher. Her skin felt sticky; her sunglasses slid down her nose.

"I'm going back to check the car, see if he might have left a note. Maybe he's somewhere nearby, watching for me to return."

"Roger that," Trace said. The others acknowledged the communication. Aside from Ziggy's brief appearance, and the text she had received, nothing had happened. And no one had seen anything out of the ordinary.

Maggie reached the parking lot, where the pavement was soft and hot beneath the soles of her sneakers, and heat rose in rippling waves. She wanted to climb inside the car and turn on the air conditioner, blast the icy coolness into her face.

At the sight of the empty windshield, she felt her

shoulders droop. Unlike the last time, there was no note, no sign that her stalker had been there. Nothing but his eerie text message, which, like before, had probably come from a throwaway phone.

"Shall I head over to the marina?" she asked into the mic.

Alex and Ben had been aboard the boat that morning, she knew, a place to have coffee and wait for the sun to come up.

"Roger that," Trace said. "We'll rendezvous at the *Lady,* get out of the sun for a while, maybe try again a little later."

Though if her stalker was watching, he would see them all together, and any chance to make contact would probably be lost.

Still, getting out of the sun sounded like a great idea to Maggie. Imagining a cold drink and some time off her feet, she didn't notice the battered old Dodge van that was parked two cars down from her Ford on the opposite side. She didn't give it much thought when the driver backed the van out of its space and pulled up in front of her.

Then the van doors rolled open and two men in tank tops and camouflage cargo pants jumped out and shot toward her, their heavy lace-up boots clattering on the asphalt. One was white with curly blond hair, the other Hispanic with a do-rag tied around his head. Both were covered with tattoos and had solid, muscular bodies.

"Trace!" Maggie screamed as one of the men grabbed her camera and started trying to drag the strap off over her head. "Let go of that!" The heavy length of black nylon was looped around her neck. Maggie hung on tight, not about to let go. "Get away from me!"

"Get her purse!" the guy yelled to his friend, who grabbed her bag, which she was wearing secured across her body messenger-style. Even if she'd wanted to give it to him, she couldn't get it free.

"Goddamn it, lady!" He tugged on the strap, trying to jerk the expensive camera off over her head, while the other guy yanked on her purse, which held credit cards and several hundred dollars in cash.

Maggie dug her heels into the pavement and pulled back as hard as she could, at the same time twisting to get free. One of them shoved her and she went down, scraping her palms as she tried to protect the camera.

The second man pulled a knife out of nowhere, cut the strap on her purse and ran for the van. "Come on, Chaz!"

Maggie staggered to her feet, still gripping the camera, determined to hold out until Trace, Ben and Alex could reach her.

"I'm not giving it to you!" Her heart was pounding, slamming against her ribs, as she tussled with the blond man.

"You bitch!" A tattooed hand slapped her hard across the face and she stumbled but didn't let go. A red-and-blue serpent wound around the arm that fought for the camera, and a skull-and-crossbones gleamed on one shoulder.

"Stop it!" Her cheek burned, making her more determined than ever not to let him win. Then, suddenly, she was free, stumbling to keep her balance and not wind up on the ground again.

In a blinding rage, Trace grabbed the first guy by the back of the neck, spun him around and hit him so hard that his feet left the ground and his head cracked against the pavement. From the corner of his eye, he saw Alex grab the second guy, a muscular Hispanic with a faint mustache and deep-set black eyes. Alex slammed the gangbanger's head against the side of the van once, twice and again, and Maggie's purse tumbled out of his hands. Through the window, Trace saw Ben jerk open the driver's-side door, drag a second Hispanic guy out of the vehicle and smash a fist into his face.

Trace turned an instant too late. His opponent was on his feet, a tattooed arm swinging a punch that split Trace's lip and sent blood flying across the front of his shirt. He rammed a fist into the thug's belly. A right, then a left, followed by third blow left the guy reeling.

Flicking a glance at Maggie, Trace saw the red mark on her cheek and punched him again, slamming him to the pavement. This time he didn't get up, until Trace grabbed the front of his tank top and hauled him to his feet, ready to hit him again.

"Trace!" Maggie's high-pitched shriek cut through the bloodlust, dragging him back to his senses. He shook his head to clear it and reined himself in, his fist shaking with his effort to stay in control. He'd known better than to make Maggie a target. The minute he spotted the van, he knew he had made a mistake.

Trace turned to see Alex mopping up the pavement with the gangbanger in the do-rag, then hauling him up beside the van. Ben goose-stepped the driver around the front of the vehicle, his arm cranked up behind him.

The guy with the serpent tattoo hadn't moved since Trace knocked him ass-over-tea-kettle onto the pavement. Trace stepped over the unconscious figure, checked the pulse beating at the side of his neck, found it strong and steady, and headed for Maggie.

She was trembling and pale, her hands scraped raw from her fall on the asphalt. Trace drew her into his arms.

"It's okay, honey, it's over. Everything's all right."

Maggie took a deep breath, but didn't let him go. All Trace could think was how glad he was that she was only scared and a little bruised, not seriously injured. She took another breath, managed to nod, and reluctantly, he released her.

A crowd was beginning to gather. In the distance, he could hear the wail of a siren.

Maggie gazed up at him. "I don't…I don't understand what's going on. Is one of these men my stalker?"

"No," Trace said darkly. "Maybe you ought to go sit in the car, turn on the AC."

Maggie firmly shook her head. "No way."

The white guy was still unconscious. Trace turned his attention to the driver of the van, who appeared to be in his late twenties, with a shaved head and small goatee. "Who hired you to follow the lady down here?"

"I don't know what you're talking about, man."

Ben whacked him on the back of the skull, summoning a belligerent glare.

A few feet away, Alex shook his guy like a rat. Trace had learned long ago that the jet jockey was a lot tougher than his sophisticated appearance made him seem. "You heard the man. Who paid you to follow the lady?"

When the guy clamped his lips shut, Alex slid a hand around his throat and hoisted him up against the side of the van. "I asked you a question."

Dear Reader,

IT'S A FACT: if you answer 4 quick questions, we'll send you **4 FREE REWARDS!**

I'm not kidding you. As a leading publisher of women's fiction, we value your opinions… and your time. That's why we are prepared to **reward** you handsomely for completing our mini-survey. In fact, we have 4 Free Rewards for you, including 2 free books and 2 free gifts.

As you may have guessed, that's why our mini-survey is called **"4 for 4".** Answer 4 questions and get 4 Free Rewards. It's that simple!

Thank you for participating in our survey,

Pam Powers

To get your 4 FREE REWARDS:
Complete the survey below and return the insert today to receive 2 FREE BOOKS and 2 FREE GIFTS guaranteed!

"4 for 4" MINI-SURVEY

1 Is reading one of your favorite hobbies?
☐ YES ☐ NO

2 Do you prefer to read instead of watch TV?
☐ YES ☐ NO

3 Do you read newspapers and magazines?
☐ YES ☐ NO

4 Do you enjoy trying new book series with FREE BOOKS?
☐ YES ☐ NO

YES! I have completed the above Mini-Survey. Please send me my 4 FREE REWARDS (worth over $20 retail). I understand that I am under no obligation to buy anything, as explained on the back of this card.

194/394 MDL GMYP

FIRST NAME

LAST NAME

ADDRESS

APT.#

CITY

STATE/PROV.

ZIP/POSTAL CODE

© 2017 HARLEQUIN ENTERPRISES LIMITED
® and ™ are trademarks owned and used by the trademark owner and/or its licensee. Printed in the U.S.A.

READER SERVICE—Here's how it works:

"Nobody paid us, man," he managed to choke out.

"Keep your mouth shut, Reggie," the driver warned. Ben whacked him again and dragged him around to the other side of the van, leaving his buddy at Alex's mercy.

Alex kept his hand around Reggie's throat, the threat more than clear, and his tough-guy facade began to crumble.

"You're going to jail for assault," Trace said to him. "Do yourself a favor and cooperate."

"Nobody paid us," he said again. Alex released him. "We just came down to drink some beer and have some fun." Reggie rubbed his throat. "Then we seen her. She was on TV so we knew she was some rich bitch photographer. We figured that fancy camera of hers had to be worth at least a grand, so we went for it."

"I'm not rich," Maggie said fiercely. "I saved for a long time to buy that camera. I didn't steal it from someone the way you tried to do. And I didn't hurt anyone trying to get it."

Under his dark skin, Reggie's homely face went red. "Oh, yeah? Well, if you woulda just handed it over, you wouldna got hurt."

Trace's jaw went tight. "Since you and your buddies are going to jail, I guess your plan didn't work out too well."

A siren sounded a couple of times before a pair of car doors swinging open ended the conversation. Two deputy sheriffs rushed up from the patrol car that had stopped in front of the van. Another car rolled up behind the vehicle and a second pair of deputies shot out.

"The sheriff'll handle it from here," Trace said to Maggie. He walked over, picked up her purse and gave it back to her.

Her hand trembled as she clutched it against her. "But we didn't get the stalker."

Trace slid an arm around her, eased her against his side. "Maybe we'll get something off the text message he sent." Not likely, but possible. He glanced over at the men and deputies next to the van. "I want you to promise me something."

"What is it?"

"Next time some guy tries to steal your camera or your purse, you give it to him, okay?" He thought of the knife Reggie had been wielding and how much worse it could have been. "I don't care what you paid for it, nothing is worth your life."

She gazed up at him, her big green eyes searching his face. Damn, she was pretty.

"I knew you were out there. All I had to do was hold them off long enough for you to reach me."

Trace looked at her hard. "Promise me."

Maggie sighed. "Okay, I promise. I suppose you're right."

He walked her back to her car to wait for one of the uniforms to come over and take a statement.

"At least he called," she said, referring to the stalker. "He made contact. That could be good. Maybe we could try this again."

Trace forced himself to smile. "We'll have to wait and see."

But no amount of convincing was going to get him to risk Maggie's life again.

Chapter Twenty-Seven

"What are you doing?" Maggie walked into the living room to find Trace adjusting his big-screen TV.

"Getting ready to look at some of your photographs. The ones you stored in Photodrive."

"All my pictures are stored there."

"I'm just interested in the ones you showed at the gallery. The fire was set after the opening—before you had time to get the sold ones reprinted. I'm thinking someone who was there that night might have seen something in one of your pictures that he didn't like."

Trace had suggested the theory before. It seemed improbable. But the world was an improbable place and she had come to trust Trace's judgment. "I suppose it could happen."

"Since the gallery wasn't torched, we have to assume if there is something in one of the photos, it's in one of those purchased that night."

Going with the theory, she started nodding. "If someone had something to hide, he would have bought the
picture to get it out of sight. He would have needed to
destroy the picture and the memory card and—"

"And hire someone to burn down your studio. That
way the photograph couldn't turn up again."

"It makes sense—if I actually did take some kind of
incriminating picture."

"We need to know which pieces were purchased and
who bought them."

"The information's on your laptop." The one he had
loaned her after the fire. "I had Faye email it to me
again. I'll print us a copy." She smiled. "You'll be happy
to know I'm almost finished with my client list. I need
to integrate the stuff Faye sent, but once it's done, the
list will be complete."

"That's great. The more information we have, the
more likely we are to figure out what the hell is going
on." He tipped his head toward the kitchen table, where
his laptop sat open. "I want you to go online and download your latest photos onto a card. We'll bring the pictures up in high-def on the TV screen. That'll make
them big enough for us to see in close detail."

"Great idea." Maggie walked over to the table and
sat down. Trace had already plugged a photo card into
the machine, so she was ready to go. Using his wireless
connection, she accessed the internet, went to www.
photodrive.com, put in her username and password and
brought up her account.

The photos were listed by collection, her latest effort entitled simply *The Sea*. It was the same name she
was using for her coffee-table book—if she ever got it
finished.

She downloaded the photos, which took a bit of time. While she was waiting, she sent the file Faye had emailed of the buyers' names and the pictures purchased at the opening off to Trace's printer, which was down the hall in his office.

They were working a two-pronged approach, searching for her stalker, but also examining the possibility that the fire was set for an entirely different reason.

Maggie looked at the screen, saw the download of the photos was complete. Trace took the photo card out of the computer and she jumped up and headed down the hall. The printer was humming, spitting out pages of names when she walked in. She picked them up and returned to the living room.

"Let me take a look." Trace walked up behind her, his hard chest pressing against her back as he read the list over her shoulder. She smiled, feeling a little curl of heat.

"Looks like half the bigwigs in the city bought one of your photos. The mayor. The chief of police. Mrs. Robert Daily—she's chairman of the university board."

"I sold fourteen that night."

"Richard Meyers's name is here—Senator Logan's aide. Logan's daughter, Cassidy, too. I remember you mentioned Matthew Bergman, the guy in the Ferrari that night. I see his name here. I don't recognize any of the others."

Maggie looked down at the list. "Mr. and Mrs. Silverman have bought from me before. Mrs. Weyman's name is here, the founder of the children's shelter. I don't know the others, though I may have met them that night." She handed Trace the pages.

"Let's match the photos with the people who bought them, see if anything comes up."

But the idea that she could have taken a photo and not noticed something important enough to drive a person to burn down her house seemed pretty far-fetched.

With a sigh, she followed Trace into the living room.

Trace stuck the photo card into the slot on the side of the TV. An instant later, the first picture popped up on the screen. This one he remembered from the gallery show, a photo of a deserted shore with palm trees blowing in unison as if dancing a ballet. He accessed the metadata, which told the time and date the photo was taken. He remembered the title: *Taste the Wind.* There were no people in it, nothing out of the ordinary. It was the print Mrs. Daily had purchased.

The next photo came up. *"Sands of Time,"* Maggie said. It wasn't on the purchased list. The next two pictures were beautiful, but when she and Trace cross-checked, neither were among the fourteen sold at the opening.

He smiled as the fourth picture came up, the tiny sailboat racing to escape the tentacles of a rapidly descending storm.

"Ferocity," Maggie announced.

He remembered her saying she had waited for the little boat to reach safety before she'd left the area, remembered how it had touched him that she had been so worried about the people on board.

"Looks like that's the one Mrs. Weyman bought." The woman was a heavyweight in high society, someone who would be concerned about her reputation.

"I don't see anything," Maggie said, carefully examining the photo.

"You said the boat reached the harbor. So nothing untoward happened to it."

"That's right."

He went to the next digital image, of surfers slicing through a curl, the sun illuminating the wave from behind, making it look like glass.

"Color of Water," Maggie said.

He looked down at the list. "Cassidy Logan bought it."

Maggie smiled. "I took it when I was out in California. Down at Laguna Beach."

He raised an eyebrow. "Visiting good ol' Roger?"

Maggie didn't take the bait. "I stopped to see him. We're friends, remember?"

And nothing more, he knew with a smug sense of satisfaction. Since Roger was gay, he was one man Trace didn't have to worry about.

The next photo came up, a wide swatch of ocean stretching out from a sandy cove. An elaborate sand castle was slowly being washed away by the surf, the kids who had built it watching with solemn expressions. Clearly, they were proud and sad at the same time.

"I call it *Life and Death,*" Maggie said, and he got it. Like building a sand castle, life was bright and fun, and yet it was fleeting.

She looked down at the list. "Someone named John Andrews bought it."

Trace studied the photo. "Just a couple of kids. I don't see anything that might be a problem for Mr. Andrews."

Maggie's gaze followed. "Neither do I."

"Still, it wouldn't hurt to have Sol do a little digging, see if there's anything we should know about him."

"Sol's the computer whiz in your office, right?"

"That'd be him. I'll have him take a look at the buyers we don't know anything about."

They ran through the first half of the photos. Not wanting to miss anything, they spent longer than they had expected, and found nothing in the pictures that looked suspicious.

"My concentration is going," Trace said with a sigh. "We could both use a break, and I need to get down to the office for a while. How about we look through the next batch when I get home?"

Maggie glanced away from the last photo on the screen. "All right." He could read her disappointment. She was hoping that something in the pictures might help them find her stalker.

Trace caught her face between his hands and gave her a soft, reassuring kiss. "Maybe this whole idea will turn out to be a wild-goose chase. But we won't know for sure until we're finished. And we've still got your client list to work. Soon as you've got it done, we'll get started."

Maggie just nodded.

"I know it doesn't seem like it, but we're making progress, darlin'. Something will break sooner or later. It always does."

She sighed. "I hope you're right. I just can't…"

"You just can't what?"

She shook her head. "Nothing."

Trace kissed her again. "Get that list done for me."

Maggie's smile looked forced. "I will, I promise."

He turned, let out a soft whistle, and Rowdy shot

out of the kitchen. A single bark said he was ready to go. Trace ruffled his coat. Rowdy loved to ride in the car. It didn't matter where. As long as it wasn't too hot, Trace usually took him along.

"Let's go, boy." He waved at Maggie as he headed out the back door, only a little concerned by the look he had seen in her eyes.

She'd be all right, he told himself. He would take her out to dinner tonight, get her out of the house for a while.

Trace thought of the evening ahead and how they would make love when they got home, and he smiled.

True to her word, Maggie finished her client list. There were dozens of people over the years who had bought one or two of her photos. There were twenty people who had purchased three pictures, ten who had purchased four and two who had purchased five. Two different art brokers had acted on behalf of clients. She had gotten in touch with them, but neither had clients who had purchased more than two pieces.

Her work was finished.

She glanced around Trace's warm, cozy house and ignored a sharp little pang at the thought of leaving. It was past time to go. Whatever was going on in her life, she couldn't live in limbo any longer. Trace didn't believe her stalker had set the fire. She had received a text from him that said the same thing.

Oddly enough, she believed him.

It didn't mean he wasn't a danger.

It didn't change what she had to do.

Grabbing her purse off the table, she headed for the back door. She set the alarm as Trace had shown her, and made her way out to the garage. Her Escape was parked next to where Trace kept his Jeep. She backed into the alley and headed for the real estate office she had phoned yesterday morning after reading an ad in the paper.

Gallagher Realty handled apartment rentals in the area near where her town house was being rebuilt. Trace was going to have a fit, but it couldn't be helped.

Maggie glanced in the mirror, but didn't see anyone. She hadn't heard from the stalker since the text she had received from him at the shore. Even if he continued to harass her, she had no choice but to move on. It was time to get back to reality, and that meant finding a place of her own.

She thought of the days and nights she had spent with Trace, and a soft ache throbbed in the middle of her chest. Both of them had known it would come to this, she told herself, known their little housekeeping interlude would have to end. She had hoped by now they would have found the stalker, but unfortunately, that hadn't happened.

It didn't matter. She had put her life on hold for as long as she could stand. It was time to take the necessary steps and move toward the future.

She swallowed past a sudden tightness in her throat. Living with Trace had been surprisingly wonderful. She could have guessed the sex would be spectacular, but hadn't expected the day-to-day living to go so smoothly, or expected how happy just being with Trace made her feel.

The trouble was, Trace wasn't looking for a long-term relationship. He'd had one failed marriage. He was gun-shy for certain.

And so was she.

She wasn't good at relationships. Sooner or later, things would go downhill, and the longer she stayed the more it would hurt.

She spotted the real estate sign, drove into the parking lot and turned off the engine. Fifteen minutes later, an agent named Mary Darwin was showing her a single-story unit on the third floor of a complex that looked out onto wide landscaped lawns dotted with huge, leafy trees. There was a single-car garage for each unit, a communal pool, and the entire complex was gated, which offered at least some sense of security.

An hour later, she walked out of the real estate office with a month-to-month lease in hand. She had rented a three-bedroom, two-bath unit so that once it was safe, there would be room for Ashley and little Robbie.

Maggie hadn't realized she would miss them the way she had. It was nice being part of a family. She hadn't foreseen how much that would mean to her.

She sighed as she leaned back in the seat and started the engine. It felt good to be out of the house and once more on her own. Instead of heading back to Trace's, she drove to the Galleria to do a little shopping.

She could easily imagine how angry Trace would be when he found out what she had done.

Maggie grinned. She definitely needed something sexy to wear when she told him.

Ashley sat hunched over the dining room table. Made of rosewood, it was elegant and gorgeous. Everything in the apartment was done in exquisite taste. French antiques were mixed with contemporary pieces; marble and glass and expensive oil paintings were everywhere.

She loved it here. Which was the reason she had to leave.

She was living on borrowed time, in a borrowed apartment, enjoying a borrowed life. She needed a life of her own and she would never have it as long as she was dependent on someone else.

So when Betty Sparks had approached her last night at the end of her shift, she had grabbed onto the opportunity the older woman had posed.

"We all know about the fire," Betty said. "I know you're okay for now, but sooner or later you're gonna need a place of your own. Me and Bill…we talked about it some." Her husband, Bill, sometimes cooked at the café. But he had a heart condition and Betty worried that he worked too hard.

"We got this place upstairs," the gray-haired woman continued. "Our daughter lived there when she went to college. Been empty since she graduated and moved off to Dallas. You been doing a real fine job here, honey. Me and Bill…we worked hard all our lives. Kinda come to us that maybe you could stay on after Eddie gets back to work. You could keep workin' nights, so we could take a little time off, and you'd have your days to go to that cooking school you've had your eye on. You and your baby could live right upstairs, you know. Just be part of the deal."

For a moment, Ashley was speechless. Then her eyes began to fill. "Oh, Betty, that would be perfect."

She had patted her on the back. "Don't cry, now. You ain't seen the place yet."

But it wasn't a bad place at all, and Betty said she was going to have it painted, and the carpet replaced, before Ashley and the baby moved in.

So she would be leaving the fabulous apartment Jason had arranged for her use, and striking out on her own.

And the first step was completing the paperwork lying on the table, an application for admission to the culinary school at the Houston Art Institute, along with an application for a student loan, a program Maggie had found for her on the internet.

Ashley filled in the last few blanks, smiled as she finished, then turned at the chiming of the doorbell. Her heart took a leap. Jason had phoned earlier. She was off work tonight and he was bringing Chinese. She had been cooking so much lately she was looking forward to the treat.

The bell chimed again as she headed for the door. He was coming over early, as he often did. Time had slipped away while she was working on the applications, so she hadn't had time to change and still wore the jeans, flat leather sandals and a T-shirt with a bunny on the front she'd put on earlier. Funny thing was, Jason never seemed to mind.

She opened the door, excited to tell him all her news, and there he stood, handsome as a god with his gleaming blond hair and tanned skin, all warm smiles, and a soft look in his gorgeous blue eyes that seemed just for her.

"May I come in?"

She didn't realize she was staring. Warm color rushed into her cheeks. "Sorry." She stepped back and he walked past her, his arms full of brown paper bags. Ashley hurried ahead of him into a kitchen that was every cook's dream, waited as he set the bags on the long granite countertop.

Jason leaned over and pressed a light kiss on her lips. It made her stomach quiver. "Hungry?" he asked.

"Starving. I didn't realize it until I smelled that delicious food."

He opened one of the bags, inhaled deeply. "Pineapple sesame prawns and lobster dumplings." He looked into another bag. "Tea-smoked duck, steamed rock cod with ginger and scallions." He opened the last bag. "Bok choy with fresh pea leaves in garlic sauce—and fortune cookies, of course."

Ashley laughed. "The leftovers will feed me for a week."

Jason smiled. "Mike Choo down at the China Palace cooks this stuff just for me. He knows how much I love Chinese."

Her smile slipped a little. Jason was used to the good life. Restaurant owners who catered to his every wish were nothing out of the ordinary. She wondered if he would still come around when she was living in a tiny apartment above the Texas Café.

She started taking down plates and getting out silverware. "I've got some news," she said as he pulled the cartons out of the bags and set them on the counter. "I just finished filling out my application for culinary school."

He looked up. "That's great, Ash." He glanced away, then back. "I know you don't have much money. I'd be happy to help you. You know I can afford it. Just tell me what you need and I'll take care of it."

She could feel her temper rising. She'd been afraid this would happen. She started shaking her head. "I don't want your money, Jason. My sister offered, too, but that isn't what I want. I'm applying for a student loan. I'm pretty sure I'll qualify." She looked up at him and managed to smile. "Besides, I'm keeping my job."

A frown appeared between his sexy blue eyes. "I thought you were just filling in."

"I was, but Mrs. Sparks wants me to stay. She says she'll work around my hours while I'm in school." She kept her smile in place. "And guess what? She's going to let me and Robbie live in the apartment upstairs. Isn't that terrific?"

Jason's frown deepened. "What's wrong with staying right here?"

"Nothing's wrong with it. It's the most beautiful apartment I've ever seen. But it isn't mine. Eventually your friend will be coming back. And the truth is, I need a place of my own."

"Jimmy's busy gallivanting all over Europe. He won't be back for weeks. I think you ought to stay here. I live close by in case you need anything and—"

"Please, Jason. Please try to understand."

He swallowed, took a deep breath. "I know how much you value your independence. It's one of the things I admire about you, Ash. But it just seems crazy when I have so much and you—"

"Don't say it! I know you want to help, but I just can't take your money!"

A lengthy silence followed. "Okay," he agreed with a sigh. "We'll do it your way."

Ashley looked up at him. "I just want to know one thing. If I move into a little apartment like that, will you still come and see me? I know you aren't used to that kind of place, but—"

He grabbed her shoulders, gently shook her. "Stop it! Stop it right now!" He bent down and kissed her, quick and hard. "I'm crazy about you, Ash. I wouldn't care if you lived in a doghouse. I'd still want to see you." And then he pulled her into his arms. "I just want you to be happy, honey. That's all I care about."

Ashley blinked back tears and clung to him. "Jason…" She loved the feel of him wrapped around her, the warmth of his body against hers. When he held her this way, it seemed as if nothing in the world could hurt her.

"It's all right," he soothed. "Everything's gonna be all right."

She nodded against his shoulder. She was falling in love with him. She had tried so hard to keep him at a distance, but he just kept breaking down her defenses. It couldn't possibly work out. Jason was a wealthy playboy and she was a working mother trying to scratch out a life for herself and her child. And yet when he held her like this, her heart swelled with love and hope.

He eased a little away. "Are we okay then?"

Ashley looked up at him and nodded.

Jason released a relieved breath, smiled and changed the subject. "So what are we doing tonight? I stopped at Blockbuster, got us a couple of movies."

Ashley smiled. "I got one, too. *The Prince and the Maiden.* I promised my sister I'd help her and Trace find the stalker. I thought if we watched it we might find a clue."

Jason grinned. "Sounds like fun." He glanced toward the bedroom. "Baby's asleep?"

"He'll probably wake up pretty soon."

"Then we'd better eat so you can give him his bottle."

He always considered Robbie. Jason smiled when he

held her infant son, and Robbie always smiled back. She was afraid her boy was falling in love with him, too.

She didn't want to think about it. Jason was a man, and though he seemed to care about her, she knew she'd be a fool to trust him.

It made her heart hurt to think how sad she was going to be when he left her.

Chapter Twenty-Eight

Trace stomped the dust from his boots, turned off the alarm and opened the back door. Rowdy trotted in beside him.

"Maggie?" He hung his hat on the peg beside the door.

"I'm in here."

He walked in that direction, more eager to see her than he wanted to be. Damn, he liked having her around. Too much, he knew, but consoled himself that there was nothing he could do about it, not until they found her stalker.

"Hello, lover." She walked up to him, kissed him softly on the mouth. "I missed you."

His groin instantly tightened. "I missed you, too." He had called her earlier, told her he wanted to take her out to supper, and she'd seemed excited about going. She was already dressed to go in a short, sexy burgundy number. One more kiss like the one she'd just given him and he would have to change the time of their dinner reservation.

"So how was your day?" she asked, reaching up to run a hand through his hair. He resisted an urge to do the same to hers, to tangle a fist in all those glorious red curls.

"Pretty busy. I talked to Mark Sayers. He already knew how our little trip to the shore turned out—unfortunately. He did have some info. He managed to come up with the location of the cell towers the stalker's calls came through. Two from one location, one from another. It might be something we can use."

"That's good, I guess."

"Sayers mentioned Parker Barrington. Says the D.A.'s case is getting stronger every day. They think they can put him away for Hewitt's murder."

"That's great. From what you've said, it couldn't happen to a nicer guy."

Trace chuckled. "Jason was damned glad to hear it. I think the kid'll be able to move on with his life now." He leaned back against the kitchen table, settled her in front of him between his legs. "How about you? You get anything done?"

"I finished my client list." She tipped her head toward the kitchen. "We can go over it whenever you're ready."

"Good girl. But not tonight. Tonight I have a date with a beautiful woman."

She smiled. "I finished my work and then I went out and rented an apartment."

Trace frowned. "What are you talking about?"

"I rented an apartment over on Baylor. It's very nice,

and it's close to Broadmoor so I can keep an eye on the construction being done on my town house."

He took a breath and worked to calm his temper. "You can't do that, Maggie. You know it isn't safe."

"I already did it, Trace. I'm moving in the day after tomorrow."

He felt a growl welling up in his throat, told himself to stay calm. "What about your stalker? He isn't going to leave you alone just because you want him to."

"No, he isn't. But other people have problems like this and they don't just move in indefinitely with their bodyguard."

His temper heated. "Your bodyguard? That's all I am to you?"

"Of course not. But I have a life to live, just like you do, and it's time for me to live it."

He clamped down on his anger. "The man set your house on fire. He nearly killed your sister and her baby. What if he does something like that again?"

"You don't believe he set the fire. You think it was something else. The stalker says he didn't do it. He says he wouldn't hurt me, and as crazy as it sounds, I believe him."

"You believe him."

"That's right."

"These guys are unpredictable, Maggie. He might mean exactly what he says, but tomorrow something could happen that changes the way he feels. You can't take that kind of chance."

"It isn't fair to you, Trace. Can't you see that? Neither of us wants to make a commitment. When things don't work out, one of us is going to get hurt."

Some of his temper seeped away, replaced by a tightness beginning to build in his chest. "Is that what this is about? You and me? It's over for you and time to move on?"

"No! I mean…I—I don't know. I just think we'd both be better off if we put things back on an even keel."

But he wouldn't be better off without Maggie. Trace was only beginning to realize how deeply he had come to care for her. He liked having her there when he came home. He liked being with her, liked everything about her. Well, almost everything. He didn't like one damned bit that she was so willing to put herself in danger.

"This is a bad idea, Maggie. But if you want out that bad, I can make it happen. I'll set up security around your place. We've got guys who make regular rounds. I'll have them put your apartment on the route. We can do some kind of temporary alarm system until you get back in your condo."

He didn't say more. His chest was clamping down, making it hard to breathe. He should have known she was getting to him, should have backed off way before now.

It was his own damned fault, and he had no one to blame but himself.

Maggie walked up and looped her arms around his neck. "You're supposed to be mad."

"I am mad."

"We were supposed to fight and then have a round of wild, unbridled sex."

He eased her arms from around his neck. He felt sick inside, sick and angry with himself. "Sorry, I'm not in the mood anymore."

Tears welled in her pretty green eyes. "It had to happen sooner or later, Trace. We both knew that."

"Did we?" He turned and started walking. "I think you'd better call out for pizza. I'm not hungry anymore."

"Trace…"

He grabbed her client list off the table and kept walking. Carly had played him for ten kinds of fool. But Maggie O'Connell, with her soft smile and big green eyes, had managed to break through the wall he had built around his heart.

The following morning, Maggie knocked on the door to Ashley's fancy, borrowed apartment. She had been there with Trace a couple times to make sure Ashley and Robbie were settled in all right. In the lobby, the security guard recognized her and phoned upstairs to let Ashley know she was on her way up. It was all very classy and very secure.

She stepped out of the elevator and started down the ninth-floor hallway, her sandals slapping the marble tiles as she wearily approached the apartment. She was exhausted. Last night, instead of sleeping, she had tossed and turned and listened for the sound of Trace's boots when he came home, yearning to see him, afraid of the way she would feel when she did.

She took a breath and knocked on the apartment door, and a few moments later, Ashley pulled it open.

"Maggie! I'm so glad you're here! I was going to call you this morning. I was just waiting until I was sure you and Trace would be up."

The words made her stomach churn. The baby started crying somewhere inside and Ashley hauled Maggie into the massive entry and closed the door.

"Hold on, I'll be right back." Her sister darted off

down a wide, marble-floored hallway and disappeared into the room she was using as a nursery.

A few minutes later she reappeared, little Robbie wrapped in a soft blue blanket and nestled snuggly in her arms.

"Jason bought a baby monitor so I can hear him wherever I am. The place is so big it's kind of hard to keep track of such a little guy." She jostled him until he stopped crying, then rubbed her nose against his until he finally smiled. "Your aunt Maggie's here. She wants to hold you, sweetheart."

And as Maggie looked down at the baby, she really did. She needed the comfort and sweetness of the little boy's tiny body pressed against her. Needed someone who could cheer her up out of the terrible despair she had fallen into after Trace had gone.

He hadn't come home last night, though he must have stopped by sometime, since there was a note on the door.

Keep your cell phone handy and the battery charged. If anything happens, ANYTHING, call me. I'll help you move your stuff whenever you're ready.

"I have some really great news," Ashley said brightly, leading her onto the plush carpet in the living room.

Maggie cuddled the baby in her arms. "I could use some good news."

"I'm keeping my job at the café while I go to culinary school." Ashley grinned. "Mrs. Sparks has it all worked out. And she's got a place for me and Robbie to live, an apartment above the café. So you don't have to worry about us anymore."

Maggie reached up and pushed a shiny blond curl back from her sister's cheek. "I never worried about you. I loved having you and Robbie with me. But I'm happy for you, Ash. Really happy."

Her sister glanced around. "I'm really gonna miss this place, but I'm excited, too, you know?"

"Yeah, I do. So is that why you were going to call?"

"No. Last night, Jason and I figured something out. Come on, I'll show you." Ashley tugged her across the thick carpet into a room with no windows. It was a giant media space with a huge viewing screen, Dolby sound and six wide reclining leather chairs.

"Jason showed me how to play this thing." She went over and turned on the DVD player. "Last night we watched the movie *The Prince and The Maiden*. That was the song the stalker played for you over the phone, right? We figured maybe we could find some kind of clue."

Maggie kissed the top of the baby's head. One of his tiny hands wrapped around her finger and she felt a soft tug in her heart. She looked over at the massive screen. "So you think you might have found something?"

"I'm not sure. We were thinking maybe it could be." Her sister started the movie, zipped forward at high speed, stopped a couple times until she found the place she was looking for. "Here's where they sing the song." The beautiful maid began to dance with the handsome prince. The couple sang the verse together. "I…saw… you…I knew you would be my one true love. I…saw… you…a vision so pure and sweet, my only true love…."

"It's a lovely song," Maggie said wistfully, trying

not to think of Trace or recall the look in his eyes when she had told him she was leaving. Trying to ignore the grinding pain in her heart that she had destroyed a relationship that had become more precious than anything she had ever known.

"You said the guy broke into your house, right? That night he left a porcelain statuette."

"That's right." She continued to watch the film until Ashley pushed the pause button.

"Well, here's the thing. The couple in the figurine were dancing, right? That's what you said."

"Yes." Maggie swung her nephew from side to side, watched his little hands fisting and his mouth working.

"Well, the song says, 'I saw you, I knew you would be my one true love.'" But in the movie, they aren't just singing, they're waltzing. Just like the couple in the figurine."

The truth hit her like a jolt of lightning, and chills rushed over her skin. She sank down in one of the leather chairs, clasping the baby in her arms.

"You're right. In the movie, they're waltzing. Just like the statuette." She looked up. "I love to dance. Until this started, Roxanne and I went all the time. That has to be it. I must have danced with him somewhere."

"I really think that's the clue. I think you danced with him and he fell in love with you."

She shook her head. "It isn't love. It's some sick infatuation."

"Not to him. He calls you, follows you. He thinks you belong to him, don't you see? Just like the maiden belonged to the prince."

Maggie's heart was pounding. She had to call Trace, tell him what they had discovered. Her palms began to sweat. She had to phone him, and half of her wanted that more than anything in the world.

The other half knew how difficult that call would be. Trace saw her actions as the end of their affair. He would be determined to get on with his life—just as she'd said she wanted to do.

Ashley reached for the baby, settled him back in the crook of her arm. "What is it, Maggie? Something's wrong. I saw it in your face when you walked through the door."

Sadness welled inside her. "I rented an apartment. I told Trace I was moving out tomorrow."

"You broke up with him?"

"I didn't break up with him. How could I? We were never really a couple. It was only a physical thing."

"That is so not true." Ashley settled into the over-size leather chair beside her. "He loves you. The way he looks at you…it's like he could just eat you up. Maybe he hasn't quite got it figured out, but he loves you."

Maggie's throat swelled. She only shook her head.

"You know what else?" Ashley gently pressed. "You love him, too."

"No…"

"You really don't think so? Look at you."

Maggie swallowed past the painful lump in her throat. "Even if I did love him, it wouldn't work. I'm really bad at relationships. I always run away when things get too involved."

"You mean like now?"

She closed her eyes. She was doing it again. Only this time, instead of escaping, feeling free, she felt as if she were falling into a deep, dark hole.

Ashley's hand settled gently on her shoulder, making small, comforting circles.

The tears in Maggie's eyes spilled over onto her cheeks. "I love him. I love him so much."

Her sister smiled. "Well, then, I don't see a problem. All you have to do is tell him how you feel."

A ragged breath seeped out. "You don't know him. He had a really bad marriage. He was only just beginning to trust me. He won't do it again."

Ashley's smile faded. "Oh, Maggie."

She rose from the chair, bent down and kissed the baby's forehead. "I have to call him. Tell him what you and Jason figured out."

Ashley stood up, too, leaned over and hugged her. "Do it. Call Trace. Don't give up on him yet. And don't give up on yourself."

Chapter Twenty-Nine

Trace leaned back in the chair behind his desk at the office. He hadn't been home for two days. He and Rowdy had been sleeping on the sofa in the back room.

He rubbed the bristles along his jaw. He needed to shower and shave. But he was still on Maggie's payroll. He still had a job to do.

He sighed into the quiet. At least he'd been working on her client list. Sol had run the names of the people who had bought her photographs, but come up with nothing useful except the addresses of where they were employed.

Trace was working on a theory. He just hadn't had time to put it all together. He needed to talk to Maggie, explain what was going on. And he needed her help to finish going over the second half of the photos sold the night of the opening.

He didn't reach for the phone. Maggie was moving out this morning. She hadn't called. Apparently, she didn't need his help.

At the sound of a knock on the door, he looked up, then rose to his feet as Jake Cantrell turned the knob and walked in.

"Hey, buddy, good to see you." Trace extended a hand. Cantrell gripped it and slapped him on the back.

"You, too, my friend." The former marine was six feet five inches of solid muscle, with dark hair and pale blue eyes. He and Trace had worked together off and on over the years, most recently with Dev Raines and Johnnie Riggs in Mexico on the child-abduction case.

"I thought you were south of the border," Trace said.

"Was. Just got back. Thought I'd take a week or two off, rest up a little before you put me back to work."

"If I don't have something by then, somebody will. There's always work for guys like us."

Men who knew how to handle themselves in tough situations, who put the job first and did whatever needed to be done to protect the good guys from the bad.

Jake sat down in the chair beside Trace's desk. His size made the office seem smaller. "So what's new around here?" he asked. "Anything exciting going on?"

Trace sighed. "I thought so for a while. It didn't work out."

Jake eyed the growth of beard along his jaw. "Another redhead?"

He nodded. "I must have a death wish."

His friend chuckled. "There's always next time."

But Trace was thinking, *not for me.* This was his last attempt at normal, his last stab at home and family. He hadn't said anything like that to Maggie. Hadn't realized it himself until it was too late. The pipe dream was over now. He wouldn't make the same mistake again.

"Unfortunately, she's still a client," he said. "Got a stalker. Maybe some other trouble, too. I can't just walk away—at least not yet." Trace filled Jake in on the fire and their failed trip to the shore.

"You need some help," he offered, "you know where to find me."

"Thanks. Alex and Ben have been pitching in. Rex did some recon. So far, nothing we've done has turned up squat."

"Like I said…" Jake stood up and headed for the door.

Trace walked him to the front of the office, watched him cross the lot and climb into his big black, open Jeep with its roll bar and oversize tires. The machine was beginning to show its age and the wear and tear Cantrell put it through.

Trace watched him drive away, the pipes rumbling a little louder than they should. When he turned, he found Annie staring out the window.

"That man makes my heart flutter, and I'm sixty-four years old."

Trace chuckled. "Well, obviously, you aren't dead yet."

She laughed. "I guess not." She turned her mother-hen glare on him. "You look like somethin' the cat dragged in. You know, I really liked this last one. I thought you two were getting along."

"I thought so, too. The lady didn't seem to agree."

"More fool she."

He released a tired breath. "I guess I'm not cut out to be a settled-down kind of guy."

"That is not true, Trace Rawlins. You were a great

husband to that rotten little witch you married. I really thought this one was different."

"So did I. Shows how dumb it is to trust your instincts."

Annie opened her mouth to argue, but the phone rang, giving him a reprieve. He turned, headed back to his office.

"Line one," Annie called after him. "It's your lady. Maybe she's wised up."

He just scowled. As he sat down at his desk and reached for the phone, his stomach knotted. He pressed the receiver against his ear. "What is it, Maggie?"

"Jason and Ashley found something. I was going to call yesterday, but I…"

He didn't try to help her find the words. He knew why she hadn't phoned. The same reason he hadn't called her.

"So what did they find?"

"Maybe nothing. I'm not sure, but it might be important." She went on to tell him about watching the movie, about the prince and the maiden and how they weren't just singing the song, they were waltzing, just like the couple in the figurine.

"I love to dance, Trace. Before all this started, Rox and I went clubbing all the time. I think…I have a feeling I danced with him somewhere."

There was a long pause.

Trace leaned back in his chair. "I guess that means we're goin' dancin'," he heard himself say. "I'll pick you up at eight."

"I wrote down my new address and the gate code, and left it on your kitchen table. I'm borrowing your laptop for a few more days, if that's okay, until I can get my new computer hooked up."

"Like I said, I'll be there at eight."

"Trace?"

"Yeah?"

"Nothing… I'll see you tonight."

Trace hung up the phone. He didn't want to go. He didn't want to see her. He didn't want to feel worse than he did already.

Heading out of his office, he called to Rowdy, asleep in the back, heard his small feet padding across the carpet. Trace ruffled the dog's fur and adjusted his collar. "Come on, ol' buddy. We're going home."

He had almost reached the front door of the office when Annie's voice stopped him. "So what did she want?"

Trace grunted. "A dancing partner," he said, and closed the door.

Maggie was ridiculously nervous. As she waited for Trace, she paced back and forth across the living room. The rented apartment was furnished, but not with any sort of style, just gray carpet, a gray sofa and chair, a black coffee table and end units, and a couple lamps. The framed artwork on the wall looked like something from Walmart.

There was none of the warmth she'd grown used to at Trace's, nothing that made her smile. She missed the comfortable atmosphere. Missed hearing the thud of boots on the carpet. She even missed Rowdy.

The only thing the apartment managed to do was show her what a stupid mistake she had made.

Maggie sighed. She should have stayed, should have

talked to him, explained her feelings, found out what he was thinking in return.

But beyond the great sex they had shared, she had no idea what Trace's feelings for her actually were, and exposing herself that way just wasn't something she was ready to do.

Ashley said he loved her. But Ashley was young and inexperienced with men, no matter that she'd had a child. And Trace had never said anything remotely giving the impression that Maggie played any role in his future.

Nor had she to him.

She had hidden her feelings behind the incredible sex, hidden them from Trace—and also from herself.

Ashley was right about one thing: Maggie was madly in love with Trace Rawlins. She didn't want to run away from him—she wanted to run straight back into his arms.

But it wasn't going to happen. She knew what he would say if she told him how she felt. He wouldn't believe her. It was just that simple.

She had moved out of his house, basically told him she didn't think it would work between them. Saying she had changed her mind was just not going to cut it.

The doorbell rang.

She checked the time, took a deep breath, walked over and opened the door. Her heart lurched at the sight of him, standing there in his perfectly creased black jeans, a short-sleeved white Western shirt and black ostrich-leather boots. The ladies in the clubs were going to be drooling.

When he smiled, he looked so handsome Maggie's heart squeezed.

"I'm ready," she said, because if she said anything else, she was going to start crying.

His gaze ran over her. "You look nice."

She had taken extra care with her hair and makeup, tried on ten outfits before choosing a short red dress she had never worn, but which seemed to fit her nicely. She managed to smile. "Thanks, so do you."

His eyes fixed on her face. "I liked having you in the house, Maggie. I just wanted you to know."

Her eyes burned. "I liked being there. More than I realized."

He just nodded, then turned away from her toward the door. "Let's go catch a stalker."

She swallowed. He was all business now, the consummate professional. He was her bodyguard and nothing more.

And it was all her fault.

"We need to hit your usual places," Trace said. "Where's our first stop?"

"Galaxy. That's my favorite. Rox and I went there a lot."

"All right, Galaxy it is."

It didn't take long to reach the trendy nightclub in the Galleria district. He could hear the music throbbing out the front door as they drove up to the parking valet. Trace tossed his hat into the backseat and climbed from the Jeep, joining Maggie as a dark-haired young man helped her out onto the walkway. Trace raked a hand through his hair, settling it back in place, then rested a hand at Maggie's waist and guided her into the club.

Music thrummed inside. The place was high-tech, all brushed chrome and dark wood, with mauve and blue lighting. There was an empty stool at the bar. Trace guided Maggie in that direction. She was wearing a very short, sexy little red dress that showed way too much leg to suit him, and left her entire back bare. His jaw felt tight. She wouldn't lack for dancing partners.

"Order a drink," he said softly, clamping down on the jealousy he didn't want to feel. "Dance when you get asked. I won't be far away."

She nodded, ordered a cosmo. He had never seen her drink anything but wine before. He wondered if she was more nervous about the stalker or about being with him.

She looked pale, tired, and he might say sad. Maybe she regretted her decision. Or maybe that was just wishful thinking.

She took a sip of her drink, then slid off the stool to accompany a heavyset man onto the dance floor. The DJ was playing a fast song. The guy should have been clumsy, given his size, but he wasn't. They danced together as if they had done it a dozen times, and Trace made a mental note to get the guy's name.

A lot of people knew Maggie. She danced again and again, but none of her partners seemed overly possessive. They were just enjoying themselves, same as she was. A slow song came on as she headed back toward the bar. Trace told himself not to move, but all of a sudden there he was, taking her hand, leading her out on the dance floor.

He drew her into his arms and heard her soft little sigh. Maggie looped her arms around his neck and snuggled up to him, and though desire curled through him, mostly he just thought how much he missed her. He'd dated a dozen redheads. None of them made him feel the way she did.

None of them had the power to hurt him the way she did.

They danced well together. He wasn't great, but he wasn't all that bad. When the next song started, a Texas two-step, he couldn't resist hanging on to her hand.

"You know this one?" he asked.

Maggie grinned. "Just try to keep up, cowboy."

Guitars and fiddles, a good, fast Western song. He loved it. For a few short minutes, he forgot he was her bodyguard, forgot he was supposed to be watching for a stalker. For a few short minutes, like everyone else, he was just enjoying himself.

When the song ended, he walked her back to the bar.

"Thanks for the dance," she said, as if he was just another partner, but she was smiling.

"My pleasure, darlin'."

Trace went back to work then, waiting and watching every man who partnered her, telling himself it didn't bother him when she laughed or smiled at something one of them said. An hour later he came up behind her.

"I want the name of the first guy you danced with. He's the only one who comes close to fitting our possible description."

"That was Doug Winston. He comes in here all the time, but I don't think it's him. He just likes to dance. He's never even asked me out."

"We'll check on him, anyway." Trace urged her toward the door. "It's still early. We've got time to hit a couple more places."

She nodded and they headed outside. As the valet brought up the Jeep, Maggie's cell phone began to ring. She dug it out of her purse and pressed it against her ear.

She stiffened for an instant, then her face went pale.

"It's him," she mouthed as she walked farther away from the music so she could hear. Close beside her, Trace bent down so he could listen to the voice on the other end of the line. It wasn't distorted this time.

"I miss you, Maggie. I'm so lonely. Won't you come out and play with me?"

She swallowed, glanced up at Trace. He motioned for her to talk, whispered, "Try to get his name."

"I'd really like to," she said into the phone. "Tell me where you are and I'll come to you."

Trace nodded in encouragement, telling her she was doing the right thing.

The voice on the phone was deep and resonant, and yet it sounded oddly childlike. "Remember how perfectly we fit together, Maggie? I remember how you laughed, the way you smiled at me."

"That was a special night, wasn't it?" A faint tremor shook her voice. "I can't quite remember exactly when it was."

Silence fell over the phone. "You don't remember?"

"Not exactly. I need you to remind me."

He didn't reply. The silence stretched out. Then the phone went dead.

Trace clenched his jaw. Maggie's hand was shaking as she hung on to the phone. "He didn't try to disguise his voice this time."

"No. He thinks you know who he is. He's escalating. This isn't good." Trace dug his own phone out of his jeans pocket and dialed Mark Sayers, who sounded sleepy when he answered.

"Mark, it's Trace. I need you to track a call or at least find the cell tower it just came from."

"Maggie's stalker?"

"Yeah."

"Give me her cell number again. And give me the exact time of the call."

Trace reached out and Maggie handed him her phone. He checked the time and rattled off the information Sayers wanted.

"I'll get back to you," Mark said.

Trace clicked off and gave Maggie back her phone.

"He didn't disguise his voice," she said, tucking it back into her purse. "Maybe he wasn't using a disposable this time."

"Maybe. But even if he was, I've been working on an idea…"

He took her hand, led her to the Jeep and helped her climb inside. They had just pulled into the parking lot in front of his office minutes later when his cell started ringing.

"Disposable," Mark said simply. "But I got the tower location." Sayers gave him the address.

"So the three night calls came from one tower, the daytime call from another."

"That's right. Good luck with it."

"Thanks, Mark." Trace signed off and they started for the office. "I've been working on a theory." He unlocked the front door, led her inside, flipped on the lights and turned off the alarm. "Come on, I'll show you."

Maggie let Trace lead her into the conference room, where a map of Houston and the surrounding area was spread open on the table.

"The white stickpins mark the locations of the two cell towers where the calls originated." He pointed at one of the pins. "The night calls, including the one you got tonight, came from here. There were three of them. My theory is the guy was at home when he made the calls."

"That makes sense."

"The text message you got at the shore was a daytime call." Trace pointed to the second white pin. "It came from this tower here. I think the guy was at work."

Maggie studied the map. "And the colored pins?"

"Sol ran your main buyers and came up with a work address for each, their home addresses already being on the list. The yellow pins mark work and home data of anyone who bought five pictures. There were only two, and neither fell into either zone. The red pins are people who bought four pictures. There are ten of them, but some live out of the city, so aren't on the map. A couple live in an area serviced by one of the towers, but unfortunately, their work addresses don't fall in the daytime zone."

Maggie picked up the list. "Twenty people bought three pictures."

"That's right. I was just getting started on those when you called. We'll make those buyers green."

They worked together to place them. Locating the addresses through Google Maps using Alex's borrowed laptop, which Trace had brought into the conference room, they tried to find a person who lived in the night tower zone and worked in the daytime tower zone. Some people lived in other areas, and those names were discarded.

Maggie shoved the last of the green pins into the map. None were in both tower areas.

Trace blew out a breath. "Well, I guess my theory sucks."

She picked up the list. "You haven't located the ones that were purchased through art brokers."

"True, but those buyers bought only two pictures."

"I know, but he just started stalking me recently, so maybe time was a factor. And maybe he used a broker to keep his identity secret."

"Worth a try. We'll make them blue."

Maggie went back to work on the laptop. The first name was Maryanne Rosemore. "Doesn't sound too ominous." She typed the home address into Google Maps.

Trace located the area on the map and shoved in a bright blue pin. "Outside either zone," he said darkly.

"The last name here is Phillip Coffman." She frowned. "I don't know why, but it sounds familiar."

"Coffman…Coffman." Trace walked up beside her, typed in the name. "President of HTM Technologies." He looked at her. "Their offices are in the Park View Towers. That's right here." He found the location on the map and marked it with a pin. It was only a couple blocks from the daytime white pin.

Maggie's heart started pounding.

"What's the home address?" Trace asked, and she could tell he was trying not to get excited.

"It's 55556 Bayou Glen."

"That's in Tanglewood. Big money lives there." He stuck a blue pin into the map. It was inside the night zone. "Bingo."

Trace went back to work on the laptop, typing far faster than she could have, pulling up information on Phillip Coffman. "The guy retired six months ago after twenty years with the company." He glanced up. "He quit right after his wife died, but continued to do consulting work at the office on a part-time basis."

"Can you find a picture?" Maggie asked. Trace clicked on a couple more websites, found what he was looking for and turned the laptop around so she could see.

Big, forties, dark hair silvered at the temples. "Oh, my God."

"You recognize him?"

"He and his wife were known for their charitable contributions. Mrs. Coffman died of breast cancer. That's where I met her husband." Maggie looked up. "I danced with him at a breast cancer awareness fund-raiser earlier this year."

Trace's voice was hard. "And let me guess…the band was playing a waltz."

Chapter Thirty

Trace phoned Mark Sayers, who sounded even grumpier than the first time he'd been awakened. "Sorry to bother you again, buddy, but I need your help."

Sayers grunted into the phone. "So you found him."

"Yeah, and I want to pay him a little late-night visit."

"What's wrong with tomorrow morning?"

"Nothing. If we had enough evidence to arrest him. We don't. All we've got are a couple of cell towers and a bunch of pins stuck in a map."

"But you're sure it's him."

"Everything fits, even the description, and Maggie recognized his picture. I'm certain it's him. We need to put the fear of God into this asshole. I need you to meet me at his house."

"I'm not supposed to be working this case."

"You aren't. The address is 55556 Bayou Glen. That's out in Tanglewood."

"Guy must have plenty of money."

"Enough to pay an arsonist to burn down Maggie's house." Seemed as if Trace had been wrong on that one. It would be interesting to see what Phillip Coffman had to say.

"I'll be there in twenty minutes." Sayers hung up, and Trace turned to Maggie. It was nearly two in the morning. She looked tired, but her eyes were bright and there was plenty of color her cheeks. She was fighting mad and he didn't blame her.

"I'm going with you," she said. "I want to talk to him."

Trace shook his head. "I'm taking you home." Back to her newly rented apartment instead of his place, which hadn't felt like home since she'd left. "We don't know how this guy is going to react when he finds out his dirty little secret isn't a secret anymore."

"Why can't they arrest him?"

"Where's the proof? We don't even have enough to get a search warrant. That's why I want Sayers there tonight. If we get any kind of probable cause, we can go in. Maybe we'll find what we need inside the house."

Maggie's chin came up. "I'm coming, Trace. You can take me home and I can drive myself, or you can let me ride with you." She gave him a sassy, belligerent smile. "I know the address, remember?"

"Dammit, Maggie!"

She didn't say more, just stood there glaring, making it clear she meant what she said.

"All right, you can come. But you have to stay in the car."

"Fine."

As he locked the office and led her outside to the Jeep, his gaze ran over her. The little red dress looked wilted, her fiery curls a little less tamed, but she was still the sexiest woman he had ever seen. And the most appealing.

They drove up in front of the house just as Sayers's dark brown unmarked police car pulled up behind them. Trace retrieved the Beretta 9 mm he'd stashed under the seat earlier, and stuck it into the waistband of his jeans, behind his back.

"Promise me you'll stay right here," he said.

Silence. "I'm in the car, aren't I?"

He didn't miss that she hadn't actually promised. He gave her a hard warning glare. "I should have handcuffed you to a chair and left you in the office."

Maggie just smiled.

Trace closed the door and walked up to Sayers, and the two of them approached the massive front doors.

"The way it looks, this guy's got money and power," Mark said. "He could cause a real shitstorm for me down at the department."

"If Coffman's as off the deep end as he seemed on the phone tonight, I don't think he'll go in that direction."

"I hope you're right. I think."

They reached the door and Sayers rang the bell. Then he started pounding. "Police! Open up!"

The residential lots in the area were huge. No lights went on, no neighborhood doors came open. Sayers pounded again and the front door swung wide, revealing Phillip Coffman, six-three, mid-forties and slightly overweight.

"Yes? What is it?"

"I'm Detective Sayers and this is Trace Rawlins with Atlas Security. May we come in?"

"I'm sorry, what is this about?"

Trace answered, stepping things up a bit. "It's about your obsession with Maggie O'Connell. It's about stalking her, breaking into her home, putting a tracking device on her car, installing video cameras. It's about setting her house on fire and nearly killing two people."

Coffman started shaking his head. "I didn't set the fire. I would never do anything to hurt her."

Sayers glanced at Trace and then leaped into the fray. "But you admit to harassing her, breaking into her home?"

Coffman started frowning. He looked unsettled, but mostly just bewildered. "I don't know what you're talking about. Ms. O'Connell and I are very close friends. We…we're planning to be married."

Trace swore softly at the sound of Maggie's voice behind him. "We aren't getting married, Mr. Coffman! We don't even know each other! We danced together once—that's it."

Coffman smiled at her. "Maggie…my dear, sweet Maggie. I knew you would come to me. I knew it was only a matter of time."

"That's it," Sayers said. "Put your hands behind your back, Mr. Coffman. You're under arrest for violating section 42.072 of the Texas penal code. That's stalking, Coffman." Gripping the bigger man's arm, Sayers turned him around and snapped a pair of handcuffs onto his thick wrists. Coffman made no move to fight him, just kept staring at Maggie over his shoulder as if she had somehow betrayed him.

Sayers called for backup and a few minutes later a patrol car rolled up in front of the house. As the officers approached, Coffman turned a pleading look on Maggie.

"I don't understand, dearest. Tell them...tell them we're in love."

Maggie's cheeks flushed. "We aren't in love, dammit!"

"That's enough," Sayers said to Coffman, and started reading him his rights. The officers asked a few questions, then maneuvered the man down the walk to the patrol car and into the backseat. The cruiser rolled away and disappeared into the darkness.

"You'll both need to come down to the station in the morning to make a statement," Mark stated.

"No problem," Trace said.

Sayers blew out a weary breath. "I should have known after the first phone call that I wasn't getting any sleep tonight."

"Sorry about that." Trace glanced around for Maggie, but she was nowhere in sight. "Dammit!"

The front door stood slightly ajar. It was clear she had gone inside. Trace and Sayers followed.

"I was planning to get a warrant, go through the house with the detective in charge of the case in the morning."

"I guess not," Trace grumbled.

The house was huge, with very high ceilings and gleaming wood floors. The walls in the living room were covered in a silk brocade that matched the sofa. The entire house was spotless. Clearly, Coffman had a staff to take care of the place, though none of them appeared to be in residence.

Trace and Mark climbed the sweeping staircase and found Maggie in the massive master bedroom.

"For heaven's sake, don't touch anything," Trace said as he walked up behind her. She was standing there frozen, staring at a wall of photographs pinned one on top of another—all of her. Next to them were pictures of Angela Coffman. Pictures of Angela and Phillip together.

"Losing his wife was the stressor," Mark said.

"Maggie's about the same size," Trace said, "and both of them have red hair."

Maggie just stared. "I can't believe how many photos he took. How could I have not noticed him?"

"I have a hunch he had people working for him. That's how he got the bug on your car and the cameras installed in your apartment."

"Oh, my God, look at those." There was a whole wall of music boxes, all with dancing couples. Except that one had been broken and the dancing couple was missing. "That's where he got the figurine."

"Your guys should have a field day tomorrow," Trace said to Sayers.

When Maggie made no comment, Trace settled an arm around her shoulders. "Let's get out of here. Let the police do their job."

He led her back downstairs and they left the house, paused on the porch as Mark secured the property.

"We'll be down to make a statement in the morning," Trace said. "Thanks, Mark."

"I'm just glad it's over."

Trace nodded. Maggie was safe and his job was finished.

He should have been glad.

He wasn't.

* * *

"I can't believe I'm saying this, but I feel sorry for him." Maggie sat in the passenger seat of the Jeep as Trace wheeled the vehicle toward home. Well, not really her home. Maybe it would feel that way, eventually.

Maybe.

Besides, the apartment was only temporary. Once her town house was rebuilt, she and Ashley could decorate it, make it feel cozy this time. It wouldn't have a cheerful 1950s kitchen, but you couldn't have everything.

"The guy *was* kind of pathetic," Trace agreed. "He's obviously got mental problems. Losing his wife sent him over the edge. Somehow he identified you with her."

She felt a sweep of sadness. "He must have loved her very much."

Trace flicked her a sideways glance. "Doesn't change the fact he almost killed your sister and her baby."

Maggie caught his eye briefly. "He says he didn't set the fire, though. He admitted to everything else, so why would he lie about that?"

"The guy's a head case, Maggie. Probably hired someone to torch the place and doesn't even remember."

"I guess so."

Trace entered the gate code for the Baylor Apartments, drove into the compound and pulled up in her guest space. The sun was coming up, soft yellow rays shooting through the branches of the trees, the sky a pinkish orange. He walked her to the elevator and they made the short ride up to the third floor.

The closer they got to the apartment, the more her stomach knotted. She didn't want Trace to go. She wanted him to come inside. She wanted him to make love to her.

She wanted to tell him that she had made a terrible mistake and desperately regretted it. She wanted to tell him that she loved him.

One look at the set of his hard, bristly jaw, the distance he kept between them, and she knew it was too late.

She forced herself to smile as she used her key to open the door. "It's been a long night. Thanks for everything."

"I just did what you hired me to do."

She nodded, felt a lump beginning to form in her throat. "I don't...don't suppose you want to come in."

He just shook his head. "Wouldn't be a good idea."

She didn't reply. She thought it was a great idea.

"I'll call you tomorrow," he said. "Take you down to make a statement. You'll need to get a restraining order. I can help you get things rolling with that, too."

She swallowed. "All right."

"Good night, Maggie."

She looked up into his face, so male, so ruggedly handsome, and her heart clenched. "Good night, Trace."

He turned and started walking, and Maggie just stood there, watching until he disappeared. Her chest was aching, her eyes wet with tears.

For the first time she knew how David Lyons had felt the night she had said goodbye and walked away.

Maggie rode with Trace to the station the following morning. He seemed so distant, so completely removed from her that she wanted to cry. When they were finished giving their statements, he drove her to Evan

Schofield's office to sign the documents necessary to file a restraining order.

The law office was first-class all the way, with dark wood paneling, shelves filled with leather-bound books, and expensive bronze statues on the tables in the reception area.

The only attorney Maggie knew well enough to call was David, and she wasn't about to do that. Trace had suggested Schofield, and she remembered him being with Shawna Jordane during Trace's fight with her rap-star husband at the Texas Café. Schofield was well known in Houston for his wealthy clientele.

The hour in his office passed in a blur. The only thing she remembered aside from signing the documents was Schofield telling Trace the judge had ordered Bobby Jordane into rehab for the next ninety days.

"You don't think Shawna will take him back when he gets out?" she'd asked.

"Shawna's one smart lady," Schofield said. "I don't think she'll go down that road again."

"Let's hope Jordane learns something while he's in there," Trace commented.

"Most of them don't," Schofield had said.

Trace drove her home after that. They barely spoke on the way. He let her out in the parking lot of the Baylor complex.

"I need to return your laptop," Maggie said, wishing he would stay. "Do you want to come up while I get it?"

"I've got to get back. I'll pick it up some other time."

Her heart sank. "All right." And then he was gone.

Maggie trudged wearily along the corridor to the apartment. No matter what happened, she vowed, no matter the risk she would be taking, she was determined to talk to him, tell him how she felt.

She just couldn't seem to find the right time.

Jason carried the last cardboard box up the stairs and set it on the new beige carpet in Ashley's tiny living room. He had helped her get settled in. Mrs. Sparks had rounded up some furniture, and he had brought a few things over. Not too many. And he had purposely dinged up the ones he'd bought. He didn't want her to guess they were new.

The little place wasn't all that bad, small but kind of cozy in a way he'd never known. All his life he'd rattled around in thousands of square feet of living space. He was so used it, he took it for granted. But he thought that spending his nights here cuddled up with Ashley wouldn't be all that bad.

"I need some green plants," she said, drawing his attention. "Soon as I get my next paycheck, I'm going down to Walmart to buy some."

He almost smiled. It was cute the way she was so thrifty. He'd never known a woman like that.

She turned to survey the placement of the sofa beneath the window, and the bookcases along the wall made out of Home Depot shelves and cement blocks she had spray-painted brown. She had a knack for decorating, he could see. Making a place as small as this look good with old, patchwork furniture was definitely a challenge, but she was doing a great job with the little she had.

"It's starting to look really good, Ash."

She came over to stand beside him. Her face was

flushed from carrying the last few boxes up the stairs, her silky curls a little damp. "You really think so?"

"Yeah, I do. It's gonna be great when you're finished."

She smiled, reached up and brushed a lock of his hair back from his face. He felt that light touch like an electric shock to the heart, and all of a sudden the words just tumbled out.

"I love you, Ashley. I can't keep it bottled up inside anymore. I love you and I love Robbie and I want to marry you." When she just stared up at him as if he had lost his mind, he added, "We can live right here if that's what you want."

Her big blue eyes welled with tears. "Oh, Jason…"

He reached for her, gathered her into his arms. "I mean it. I love you so much. Say you'll marry me."

She clung to his neck and he could feel the wetness tracking down her cheeks. He prayed he hadn't rushed her too much, that in his haste to tell her how he felt, he hadn't driven her away.

"Ashley…?"

She eased back a little to look at him. "I love you, too, Jason. I've never felt this way about anyone. You're the sweetest man I've ever known."

He started shaking his head. "Don't say that. Don't say 'sweet.' Nobody marries a man who's sweet."

She smiled, reached up and touched his cheek. "You are sweet, but you're right, I won't marry you. Not now. Not until I get my life together."

A crushing weight seemed to settle on his chest.

"Besides," she continued, her moist eyes still smiling up at him, making him want to pull her back into his arms, "we haven't even made love."

She glanced toward the bedroom. "Mrs. Epstein is watching the baby. We have the apartment all to ourselves. I think…if it's what you want, too…now would be the perfect time."

His spirits lifted at the same instant his body went hard. "I want to make love to you more than anything in the world. I just…I didn't want to rush you."

She reached over and caught his hand. "We've waited long enough."

He let her lead him into the bedroom, his heart hammering away inside his chest. The queen-size bed he had told her came from a friend who was upsizing to a king had in fact come from Macy's. He hadn't dared buy her new sheets, so she was using some that Mrs. Sparks had loaned her.

He looked at the bed and then at her, saw that now she had made her decision, she was getting nervous.

"It's okay," he said, gently cupping her cheek. Leaning down, he very softly kissed her. "You don't have to do anything more. I can take it from here."

She smiled at him with such yearning his heart hurt. "I love you, Jason."

"I love you, too." And then he kissed her again and Ashley kissed him back, and everything seemed to fall exactly into place.

She was his, he knew. And no matter how long he had to wait, one day she was going to marry him.

Chapter Thirty-One

Trace sat at the kitchen table sipping a cup of thick black coffee. Unable to sleep, he had made the pot hours ago and now was brooding over the dregs.

He tried not to think about Maggie, but his mind kept going there. He kept wondering what would have happened if he had told her how he felt. He wondered if it would have made a difference. The problem was, until she was gone, he hadn't really figured out that he was in love.

By then it was too late.

It was never going to happen between them; he had to accept that. But there was this last nagging worry that wouldn't leave him.

He rubbed the bristles on his jaw as he walked into the living room and turned on the TV. The photo card with Maggie's latest collection was still in place. The list with the names of the photos sold the night of the opening sat on the end table. He picked up the list, then used the tuner to pull up the photo next in line from where they'd left off.

He recognized the picture, but didn't remember the title. He wished Maggie was there to help him.

Damn, he just wished Maggie was there, period.

He ran through the first few photos. Without knowing the names of the pieces, he couldn't compare them to the ones on the sold list, but he didn't notice anything incriminating. He went through a few more, not sure what he was looking for.

The police believed Phillip Coffman had set the fire. Coffman had admitted paying people to take photos of Maggie, to place the cameras in her house and the GPS on her car. But there wasn't anything to connect him to the fire, nothing in his house or garage, and his attorney had been adamant that his client was innocent of arson.

And the nagging suspicion Trace had had all along refused to go away.

The morning was slipping by. He needed to shower and get down to the office. He brought up another photo, tried to compare it to the titles and buyers on the list, then looked up at the sound of the doorbell.

Trace was wearing only his jeans, no shirt, no shoes; and smiled to think he couldn't get past the no-service sign on the door of the Texas Café. He looked through the peephole, saw Maggie standing on his porch, and his chest squeezed.

Dammit. He'd promised himself he would never let a woman make him feel this way again.

He opened the door.

"Good morning," she said brightly. Too brightly, he

thought. "I took a chance you'd still be home. I brought your laptop back. I figured you might need it."

He stepped out of the way to let her pass, got a whiff of her flowery perfume. "Thanks," he said gruffly, raking a hand through his sleep-mussed hair.

He took the laptop from her hand, but she made no move to leave, and he didn't want her to. "Listen, if you've got a few minutes, I could use your help." Damn, she looked pretty with her fiery hair loose. He tried not to think about how lonely he'd been without her. "I could make us a fresh pot of coffee."

"Yes! I—I mean, coffee sounds great." There was something in her eyes he had never seen there before. Something that made his pulse begin to hammer.

"So what kind of help do you need?" she asked, following him into the kitchen.

"I thought I'd finish going through those pictures you took. Just, you know, to satisfy my curiosity and tie up any loose ends."

"I think that's a good idea. What could it hurt, right?" She waited while he made the coffee, and he thought how good it felt to have her back in his house. How much more homey it seemed. Rowdy must have felt the same, because at the sound of her voice, he came trotting into the kitchen and made a beeline straight for her.

"Hello, boy." She petted his thick, black-and-white fur. "I missed you."

Trace wondered if there was any chance she had missed him, too. Wondered what would happen if he just blurted out that he was crazy about her. That he wanted her to move back in.

He didn't, of course. Common sense prevailed. If she wanted to be there, she would have stayed.

While the coffee was dripping, he went back to the living room and put the next photo up on the screen.

"That's called *Magnificent Storm,*" Maggie said, walking up beside him.

He tried not to think of kissing her, lifting her up in his arms and carrying her off to bed. He focused his attention on the list.

"It was one of those sold that night, but it's a seascape. No people in it."

"No."

The next photo came up. *"Rising Tide,"* she said. People playing in the surf, some lying on beach towels in the sand. Most were too far away to see, but a young couple was kissing on a blanket closer to the camera, and there was such an innocence about them it made his chest ache.

"Plenty of people in that one but I don't see anybody doing anything wrong." He smiled. "Unless that couple has something to hide."

"They were newlyweds." Maggie returned the smile. "I talked to them, got them to sign a release, since they appeared so prominently in the photo."

"Probably not about them then, and no one else stands out." He clicked up another picture, the harbor shot he had liked the night of the show.

"I know this one. *Harbor Sunset.* I remember it made me want to go sailing."

"It was taken down at the Blue Fin Marina just as the sun was setting."

"That's near Seabrook. Lots of boats and lots of people."

"It was the end of a perfect day. Most of the boats were back in their slips and people were sitting out on their decks. You can see the names on the back of the yachts along the dock. The sun was coming in at just the right angle. The lighting was perfect. It made a great shot."

"Metadata says it was taken April 20 at 5:42 p.m."

"That sounds about right."

Trace looked down at the list. "Richard Meyers, Senator Logan's aide, bought it."

Maggie walked closer to the screen. "I wonder if Logan owns one of the yachts in the picture."

"As I think back, Cassidy said once that her dad had a really nice boat."

Maggie pointed to one of the expensive white yachts in the picture. "I bet that's his—*Capitol Expense*." It was big and flashy, something a guy like Logan would own.

She studied the photo, which was blown up to fifty-two inches, but in high-definition was relatively clear. "I think that's him—the guy with the silver hair sitting on the deck."

Trace moved nearer. "I think you're right." He studied the photo, beginning to get one of those niggling feelings at the back of his neck. "There's a woman sitting across from him."

"She's got really dark hair, so she isn't his wife."

"Then it's not his daughter, either. Both of them are blonde. Just for fun, let's find out who she is."

"How do we do that? Mainly, we just see her profile."

"We can tell one thing. She's wearing a bikini and she looks damned good in it."

Maggie laughed. "She looks young."

"Young and pretty. I don't think this is one of the senator's constituents."

Maggie looked up at him. "He's running for governor. It wouldn't help him any for word to get out he's having an affair."

Trace studied the photo. The woman was definitely not Cassidy or Teresa Logan. "Hard to believe he'd be willing to burn down your house, though, to keep it quiet."

"I guess it depends on how badly he wants to win."

Trace walked over and touched the screen. "There's something here, on the woman's shoulder. Some kind of colored mark. I can't quite make it out..."

Maggie leaned forward, close enough he could feel her warmth, breathe in that familiar perfume. His body tightened. Damn.

"Might be a tattoo," she said. "She's young. It's kind of the thing to do."

"Maybe." He pulled the card out of the slot in the side of the screen. "I know someone who can help us. He can give us a better look at the woman's face, and we'll find out what the mark is on her shoulder."

The coffee was done, the rich aroma filling the house, but Trace no longer cared. His instincts were screaming, telling him he had just hit the mother lode.

"Can I come with you?" Maggie asked, looking up at him with those pale green eyes that had drawn him in since he had seen her that day at the Texas Café. And though he knew he was being a fool, knew he would only feel worse when she left again, he opened his mouth and said, "Yes."

Maggie waited as Trace made a phone call. When he hung up, he led her out to his Jeep.

"Where are we going?" she asked.

"An old friend of my dad's. Pete Wilkinson. He's retired from NASA. Still does consulting work for them on occasion."

She snapped her seat belt in place, then sat back as Trace headed out of town, driving southeast, winding up in a subdivision in Pasadena. His father's friend must have been watching for them. A man in his late fifties, with iron-gray hair and a paunch around his middle, opened the door and stepped out on the porch as they pulled up in front of his single-story brick house.

"Come on," Trace said, leading Maggie up the walkway. The men shook hands. Introductions were made and Pete led them into his home.

"Thanks for seeing us, Pete. I have a feeling this may be important."

"Well, then, I hope I can help."

Maggie followed the men into Wilkinson's study, which was surprisingly high-tech, considering the rest of the house was simply furnished, with a dark brown overstuffed sofa, newspapers stacked on the coffee table and a dog bowl on the floor next to the kitchen counter. She could tell Pete lived alone.

In comparison, the office looked very space-age, with big screens filling the walls, and banks of computers. Photos of the space shuttle, pictures of the moon landing and impressive colored images from the Hubble telescope hung on what few walls were not otherwise occupied, next to an impressive array of gilt-framed awards.

"Pete worked on the software NASA developed to study the photos sent back to earth from space. They're still using a lot of it." Trace's mouth edged up. "Pete does consulting for the space center when they can't figure things out by themselves."

The older man just smiled. "Keeps me busy. I'm a widower, you see, and not the type to go out and play golf."

"Pete helped my dad with some of his tougher surveillance cases." Trace handed him the digital imaging card. "We're trying to identify a girl in one of the photos."

The photo expert stuck the card into one of his computers and used the keyboard to shoot forward through the pictures.

"There!" Trace stopped him. "That's the one we're interested in."

Pete shoved on a pair of thick-rimmed glasses and peered at the screen. "All right, let's see what we can see." He fiddled with the controls and the computer started enlarging then clarifying the image on the monitor. Enlarging, then clarifying. It didn't take long before they could clearly see Senator Logan's handsome, smiling face on the screen.

"That appears to be our illustrious senator," Pete said.

"That's right."

He went to work on the girl's profile, enlarging and clarifying until her image came sharply into view.

"Can't really see enough of her face to recognize her," Pete said.

Trace turned to Maggie. "Any idea who it might be?"

She shook her head. "No."

Pete went back to work, using his equipment to bring up the patchy image on the young woman's shoulder.

"It's a tattoo, all right," Trace said as the colored design came into focus. "Pretty fancy work."

"Looks like a small, extremely detailed fairy," Pete said, assessing the drawing, which was perfect in every way.

"Yeah. I don't think it's something you'd find in your average tattoo parlor. Guy's a real artist. This is extremely specialized work." Trace looked at Pete. "Can you get us some prints?"

"You bet I can."

A few minutes later, magnified photos of the senator and his lady friend buzzed out of the printer, followed by close-ups of her colorful tattoo. Pete plucked them out of the tray and handed them to Trace.

"Thanks, Pete."

"Let me know how it all turns out, will you?"

"You bet."

"Too bad about your dad," Pete said as he walked them back through the house. "Heart attack." He shook his head. "I always thought he'd go down in a blaze of gunfire."

Trace's smile was tinged with sadness. "I'm sure there were times he thought so, too."

Pete stopped at to the door. "Nice to meet you, Maggie."

"You, too, Pete. We really appreciate your help."

She and Trace left the house, enlargements in hand, and he headed the Jeep toward downtown Houston.

"Where to now?" Maggie asked.

"I've got a friend in the department. Danny Castillo. He's head of the Houston gang division and knows tattoos backward and forward. With a design as intricate as this one, he should be able to tell us who did the work. With any luck, the artist will be able to give us his customer's name."

"You think Castillo will be in?"

"We'll run him down sooner or later. My gut is telling me we're onto something here."

"Maybe the girl was just a friend of a friend."

"Could be. I have a hunch we're going to find out."

As they pushed through the glass doors, Maggie's nerves kicked in. She couldn't help remembering the night she had gone to the police station hoping to get help with a stalker. Instead, she had garnered snide looks and knowing glances, and very little interest in her troubles. She told herself this time would be different.

"He's here," Trace said, returning from a visit to the front desk. "He'll be out in a minute."

Maggie just nodded. Her stomach was in knots, though she told herself this had nothing to do with her, and was probably a waste of time. It didn't take long before a tall, good-looking Hispanic with short black hair combed straight back, and very black eyes, walked toward them.

"Hey, man, good to see you." Castillo shook hands with Trace.

"Danny, this is Maggie O'Connell. She's been dealing with a stalker. We're hoping you can help us run down a lead on something that might be pertinent to the case."

"Sure, whatever I can do. Come on back." Castillo led them down a long hall into a white-walled room that was worn and Spartan, the linoleum floors chipped in places, the baseboards scuffed with shoe marks. The

wooden chairs around the battered table had seen plenty
of wear. "You want some coffee or something?"

"Not for me," Maggie said.

"We're fine," Trace agreed. "We just need you to take
a look at this picture. The tattoo is pretty impressive.
Whoever did it knew what he was doing. We're hoping
you can tell us the name of the artist."

Danny studied the photo and started to frown. "It
was done by a guy named Caesar Hernandez. He's one
of the hottest ink men in Houston. Caesar does one-of-a-
kind tats. Designs the images himself by hand." Danny
glanced up, his expression less friendly than it had been
when they walked in. "Where'd you get this picture?"

"Maggie took it. She's a professional photographer.
What you're looking at is a digital of a shot taken down
at the Blue Fin Marina." Trace handed him the other
close-up images.

"That's Senator Logan," Danny said.

"That's right. We're trying to locate the girl."

Danny's hard gaze zeroed in on Maggie. "When was
this taken?"

Her shoulders tightened. The night she had gone to
the police she had seen that same look on the detectives' faces. "I took it around sunset on April 20. The
date and time is on the original photo."

"Stay right here." Danny left the room, closing the
door solidly behind him.

"What's going on?" Maggie asked, looking up at
Trace, a sick feeling curling in her stomach.

"I don't know. But it looks like Danny knows something that might help us."

"Or maybe he's figured out who I am, and he won't
help us at all."

The door swung open just then and Castillo walked back into the small, suddenly airless room. Another man walked in behind him, stocky, balding, solid as a rock, his expression deadly serious.

"Ms. O'Connell, I'm Captain Roberts. I understand you took this photo April 20 of this year."

"That's right. Around five in the evening."

"The woman in the photo is Isabel Garner. You may have read about her in the papers. She went missing on April 20, but it wasn't reported till the next day."

"Oh, my God." Maggie remembered, all right. She had seen the report on TV.

"A week later, her body washed ashore. Cause of death was blunt force trauma to the head. I'm afraid Ms. Garner was murdered."

Maggie's gaze shot to Trace. His face appeared to be carved in stone.

"Then I guess you'll want to talk to Senator Logan," he drawled. "Since the senator appears to have gone to great lengths to keep this photo from being seen."

"Is that right?" the captain said.

"That's right. You might want to ask him about the man he hired to burn down Ms. O'Connell's studio— a torch job meant to destroy the photo you're looking at now."

The captain gave Maggie the first friendly smile she had received. "That sounds extremely interesting. I believe we'll do just that."

Chapter Thirty-Two

It was over. Garrett Logan and Richard Meyers had been arrested for the murder of Isabel Garner—though they were already out on bail.

Maggie was back in her apartment. Trace was back in his house. She was taking photos again. She was living by herself.

And her heart was broken.

She'd never had the chance to talk to Trace, never summoned the courage to tell him how she felt. Instead, for a long, miserable week she had tried to pull her life back together, put things back the way they were, only to discover she wasn't the same person she had been before.

And she didn't want to be.

Sitting behind the new computer monitor in her half-baked, makeshift office, she thought of Trace and wondered for the hundredth time what would happen if she just drove over to his house, barged in and told him she was in love with him.

Maybe she would, she told herself. But then the telephone started to ring, another excuse that momentarily saved her. For an instant she thought it might be Trace, and she grabbed the receiver.

It was Ashley. "Hi, sis. I just…I wanted to check on you, make sure you were all right."

Things had slipped badly, Maggie realized, when little sister worried about big sister instead of the other way around.

"I'm fine."

"I guess, um, you haven't heard from Trace."

Maggie sighed. "I didn't really expect to. I'm sure he's busy. I'm not his client anymore. I'm sure he has other people to worry about now."

"I guess…."

She forced a little cheer into her voice. "How about you? Everything good with you and Jason? Are you still walking on clouds?"

She could almost see her sister's dreamy smile. "It's just like you said. Jason's amazing, Maggie. I finally found a guy I really have the hots for. I never thought it would be this way—not for me."

Maggie smiled into the phone. "That's wonderful, Ash. I'm happy for both of you."

"Listen, I gotta go. I'll be late for work. I just wanted to check on you."

"I'm fine, really. Call me when you have time to talk."

"I will." The line went dead.

Maggie wandered around the apartment, trying to

get enthused about working. She had some new photos downloaded onto the computer. She told herself they were reasonably good, that with a little tweaking here and there she could use them in her coffee-table book.

She wasn't convinced.

A knock sounded on the door and she brightened at the thought of a distraction—Roxanne, perhaps. Or maybe it was Trace.

Her heart kicked up. She looked down at her T-shirt, which had a camera on the front and Flash Dancer printed underneath, and wished she had time to change. Instead, she hurried to the door.

She hadn't gotten around to upgrading the locks or installing a peephole, but it wasn't as important as it had been. Maggie turned the knob and pulled open the door, and the breath rushed out of her lungs.

"Hello, my dear. I've missed you."

Her chest clenched and for an instant she couldn't breathe. As Phillip Coffman shoved his way into her apartment, she thought of the dozens of photos of herself she had seen on his bedroom walls, and fear made her legs feel weak. She told herself to stay calm. Phillip had never actually hurt her. He hadn't set the fire, they now knew. Senator Logan was responsible for that. Phillip had mostly just spied on her and followed her and made eerie phone calls. And aside from his size, he seemed more pathetic than dangerous.

Still, she eyed the door, trying to judge whether or not she could get past him and make a run for it.

She might have tried—if he hadn't pulled a gun out of his jacket pocket. A big black semiautomatic, something like the one Trace carried.

"Phillip..." she said with a disbelieving breath.

"I've come for you, my dear. It's time for us to be together. Just the way I promised."

Her pulse raced. Her heart hammered so hard she could hear it.

"I thought…I thought you were in the hospital." In for psychic evaluation. Dear God, had they released him and not told her?

"My daughter, Susan, is such a good girl. She and her friend Clayton Arnold made arrangements for me to be released. Clay's a lawyer, you see."

Oh, she saw, all right. Clearly, Coffman had enough lucid moments or his daughter had enough money to pressure the right people into letting him go.

"I was feeling much better, so I came here first thing."

"Why…why did you bring the gun?" she asked.

Coffman looked down at the weapon as if he didn't know he held it in his hand. Then he smiled. "Because it's time, my dear, for us to fulfill our destiny."

Oh, my God, the guy was even further over the edge than he had been before. She started inching around him, moving a tiny bit at a time toward the door.

"I wouldn't do that if I were you." He swung the gun in her direction. "Don't you see, my love? I'm the only one who can save you." He leveled the weapon at her chest, freezing her where she stood. "But first we need some together time to talk about our future."

What future? she thought. *We won't have much of a future if we're dead!*

Phillip motioned with the pistol toward the living room. "Why don't we sit down and make ourselves comfortable? We don't have much time."

Maggie swallowed. If she ran, he might just shoot

her, end things now. But maybe if she bided her time, she could talk him down, or find some way to distract him long enough to escape.

She forced herself to smile. "That's a good idea... dearest."

Trace's fingers felt damp where they held the bouquet of red roses. He hadn't been sure what to buy, but most women liked roses and red ones always seemed the most romantic.

He figured he needed all the help he could get.

For nearly a week, he had talked himself out of coming here, just showing up unannounced at Maggie's door. But the longer he stayed away from her, the more he realized how much he loved her. And he was afraid if he called, he would say the wrong thing.

He might do that anyway. He wasn't great at this love stuff. It had been easy to say the *L* word to Carly, because at the time he didn't really know what love was, and he just figured it was the right thing to do if he was going to marry her.

This time he meant it. He was in love, big-time, and he wasn't going to let this last chance at happiness slip away without a fight. He was a Ranger, wasn't he? At least he had been. Surely he was tough enough to fight for what he wanted.

The only trouble was, he had no real idea what Maggie felt for him, and the last thing he wanted was to marry a woman who didn't love him.

Been there, done that.

There was only one way to find out, he figured, and that was just to straight-out ask her. After all they had been through, he believed she would tell him the truth.

He stepped out of the elevator onto the third floor and started down the corridor to her apartment. Outside the door, he paused long enough to shine his boots on his pant legs. He'd reached for the bell when he heard voices. Maggie's he recognized, the other was clearly male. Trace's chest tightened. Maggie was in there with a man.

His hand squeezed around the stems of the bouquet. He considered tossing the roses away and just leaving, but he had come this far and he wasn't a quitter. Maybe the guy was a client or something. Trace couldn't hear what they were saying, but if that wasn't it, at least he would know the truth.

He reached out and rang the bell, and the conversation inside the apartment instantly stopped. No one came to the door, and he felt as if his heart had stopped, as well.

He summoned his courage. "Maggie?" He rang the bell one last time, knowing she was in there.

No answer. Clearly, she was too busy with her visitor to care if he had come. He dropped the bouquet beside the door and turned to leave, heard the crash of something breaking, then Maggie's high-pitched scream.

"Trace!" she cried out.

Adrenaline shot into every muscle in his body. He raised a booted foot and kicked as hard as he could, felt the door give way and knew a moment of gratitude that there wasn't a dead bolt. "Maggie!"

She stood in the living room, Phillip Coffman behind her with a big-ass semiauto pressed against her head.

"You need to leave," the man said. "This is a private conversation." Coffman's thick arm wrapped around her neck and dragged her more solidly against him. "Get out now."

"Take it easy," Trace soothed. "We're going to work all of this out."

"You aren't supposed to be here. You're interfering with our destiny."

"Put the gun down, Phillip, so we can talk."

The big man shook his head. "You're making this happen too fast. Maggie and I…we need time to make plans for our life together once we reach the astral plane."

She made a little whimpering sound in her throat. Trace wished he could look at her, try to reassure her, but he needed to keep his focus on Coffman. Sometimes he carried a little .25 in his boot, a habit that had served him well on occasion, but it hadn't seemed appropriate to bring it with him today.

"So that's your plan?" he asked Phillip, just to keep him talking. "You both die and go on to live in some other world? What about staying here? You and Maggie making a life together right now?"

Coffman frowned, seeming confused. "Could we do that?"

"I don't see why not. What do you think, Maggie? Don't you think that's a better idea?"

She swallowed, her fingers digging into the arm beneath her chin. "I think it's a fine idea. Phillip and I could get married. We could live right there in his house."

The older man stiffened. "That was Angela's house. We couldn't live there. We have to go somewhere else." He adjusted the gun, pressing it more squarely against her temple. "It's time for us to leave."

"Wait!" Trace moved closer. "If you stayed here, the

two of you could go dancing. Remember that night? Remember the way you danced together? Don't you want to dance like that again?"

Coffman smiled. "I remember. Maggie looked so beautiful that night."

"And you…you were so handsome," she said. "It… it felt wonderful to be held in your arms."

Trace eased closer and Phillip's gaze sharpened. He turned the gun away from Maggie and pointed it squarely at Trace's chest.

"You don't belong here." Something hard and determined moved across his features. There wouldn't be any more words.

Maggie must have read his intent, for just as Phillip squeezed the trigger, she jerked away, knocking his gun hand sideways, destroying his aim. A shot went off with a violent roar. Maggie grabbed for the pistol at the same instant Trace leaped forward. The three of them went down in a heap. Maggie struggled with Coffman, the gun wedged between them. Trace fought to pull her out of danger, and the pistol exploded again.

"Maggie!" Blood poured onto the carpet. Trace heard her soft moan as he leaped to his feet. She lay motionless on top of Coffman. "Maggie!"

She moved just then and he saw it, realized the bullet hadn't hit her but had fired into Coffman's chest. That the blood soaking her clothes belonged to Phillip and not to her. Relief hit him so hard he swayed on his feet.

"Trace…?"

He pulled the gun from Coffman's limp fingers and tossed it away, saw that the shot had torn a ragged hole in the big man's heart. Trace drew Maggie to her feet and eased her into his arms.

"Easy, sweetheart, I've got you."

"Oh, God, Trace." She just hung on and so did he. He wasn't letting her go. Not this time.

"You okay?" he finally asked, though he could feel her trembling.

Maggie clung to him. "I'm okay."

Trace dug his cell phone out of his jeans pocket and punched 911. He reported what had happened and gave the police the address.

The call ended. Maggie still held on to him and a faint sob escaped. "I thought I was going to die," she said. "I thought I would never have a chance to tell you how I feel." She looked up at him, her heart in her eyes. "I love you, Trace. I love you so much. I wanted to tell you, but I was afraid."

He clasped her closer. "I love you, too, Maggie, darlin'. And I'm an even bigger coward than you."

Her pretty green eyes sparkled with tears. "Can I… can I come home?"

His heart swelled with love for her. "That's what I'm here for, darlin'. I came to take you home."

Maggie packed an overnight bag, and once the police allowed them to leave, Trace drove her back to his house.

She had thought all this was finished, first when Phillip Coffman was taken into custody, then two days ago, when the police arrested Garrett Logan for the murder of Isabel Garner. Confronted with traces of the murdered woman's blood on the deck of his yacht, Logan hadn't denied his involvement with the beautiful young woman, but claimed her death was an accident.

His story was that Isabel, who had moved from

Memphis to Houston only two months before she disappeared, had tried to extort him for money. Logan had overreacted, pushed her too hard, and she had hit her head on the railing of his yacht. He'd been frightened and confused, he had said. He had called his aide, and Richard had urged him to take the boat out to sea and dispose of the body.

Meyers had also been arrested.

Both men had denied any knowledge of the fire that destroyed Maggie's town house, though there wasn't much doubt who was responsible.

Logan and Meyers were going to stand trial, and Phillip Coffman was dead. Maggie felt sorry for Coffman's daughter. According to Detective Sayers, Susan Coffman had taken the news of her father's death extremely hard. She had blamed herself for what had happened. Considering Susan was responsible for her father's early release from the psychiatric ward, to some extent, Maggie agreed.

But all that was behind her now. Her life was her own once more, and this time she meant to make the most of it.

It was evening. A soft spring rain had started to fall, pattering softly against the roof. Maggie had showered away some of her fatigue, washed and dried her hair, and put on the white satin peignoir set she had bought after the fire to wear for Trace, but never got around to using.

As for Trace, he had been oddly quiet. Now, watching him walk out of the bedroom barefoot in just his jeans, she wondered what he was thinking. His dark hair still glistened from his recent shower. Drops of water beaded on his powerful chest and the six-pack muscles across his flat stomach.

She walked toward him, the peignoir floating around her ankles. The garment was almost virginal, and she felt that way tonight, as if this would be the first time they made love.

Trace reached out and ran a hand through her hair, pushed a curl behind her ear. "You look beautiful, dar-lin'."

She glanced away, feeling strangely shy. "Thank you."

He cupped her cheek, drawing her attention back to his face. "It feels different now, doesn't it?"

"Yes. Different in a wonderful way."

"I meant what I said. I love you, Maggie. I think I was attracted to those redheads over the years because I was searching for you."

Her eyes filled. "As soon as I moved out, I knew I'd made a mistake. I just didn't know how to undo it. By then I knew I'd found Mr. Right, but it was too late."

He kissed her softly. "Will you marry me, Maggie?"

Her throat closed up. She hadn't expected this, but she knew the answer, had no more doubts about what she wanted. The tears in her eyes spilled onto her cheeks. "I would be honored to marry you."

Trace kissed her again, tenderly at first, then more deeply. Lifting her in his arms, he carried her into the bedroom, her white satin robe spilling over his arm until he set her on her feet beside the bed. He eased the pei-gnoir off her shoulders, leaving on the gown, then lifted and settled her on the mattress, following her down.

His mouth found hers and he kissed her once more, a slow, languid kiss that seemed to have no end. He smelled of soap and man, and tasted fresh and incredibly sexy. She ran her fingers over the muscles of his chest, thinking she would never get tired of touching him, of having him touch her.

Trace just kept kissing her, as if he had all the time in the world, moving lower, trailing hot, moist kisses over her throat and shoulders, down to her breasts. He kissed each one through the slick white satin, ran his tongue over the hardened crests, leaving them damp and aching when he peeled down the narrow satin straps, bent and took the nipples into his mouth.

Maggie arched beneath him, wanting more, wanting him naked and his hard length inside her. She had never desired a man this way, never trusted a man enough to give him her heart.

But she knew this man she loved, knew him to be honorable, caring and generous. Knew him to be truthful in his feelings. Knew that when he said he loved her, he meant the forever kind of love, the kind she was willing to give in return.

Trace eased her nightgown over her head, then left her long enough to dispense with his jeans. Naked, he settled himself between her legs, his beautiful whiskey-brown eyes on her face. He kissed the inside of her thighs and had her trembling. Her body wept for him and her heart ached with love.

There was something different in his lovemaking tonight, something that made her feel worshipped and adored. Something that told her she had found what she had been searching for so long.

Her body heated, turned hot and liquid. Trace knew exactly how to bring her to the peak and beyond, how to use his hands and mouth, just where to touch her to make her fly apart.

She cried out his name, but he didn't stop, not until he had carried her to the peak a second time. Then he came up over her, slid himself deeply inside. Slow and easy, propping himself on his elbows, kissing her and kissing her, stirring back to life the fires that he had so recently tamed.

Outside, the rain fell softly, pattering against the windowpanes. A slight breeze slipped through the trees. Inside the bedroom, the heat of their bodies increased with the friction of their movements. Maggie slid her hands into Trace's silky dark hair, gave herself up to the slow, tantalizing rhythm he set. Deep and penetrating, lazy, sensual strokes that had her moving beneath him, silently begging for more.

His rhythm increased along with his breathing, the pace spiraling upward, her need building. She was close, so very close.

Then she was there, crying out his name as she soared. Trace followed her to release and Maggie clung to him, feeling the rightness of it. The blazing joy.

They floated down together. Trace kissed her one last time.

"You said yes," he whispered against the side of her neck. "You can't change your mind."

Maggie smiled into the darkness. "I found Mr. Right. I'm not going to change my mind."

He rolled onto his back, taking her with him. "When, then?"

Maggie softly kissed him. "How about tomorrow?" she said, and heard a rumble of male satisfaction coming from Trace's hard chest.

Epilogue

They were married two weeks later. Trace didn't want to wait, and Maggie foolishly agreed to the hastily organized wedding that Annie and Ashley helped her arrange.

Damn, he loved her. And this time, he knew he had a woman who loved him in return. A woman he could count on, one who had stood up to a lunatic, put her own life at risk to save his.

The wedding was held in a chapel behind the Methodist Church, a place just the size to hold their small but valued group of friends.

Ashley was Maggie's maid of honor, Roxanne a bridesmaid. Trace asked Devlin Raines to stand as his best man, and Jake Cantrell partnered with Roxanne. Jason was there, grinning like a fool at Ashley, who had finally agreed to wear the beautiful, flawless but unpretentious diamond engagement ring he had bought her.

The rest of Trace's bachelor friends were there. Alex and Ben, and Johnnie Riggs. Once Riggs and Cantrell had met Maggie and seen the two of them together, they resisted ragging him about marrying a redhead. Trace thought maybe they had fallen a little in love with her themselves.

Dev's two brothers, Jackson and Gabriel, flew in for the festivities with their wives, Sarah and Mattie. Evan Schofield was there and Mark Sayers.

Amazingly, Maggie's mom showed up for the wedding. It turned out to be a surprisingly touching reunion between a mother and her daughters.

The reception was held at the Texas Café, which they took over for the evening, and they partied there, dancing to the music of a country band until late into the night.

After the party, a limo took Trace and his bride out to the old family ranch house. He'd prepared it especially for their stay, with rose petals scattered over satin sheets on the old-fashioned four-poster bed, champagne and chocolate-covered strawberries on hand, and enough food laid in for a week.

They hadn't decided yet where they wanted to go for their real honeymoon. Italy, maybe, or Tahiti, or perhaps Australia. A trip Down Under might be an interesting place to visit, and provide some good photo ops for Maggie, give her what she needed to finish her coffee-table book. It really didn't matter as long as they were together.

This morning before the sun was up, he had saddled a couple horses, good, solid, easy-to-handle mounts he rode when he came out to the ranch. Maggie was excited. She hadn't ridden much over the years, she'd said, but she had always enjoyed it.

Most days they weren't doing much but making love, and whatever else hit their fancy.

"You know, darlin'," he said as he helped her swing up in the saddle, waited till she shoved the boots he'd bought her into the stirrups. She looked real good up there, in the white straw cowboy hat that went with the boots, her fiery hair tucked up under the crown. "We haven't talked much about kids."

Her head came up. "Kids? What about them?"

Trace swung into his own horse's saddle, tugged the brim of his hat down over his forehead. Rowdy sniffed the ground at the horses' feet. "You want some, right?"

Maggie grinned. "Oh, yeah. I want a houseful."

Trace hadn't noticed the tension in his shoulders until he heard those words. He relaxed and grinned right back. "Then I guess we'd better get started as soon as we get home."

Maggie laughed and nudged the little sorrel into a trot. "Looks like this ride is going to be shorter than I thought."

Trace's grin widened and Rowdy barked. As the morning sun broke over the horizon, he nudged his horse forward and came up beside her. Together they rode into the glorious future that dawned ahead of them.

* * * * *

Author's Note

I hope you enjoyed Trace and Maggie in *Against the Storm,* the fourth book in my Raines of Wind Canyon series. The novels, all tales of contemporary romantic suspense, began with the Raines brothers, Jackson, Gabriel and Devlin, in *Against the Wind, Against the Fire* and *Against the Law.*

In the next book, *Against the Night,* Trace's friend Johnnie Riggs, who first appeared in *Against the Law,* gets a chance to find love with a sexy little blonde schoolteacher posing as a stripper to find her sister, who has disappeared without a trace. Amy Brewer is willing to do whatever it takes to enlist John Riggs's aid—even if it means giving in to his determined seduction.

It's a tale of romance and high adventure that leads

to true love. I hope you'll watch for *Against the Night,* the next book in the series.

Till then, all best wishes and happy reading.
Kat

Visit the Author Profile page
at Harlequin.com for more titles.

WANTED WOMAN

B.J. Daniels

This book is gratefully dedicated to the Bozeman Writers' Group for all their wonderful support and encouragement. Thank you, Randle, Wenda, Kitty, Bob, LuAnn and Mark. You're the best!

Chapter One

Puget Sound, Seattle

The smell of fish and sea rolled up off the dark water on the late-night air. Restless waves from the earlier storm crashed into pilings under the pier and in the distance a horn groaned through the thick fog.

Maggie shut off the motorcycle and coasted through the shadows and damp fog. She couldn't see a thing. But she figured that was good since he wouldn't be able to see her. Nor hear her coming.

She'd dressed in her black leathers and boots. Even the bulging bike saddlebag was black as the night. She told herself she was being paranoid as she hid the bike and walked several blocks through the dark old warehouses and fish plants before she started down the long pier.

He would be waiting for her somewhere on the pier.

With the dense fog and the crashing surf, she wouldn't know where until she was practically on top of him. She assured herself that she had taken every precaution—short of bringing a weapon.

But she was no fool. He had the advantage. He'd picked the meeting place. He was expecting her. And because of the fog, she wouldn't know what was waiting for her at the end of the deserted pier until she reached it.

Fortunately, she was a woman used to taking chances. Except tonight, the stakes were higher than they'd ever been.

The sound of the sea breaking against the pilings grew louder and louder, the wet fog thicker and blinding white. She knew she had to be nearing the end of the pier.

And suddenly Norman Drake materialized out of the fog.

He looked like hell. Like a man who'd been on the run from the police for three days. He looked scared and dangerous—right down to the gun he had clutched in his right hand.

He waved it at her, his pale blue eyes wide with alarm. And she wondered where he'd gotten the gun and if he knew how to use it. He was young and smart and completely out of his league—a tall, thin bookworm-turned-law-student-turned-law-assistant. She could smell the nervous sweat coming off him, the fear.

"You alone?" he whispered hoarsely.

She nodded.

"You sure you weren't followed?"

"Positive."

He exhaled loudly and wiped his free hand over his mouth. "You bring the money?"

She nodded. The ten thousand dollars he'd demanded weighted down the saddlebag. She reached in slowly and held up one bundle. Unmarked, all old, small denomination bills, dozens of bundles making the bag bulge.

It took him a minute to lower the weapon. His hands shook as he shoved it into the front waistband of his wrinkled, soiled slacks. Not a good idea under any circumstances. As nervous as he was, he'd shoot his nuts off.

"I didn't know who else to call but you," he said, his gaze jumping back and forth between her and the fogged-in pier behind her. "They killed Iverson and they'll kill me, too, if I don't get out of town."

Clark Iverson, her father's longtime attorney, had been murdered three days ago. The police had determined that his temporary student legal assistant was in the building at the time. There was no sign of forced entry. No sign of a struggle. Visitors had to be buzzed in. That's why the cops were actively looking for Norman.

"You told me on the phone you had important information for me about my father's plane crash," she said, keeping her hand clamped on the saddlebag, keeping her tone neutral.

He nodded, a jittery nod that set her teeth on edge. "It wasn't an accident. The same person who murdered Iverson killed your father."

She felt shock ricochet through her. Then disbelief. "It was determined an accident. Pilot failure."

Norman shook his head. "A week before the crash,

your father came into the office. He seemed upset. Later, after he left, I overheard Iverson on the phone telling someone he couldn't talk your dad out of it."

"That's not enough evidence—"

"I was there three nights ago. I heard them talking about the plane crash. Iverson had figured out that the plane had gone down to keep your father from talking. He threatened to go to the Feds. I heard them kill him—" Emotion choked off the last of his words.

"You actually heard someone admit to murdering my father?"

He nodded, his Adam's apple going up and down, up and down. She watched him, shock and pain and anger mixing with the grief of the past two months since the single passenger plane had gone down on a routine business flight. She fought to keep her voice calm. "You said *they?*"

He seemed surprised by the question. "Did I? I only heard one man talk but—" He frowned and looked away. "I remember thinking I heard two people coming down the hall after the elevator opened." He was lying and doing a poor job of it. Why lie about how many killers there were? "You believe me, don't you?"

She didn't know what to believe now. But her father had liked Norman, thought he was going to make a good lawyer someday. Good lawyer, an oxymoron if there ever was one, her father would have joked. "Norman, how did they get in? The building was locked, right?"

He nodded, looking confused. "I guess Iverson buzzed them up. All I know is that I heard the elevator and—" He looked behind her again as if he'd heard something. "I somehow knew not to let them know I was there."

A foghorn let out a mournful moan from out beyond the city.

"You're telling me Clark didn't *know* you were still in the office?"

Norman fidgeted. "I'd fallen asleep in the library doing some research for him. The door to his office was closed. Earlier, he'd told me to leave, to do the rest in the morning. I guess he thought I'd left by the door to the hallway. The elevator woke me, then I heard voices arguing."

Just seconds before he'd said he'd heard two sets of footsteps coming down the hall after the elevator opened. No wonder Norman hadn't gone to the police. His story had so many holes it wouldn't even make good Swiss cheese.

"You heard them arguing?" she asked.

He nodded. "Then I heard this like…grunt and glass breaking—" He closed his eyes as if imagining Clark Iverson's body, the lamp he'd grabbed as he went down shattered on the floor next to him, his eyes open staring blindly upward, a knife sticking out of his chest at heart level, just as he'd looked when his secretary and Maggie had found him the next morning. Just as he must have looked when Norman saw him.

"You didn't see the killer."

"No, I told you, I just ran."

"Why didn't you call the police?" It was the same question the cops wanted to ask him.

Norman closed his eyes tightly as if in pain. "After they killed him, they rummaged around in his desk drawers, in his file cabinets. I could hear them. I was afraid that at any minute they'd come into the library and find me." Another look away, another lie. "I just ran. I took the stairs, let myself out the back way and I've been running ever since. If they find me, they'll kill me."

"Did you recognize the one voice you heard?"

He shook his head.

"But you heard what they were arguing about."

"Iverson said the secret wasn't worth killing people over."

"What secret?"

Norman squirmed, his gaze flicking past her. "An illegal adoption."

She felt a chill come off the ocean as if she already knew what his next words would be.

"You were the baby," Norman said, the words tumbling over themselves in their struggle to get out. "Iverson wanted to tell you the truth. That's why they killed him. He said your father had found out and was going to tell you."

"Found out what?" So her parents hadn't gone through the proper channels. So what? "I'm twenty-seven years old. Why would anyone kill over my adoption no matter how it went down?"

"It was the way you were…acquired," Norman said. "Your father had found out that you were kidnapped."

Kidnapped? She'd always known she was adopted and that was the reason she looked nothing like her parents. Nor was anything like them.

Mildred and Paul Randolph had always seemed a little surprised by their only child, a little leery. Maggie had come into their life after they'd tried numerous adoption agencies, they'd told her. She'd been a miracle, they'd said. A gift from God.

Maybe not quite.

Although well-off financially, her parents weren't the ideal adoptive candidates. Her mother had been confined to a wheelchair since childhood polio and her father was considered too old. He'd been fifty when Maggie had come along. But, according to both Mildred and Paul, they'd finally found an agency that understood how desperately they wanted a child and had given Maggie to them to love.

No child could have asked for more loving parents. But they'd been horribly overprotective, so afraid something would happen to her, that Maggie had become fearless in self-defense. By the age of twenty-seven, she'd tried everything from skydiving and bungee jumping to motorcross, heli-skiing and speedboat racing.

Her parents had been terrified. Now she realized they'd been afraid long before their only child had become a thrill-seeker. Now she knew why she'd seen fear in her father's eyes all of her life. He'd been waiting all these years for the other shoe to drop.

It had finally dropped. He'd found out she was kidnapped and couldn't live with the knowledge.

She heard a board creak behind her, heavy with a tentative step. "Norman, you have to tell the police what you told me. They'll protect you."

"Are you *nuts?* You can't trust anyone. These people have already killed twice to keep their secret. Who knows how influential they are or what connections they might have."

He'd seen the killer and knew something he wasn't telling her. That's why he was so afraid. Well, maybe the cops could get the truth out of him. "Norman, I called the detective on the case after I talked to you. Detective Blackmore."

"What?" He looked around wildly. "Don't you realize what you've done?" He grabbed for the saddlebag. "Give me the money. I have to get out of here. Quick. He'll kill us both if—" Norman broke off, his gaze riveted on something just over her left shoulder, eyes widening in horror.

She heard the soft pop, didn't recognize the sound until she saw blood bloom across the shoulder of Norman's jacket. The second shot—right on the heels of the first—caught him in the chest, dead-on.

His grip on the saddlebag pulled her down with him as he fell to the weathered boards, dropping her to her knees beside him.

"Oh, Norman. Oh, God." Her mind reeled. The police wouldn't have shot him. Not without a warning first. But who else had known about their meeting?

The third shot sent a shaft of pain tearing through her left arm as she tried to free herself of the saddlebag strap and Norman's death grip.

"Timber Falls," he whispered, blood running from the corner of his mouth as his fingers released the bag of money and her. "That's where they got you." Adding on his last breath, "Run."

But there was no place to run. She was trapped. Behind her, she heard the groan of a board, caught the scent of the killer on the breeze, a nauseating mix of perspiration, cheap cologne and stale cigar smoke.

She had only one choice. She fell over Norman, rolling him with her, using his body as a shield as a fourth shot thudded into his dead body.

As she fell, she looked up, saw the man with the gun come out of the fog. Shock paralyzed her as her eyes met his and she realized she knew him.

She let out a cry as he raised the gun and pulled the trigger. Two more shots thudded into Norman's riddled body as she rolled off the end of the pier, taking Norman and the saddlebag with her, dropping for what seemed an eternity before plunging into the cold, dark roiling water below.

Chapter Two

Outside Timber Falls, Oregon

Jesse Tanner had been restless for days. He stood on his deck, looking down the steep timbered mountain into the darkness, wishing for sleep. It had been raining earlier. Wisps of clouds scooted by on a light breeze.

He sniffed the cedar-scented air as if he could smell trouble, sense danger, find something to explain the restlessness that haunted his nights and gave him no peace.

But whatever was bothering him remained as elusive as slumber.

A sound drew him from his thoughts. A recognizable throaty rumble. He looked toward the break in the trees below him on the steep mountain to the strip of pavement that was only visible in daylight. Or for those few moments when headlights could be seen at night on the isolated stretch of highway below him.

The single light came out of the trees headed in the direction of Timber Falls. A biker, moving fast, the throb of the big cycle echoing up to him.

Jesse watched the motorcycle glide like warm butter over the wet, dark pavement and wished that he was on it, headed wherever, destination unknown.

But that was the old Jesse Tanner. This Jesse was through wandering. Through with the open road. This Jesse had settled down.

Not that he still couldn't envy the biker below him on the highway. Or remember that heady feeling of speed and darkness and freedom. There was nothing like it late at night when he had the road to himself. Just an endless ribbon of black pavement stretched in front of him and infinite possibilities just over the next rise.

He started to turn away but a set of headlights flickered in the trees as a car came roaring out of a side road across the highway below him. He watched, frozen in horror as the car tore out of Maple Creek Road and onto the highway—directly into the path of the motorcycle.

He caught a flash of bright red in the headlamp of the bike and saw the car, a convertible, the top down and the dark hair of the woman behind the wheel blowing back, in that instant before the bike collided with the side of the car, clipping it. The bike and rider went down.

Jesse gripped the railing as the bike slid on its side down the pavement, sparks flying as the car sped away into the darkness and trees, headed toward Timber Falls, five miles away.

He was already running for the old pickup he kept for getting firewood. Other than that, all he had was his Harley. Taking off down his jeep trail of a road in the truck, he dropped down the face of the mountain, fearing what he'd find when he reached the pavement.

At the highway, he turned north. It was darker down here with the forest towering on each side of the two-lane. In the slit of sky overhead, clouds scudded past, giving only brief glimpses of stars and a silver sliver of moon.

He hadn't gone far when he spotted the fallen bike in his headlights. It lay on its side in the ditch, the single headlamp casting a stationary beam of gold across the wet highway. Where was the biker?

Driving slowly up the road, he scanned the path with his headlights looking for the downed rider, bracing himself for what he'd find.

A dozen yards back up the highway from the bike, something gleamed in his headlights. The shiny top of a bike helmet. The biker lay on his side at the edge of the road, unmoving.

Jesse swore and stopped, turning on his emergency flashers to block any traffic that might come along. He didn't expect any given the time of the night—or the season. Early spring—the rainy season in this part of the country. People with any sense stayed clear of the Pacific side of the Cascades where, at this time of year, two hundred inches of rain fell pretty much steadily for seven months. The ones who lived here just tried not to go crazy during the rainy season. Some didn't succeed.

Following the beams of his headlights, he jumped out of the pickup and ran across the wet pavement toward the biker, unconsciously calculating the odds that the guy was still alive, already debating whether to get him into the back of the truck and run him to the hospital or not move him and go for help.

As he neared, he heard a soft moan and saw movement as the biker came around. Jesse figured he was witnessing a miracle given how fast the motorcycle had been traveling.

"Take it easy," he said as the figure in all black leathers coughed as if gasping for breath and tried to sit up. The biker was small, slim and a damned lucky dude.

As Jesse knelt down beside him in the glow of the pickup's headlights, he saw with shock that he'd been wrong and let out an oath as a hand with recently manicured nails pulled off the helmet. A full head of long dark curly hair tumbled out and a distinctly female voice said, "I'm okay."

"Holy…" he said, rocking back on his heels. This was one damned lucky…*chick*.

She had her head down as if a little groggy.

He watched her test each leg, then each arm. "Are you sure you're not hurt?" He couldn't believe everything was working right. "Nothing's broken?"

She shook her head, still bent over as if trying to catch her breath.

He waited, amazed as he took in the leather-clad body. Amazed by the bod and the bike. She was wheeling a forty-thousand-dollar ride that most men couldn't handle. A hell of a bike for a girl. It was too heavy for anyone but an expert rider. No wonder she'd been able to dump the bike and not get hurt.

She tried to get up again.

"Give it another minute. No hurry," he said, looking from her back up the highway to her bike. This gal had nine lives, a whole lot of luck and she knew how to ride that fancy bike. He wasn't sure what impressed him more.

"I'm all right." Her voice surprised him. It was all female, cultured and educated-sounding and in stark contrast to her getup and her chosen mode of transportation.

But the real shocker was when she lifted her head, flipping back her hair, and he saw her face.

All the air went out of him as if she'd sucker punched him. "Sweet mother—" he muttered, rearing back again. She was breathtaking. Her skin was the color of warm honey, sprinkled with cinnamon-and-sugar freckles across high cheekbones. And her eyes... They were wide and the color of cedar, warm and rich. She was exquisite. A natural beauty.

And there was something almost familiar about her...

She tried to get to her feet, bringing him out of his dumbfounded inertia.

"Here, let me help you," he said and reached under her armpits to lift her to her feet. She was amazingly light and small next to him.

She accepted his help with grace and gratitude even though it was clear she liked doing things for herself.

She took a step. "Ouch," she said under her breath and swayed a little on her feet.

"What is it?"

"My left ankle. It's just sprained."

Maybe. Maybe not. "I'll take you to the hospital emergency room to see a doctor."

She shook her head. "Just get me to my bike."

"It's not rideable." He'd seen enough twisted metal on it even in passing to know that. "I'll load it into my pickup. There's not a bike shop for a hundred miles but I've worked on a few of my own. I might be able to fix it."

She looked up at him then as if seeing him for the first time. Her eyes narrowed as she took in the boots, jeans, bike rally T-shirt and his long dark ponytail. Her gaze settled on the single gold ring in his earlobe. "You live around here?"

"Right up that mountain," he said, pointing to the light he'd left on. It glowed faintly high up the mountainside.

She studied it. Then him.

It was three in the morning but he had to ask. "Is anyone expecting you up the road, anyone who'll be worried about you? Because I don't have a phone yet."

She didn't seem to hear him. "You have ice for my ankle at your place?"

He nodded.

"Good. That's all I need."

"I have a clean bed you're welcome to for what's left of the night," he offered.

She flashed him an in-your-dreams look.

He smiled and shook his head. "All I'm offering is a bed. Maybe something to eat or drink. Some ice. Nothing more."

She cocked her head at him, looking more curious than anything else. He wondered what she saw. Whatever it was, he must have looked harmless enough before she started to limp toward her bike. "I need my saddlebag."

"I'll get it," he said, catching up to her and offering a hand. "No reason to walk on that ankle any more than you have to." She quirked an eyebrow at him but said nothing as she slipped one arm around his shoulder and let him take her weight as she hobbled to the pickup.

As he opened the passenger-side door and slid her into his old truck, he felt way too damned chivalrous. Also a little embarrassed by his old truck.

She glanced around the cab, then settled back into the seat and closed her eyes. He slammed the door and went to load her bike.

He'd only seen a couple of these bikes. Too expensive for most riders. It definitely made him wonder about the woman in his pickup. The bike didn't look as if it was hurt bad. He figured he should be able to fix it. He liked the idea of working on it. The bike intrigued him almost as much as the woman who'd been riding it.

He rolled the bike up the plank he kept in the back of his pickup, retrieved her saddlebag and, slamming the tailgate, went around to climb into the cab of the truck beside her. He set the heavy, bulging saddlebag on the seat beside them.

She cracked an eyelid to see that the bag was there, then closed her eyes again.

"The name's Jesse. Jesse Tanner."

She didn't move, didn't open her eyes. "Maggie," she said, but offered no more.

He started the engine, shifted into first gear and headed back up the mountain to his new place. The road was steep and rough, but he liked being a little inaccessible. He saw her grimace a couple of times as he took the bumps, but she didn't open her eyes until he parked in front of the cabin.

She looked up at the structure on the hillside, only the living-room light glowing in the darkness.

"This is where you live?" she said and, opening her

door, got out, slipping the saddlebag over her shoulder protectively.

Something in her tone made him wonder if she meant the cabin or the isolated location. The only visitors he'd had so far were his younger brother, Mitch, and his dad. He figured if he wanted to be social, he knew the way to town and it was only five miles. Not nearly far enough some days.

He looked at the cabin, trying to see it through her eyes. It was tall and narrow, a crude place, built of logs and recycled cedar, but he was proud of it since he'd designed and built it over the winter with the help of his dad and brother. It had gone up fast.

Three stories, the first the living room and kitchen, the second a bedroom and bath with a screened-in deck where he planned to sleep come summer, the third his studio, a floor flanked with windows, the view incredible.

Unfortunately, it was pretty much a shell. He hadn't furnished the inside yet. Hadn't had time. So all he had was the minimal furniture he'd picked up.

Lately, he'd been busy getting some paintings ready for an exhibit in June, his first, and— He started to tell her all of that, but stopped himself. It wasn't like she would be here more than a few hours and then she'd be gone. She didn't want his life history, he could see that from her expression.

He'd been there himself. No roots. No desire to grow any. Especially no desire to be weighed down even with someone's life story.

She was standing beside the pickup staring up at his cabin as he climbed out of the truck.

"It's still under construction," he said, irritated with

himself for wanting her to like it. But hell, she *was* the first woman he'd had up here since it was built.

"It's perfect," she said. "Neoclassical, right?"

He smiled, surprised at her knowledge of architecture. But then again, she was riding a forty-thousand-dollar bike and had another couple grand in leather on her back, spoke like she'd been to finishing school and carried herself as if she knew her way around the streets. All of that came from either education, money or experience. In her case, he wondered if it wasn't all three.

She caught him admiring the way her leathers fit her.

"Let's get you inside," he said quickly. "You hungry?"

She shook her head and grabbed the railing, limping up the steps to the first floor, making it clear she didn't need his help.

"You sure you don't want to see a doctor? I could run you into town—"

"No." Her tone didn't leave any doubt.

"Okay." He'd had to try.

They'd reached the front door. She seemed surprised it wasn't locked. "I haven't much to steal and most thieves are too lazy to make the trek up here." He swung the door open and she stepped inside, her gaze going at once to his paintings he'd done of his years in Mexico.

He had a half dozen leaning against the bare living-room wall waiting to go to the framer for the exhibit. She limped over to them, staring at one and then another.

"How about coffee?" he offered, uncomfortable with the way she continued to study his work as if she were seeing something in the paintings he didn't want exposed.

He couldn't decide if she liked them or not. He wasn't about to ask. He had a feeling she might tell him.

While she'd been studying the paintings he'd been studying her. As she shrugged out of her jacket, he saw that she wore a short-sleeved white T-shirt that molded her breasts and the muscles of her back. She was in good shape and her body was just as exquisite as he'd thought it would be beneath the leather.

But what stole his attention was the hole he'd seen in the jacket just below her left shoulder—and the corresponding fresh wound on her left biceps. He'd seen enough gunshot wounds in his day to recognize one even without the telltale hole in the leather jacket.

The bullet had grazed her flesh and would leave a scar. It wasn't her first scar, though. There was another one on her right forearm, an older one that had required stitches.

Who the hell was this woman and what was it about her?

"These are all yours," she said, studying the paintings again. It was a statement of fact as if there was no doubt in her mind that he'd painted them.

"I have tea if you don't like coffee."

"Do you have anything stronger?" she asked without turning around.

He lifted a brow behind her back and went to the cupboard. "I have some whiskey." He turned to find her glancing around the cabin. Her gaze had settled on an old rocker he'd picked up at a flea market in Portland.

"That chair is pretty comfortable if you'd like to sit down," he said, as he watched her run her fingers over the oak arm of the antique rocker.

She looked at him as she turned and lowered herself

into the rocker, obviously trying hard not to let him see that her ankle was hurting her if not the rest of her body. Maybe nothing was broken but she'd been beat up. Wait until tomorrow. She was going to be hurtin' for certain.

He handed her half a glass of whiskey. He poured himself a tall glass of lemonade. The whiskey had been a housewarming gift from a well-meaning friend in town. He'd given up alcohol when he'd decided it was time to settle down. He'd seen what alcohol had done for his old man and he'd never *needed* the stuff, especially now that he was painting again.

He watched Maggie over the rim of his glass as he took a drink. He'd made the lemonade from real lemons. It wasn't half-bad. Could use a little more sugar, though.

She sniffed the whiskey, then drained the glass and grimaced, nose wrinkling, as if she'd just downed paint thinner. Then she pushed herself to her feet, limped over to him and handed him the glass. "Thank you."

"Feeling better?" he asked, worried about her and not just because of her bike wreck.

"Fine."

He nodded, doubting it. He wanted to ask her how she'd gotten the bullet wound, what she'd been doing on the highway below his place at three in the morning, where she was headed and what kind of trouble she was in. But he knew better. He'd been there and he wasn't so far from that life that he didn't know how she would react to even well-meaning questions.

"I promised you ice," he said, and finished his lemonade, then put their glasses in the sink and filled a plastic bag with ice cubes for her ankle. "And a place to lie down while I take a look at your bike." He met her gaze. She still wasn't sure about him.

He realized just how badly he wanted her to trust him as he gazed into those brown eyes. Like her face, there was something startlingly familiar about them.

She took the bag of ice cubes and he led her up the stairs, stopping at his bedroom door.

"You can have this room. The sheets are clean." He hadn't slept on them since he'd changed them.

"No, that one's yours," she said and turned toward the open doorway to the screened-in deck. There was an old futon out there and a pine dresser he planned to refinish when he had time. "I'll sleep in here."

He started to argue, but without turning on the light, she took the bag of ice and limped over to the screened windows, her back to him as she looked out into the darkness beyond.

Fetching a towel from the bathroom, he returned to find her still standing at the window. She didn't turn when he put the towel on the futon, just said, "Thank you."

"De nada." He was struck with the thought that if he had been able to sleep he would never have seen her accident, would never have met her. For some reason that seemed important as if cosmically it had all been planned. He was starting to think like his future sister-in-law, Charity, and her crazy aunt Florie, the self-proclaimed psychic.

He really needed to get some decent sleep, he concluded wryly, if he was going to start thinking crap like that. "There are sheets and blankets in the dresser and more towels in the bathroom." He would have gladly made a bed for her but he knew instinctively that she needed to be alone.

"About my bike—"

"I think I can fix it," he said. "Otherwise, I can give you and the bike a lift into Eugene."

She turned then to frown at him. "You'd do that?"

He nodded. "I used to travel a lot on my bike and people helped me. Payback. I need the karma." He smiled.

Her expression softened with her smile. She really was exquisite. For some reason, he thought of Desiree Dennison, the woman he'd seen driving the red sports car that had hit Maggie. "I can also take you in to see the sheriff in the morning. I know him pretty well."

"Why would I want to see him?" she asked, frowning and looking leery again.

"You'll want to press charges against the driver of the car that hit you."

She said nothing, but he saw the answer in her eyes. No chance in hell was she sticking around to press charges against anyone.

"Just give a holler if you need anything," he said.

Her gaze softened again and for an instant he thought he glimpsed vulnerability. The instant passed. "Thank you again for everything."

My pleasure. He left the bathroom door open and a light on so she could find it if she needed it, then went downstairs, smiling as he recalled the face she'd made after chugging the whiskey. Who the hell was she? Ruefully, he realized the chances were good that he would never know.

Maggie hurt all over. She put the ice down on the futon and limped closer to the screened window. The night air was damp and cool, but not cold.

She stared out, still shaken by what had happened on the dock, what she'd learned, what she'd witnessed.

She'd gotten Norman killed because she'd called Detective Rupert Blackmore.

Below, a door opened and closed. She watched Jesse Tanner cross the mountainside to a garage, open the door and turn on the light. An older classic Harley was parked inside, the garage neat and clean.

She watched from the darkness as he went to the truck, dropped the tailgate, pulled out the plank then climbed up and carefully rolled her bike down and over to the garage.

For a long moment he stood back as if admiring the cycle, then slowly he approached it. She caught her breath as he ran his big hands over it, gentle hands, caressing the bike the way a man caressed a woman he cherished.

She moved away from the window, letting the night air slow her throbbing pulse and cool the heat that burned across her bare skin. She told herself it was the effects of the whiskey not the man below her window as she tried to close her mind to the feelings he evoked in her. How could she feel desire when her life was in danger?

She'd been running on adrenaline for almost thirty-six hours now, too keyed up to sleep or eat. Her stomach growled but she knew she needed rest more than food at this point. She could hear the soft clink of tools in the garage, almost feel the warm glow of the light drifting up to her.

She took a couple of blankets from the chest of drawers. Wrapping the towel he'd left her around the bag of ice, she curled up on the futon bed, put the ice on her ankle and pulled the blankets up over her.

The bed smelled of the forest and the night and possibly the man who lived here. She breathed it in finding a strange kind of comfort in the smell and sound of him below her.

She closed her eyes tighter, just planning to rest until he was through with her bike, knowing she would never be able to sleep. Not when she was this close to Timber Falls. This close to learning the truth. Just a few more miles. A few more hours.

Tonight on the highway when the car had pulled out in front of her, she'd thought at first it was Detective Rupert Blackmore trying to kill her again.

But then she'd caught a glimpse of the female driver in that instant before she'd hit the bright red sports car.

She'd seen the young woman's startled face in the bike's headlight, seen the long dark hair and wide eyes, and as Maggie had laid the bike on its side, she'd heard the car speed off into the night all the time knowing that the cop would have never left. He would have finished her off.

She feared that Norman's body had washed up by now. And it was only a matter of time before Blackmore realized her body wouldn't be washing up because she hadn't drowned.

How soon would he figure out where she'd gone and what she was up to and come here to stop her?

But what was it he didn't want her finding out? That she was kidnapped? Or was there something more, something he feared even worse that she would uncover?

Right now, all she knew was that people were dying because of *her.* Because her parents had wanted a baby so desperately that they'd bought one, not knowing that she'd been kidnapped from a family in Timber Falls, Oregon.

Her ankle ached. She tried not to think. Detective Rupert Blackmore was bound to follow her to Timber Falls. Unless he was already in town waiting for her.

Sleep came like a dark black cloak that enveloped her. She didn't see the fog or Norman lying dead at her feet or the cop on the pier with the gun coming after her. And for a while, she felt safe.

Chapter Three

Maggie woke with a start, her heart pounding. Her eyes flew open but she stayed perfectly still, listening for the thing she feared most.

The creak of a floorboard nearby. The soft rustle of clothing. The sound of a furtive breath taken and held.

She heard nothing but the cry of a blue jay and the soft whisper of the breeze in the swaying dark pines beyond her bed.

She opened her eyes, surprised to see that the soft pale hues of dawn had lightened the screened-in room. She'd slept. That surprised her. Obviously she'd been tired, but to sleep in a perfect stranger's house knowing there was someone out there who wanted her dead? She must have been more exhausted than she'd thought.

She listened for a moment, wondering what sound had awakened her and if it was one she needed to worry about. Silence emanated from within the house and there was no longer the soft clink of tools.

Sitting up, she retrieved the bag and towel, and swung her legs over the side of the bed. The ice she'd had on her ankle had melted. Some of the water had leaked onto the futon. The towel was soaked and cold to the touch.

She scooped up both towel and bag and pushed to her feet to test her ankle. Last night she'd been scared that her ankle was hurt badly. Anything that slowed her down would be deadly.

Her ankle was stiff and painful, but she could walk well enough. And ride. She stood on the worn wood-plank flooring and took a few tentative steps toward the screened windows. That is, she could ride if her bike was fixed.

She glanced out. The garage door was shut, the light out. The back of the pickup was empty. Her bike sat in front of the house, resting on its kickstand, her helmet sitting on top, waiting for her. He'd fixed it.

The swell of relief and gratitude that washed over her made her sway a little on her weak ankle. Tears burned her eyes. His kindness felt like too much right now. She turned toward the open doorway. She'd left her door open and so it seemed had he. As she neared the short hallway between the rooms, she could see him sleeping in his double bed, the covers thrown back, only the sheet over him.

He was curled around his pillow on his side facing her, his masculine features soft in sleep. A lock of his long, straight black hair fell over one cheek, shiny and dark as a raven's wing. She caught the glint of his earring beneath the silken strands, the shadow of his strong stubbled jaw, the dark silken fringe of his eye-lashes against his skin.

Even asleep the man still held her attention, still ex-uded a wild sensuality, a rare sexuality. This man would be dangerous to a woman. And she didn't doubt he'd known his share. Intimately. Or that he was a good lover. She'd seen the way he'd touched her bike. She'd seen his artwork. Both had made her ache. Fear for her life hadn't stolen her most primitive desires last night. Nor this morning.

But what surprised her wasn't her attraction to the man, but that she felt safe with him. Too safe.

She moved silently down the hallway. He'd left a small light burning in the bathroom for her. That gesture even more than the others touched her deeply. She closed the door behind her and poured what water was left in the plastic bag down the drain, then hung up the towel.

She washed her face, avoiding looking at the stranger in the mirror. She'd spent too many years questioning who she was. Now she was about to find out and she didn't want to face it or what her adoptive parents might have done in their desperation for a child.

She knew money had exchanged hands. Most adoptions involved an exchange of money, although she hated to think what her parents had paid for her. What frightened her was how the purchase had been made. And why someone was now trying to kill her to keep her from finding out.

No one committed multiple murders to cover up an illegal adoption or even a kidnapping. Especially after twenty-seven years. There had to be more to it. What was someone afraid would come to light?

According to Norman, the answer was in Timber Falls—just a few miles away now. She had raced here, running for her life, rocketing through the darkness toward the truth. But now that she was so close, she feared what she would find.

When she was younger, she'd often thought about finding her biological parents. Of course, her adoptive parents had discouraged her. Now she knew it wasn't just because they didn't want to share her.

Unfortunately, now she had no choice but to find out who she really was. And hopefully the answer would save her life. But what would her life be worth once she knew the truth?

As she turned to leave the bathroom, she froze. A sheriff deputy's uniform hung on the hook of the closed door.

The call came before daylight. Detective Rupert Blackmore was lying on his bed, fully clothed, flat on his back, staring up at the ceiling. Certainly not asleep. He'd been waiting for the phone to ring, willing it to ring with the news he needed.

Praying for it. Although praying might not have been exactly what he'd been doing. Right now he would have sold his soul to the devil if he hadn't already traded it to Satan a long time ago.

He let the phone ring three times, then picked up the receiver. "Detective Blackmore."

"Just fished a body out of the sea near the old pier," said his subordinate, a young new detective by the name of Williams. "Six gunshot wounds. Dead before the body hit the water. Definitely a homicide."

Rupert Blackmore held his breath as he got to his feet beside the bed. "Has the body been IDed?"

"Affirmative. Norman Drake. Wallet was in his pocket. The guy we've been looking for in connection with the murder of his boss, attorney Clark Iverson."

As if Rupert didn't know that. He tried not to let Williams hear his disappointment that Norman's body was the only one found so far. "Close off the entire area. I want it searched thoroughly. Drake didn't act alone and now it appears there's been a falling out among murderers."

He hung up and cursed, then in a fit of rage and frustration, knocked the phone off the nightstand, sending it crashing to the floor.

He sat down on the edge of the bed and lowered his head to his hands. Her body would wash up. Then all of this would be over. He took a deep breath, rose and picked up the phone. Carefully he put it back on the nightstand, thanking God that his wife, Teresa, was at her mother's and wouldn't be back for a few more days. Plenty of time to get this taken care of before she returned.

As he headed for the door, he tried not to worry. Once Margaret Randolph was dead, no one would ever find out the truth. And it would never get back that he hadn't taken care of this problem twenty-seven years ago as he'd been paid to do.

One moment of kindness… He scoffed at his own worn lie. He'd done it for the money. Plain and simple. He'd sold the baby instead of disposing of it. And he'd never regretted it—until Paul Randolph found out the truth. Now Rupert had to take care of things quickly and efficiently before everything blew up in his face. No more mistakes like the one he'd made the other night at the pier. There was no way he should have missed her. He'd been too close and was too good of a shot.

He tried to put the mistakes behind him. Look to the future. And the future was simple. If Margaret Randolph wasn't floating in Puget Sound with the fish, she soon would be.

Maggie stared at the sheriff's deputy uniform and tried to breathe. Jesse Tanner was a cop? Last night he'd said he knew the sheriff. She'd just assumed because it was a small town, everyone knew everyone else.

She stifled a groan. Not only had she stayed in the house of the local deputy, but now he might have the plate number on her bike. If he'd had reason to take it down.

Fear turned her blood to ice. He could find out her last name—if he didn't already know. Worse, he could tell Blackmore that not only was she alive but that she was in Timber Falls.

But why would Jesse Tanner run the plate number on her bike? She hadn't given him any reason to. Cops didn't need a reason, though. And everyone knew they stuck together.

Except Jesse was different. He didn't act like a cop. Didn't insist she go to the doctor last night or the sheriff this morning. Didn't ask a lot of questions.

She tried to calm her pounding heart. Her hands were shaking as she wiped down the faucets and anything else she might have touched. Were her fingerprints on a file somewhere? She didn't know.

She thought she remembered being fingerprinted as a child. She knew her parents had worried about her being kidnapped. How ironic. And she'd always thought it was because of their wealth.

As she opened the bathroom door, she half expected the deputy to be waiting for her just outside. The hallway was empty. She stood listening.

Silence. Tiptoeing down the hall, she passed his open doorway again. He had rolled over, his back to her now. She prayed he would stay asleep as she eased into the screened-in deck where she'd slept.

She picked up her boots, her jacket and the saddlebag stuffed with most of the ten grand from the pier. Then she looked around to make sure she hadn't left anything behind before she limped quietly down the stairs.

At the bottom, she glanced at his paintings as she pulled on her boots, the left going on painfully because of her ankle. What she now knew about the man upstairs seemed at odds with his art. Jesse Tanner and his chisel-cut features, the deep set of matching dimples, the obsidian black eyes and hair, the ponytail and the gold earring didn't go with the deputy sheriff's uniform.

There was a wildness about the man, something he seemed to be trying to keep contained, but couldn't hide in his artwork. The large, bold strokes, the use of color, the way he portrayed his subjects.

Her favorite of the six paintings propped against the wall was a scene from a Mexican cantina. A series of men were watching a Latin woman dance. The sexual tension was like a coiled spring. In both the work and the painter.

He was talented, too talented not to be painting full-time. So why was he working as a sheriff's deputy? He didn't seem like the type who liked busting people for a living. Quite the opposite.

She glanced around the cabin. She liked it. Liked him. Wished he wasn't a cop. She told herself she shouldn't feel guilty for just running out on him.

Last night she'd been shaken from her accident, hurt and exhausted. She had needed a refuge and he'd provided it, asking nothing in return. He would never know how much that meant to her.

Under other circumstances, she would never have left without thanking him. But these were far from normal circumstances, she reminded herself and remembered the glass of whiskey she'd drunk last night.

Going to the sink, she turned on the faucet and washed both glasses thoroughly, then dried them. Being careful not to leave her prints anywhere, she set the glasses back on the cabinet shelf with the others and wiped down the faucet and handles just as she had in the bathroom upstairs.

She knew she was being overly cautious. But maybe that was why she was still alive.

Her bike was sitting outside, her helmet on the seat as if he'd put it there to let her know it was ready to go. He'd fixed the kickstand and straightened the twisted metal, as well as the handlebars. The bike was scraped up but didn't look too bad considering how close a call she'd had. Now if it would just run as well as it had.

She strapped on the saddlebag, then climbed on the bike, rolled it off the kickstand and turned the key.

The powerful motor rumbled to life and she felt a swell of relief—and appreciation for the man who'd fixed it. As she popped it into gear, she couldn't help herself. She glanced up at the house, then quickly looked away. He was a cop. She had learned the hard way not to trust them. Not to trust anyone. If she hoped to stay alive, she had to keep it that way.

Jesse Tanner stood at the screened window watching her leave. He'd been awakened by the sound of running water downstairs and had half hoped she was making coffee. He should have known better.

But he couldn't help worrying as he watched her ride off into the dawn. Last night after he'd finished with the bike, he'd looked in on her. He felt guilty for snooping but he'd looked into the heavy saddlebag and seen the bundles of money. Maybe she didn't believe in traveler's checks. Maybe she'd withdrawn all of her savings from the bank for a long bike trip. Or maybe she'd robbed a savings and loan.

Either way, she was gone and not his problem.

Nor should he be surprised she would leave like this without a word. Last night he'd gotten the impression she wasn't one for long goodbyes.

Still, he would have made her pancakes for breakfast if she'd hung around. Hell, he hadn't had pancakes in months, but he would have made them for her.

He went downstairs, foolishly hoping she'd left him a note. He knew better. Her kind didn't leave notes. No happy faces on Post-its on the fridge, no little heart dotting the *i* in her name. She was not that kind of girl.

He made a pot of coffee and saw that she'd washed their glasses and put them away. He stood for a long time just staring at the clean glasses as the coffee brewed, then he poured himself a cup and took it back upstairs while he showered and dressed in his uniform hanging on the back of the bathroom door, all the time dreading the day ahead.

It wasn't just the biker chick with the bag of money and worry over what she might be running from that had him bummed. She was miles away by now.

His problem was Desiree Dennison. He'd recognized the little red sports car that had sideswiped the biker last night. He couldn't turn a blind eye to what he'd seen: Desiree leaving the scene of an accident.

But the last thing he wanted to do was go out to the Dennisons and with good reason.

Chapter Four

Maggie cruised through Timber Falls in the early morning, surprised to find the town even smaller than the map had led her to believe. The main drag was only a few blocks long. Ho Hum Motel, Betty's Café, the Busy Bee antique shop, the Spit Curl, Harry's Hardware, a small post office, bank and auto body shop.

Past the *Cascade Courier* newspaper office she spotted the cop shop. She turned down a side street, avoiding driving by the sheriff's department even though she knew Jesse Tanner couldn't have beat her to town. But she had no way of knowing how many officers there were in this little burg, or who might be looking for her.

When she'd rolled off the pier, she'd taken Norman's body with her into the water. The surf was rough that night. As far as she knew Norman's body hadn't turned up yet, but then, she hadn't had a chance to check a newspaper. Until Norman's body was found, Blackmore might not be aware that she was still alive.

Last night she hadn't gone home. Fortunately, she'd been smart enough to hide her motorcycle before going down to the pier to meet Norman. When she'd crawled out of the water after being shot, she'd come up a hundred yards down the beach near a small seafood shack.

Keeping to the shadows, she'd broken in, stripped off her leathers down to the shorts and tank top she wore underneath and bandaged her arm as best she could with the first-aid kit she found behind the counter.

Then she'd set off the fire alarm, hiding until the fire trucks arrived. In the commotion, she'd worked her way back to her bike, carrying her leathers in a garbage bag she'd taken from the café's kitchen.

She'd feared the cop would have found her bike and have it staked out but she didn't see anyone. Nor had she found any tracking devices on it when she'd checked later.

Running scared, she'd gone the only direction she could. Toward Timber Falls, Oregon, a tiny dot she'd found on a service station map. With luck, she'd bought herself a little time. Once Norman's body washed up and hers didn't, they were bound to get suspicious. Whoever they were.

Norman. Oh, Norman. She still felt sick and still blamed herself for his death. If she hadn't called Blackmore...

She'd called Rupert Blackmore because he was the detective investigating Clark Iverson's murder and she'd read in the paper that he was actively looking for the attorney's legal assistant, Norman Drake, for question-

ing. She knew nothing about the cop, let alone if he had
a tie in with Timber Falls. Or her.

But she understood now why Norman was so freaked
out. He had seen Detective Blackmore kill Iverson and,
like Maggie, he had probably seen the recent photograph of Blackmore in the paper getting some award
from the mayor for bravery and years of distinguished
service in the Seattle Police Department.

Who would believe that a cop who'd been on the
force for thirty years and received so many commendations was a killer? No one. That's why Norman hadn't
gone to the cops. That's why Maggie knew she couldn't
until she knew why Blackmore had murdered the others—and tried to kill her, as well.

Now she passed through a small residential area of
town, coming out next to the Duck-In bar and Harper's
Grocery. Her stomach growled and she tried to remember the last time she'd eaten and couldn't.

Parking beside the market in the empty lot, she went
in and bought herself a bag of doughnuts and a carton of milk, downing most of the milk as she gathered
supplies. She purchased some fruit and lunch meat for
later and a bottle of water. She wouldn't be back to
town for hours.

As she started to check out she saw a rack of newspapers and braced herself. But before she could look for
a story in one of the larger West Coast papers about a
body floating up on a beach, she spotted a headline in
the *Cascade Courier* that stopped her heart cold.

"Here, you forgot this," Sheriff Mitch Tanner said
from his recliner as Jesse walked through the door.
Jesse's first stop in town was to see how his brother was

doing—and talk to him about the accident last night on the highway.

Mitch had always been the good one. College right after high school, then he'd taken the job as sheriff and bought a house. Mr. Law-Abiding.

Jesse on the other hand had been the wild older brother. Always in trouble. When he'd left Timber Falls it had been in handcuffs. After that little misunderstanding was cleared up, he'd headed for Mexico and had spent years down there, half-afraid to come home and yet missing his brother and dad.

"It's required that you have it with you at all times—and keep it turned *on,*" Mitch said, tossing him a cell phone.

Jesse groaned as he caught the damned thing. It was bad enough being a cop, let alone having to carry a cell phone. He stuffed it into his pants pocket, telling himself it was only for a couple of months tops. "It's one of those that vibrates, right?" he asked with a wink. "Maybe it won't be so bad."

Mitch rolled his eyes and lay back in the recliner, his left leg in a huge cast and a pair of crutches leaning against the wall next to him. He'd taken two bullets: one had broken the tibia of his left leg. The other had just passed through his side. Both had laid him low, though.

Worse, Mitch hadn't taken it well that his first bullet wound in uniform would be from someone he knew—the most famous man in Timber Falls, Wade Dennison. Wade had shot Mitch while struggling over a .38 with his estranged wife, Daisy. Mitch had just been in the wrong place at the wrong time.

Or at least that was Wade's story.

Jesse thought being behind bars was the perfect place

for Wade. The man owned Dennison Ducks, the wooden decoy carving plant and pretty much the reason for the town's existence, and because of that Wade Dennison had thrown his weight around for years.

Well, after being patched up at the hospital he was now behind bars facing all kinds of charges, including assault with a deadly weapon, resisting arrest and domestic abuse. His wife, Daisy, was fighting for no bail, saying she feared for her life should Wade be released.

Needless to say, it made great headlines in the *Cascade Courier,* the weekly local paper run by Mitch's fiancée, Charity Jenkins. In fact, Charity seemed to be doing everything she could to keep the story page one.

And, as always, the news kept the gossips going at Betty's Café.

Jesse knew a lot of people in town resented Wade because of his money and his overbearing attitude and were hoping when the trial rolled around that Wade got the book thrown at him. Jesse just hoped Wade never went gunning for Mitch again. He would definitely take it personally next time.

Meanwhile, since Mitch was off his feet, he'd asked Jesse to stand in as acting deputy until he was completely recovered. Jesse had helped him out before since his return to Timber Falls. Because the town was in a remote part of Oregon, the sheriff had the authority to deputize whatever help he needed.

Jesse suspected Mitch thought putting him in a uniform would help straighten him up. He smiled at the thought because the job was a mixed blessing. He had only started this morning and already hated it. Still, he figured he was doing Mitch a favor and he could use the money, but he'd never been wild about cops since his wild youth and now he was one. The only one in Timber Falls.

The good news was that Timber Falls seldom had any real crime. Although this rainy season had had more than its share. But Jesse was hoping that with Wade Dennison locked up in jail and no more Bigfoot sightings, things would quiet down.

"You look like you're doing all right," he said to his brother as Charity came into the room with a tray of coffee, freshly squeezed orange juice, scrambled eggs, bacon and toast. She put it down on Mitch's lap.

Jesse raised a brow. "Damn, the woman can even cook?"

"Very funny," Charity quipped. "It's genetic. All women are born to cook and clean. Men are born to be asses."

Jesse faked a hurt expression.

"Except for Mitch," she added with a smile as she touched his shoulder. Charity had been crazy about Jesse's younger brother since she was a kid and he couldn't be more excited that the two of them were finally getting married. Mitch, while lying in a pool of his own blood, finally got smart and proposed to her after she'd helped save his life. The man was slow, but not stupid.

"I need to talk to my little brother for a moment," Jesse said. Mitch was two years younger, but several inches taller than Jesse. "Sheriff's department business."

Mitch groaned. "That's like waving a red flag in front of a bull to talk sheriff's department business in front of Charity, ace reporter."

"It's nothing you'd find interesting for the newspaper," Jesse assured Charity as he sat down next to Mitch and stole a piece of his bacon. Charity stuck around just in case. She was the owner, editor and reporter of the *Cascade Courier* and she was a bloodhound when it came to a good story.

"You know those forms you said I have to file every week?" Jesse said, chewing the bacon. "Where again do you keep them?"

Charity picked up her purse and headed for the front door. "Jesse, if you're going to be here for a few minutes, I need to run by the paper."

"I *can* be left alone, you know," Mitch called to her. "I'm not a complete invalid."

Charity paid him no mind.

"I'll stay here until you come back," Jesse proposed so she would finally leave.

"Forms?" Mitch said after she'd gone.

Jesse shrugged. "Couldn't think of anything else off the top of my head. The real reason I wanted to talk to you is that I witnessed an accident last night. Desiree Dennison ran a biker off the road."

Mitch swore. "Anyone hurt?"

Jesse shook his head. "It was a hit-and-run, though. She didn't even stop to see if the biker was okay."

"You're sure it was Desiree?"

"Saw the car with my own eyes. She had the top down. No one has a head of hair like her." Desiree took great pride in that wild mane of hers.

He was trying to put his finger on just what color it was when he was reminded of the biker's hair. It was long and fell in soft curls down her back and was a dark mahogany color that only nature could create. Desiree's was darker than he remembered and he realized she must have put something on it.

"Any other witnesses?" Mitch asked.

"Not at 3:00 a.m."

"What about the biker?"

"Wasn't interested in pressing charges. You know bikers."

Mitch grunted. He knew Jesse and that was enough.

"There's going to be damage to the car. The biker hit the passenger-door side. I'd say pretty extensive damage and I took a sample of the paint from the bike."

Mitch was nodding. "You have to write Desiree up. The judge is going to take her license, has to after all her speeding tickets."

Jesse nodded. "I just wanted to tell you before I go up there. I'm sure there will be repercussions."

Mitch snorted. "With a Dennison?"

"I heard Wade might make bail."

"No way. Daisy's fighting it. So am I. He's too much of a risk."

"I hope the judge sees it that way," Jesse said as he took a piece of Mitch's toast. He'd never had much faith in the system. And Charity had been writing some pretty inflammatory news articles about Wade and the rest of the Dennisons, dragging up a lot of old dirt.

If Wade got out, who knew what he would do. He'd threatened to kill Charity at least once that Jesse knew of.

"Have you considered cutting your hair?" Mitch asked, eyeing him as Jesse wiped his bacon-greasy hands on his brother's napkin.

"Nope." That was the good part about being deputized in this part of Oregon. A lot of the rules in the big city just didn't apply. How else could someone like Jesse become an officer of the law?

He heard Charity's VW pull up. "Your woman's back. Better eat your breakfast."

"What's left of it," Mitch grumbled. "Be careful up there at the Dennisons'. I swear they're all crazy."

Jesse wouldn't argue that.

Maggie stared at the newspaper headline. After Twenty-Seven Years in Hiding Following Daughter's Kidnapping, Daisy Dennison Ready for New Life.

"Is that all?" the grocery clerk asked.

Maggie dragged her gaze away from the newspaper to look at the older woman behind the counter. Twenty-seven years. Kidnapping. "What?"

"Is there anything else?"

"I'll take a few papers," Maggie said, feeling light-headed and nauseous as she grabbed the two larger West Coast papers and one of the tiny *Cascade Courier.* She shoved them into the grocery bag with her other purchases, her hands shaking.

The clerk eyed her for a moment, then rang up the newspapers. Maggie gave her a twenty and accepted the change the woman insisted on counting out into her trembling palm. Stuffing the change into the bag with the groceries, Maggie left, trying not to run.

Outside she gulped the damp morning air as she scanned the streets, not sure if she was looking for the face of a killer, that of a handsome dimpled sheriff's deputy or maybe a face that resembled her own.

The streets were empty at this early hour. She looked back to find the clerk still watching her.

Climbing onto her bike, Maggie backtracked a few blocks to make sure no one was following her, then rode south out of town to one of the dozens of state campgrounds she'd seen on the map. She picked a closed one, wound her way around the barrier until she found a campsite farthest from the highway, deep in the woods and near the river.

It wasn't until she was pretty sure she was safe that she dragged out the newspapers, starting with the article in the *Cascade Courier*.

She read it in its entirety twice. There was little about the original kidnapping. Mostly it was a story about a woman named Daisy Dennison who had been a recluse for twenty-seven years after her baby daughter had been stolen from her crib.

Her husband, Wade, the founder of Dennison Ducks, a local decoy carving plant, was behind bars for a variety of things including shooting the sheriff during a recent domestic dispute with Daisy.

Wade Dennison's attempts to make bail had been thwarted by his wife. Daisy, it was alleged, had filed for divorce and had started a new life.

What a great family, Maggie thought sarcastically.

But what Maggie did get from the story was that the couple's youngest daughter, Angela, had been kidnapped twenty-seven years ago. No ransom had ever been demanded. Angela was never seen again.

Angela Dennison. Was it possible Maggie was this person? If what Norman had told her was correct, she had to be. How many other babies had been kidnapped from this tiny town twenty-seven years ago?

She quickly set up her two-man tent and finished off the milk and a couple more doughnuts before going through the larger newspapers. Nothing about Norman. She breathed a sigh of relief.

She knew she should try to get some sleep but the river pooled just through the trees near her campsite, clear and welcoming. She left the tent and walked over to the small pool, stripped down and took a bath. The icy-cold water did more than clean and refresh her. It assured her she was alive. At least for the time being.

Full and feeling better, she still felt restless—anxious for the cloak of darkness so she could return to town—and worried about the deputy she'd stayed with part of the night. He had no reason to come looking for her. Unless he'd been warned she might be headed to Timber Falls. But then, that would mean Jesse Tanner had been in contact with Detective Rupert Blackmore and Blackmore knew she was alive.

Would the deputy help Blackmore find her? Why wouldn't he? It would be her word against a respected detective. No contest.

She hid her bike in the trees, then brought the saddle-bag full of money and her meager toiletries and clothing into the tent to wait until dark.

Chapter Five

Jesse had made a point of steering clear of the Dennisons since the time he was a boy. The last thing he wanted to do was ruin the morning by confronting Desiree, let alone her mother, Daisy.

But he stopped by the sheriff's department just long enough to leave his Harley and pick up the patrol car Mitch insisted he use along with that damned cell phone.

The Dennisons lived a few miles outside of town not far from Dennison Ducks.

Jesse hadn't seen Wade and Daisy's daughter Desiree since the shooting at the Dennison house when his brother had been wounded.

But he'd heard Desiree had been frequenting the Duck-In bar more than usual and driving like a bat out of hell in that cute little sports car Daddy had bought her before he went to jail.

The last time he was at the house he'd found them all in the pool house, Mitch lying on the floor bleeding and Daisy with the gun trying to kill Wade. Fun family. Charity had saved the day—and Mitch—and all Jesse had needed to do was handcuff Wade and haul him off to the hospital then jail, adding to the scandal that had been a part of that family from as far back as Jesse could remember. Long before their youngest daughter had been kidnapped twenty-seven years before.

Needless to say, neither Daisy nor Desiree was going to be anxious to see him again. The feeling was mutual.

He parked his patrol car near the four-car garage and climbed out, the Dennison mansion looming out of the forest in front of him.

The place had been built with one thing in mind, letting everyone know just how much money Wade had and how much more could be made through duck decoys. It was an overdone plantation house straight out of *Gone with the Wind.* Antebellum style with huge pillars, a massive veranda complete with white wicker and inside, a Timber Falls' version of Southern belles. Except Daisy, like her daughter Desiree, was no Southerner. Nor was either a belle.

He checked the garage first, peeking in the windows. There was Wade's SUV. Daisy's SUV. And Desiree's little red sports car, the passenger side caved in. He opened the garage door and stepped in, taking the chip of paint he'd scraped from the bike out of his pocket and holding it up against the car door panel. Perfect match. As if there had ever been any doubt. Then he headed for the main house.

"Would you please get Miss Desiree up, ma'am," he said in his best Rhett Butler imitation when the housekeeper answered the front door of the house a few minutes later. "It's the law come a calling." He flashed his credentials.

The German housekeeper didn't get the accent or the humor, what little there was. Nor did she look the least bit concerned. It wasn't as if this was the first time a uniformed officer had come to the door looking for Desiree.

"She is indisposed."

Jesse laughed. "She's still in bed. If I have to come back it will be with a warrant for her arrest."

"I'll take care of this," said a female voice from the cool darkness of the house. Daisy stepped from the shadows. She was close to fifty and still a very attractive woman. It seemed as if the years she'd spent in seclusion after Angela's kidnapping had made her more reserved, less haughty. Her dark hair had been recently highlighted with blond streaks and cut to the nape of her neck so that it floated nicely around her pretty face.

But Jesse would always see her as he had at the age of nine, a goddess with long dark hair and a lush body, riding bareback through the tall grass behind his house, smelling of fancy flowers and what he later realized was sex.

"Hello, Jesse. Can I offer you some coffee? Or perhaps a glass of iced tea? Zinnia just made some."

"No, thank you, Mrs. Dennison." He supposed it was natural he was disposed not to like the woman even if he had never spoken more than two words to her before. "I need to see Desiree."

"I'm sure she's still in bed. Please. Call me Daisy."

"I'm going to have to insist you get her up, Mrs. Dennison."

Daisy's back stiffened. So did her features. "It's that important?"

"Yes, ma'am, it is."

She sighed. "Very well. If you'd care to wait in there." She pointed toward a small sitting room, the walls lined with books. "I'll go get her." Her look said Desiree would not be happy about this.

Too bad. He was a hell of a lot less happy about this than the princess of the house.

It was a good forty-five minutes later before Desiree made an appearance. Jesse had reacquainted himself with several classics in the small library by the time she burst into the room.

Her scent preceded her. She smelled of jasmine, her hair still wet from her shower, her face perfectly made-up. She was wearing all white, a blouse that floated over her curves and white Capri pants that set off her sun-bed tanned legs. She gave him her come-hither look, but being seductive came as easily as breathing for Desiree.

"Jesse," she cooed. "You really should call a girl before you drop by so she can be presentable."

He was struck by the color of her eyes. But it wasn't just the eyes, he realized.

She moved past him, darting to plant a kiss on his cheek and brushing one of her full breasts against his arm as she did.

He found his voice. "This is not a social occasion and you know it."

She turned to smile at him. Desiree Dennison had found that she possessed a power over men and she loved it.

"I'm here on sheriff's department business," he said. "I witnessed an accident last night on the highway by my place. I saw you hit a motorcyclist when you pulled out from Maple Creek Road."

She drew back, gave him a get-real look, then lied right to his face. "I don't know what you're talking about."

"Where were you at three in the morning, after the bars closed?"

A brow shot up. "In bed."

"Anyone's bed I know who can give you an alibi?"

She pouted. "In my own bed, alone."

He shook his head. "Give me your car keys."

"What?"

"Your car keys. Now."

"I'll have to go upstairs and get them." Her cheeks flamed with obvious anger as if the walk was more than she was up to this morning. Or maybe it was being caught.

"I'll wait."

She turned her back on him to buzz the housekeeper on the intercom. "Get me some juice," she snapped. "Orange juice. A large glass." Then she left the room.

He half expected to hear the sports car engine roar to life, but Desiree was too used to getting out of scrapes to make a run for it. Daddy always bailed her out. Only Daddy couldn't even make bail himself right now. And maybe Mommy was over Desiree's shenanigans.

But it was Daisy who returned with the car keys. "If you had told me why you were here, I could have saved you the trouble of waking Desiree. I was driving my daughter's car last night."

He stared at her, not bothering to take the keys she held out to him. "You were the one up Maple Creek Road? You realize that's the local make-out spot?"

She smiled. "Is it? I'm afraid I was only turning around. I took Desiree's car because I felt like having the top down. I pulled into the turnoff at Maple Creek Road. I didn't see the biker. I know I should have reported it at once."

"Or maybe stopped to see if the biker wasn't killed."

Daisy blanched. "Is he all right?"

Jesse didn't correct her on the rider's gender. "Yeah."

Her expression said she expected charges to be filed, probably a lawsuit by the biker, maybe even her own arrest, but she was ready. Like her daughter, she'd always come away from scrapes unscathed. Except for the loss of her youngest daughter, Angela, when Desiree was two.

"Are you sure you want to take the rap for your daughter?" Jesse asked, holding her gaze. "I know Desiree was driving the car. I saw her."

"Really? You were making out on Maple Creek Road last night, deputy?" Daisy asked.

He smiled. "No, I was standing on the deck of my cabin. I can see the highway from there."

"From your house?" Daisy repeated. "From that distance and in the dark you are absolutely sure it was Desiree behind the wheel?"

"Yes."

"How is that possible when I was the one driving her car?" Daisy asked.

He knew exactly what she was saying. He could call her a liar and press this. It would be his word against hers. He might be wearing a deputy's uniform but she would be more credible—even after the shoot-out in her pool house. Maybe more so because she had come off as the victim. Plus she would hire the best attorney money could buy.

"Look, the worst that will happen is Desiree will lose her driver's license," he said patiently. "And you know that's probably the best thing that could happen, getting her off the streets for a while. Next time she might kill someone. Or herself. And there *will* be a next time."

"I told you I was the one—"

"I know what you told me," Jesse interrupted. "You also told me that Wade was the one who shot my brother but it was your gun and your hand over Wade's when the shots were fired."

Daisy's gaze turned to granite. "I'm sorry about Mitch. I was only trying to defend myself."

Or make sure Wade was out of her life—and without the money, the house, the business. Jesse fought to hold his temper in check. "Isn't that the same thing Wade said when he killed Bud Farnsworth?"

She flinched imperceptibly. The former production manager at Dennison Ducks had pretty much confessed to kidnapping baby Angela from her crib twenty-seven years ago. Unfortunately, Bud never had the chance to implicate the person believed to have masterminded the kidnapping—or tell anyone what he'd done with Angela.

According to Charity, who'd been there, Bud had been trying to say something when Wade shot and killed him. Wade's defense was that he was protecting Charity and Daisy.

"In two months' time, you've been involved in two shootings," Jesse pointed out.

"I was shot myself by Mr. Farnsworth, you might recall," Daisy said. "And almost killed by my estranged husband. In my emotional state is it any wonder I didn't see that motorcycle last night let alone that I panicked and foolishly didn't stop?"

He had to laugh. She would play whatever card it took to get herself out of this—and damned if she wouldn't walk.

"Are you going to arrest me?" she asked. "If so, I'd like to call my lawyer."

"You can call your lawyer from the sheriff's office," Jesse said. "Sure you don't want to rethink what you're doing, Mrs. Dennison?"

She hesitated but only for a moment, then held out her wrists to be handcuffed.

It was a temptation. "I don't think that will be necessary as long as you promise to come along without any trouble."

She smiled and walked to the intercom. "I'll be back shortly, Desiree."

Desiree didn't come back downstairs. Not even when Zinnia showed up with a large glass of freshly squeezed orange juice.

Charity checked to make sure Mitch had fallen asleep before she let Aunt Florie in the front door and took her aside.

"Don't try to force anything with tofu in it on him, all right?" Charity whispered so as to not disturb Mitch who was snoring softly in his recliner. "Or zucchini."

"He likes my zucchini bread," Florie said.

Sure Mitch did. If Charity hadn't been desperate, she would never have even considered leaving Florie with Mitch, but Wade Dennison's sister, Lydia Abernathy, had asked her to stop by the antique shop. Charity was dying to know what that was about. Wade and his recent arrest probably. Charity had always suspected Lydia knew a lot more about what went on at her brother's house than she was telling.

"And no reading his palm or his tea leaves, got it?" Mitch wouldn't be happy to wake up to Florie. But Charity's aunt and all her other screwball relatives came with the marriage package. No wonder Mitch had taken so long to pop the question.

"Whatever." Florie smiled. She'd been doing that a lot lately. Ever since Liam Sawyer had become single again. "Just a minute. I don't know what to wear to the party this weekend." She whipped two caftans out of her bag, one in swirls of bright colors, the other in splashes of bright colors. "Which do you like best?"

That was a tough one. They were both garish at best. "I have an idea," Charity said, looking at her aunt. "I think it's time for a makeover."

Florie, now hugging seventy, was the local psychic and ran her business, Madam Florie's, via email from an old motel on the south end of town. The motel units were now bungalow rentals and Florie did readings out of the office-slash-apartment, as well as on the internet.

Whether or not Florie was clairvoyant was debatable. But she definitely played the part. She wore her long dyed red hair wound around her head like a turban, and dressed in bright caftans that mirrored the turquoise eye shadow she wore to highlight her blue eyes. Her fingers were adorned with dozens of rings and her slim wrists jangled with an array of colorful bracelets. She looked like an exotic bird, blinding in its plumage.

"What's wrong with the way I look?" Florie asked.

Charity didn't have enough time to get into that. "I

just think maybe Roz and I could give you a new look for the party." Roz was Liam Sawyer's daughter. The party was to celebrate the fact that her best friend Rozalyn was back in town to stay. Also, Charity suspected, to announce Roz's engagement to Ford Lancaster.

"A new look?" Florie repeated.

Charity nodded enthusiastically. "A surprise for Liam."

The older woman's eyes brightened and Charity knew she had her. Florie had been in love with Liam for years.

"I'll talk to Roz. Don't you worry. It's going to be great," Charity whispered, backing toward the door. "I'll be back as soon as I can. Don't forget, nothing funny on Mitch."

Florie had that dreamy look on her face, obviously lost in thought about Liam, as she waved from the front porch.

Charity had to smile as she climbed into her VW Bug. It was nice to know that falling in love had no age limit. She hoped things worked out for her aunt and Liam. Meanwhile, she couldn't wait to find out what Lydia Abernathy wanted. Lydia only called when something was up.

After locking up Daisy Dennison, Jesse drove through town, fighting a bad mood, hoping to see that fancy motorbike he'd rolled into the back of his pickup last night.

He couldn't get Maggie—if that was her real name—off his mind. Or the money he'd seen in her saddlebag. But there was no sign of her.

Back at the office, he whizzed past Sissy, taking the handful of messages she waved at him as he went by.

Sissy, a thirtysomething large woman with an attitude, managed to get in one of her your-name-is-mud looks before he closed the door.

He sat down behind his brother's desk, glaring at the computer. After a moment, he looked through the messages. Barking dog, missing trash can, abandoned car, noise complaint. He recognized the names of the people who had called. Constant complainers. All people his brother had to deal with on a daily basis—especially this time of year when the constant rain caused a bad case of cabin fever. Jesse wondered how Mitch did it.

Dropping the messages on his desk, he stared at the computer. He'd written down the license number from Maggie's bike last night when he'd hoped she would press charges. Now he hesitated.

"Sissy?" he said, buzzing the clerk.

"Yeesss?"

He cringed; only desperation would make him call her in here, but he was about as wild about computers as he was cell phones. "I need help."

That soft knowing chuckle of hers. "Don't I know it."

A minute later she opened the office door and stepped in, hands on hips. "If you want coffee, you get it yourself. Doughnuts, I get 'em every morning, anyway, so I don't mind picking up a couple for the sheriff. He liked lemon-filled."

"Lemon-filled works for me," Jesse said.

"And it would help if you told me where you were going when you left. Better yet," she said, swinging her head to one side with obvious attitude, "if you bothered to show up in the morning at all. People call wanting to know there is someone in charge and what am I supposed to tell them?"

"I thought *you* were in charge," he said and smiled.

She mugged a face at him. "You better believe it."

He reminded himself that he only had to do this for a couple of months tops and if he could deal with Daisy and Desiree Dennison he could put up with Sissy Walker. As long as he didn't spend too much time in the office.

"You know how to run this damned thing?" he said, motioning to the computer.

She smiled that smug smile of hers. "The Pope wear boxers?"

He didn't have a clue. But she hadn't moved. "Can you *show* me how to use it?" She still didn't move. "Please? Pretty please and I buy the doughnuts?"

A smile burst across her ample face and she sashayed over, shooed him up and planted her wide hips in his chair. "What you want?"

"Show me how to find out things. Like…how do I track down a name from a license plate number?"

"What state?"

"Washington. A motorcycle license."

She kicked up an eyebrow and gave him a look but began to tap the keys. He paid attention. He might not like computers, but he was a fast learner and he wasn't going to call in Sissy every time he needed to look up a plate number.

"What's the number?"

He told her, then watched the screen anxiously to see what she came up with.

Sissy let out an "uh-huh," as the name appeared on the screen. "I should have known it would be some broad."

"Biker chick," he corrected, reading the name Margaret Jane Randolph—Maggie—and the address, a better-known wealthy residential area in West Seattle. He hadn't expected anything less.

Sissy started to get up.

"Wait, one more thing. How would I see if there are any priors on her?"

Sissy gave him that eyebrow thing again but continued typing. "You know how to pick 'em," she said as an APB came up for the woman in question.

Margaret Jane Randolph was wanted for questioning in a murder investigation in West Seattle. Murder? The photo accompanying the APB looked as if it was her mug shot from her driver's license. Her hair was different but she was obviously the woman he'd picked up off the highway last night. No two women had a face like that even if some of her features might remind him of another woman.

He swore softly under his breath.

"Anything else?" Sissy asked, sounding disgusted as she pushed herself up and started toward the door.

"No. Thanks," he said as he lowered himself into the chair she'd vacated.

Sissy stopped in the doorway. He glanced up at her. She was shaking her head, giving him the once-over, her gaze halting on his ponytail for a moment.

"How do I make a printout?" he called after her.

"Press Print. Some deputy you make," she said under her breath as she left the room, closing the door behind her.

He turned back to the screen.

An instant message box had flashed up, advising any inquiries to be routed to Detective Rupert Blackmore of the West Seattle Police Department. The message was marked urgent and included the detective's phone number.

Jesse stared at the message and swore. What the hell? It seemed pretty clear Maggie wasn't just wanted for questioning. Was it possible she was a suspect in the murder investigation? And where did all the cash fit in? Or did it?

Jesse got up and walked to the window, telling himself there was no reason to call the detective. No reason to pursue this. She was long gone. Hell, she could be halfway to Mexico by now. Or at least California.

Outside, it had started to rain again, another gray day. Nothing new there.

The woman was wanted for questioning in a murder investigation? Damn.

He went back to the computer, jotted down the detective's name and number on a piece of scrap paper.

Then he hit the close key.

It took a long moment for the screen to clear and as he watched it, he wondered if Detective Rupert Blackmore was at this very moment wondering why someone at the sheriff's department in Timber Falls, Oregon, was interested in Maggie Randolph.

Chapter Six

Detective Rupert Blackmore left the crime scene trying not to panic. Margaret Randolph's body hadn't floated up and now he knew it wouldn't.

Williams had informed him that a fire alarm had been set off at a café a quarter mile downstream. A false alarm. Not just that, the owner of the café had told Williams that the place had been broken into, there were drops of blood on the floor and someone had used the first-aid kit kept behind the counter.

After Rupert had shot them both, he'd waited in the fog for the bodies to float ashore. Waited until he heard the fire trucks and saw the flashing lights a quarter mile down the water at some wharfside café. He hadn't put it together then because he'd been so sure they were dead.

Hell, she'd gone down with the geek and she'd been hit. Even if the bullets hadn't killed her, the fall and the cold churning water would have, his mind argued. But the fog had been too damned thick to tell if she'd surfaced.

He reminded himself that she'd had on all leather. It would have acted like a wetsuit. And the woman was an athlete.

Rupert knew it was time to quit lying to himself. Margaret Randolph's body wasn't going to float up. Worse, he couldn't forget those last few moments on the pier when she'd looked up at him. *Recognized* him.

He sat down at his desk and began to fish around in the top drawer for some Tums. His stomach was killing him.

He'd made the mistake of keeping an eye on her over the years. It was crazy, but he felt as if she were his kid. Like he'd been the one to give her life. Hell, he had. If he'd done what he'd been paid to do, she would have died as a baby and been buried up in the mountains.

Was that why he'd blown it at the pier?

But if she was alive, then why hadn't she contacted his superiors? Or the Feds? If she was alive, wouldn't she tell someone what she knew?

Out of the corner of his eye he caught the flashing icon on his computer screen. His gaze jerked to it and he felt his heart take off like a thief.

He shot a quick glance behind him and saw that Williams was on the phone with someone and paying no attention. Hands shaking, he clicked on the icon and tried to catch his breath.

As the inquiry came up, his chest ached as if he'd been shot and for a moment he couldn't think, couldn't breathe. Funny, but he didn't even mind the thought of falling over dead at his desk. At least he didn't mind for those first few seconds. A heart attack seemed a better way out than any of the other alternatives right now.

But then he caught his breath, regained his senses, felt that primal survival instinct kick in. He wasn't ready to go out feetfirst. Hell, if he could weather this storm, he would retire like Teresa had been trying to get him to do. And he'd buy that damned RV she had her heart set on and the two of them would head south. No more rainy winters in the Northwest. They'd go to Arizona and he'd sit in the sun by the pool. Hell, yes. Maybe he'd take up shuffleboard or bingo. Why not?

He deleted the information on the screen, grabbed his coat and left the police station, driving around aimlessly, trying to think.

He'd tagged inquiries about Margaret Randolph only so he'd know firsthand when any evidence surfaced. He'd never dreamed he'd get a hit from some hick sheriff's department. And in Timber Falls, Oregon, of all places. Margaret Randolph's motorcycle tags had been run along with a check for any outstanding warrants on her. What the hell? Did that mean what he feared it did?

He tried to convince himself that someone else had her bike. Maybe had stolen it since he hadn't been able to find the bike after he'd seen her go off the end of the pier and into the icy, churning water below. She'd been wearing her biker outfit so he'd known she'd come by bike. He'd looked for it but was forced to leave for fear of being seen by emergency personnel. Her bike must have been hidden.

So where the hell was it now?

In Timber Falls, Oregon.

And how had it gotten there?

If Margaret Randolph had been riding it then… Hell,

then she knew. Norman Drake must have overheard more than Rupert thought he did. Damn. If only he'd gotten to Norman Drake sooner. If only…

He pulled the car over, his hands still shaking, and waited for his heart rate to return to normal, knowing it wouldn't until he found her and finished the job.

Maybe her bike had been stolen, though. Maybe her body *would* wash up.

His cell phone rang as if on cue. He fumbled it open, his pulse a deafening pounding in his ears. "Blackmore."

"It's Williams. The boys are done. It's raining and they haven't found anything else. You want me to leave a man down there? I'm not sure what else you were hoping we would find."

Another damned body. But then he couldn't very well tell Williams that, could he? "Tell them to pack it in. Listen, I'm not feeling very well."

"Ulcers again?"

"Goes with the job," he said. "I'm thinking I might take a day or two of sick pay. If there's anything new on the Iverson and Drake homicides just call me on my cell."

"Hope you get to feeling better," Williams said, but Rupert could hear his relief. The fool thought he could solve both cases and make a name for himself with the guys upstairs in the next forty-eight hours.

Down the block Rupert spotted a phone booth. He didn't want to use the company cell for this call. He parked, got out and ran through the pouring rain. He was soaked to the skin and breathing hard from the exertion by the time he ducked inside the booth. He promised himself he'd get in shape once he got to Arizona.

He dug out a handful of coins from his pocket, dialed the long-distance number and listened to it ring twice as he lit a cigarette and tried to calm down.

"Hello."

Teresa's voice brought tears to his eyes. He wiped at them with the back of his hand. "Hey, baby," he said, his voice breaking. "I was hoping I'd catch you."

"Is everything all right?" He could hear the worry in her tone. She knew him too well. But she didn't know the half of it. And he would die before he'd let her find out.

"I've got to go out of town for a couple of days on a case," he said. "I just wanted to let you know so you wouldn't worry about me if you called the house. How's your mom?"

"Better. She says to tell her favorite son-in-law hello."

It was an old joke between the three of them. "If I see him, I will."

Teresa laughed as she always did. "I miss you."

"Me, too." He could feel himself getting choked up again. He wished they'd had kids. Wished to hell he'd retired last year. Wished they were in Arizona right now.

But even as he thought it, he knew this wasn't something he could have avoided. Not even in Arizona.

"I'll call you when I finish this job," he said. "I've got to go."

"You take care of yourself, you hear?" It was what she always said.

"For you," he answered as he always did. He started to tell her he'd decided to retire. That they would buy that RV she liked as soon as she got back from her mother's so it would be all ready for them to go south at the first drop of rain next fall, but she'd already hung up.

As he put the receiver back and stood staring out through the soiled glass at the driving rain, Rupert realized what else had been bothering him.

The officer in Timber Falls who'd made the inquiry about Margaret Randolph hadn't called him. Why, when the hick cop had to have seen the message that he was to notify Detective Rupert Blackmore immediately?

He swore under his breath. He was sweating profusely even with the rain hammering the phone booth and a cold wet wind blowing up under the door.

He wasn't spending his golden years behind bars with criminals he'd put there. But he doubted that was even an option. If the person who'd hired him all those years ago found out who Margaret Randolph really was, then it would be clear that he hadn't killed her twenty-seven years ago. That he'd sold her instead and pocketed the cash. And then he'd be a dead man.

He watched the rain drum the glass of the phone booth without even hearing it or feeling the cold or the damp. After a few minutes, he started to breathe a little easier. He felt better. There was nothing like a plan.

He was going to Timber Falls. He'd put an end to this mess once and for all.

Pushing open the phone-booth door, he took a deep breath of the damp Seattle air and thought about Arizona.

Hell, by this time next year he could have a tan.

Jesse had just looked up from the computer when he caught a flash of color streak by on the street beyond his window. For just an instant, he thought it might be Maggie Randolph on that bike of hers.

But as he peered out the window, he saw it was Desiree's bright red sports car.

"I'll be a son of a—" He ran outside just as Desiree swung the car into Betty's Café and came to a dust-whirling stop.

He swore again and went after her.

Desiree was already sitting in a booth when Jesse walked in. She groaned when she saw him coming toward her. At least she knew she was in trouble. That was a start. He went straight to her booth and slid in across from her.

For a long moment, he just looked at her. She really was a pretty young woman, great bones, nice eyes. There was no denying that. But Desiree lacked something that the woman he'd met last night had in spades. Something beyond looks that had made her impossible to forget.

"What?" Desiree asked peevishly.

"I know your mother took the blame for you this morning," he said quietly. She started to argue but he held up his hand. "You don't learn. I just saw you speeding down Main Street. You're going to kill someone. Or yourself."

"Are you going to write me a ticket?" she asked, as if bored with this particular lecture.

"Desiree…"

She smiled and leaned toward him. "Yes?"

"Get a job. Do something with your life before it's too late." He couldn't believe those words had come out of his mouth.

Neither could she. "Jesse Tanner telling *me* to do something with *my* life?"

He smiled then and shook his head. "I know I'm the last person who should be giving career advice since I'm just starting to get my act together and you're six years younger than me."

"No kidding."

He tried another tack. "Is this about your father? Some sort of rebellion? Because if it is, I can relate."

Her eyes narrowed at him in warning. "Your father isn't in jail."

"No, but I spent a few nights there as a juvenile and I can see a cell in your future if you don't stop acting out."

She rolled her eyes.

"I'm trying to cut you some slack here," he said.

"Don't."

"Okay." He pulled out his ticket book and wrote her up for speeding. He handed the ticket across the table to her as Desiree's lunch arrived.

She stuffed the ticket into her purse without looking at it, picked up a piece of bacon that had fallen out of her BLT and took a bite, licking her lips as her gaze met his. "You want a bite?"

"No."

"Sure?" She cranked up the seduction, obviously in her comfort zone again.

He got to his feet. He'd hoped maybe he could talk some sense into her. Or at least reach out to her in a brotherly sort of way. He felt as if he owed her that for reasons he didn't want to touch.

As he left, he felt it again—something in the air. The way he could sense a storm coming. As if the atmosphere were electrically charged. He stopped to sniff the breeze, unable to shake the bad feeling he had. It was as if something was about to happen and nothing could stop it. Least of all Acting Deputy Jesse Tanner.

"Charity, punctual as always," Lydia Abernathy called from the back as Charity walked through the door of the Busy Bee antique shop a few minutes later.

Lydia smiled and waved from her wheelchair. She was a tiny woman, her hair a white downy halo around her head, her blue eyes bright. She looked older than Charity knew her to be. No doubt because of the accident that had severed her spinal cord and killed her beloved husband, Henry.

It had happened thirty years ago, before Charity was born, but she remembered Florie telling her that Wade had been driving the car. Henry had died instantly, Lydia had ended up in a wheelchair and Wade had gotten off without a scratch.

It was no secret that Wade felt responsible. He'd taken care of his sister for years, supporting her financially, opening the antique shop she'd always wanted and making sure she had live-in help.

They were close in spite of the past. Although Lydia, like most siblings, did take perverse pleasure in her brother's troubles. And Wade had his share right now.

"I heard about your upcoming nuptials," Lydia said as she moved her wheelchair over to the hot plate to collect the teapot. "I thought we'd celebrate with a cup of tea and a few of my sugar cookies."

"You know I can't resist your sugar cookies," Charity said with a groan. "The ones with the sprinkles on top?"

Lydia beamed. "Of course. Angus insists I do too much. He says he's taking over the baking."

Angus Smythe was Timber Falls' version of an English butler. Silent unless spoken to, always painfully polite, and very protective and attentive of Lydia. Plus, he was from England and came complete with the accent. He'd been a close friend of both Lydia and Henry. He was obviously devoted to her.

Charity dragged up a chair, glancing around the shop. The merchandise hardly ever changed. Lydia had collected pieces via the internet but had marked them up so much they weren't likely to sell. Charity suspected she just liked having pretty things around and wasn't in the antique business to make money. Fortunately, she didn't have to show a profit. She had her brother, Wade, when she needed money.

"So when is the wedding?" Lydia asked, handing her a cup of tea, a sugar cookie lounging on the saucer next to it.

Charity knew this wasn't why Lydia had asked to see her. "June. Everyone in town will be invited. I'm just starting the planning."

The older woman nodded. "Henry and I had a lovely wedding." Her eyes clouded over for a moment as if lost in memory. "Henry's buried back East, you know, in the family plot. I will join him when the time comes. I only stayed out here to be close to Wade." She grimaced. "Can you believe the mess he has himself in now? And all because he married beneath his class."

Lydia took a sip of her tea and settled the cup on the saucer. "I've never understood what he saw in that woman. I wish he'd had the sense to shoot her. That lie she told about him calling to say he was on his way to the house to kill her. What man would warn a stupid woman he was coming up to kill her? Although, Daisy could drive anyone to murder. Except *Wade*." She made it sound like a flaw in her brother's character.

Charity took a bite of her cookie. Lydia did make the most amazing sugar cookies. "What is the flavoring you put in these?" she asked, wondering if this was why Lydia had called her, to talk about Wade.

"It's my secret ingredient." Lydia took a sip of tea, then put down her cup, drawing herself up in the wheelchair. "I didn't call you over to talk about Wade or that woman he married. I need a favor."

Uh-oh.

Lydia leaned forward and whispered, "Have you seen that man Betty is with?"

"Bruno?" Everyone in town was talking about him. Drove an old trashed-out car and warmed a bar stool at the Duck-In bar when he wasn't hanging out at Betty's bumming free meals.

"Bruno. Is that his name? Well, I've noticed him walking by the shop and looking in as if he were casing the joint," Lydia said.

Casing the joint?

"What do you know about him?" she asked.

"Nothing." Charity was still trying to imagine Bruno "casing" the antique store. Sure, there were some valuable pieces and some small collectibles but she doubted Bruno would know the good stuff from the junk. And if he stole a pricey ornate oak buffet, how would he carry it? On his back? It certainly wouldn't fit in that old car of his.

"I want you to find out everything you can about him," Lydia said, glancing toward the front window.

Charity knew her shock must have shown. The Busy Bee was anything but busy this time of year and as far as Charity knew, Lydia never had more than a little cash in the till. Most people paid with credit cards or checks and that was when there was actually a customer. "I really don't—" Charity hedged.

"There he is," Lydia whispered.

Charity turned in time to see Bruno walk by. He was a large, not bad-looking man, with a thick head of shaggy blond hair. Bruno looked to be in his forties—a good ten years younger than Betty. Just the way she liked them.

"If you really think he's planning to rob you, shouldn't you talk to Jesse?" Charity suggested. "He's filling in as deputy until Mitch is well enough to go back to work."

Lydia was shaking her head. "I would look like a silly old woman crying wolf. No, I need to know more about him before I say anything to anyone but you. You're the one with the talent for finding out everything about everyone."

Compliments worked every time. "Okay, I could do some checking on him," Charity said.

"Good," Lydia said, sounding relieved. "He…scares me."

"Angus would never let anything happen to you."

"Angus is a dear but he is no spring chicken," Lydia said.

Angus still looked plenty capable of protecting his mistress. He had always been a large, muscular man and he'd stayed in shape, which made him seem younger than his sixtysomething years.

"I also have my own pistol in my nightstand," Lydia added with a glint in her eyes. "A woman can't be too careful. Especially one with my…disabilities."

There was a sound behind them on the back stairs, a door opening, footfalls as someone came down the steps toward them. It had to be Angus. He never used the elevator Wade had put in for Lydia.

"Don't say anything about Bruno to Angus," Lydia whispered. "Or about my gun. I hate to worry the old dear."

Angus appeared from behind a cloth curtain. "You need anything from the store, Lydia?" he inquired in that wonderful English accent Charity adored.

"No, thank you, Angus."

"I'll only be a short while," he said and, nodding to Charity, left by the back door.

"He thinks I should sell the store, you know. Angus," she added as if Charity wasn't following. "He says I should travel while I can still enjoy it and that he would gladly take me around the world if I like. Did you know he's quite wealthy in his own right? But how can I leave Wade, especially now when he needs me?"

"He might be going to prison," Charity pointed out before she could catch herself.

"Yes," Lydia said. "I guess then there would be nothing but the store keeping me here."

"I should get going," Charity said, rising to her feet.

"Here, take a couple of cookies for later and maybe a few for Mitch?"

Charity could never turn down cookies. As she left, munching one of the cookies on her way to the newspaper office, she had an uneasy feeling about Lydia's fears over Bruno.

Chapter Seven

After leaving Desiree at Betty's, Jesse cruised around town, too restless to go back to the office. Timber Falls was dead. It had been weeks since there'd been a Bigfoot sighting and it was still the rainy season so there were only locals left in town and most of those had holed up to wait out spring.

Jesse always thought it was the isolation and the cabin fever—locked inside for months while it rained day in and day out—that caused the craziness in Timber Falls. It was one of the reasons he'd gone to Mexico.

But it was his family that had brought him home. He could put up with the rain, he told himself. In a few months tourists would descend on the town to escape the heat in the valleys and residents would take a large collective sigh as if saying, "Made it through another one."

He made a wider circle around the small town. He didn't kid himself. He was looking for Maggie and her fancy motorcycle.

Common sense told him she wouldn't be hanging around Timber Falls. Not with thousands of dollars in one of her saddlebags and an APB out on her. But what was she doing even passing through this time of year? If she was headed out of the country, she was taking the long route. Timber Falls wasn't even off secondary roads.

But a biker *could* disappear in the woods around here if she wanted to though. Or needed to.

What bothered him was the feeling that she hadn't left. That coming to Timber Falls hadn't been just a flip of the coin or a wrong turn.

It didn't take Charity long to get the lowdown on Bruno once she had his real name and even that was pretty simple once she had the license plate number off his old car.

His name was Jerome Lovelace. That explained why he preferred Bruno.

For a moment she thought about asking Jesse to run a check on Lovelace, but she knew he would tell Mitch and she didn't want to worry Mitch. He hated it when she got involved in anything even remotely dangerous. Also she had her own sources.

She called her friend who worked at one of the Oregon law enforcement agencies and waited while Nancy tapped the computer keys and chewed nervously at her gum.

"Whoo-whee," Nancy whispered. "This boy's got a rap sheet as long as my arm."

"What kind of offenses? Any burglary or robbery?"

"Looks mostly like driving while intoxicated, drunk and disorderly, aggravated assault, domestic abuse, driving without a valid license, driving without insurance. He did some time for criminal mischief and for fraud. Most are just misdemeanors. The guy's a loser."

"I gathered that just looking at him." Definitely Betty's type.

"Oh, here's one. He got picked up for fencing stolen goods but got off," Nancy said. "Doesn't say what kind of goods."

"How about last known address?"

"A post office box in Seattle. You want it?"

"No." Seattle? So what had brought him to Timber Falls? Fencing stolen goods. Like antiques, she wondered. "Thanks. I owe you."

"So true."

Charity hung up and considered what she'd learned. Maybe Bruno wanted to advance his criminal career. Maybe he was contemplating burglary. But Charity didn't buy it.

She grabbed her purse and, leaving the newspaper office, started down the street toward the Busy Bee antique shop. As she neared the shop, she slowed. Wasn't that Bruno ahead of her?

She ducked into one of the store entrances as he started to look over his shoulder. She didn't think he'd seen her. She waited a minute, then peered around the corner of the building and down Main Street.

Bruno had just reached the Busy Bee. She scooted up the street, keeping to the edge of the buildings.

He slowed, looking into the large plate-glass windows at the front of the antique shop, then swung into the entryway as if also not wanting to be seen.

Charity's heart was in her throat. Was it possible Lydia was right? That Bruno really did plan to rob the place?

Bruno had disappeared from view. She ran up the street after him. Had he gone into the antique shop or was he just hidden in the recessed entrance?

Was it possible he'd spotted her, thought she was following him and was waiting for her?

She was almost to the setback entry of the shop. She glanced toward the window, pretending to study her reflection critically in the glass.

Bruno was inside the shop. He was admiring a purple vase, one Charity remembered as being marked four hundred dollars—certainly more than Bruno could afford, she would bet.

But it wasn't Lydia waiting on him. It was Angus. He was frowning, obviously suspicious of the man and maybe a little wary that Bruno might drop the expensive vase and have no way to pay for it.

As Charity walked on past the shop, she saw Angus snatch the vase from him and put it back. Angus looked up and saw her. With a small nod, he watched her pass. Bruno turned, too, frowning. A moment later Charity heard the shop doorbell tinkle behind her, heard the heavy footsteps and knew it was Bruno.

She pushed into the Spit Curl, pulled the door closed after her. She hadn't realized she was holding her breath until she saw Bruno's shadow fall across the front window, then retreat on down the street.

"You look like you've seen a ghost," Mary Jane Clark

said from the beauty-shop chair. Mary Jane was getting a blond dye job to her dark roots.

As she watched Bruno saunter on up the street toward Betty's, Charity ignored Mary Jane just as she had throughout high school when Mary Jane had shown an interest in Mitch.

Bruno peered back just once and smiled as if he knew Charity was watching him. Clearly, he was enjoying her fear.

After not finding a brightly colored motorcycle or the woman who'd been riding it, Jesse returned to his office, wondering if Detective Rupert Blackmore would be waiting for him. Or at least have called.

"She already made bail," Sissy said as Jesse walked into the office.

He didn't have to ask who she was. Daisy Dennison. He'd known she would be out before the fingerprint ink dried.

Sissy handed him another stack of messages. He flipped through them. None from Blackmore. He'd been so sure the cop would have all inquiries red-flagged. Maybe Blackmore really did just want to talk to Maggie about the murder. Maybe she wasn't a suspect.

But there were lots of messages from whiners about everything from a nasty smell coming from the neighbor's garbage cans to cars parked incorrectly along Main Street.

"Damn, don't these people have anything else to do?" he said as he headed for his office.

Sissy gave him her some-deputy-you-are look.

He sat down behind the desk and began making calls, pretending he was Mitch, pretending diplomacy was his middle name. Before he realized it, the afternoon had turned into evening. Sissy stuck her head in the door to say she was leaving and it was time to ante up for the next morning's doughnuts.

It wasn't until he'd gotten to the bottom of the pile of messages that he found Detective Rupert Blackmore's name and number where he'd scribbled it down earlier. He vaguely remembered doing it—just before he'd seen Desiree speed by.

If the cop was tagging inquiries, then he already knew that Maggie had been in Timber Falls. If the detective was really concerned, he would have called.

So a phone call from Jesse wouldn't make any difference at this point since she was long gone, anyway.

But with one phone call, Jesse would know why the detective wanted to talk to Maggie. It would satisfy his curiosity. He started to pick up the phone. Hesitated. What was he afraid he was going to find out? It wasn't fear holding him back and he knew it. He knew he was crazy for not calling. Not to mention irresponsible. But his gut instincts were telling him to wait. And he'd always gone with his instincts. Right or wrong.

His stomach rumbled. He glanced at his watch. The detective wouldn't be in his office this late. Maybe in the morning. His stomach rumbled again. And Jesse had just enough time to get to Betty's before she closed. Idly, he wondered what Maggie Randolph was having for dinner tonight.

"Will you be all right alone for a little while?" Charity asked from the doorway.

"Call Florie again and you're dead," Mitch said from his recliner.

She smiled at him. "I was desperate."

"Uh-huh. You were paying me back for the times I insisted Florie stay with you." He motioned her closer, reached out and pulled her down to him. She was never more beautiful than when she was hot on a story. Unfortunately, he knew the look all too well. "Want to tell me about it?"

"Not yet." She smiled that secret little smile of hers, the one that gave him ulcers.

The only reason she wouldn't tell him would be if she thought he would try to stop her because it was dangerous. Damn. He wished he *could* stop her. But he'd been here before and knew stopping Charity was like trying to rein in a speeding bullet. He reminded himself that this was his future, worrying about Charity. "Be *careful*."

She kissed him. "You know me."

He groaned but didn't let go of her, trailing kisses along her silken throat. At least this story had gotten her mind off the wedding. She'd been driving him crazy with discussions about orchids versus roses versus daisies, let alone all the choices for the reception.

If that wasn't bad enough, Florie had to start warning Charity about bad luck wedding superstitions. Charity pretended she wasn't superstitious. Uh-huh. But then later she'd asked him if he'd seen a blind man, a monk or a pregnant woman on his way to the Dennisons' the night he was shot.

All it seemed were bad luck before a proposal of marriage. But if he'd seen nanny goats, pigeons or wolves, then this would be a good omen that would bring good fortune to the marriage.

"I saw an entire flock of pigeons," he said, which made Charity laugh, but also look secretly relieved.

"Promise me that you'll call me at the paper if you need anything," she said now, her voice breaking a little as he nibbled at her ear.

"Promise."

She kissed him, a slow, sensuous kiss that made him desperately want to take her in his arms and make love to her. But even if he could with the cast and bandages, Charity was holding out for their wedding night.

He let go of her, not about to disappoint her now. She would get the wedding she wanted. A white one. And everyone knew "married in white, she'd chosen right."

The moment she was gone, though, he called Jesse.

"I'd venture to guess she's chasing something to do with the Dennisons," Mitch told him. Charity had been chasing one story or another about them ever since she started the *Cascade Courier* right out of college. When news was slow there was always the town's only big mystery: the disappearance of Angela Dennison twenty-seven years before. It had become the stuff local legends are made of and Charity couldn't pass up a good mystery.

"Charity went to see Lydia Abernathy this afternoon," Mitch told his brother. Florie had slipped and told him. "And now she's headed for the newspaper office." With Lydia being Wade Dennison's sister he figured whatever reason she'd wanted to see Charity couldn't be good.

"Kinda late to be going to the newspaper. Damn, that woman is obstinate, isn't she," Jesse said, unable to hide the admiration in his voice. "Glad I'm not marrying her."

"Sure you are. Are you still in town?"

"I'm at Betty's." She was making him a sandwich to go. It had been the kind of day that made him anxious to get home and as far away from being a deputy as he could. Except he wouldn't sleep once he got home, anyway. "You want me to check on Charity? No problem."

"Thanks. I'd suggest taking Charity a piece of pie. Banana cream, if Betty still has some. That way Charity won't take your head off."

Jesse grinned to himself as he hung up. It was great seeing his brother in love—and admitting it. If Mitch could fall so hard, wasn't there a chance for Jesse to find true love?

Betty bagged up the sandwich, a slice of banana cream and a slice of cherry for him.

As he drove down Main to the newspaper office, Charity was just getting out of her VW. He pulled in beside her and got out. "Here, let me get that for you," he said as she started to unlock the office. He smiled and, holding the bag from Betty's in one hand, took the keys from her.

"Mitch called you," she accused, not sounding pleased about it.

Jesse tried to look innocent, gave up and said, "I have pie. Banana cream."

She tried to hide a smile as he opened the door for her and turned on the light. "You can tell Mitch—" She stopped in midsentence, her eyes widening as she surveyed her office.

The newspaper was small, the office consisting of only three desks, a light table, copy machine, darkroom and a small press.

Everything looked fine to him. "What's wrong?"

Charity said nothing, just walked slowly into the room and headed straight for one of the large filing cabinets against the wall. The top drawer was open and when he looked past her, he saw a newspaper clipping lying on the floor between Charity and the darkroom.

He moved to her, touched her arm and motioned for her to be quiet as he headed toward the darkroom. Using his shirttail, he turned the knob. The door swung in. He flicked on the light.

The metal grate that covered a large air vent in the ceiling hung down exposing a gaping hole to the roof.

Dragging up a chair, Jesse peered into the ventilation system, careful not to touch anything. The opening was accessible from the roof and large enough for a small person to crawl through. He climbed down and checked the back door. It wasn't just unlocked. It wasn't even latched. He glanced down the alley. Empty.

"You always lock the back door?" he asked Charity.

She nodded. She hadn't moved, seemed to be frozen in her spot, eyes still wide. He figured she was reliving the last time someone had broken into the newspaper. That time she'd been in the darkroom and the burglar had grabbed her, bound her with duct tape and stuffed her in the storage closet. Obviously that incident had made a lasting impression on her.

"The door was definitely locked," she said in a whisper.

"Well, it looks like your intruder came through the air vent on the roof down into the darkroom and then made a hasty retreat out the back door. Could have been a kid—"

"No," she interrupted, shaking her head and seeming to pull herself together. "A kid wouldn't break in to steal a file of newspaper clippings. One of my files is missing."

He frowned. "How can you tell that?"

She didn't answer, just moved to the clipping on the floor and, using the pencil she'd picked up, she flipped the article over.

The headline read: Whatever Happened to Baby Angela?

Charity motioned toward the computer on the desk. Even from here he could see that the burglar had typed in the search keyword KIDNAPPING to access the file number.

"Someone is interested in the Angela Dennison case," she said.

"The file is missing?"

She nodded.

He swore under his breath. His bad feeling from earlier had settled deep in his gut.

"Interested enough to break in rather than wait until the office was open," Charity was saying. "Obviously, he doesn't want us to know who he is or why he's interested."

"Any idea who it could be?" he asked, hoping there was some weirdo in town who'd shown an interest in the case who was nuts enough to break in to read the file in private. No such luck.

She shook her head.

"Well, I think we scared whoever it was away, but there is no way you're staying here alone tonight to work."

Charity surprised him by not arguing. "It can wait until tomorrow."

Clearly she saw the potential for another story after this break-in. "You want to dust this clipping?" she asked.

He nodded and saw her glance at the sack from Betty's. "Just take the banana cream. The cherry pie and sandwich is mine."

She grinned at him as she drew out the carton with the slice of cream pie inside and took a whiff, closing her eyes for a moment, a smile on her lips.

"My brother is one lucky man."

She opened her eyes. "You know it."

Jesse walked her out to her car. "Straight home?"

"You're going to call Mitch the moment I pull away, aren't you?"

He smiled. "You know it." He watched her drive away, then took the investigation kit out of the back of the patrol car. He'd seen Mitch do this a few times and figured at this point there was no reason to call in the state crime lab boys. Not yet, anyway.

He got a half-dozen latents off the newspaper clipping and one good clear one from the back doorknob. He was hoping the burglar had taken off his gloves to peek at the articles. Maybe he hadn't planned to steal the file, didn't want to throw up a red flag when Charity found it missing.

So when he heard Jesse's and Charity's cars pull up out front after everything in town was closed and the sidewalks practically rolled up for the night, he'd just grabbed the file and run, dropping the one clipping and leaving a print on the back doorknob.

Of course, there was a good chance the prints would all turn out to be Charity's. Or Blaine's, the high-school kid who worked for her.

Back at his office, Jesse called Mitch. Charity had made it home safe and sound although Mitch was upset that someone had broken into the newspaper office, especially after the last time.

"Can you walk me through the process for sending fingerprints to the state lab?" Jesse asked his brother, taking a bite of his sandwich and booting up the computer.

Jesse did as he was instructed, figuring it would take a while to get an ID, if he got one at all tonight.

But to his surprise, the results came up immediately. He let out a curse and pushed the remaining sandwich aside.

"What?" Mitch said on the other end of the line.

"I didn't think they would come back so fast," Jesse told him. One print, the one from the back door, had come up with a match.

"That means there's an APB out on this person," Mitch said.

No kidding. The clean print on the back doorknob belonged to Margaret Jane Randolph of West Seattle.

"Tell me Charity hasn't gotten herself into trouble," Mitch said.

"Not to worry, little brother," Jesse said. No reason to tell him about Maggie just yet. "I'll call and see what's up and get back to you in the morning." He hung up before Mitch could argue.

Jesse stared at the number on the screen. Damn. Maggie wasn't on her way to Mexico. She was busy breaking into the newspaper to read the Angela Dennison file. For some reason this woman on the run from a murder investigation had stopped long enough to read a newspaper file on kidnapping.

Now what kind of sense did that make? None. And yet, it made perfect sense to him.

He opened the container with the cherry pie inside and took a few bites before he dialed the telephone number he'd scribbled down earlier. It was way too late but maybe big-city detectives worked late.

Maggie had broken into his soon-to-be sister-in-law's newspaper. It was high time he found out just what the hell was the story with his mystery biker.

He got Detective Rupert Blackmore's voice mail. Blackmore had a deep, rough-sounding voice. An older cop, hardened from time and the streets, Jesse thought. He'd met a few of them. He hung up without leaving a message.

"Now why the hell did you do that?" he asked himself and swore.

He couldn't explain it. Just a gut feeling that he needed to talk to Maggie Randolph before he talked to the cop.

Disgusted with himself, he got up from the desk and went to the window. "Some deputy you are." He stared out at the dark night. It had started to rain again. Soon he would have webbed feet if he stayed in this town.

He'd have to find her. Find out what the hell she was doing in Timber Falls. What she was searching for. But he had a bad feeling he already knew, had known longer than he wanted to admit.

Chapter Eight

In the dark tent, Maggie stared at the thick file. Her heart was still pounding. That had been a close call back at the newspaper. She'd never expected anyone to show up, not after hours and certainly not in a town that was dead by eight at night.

How long would it take the deputy to find out that she'd broken into the paper and taken the Angela Dennison file? How long before he notified Blackmore?

She should have left the file, but there wasn't time to cover her tracks, and she had to know what was in it. She'd only just started reading through the clippings, hiding in the darkroom with her flashlight, when she'd heard the cars pull up out front.

Would they have realized by now that she took the file? Maybe not. Maybe no one would know for a while.

But if it came out, then Blackmore would not only know she was in town but that she'd stumbled onto the truth.

She shone the flashlight on the file, her fingers brushing the bulging worn folder. It seemed she had been the news for twenty-seven years.

After reading for a few minutes, there was no doubt in her mind that she was the baby who had been kidnapped twenty-seven years ago from her crib in a house a few miles from here. She was Angela Dennison, youngest daughter of Wade and Daisy Dennison, owners of Dennison Ducks, a plant where decoys were carved.

The file contained not only articles published by the *Cascade Courier,* but copies of ones from larger newspapers where the kidnapping had made front-page news when it happened years ago.

Angela Dennison was only a few weeks old when she was taken from her crib in the dark of night, never to be seen again. Not only was Angela the same age as Maggie, they shared the same birthday—March ninth.

And Maggie had been adopted not twenty-four hours after Angela Dennison's disappearance.

Many of the local stories had been written by Charity Jenkins for the *Cascade Courier.* She read through all the articles again. If she was right, she was the daughter of the most written about family in town.

Maggie put the articles back in the file and snapped off the light, plunging the tent in darkness. Her head ached and she felt sick to her stomach. Closing her eyes, she listened to the sound of the river and the wind in the trees…and the frantic beat of her heart.

It was all mind-blowing. According to the articles, the mystery had been solved a few months ago when the plant production manager had been killed after admitting to Charity Jenkins right before he died that he had taken the baby. But it was clear from the newspaper articles written after his death that he had not acted alone.

Apparently both parents, Daisy and Wade Dennison, had been suspects. Might still be suspects. She had studied the photo of Wade and Daisy Dennison for a long time. It was a black-and-white, grainy and not clear enough to see any resemblance.

Or maybe she just didn't want to see a resemblance. Didn't want to be part of this infamous family.

As she sat in the darkness, she tried to tell herself it could be worse. Wade Dennison was in jail for shooting the Timber Falls sheriff during a recent domestic dispute with his estranged wife, Daisy. How could it be worse than that?

Maggie felt hot tears on her cheeks. She hadn't let herself cry. Not at the pier when Norman had been killed. Not after, when she knew it was only a matter of time before Blackmore caught up with her.

She'd focused on only one thing: learning the truth. Once she knew, she'd thought that she would be safe.

But now she saw that that wasn't the case. She still had no idea why Blackmore wanted her dead. Her throat constricted as she fought back the sobs that made her chest ache. Scared and tired and sick over what she'd found, she curled around the pain as the sobs racked her body and tears burned down her cheeks.

She was Angela Dennison. Like it or not. And for some reason, her life was in danger because of it.

After a few minutes, she dried her tears and pulled herself together. Enough crying. She couldn't just hide out in this tent and feel sorry for herself.

If Blackmore had been behind the kidnapping, that would explain why he didn't want the truth coming out. So he must have had some connection to Timber Falls. All she had to do was find it.

The obvious place to start seemed to be her biological family. Wade Dennison was a powerful man in this town but he was in jail. Was it possible he had influence as far away as Seattle? Or was it his wife, Daisy, who might have known Blackmore?

Maggie turned on the flashlight long enough to hide the stolen file under her mat, then pocketing the light, she left the tent and headed for her bike. She had hours before daylight and a lot to do before then. It was only a matter of time before Blackmore found out she was in Timber Falls and came to finish what he'd started.

Detective Rupert Blackmore was tired and cranky and his whole body ached after driving for hours. He still had miles to go to get to Timber Falls, Oregon. A waitress in an all-night truck stop refilled his coffee cup. He'd drunk too much coffee to try to stay awake and his stomach was killing him.

"Can I get you anything else?" she asked, drawing her order pad from her uniform pocket. She didn't look up as she tore off his bill and laid it on the table. She glanced at him then.

"No." He shook his head. "Thank you."

She gave him a smile, a granddaughterly smile. "Good luck. Hope you catch a bunch."

He watched her walk away. *Hope you catch a bunch.* Fish. She'd gotten the idea that he was going fishing no doubt from his hat with the lures on it and the old jacket and flannel shirt he was wearing. He smiled to himself.

Yesterday, he'd only gone home long enough to take a shower, change his clothing and collect several of the unregistered weapons he'd picked up over the years. At least the weapons weren't registered to him. They'd been ones he'd found at drug busts, ones tossed out of moving vehicles he'd chased down, ones he'd taken off dead gang members. Ones that could never be traced back to him.

At first he'd just collected them, like trophies of wild game kills. At least he thought he had. But maybe he'd known all along that the day would come when he would need a gun.

Blackmail was an insidious thing. Even when you didn't hear from the blackmailer for years, you always knew the day would come when payment would be demanded. And unless you wanted your entire world to unravel like the yarn of a slashed sweater, then you paid—no matter the price.

He'd taken the pickup he used for his fishing trips. Thrown in his tent for good measure, along with his fishing jacket and hat. When he'd finally gotten everything loaded into the pickup and slipped behind the wheel, the fishing hat perched on his head, he'd glanced in the rearview mirror.

He'd been shocked at how much he'd aged. It was as if his hair and beard had turned completely gray overnight. When was the last time he'd looked into the mirror, really looked? Obviously not when he shaved in the morning.

He recalled old fishermen he'd met over the years, tottering along the edge of the water, squinting into the sun from a face wrinkled and weathered with age and water and wind, and realized he could have been one of them.

That's when it hit him. What the people of Timber Falls, Oregon, would see. An old fisherman. Not a cop.

Not unless they looked into his eyes. That was the only part of him that would give him away. The life-hardened ice-blue eyes that even he didn't like to look into.

He'd picked up a pair of sunglasses off the dash of the truck, put them on and looked in the mirror again. He couldn't have picked a better disguise.

He left the waitress a good tip, paid his bill at the cash register and bought himself two of the best cigars the truck stop had to offer. As he headed for his pickup, he felt better than he had in days.

Maggie Randolph would never see him coming.

Jesse stared at the computer in the empty office. He knew he should go home and try to get some sleep. He could start looking for Maggie in the morning.

He leaned toward the computer, remembering what Sissy had shown him. Maggie Randolph had broken into the newspaper to research the Angela Dennison kidnapping case. While Charity's paper was too small to have an online morgue, a large paper in the Seattle area would, wouldn't it?

He went online, called up one of the two largest newspapers there, typed in the name Margaret Randolph and waited. Maybe there wouldn't be anything on her. Maybe she hadn't lived there long enough. Maybe—

A long list of articles appeared on the screen. He scanned down them surprised that most had run on the

sports pages. He shook his head in wonder. It seemed
Maggie liked to race motorcycles, participate in extreme
skiing competitions and scuba dive in dangerous wa-
ters. How about that?

He started back up the list, spotted one marked Obit
and clicked on it. Maggie's name was listed as the only
surviving child of Paul Randolph who had been killed
in a plane crash less than two months ago. He started
to click off the obituary when he spotted another one
farther down. He clicked on it. Again Maggie's name
was listed as the only child. The obit was for Mildred
Randolph, Maggie's mother. He skimmed it, noted that
the mother had contracted polio as a child and had been
in a wheelchair, and at the bottom saw something that
made him catch his breath.

Memorials were to be made to an organization the
Randolphs had started to assist older, disabled couples
in adopting a child.

What were the odds that Maggie was adopted?

Jesse swore, more sure than ever he was on the right
track. He moved the cursor back to the top of the list
and clicked on the most recent article under Margaret
Jane Randolph.

It was a story about a legal assistant named Norman
Drake. His body had been fished out of the water near
an abandoned pier on Puget Sound this morning. His
death was being investigated as a homicide. Margaret Randolph was wanted for questioning in the man's
murder along with that of Drake's boss, a local attorney
named Clark Iverson who was murdered in his office
last week. Iverson had been a longtime family friend
and attorney for Randolph's father, the recently deceased Paul Randolph.

Jesse let out a low whistle. Maggie seemed to have left a trail of bodies behind her. And now she was in Timber Falls doing a little B and E to research an old kidnapping case?

Locking up the office, Jesse climbed on his bike. It was late but there was something that couldn't wait. He'd put it off for too many years already.

Lee Tanner came out onto his deck, squinting into the darkness, as Jesse shut off his motorcycle. "Son, I was hoping that was you."

Jesse saw with relief that his father was sober. It had been a long time now but he wondered if he would always feel that instant of fear just before the relief no matter how many years his father had been on the wagon. "I know it's late…."

Lee shook his head. "I'm glad you stopped by. I was just enjoying the night sky." The rain shower had passed, leaving the sky clear and full of stars.

Jesse joined him at the deck railing, trying to see his father the way Daisy Dennison must have almost thirty years ago. Lee still had a thick head of dark hair, but at fifty-five it was shot with silver. When Lee Tanner used to ride horses in the woods behind the house with Daisy his hair had been as black as Jesse's.

His father was still an attractive man, strong and lean, his dark eyes more solemn than Jesse remembered them, his demeanor more serene. Was that just from being sober? Or had his father found some kind of peace with the past?

Jesse was reminded that he'd thought the same thing of Daisy, that the years had mellowed her, as well.

"What's on your mind, son?" Lee asked, tilting his

head back as he looked up at the glittering stars and sliver of silver moon overhead. A light breeze stirred the tops of the nearby pines, whispering softly to the night.

Jesse hesitated, afraid he was about to destroy any peace his father had found and send him back to the bottle. "The newspaper office was broken into tonight."

Lee looked over at him in surprise. This rainy season had been the worst. Murders and shootings and all interrelated in some way to the Dennisons.

"The burglar took Angela Dennison's kidnapping file." Jesse saw his father tense. A deep silence stretched between them. "There's something I need to ask you."

"As a lawman or my son?" Lee inquired quietly.

"Both. I need to know if there is any chance Angela Dennison is your daughter."

Lee closed his eyes and sighed softly. "Why would you ask me that after all these years? What possible difference could it make now?"

"I think she's alive," Jesse said, the words tumbling out, words he hadn't dared even think let alone say until this moment. "I think she's in Timber Falls. And I think she's in bad trouble. I have to know the truth. It might be the only way I can help her."

His father's eyes came open slowly. He stared at his son, his whole body seeming to quake as he gripped the rail. "Angela alive?" Tears welled in his dark eyes, now no longer at peace. "Does Daisy know?"

"I don't even know for sure myself yet," Jesse said, but maybe part of him had known from the moment Maggie had lifted her head beside that rain-soaked highway last night and he'd felt as if he'd been hit between the eyes with a two-by-four. He hadn't wanted to see the resemblance. So like Desiree and yet so different.

"My God, if Angela really is alive…" Lee Tanner stumbled over to one of the deck chairs and lowered himself into it, looking suddenly older than his fifty-five years.

"I have to know, Dad."

His father was shaking his head in wonder, staring off into the darkness as if caught in the past again. "Everyone thought she was dead."

"Dad? Is there a chance that Angela is your daughter?"

Lee Tanner looked up. "It's been so long, Jesse. You have to understand, we're different people than we were then. I know part of you believes the affair was why your mother left me—"

"I don't care about that. I *have* to know if Angela could be your daughter. My…half sister."

"Why would the truth ever have to come out? What difference—" Lee Tanner seemed to see the answer in Jesse's gaze. "Don't tell me that you're—"

"I've only laid eyes on her once," Jesse said quickly. "But if I'm right about her…" How could he explain to his father that he was instantly drawn to this woman, felt things he'd never felt? He couldn't explain it to himself. And his greatest fear was that this woman would always be forbidden to him.

"Oh, Jesse."

"I need to know the time frame."

His father seemed about to deny it, then said quietly, "I honestly don't know. But it's possible both girls could be mine."

Desiree, too. Hadn't Jesse always suspected as much? Wasn't that why he'd never taken her up on her many offers? Why he'd felt brotherly toward her?

Well, he didn't feel that way toward Maggie.

"Didn't you ever bother to ask Daisy?" he demanded.

His father looked up at him. "She went back to Wade for a while and swore that Desiree was his."

"And Angela?"

"We never spoke about Angela."

Jesse cursed under his breath. "When did Daisy break it off?"

His father seemed surprised by the question. "Daisy didn't. I did."

So that's how it had gone down. Mitch told him not long ago that Daisy had said she loved their father. Did she still? "When was that?"

"Before I knew she was pregnant," he said and looked out across the dense forest that stretched in front of his place. "I couldn't keep having an affair, not while I was married to your mother. I knew it was wrong but Daisy and I— I suppose that's why Daisy never told me she was pregnant. I didn't talk to her again until—"

"Until my mother left," Jesse guessed. "Daisy must have called you to tell you that your wife had been up to the house demanding blackmail money."

Lee closed his eyes again in silent acknowledgment.

"That's when you changed your mind and gave her the money to leave," Jesse said, seeing now how it had happened. His mother had never loved his father. As far back as he could remember, Jesse had known she wanted to leave the three of them, had just waited for her husband to grant her a divorce—and pay her off.

His father said nothing. What could he say about a woman who was that desperate to abandon her two sons and husband and had been long before her husband had taken up with Daisy Dennison.

"Why did Daisy tell you about Mother going up there?" Wasn't it obvious? "She wanted you to face how badly my mother wanted to leave, didn't she?"

He opened his eyes. "Ruth was a good woman—"

"Don't even try to sell me on her, okay?"

Lee looked down at his boots. All these years he'd tried to spare Jesse and Mitch, pretending their mother had wanted them, just couldn't handle marriage to him, always blaming himself and making excuses for her.

"Did Daisy hope you two would resume your affair after that?" Jesse asked.

A few minutes stretched past. "Daisy wanted more than I could offer her then."

That surprised Jesse. Was it possible his dad had been serious about Daisy?

"Whatever Daisy was thinking, Angela's kidnapping changed everything for her," Lee Tanner continued, turning to look at Jesse. "If this woman really is Angela…"

Jesse nodded. "It could open up a can of worms that will make everything else pale by comparison."

They fell into a deep silence again.

Jesse reached into his jacket pocket and handed his father the DNA test. "I need this now."

He nodded, went into the house and returned a few minutes later. He handed his son the boxed-up test. It was hard to tell what his father was thinking, let alone feeling at that moment.

"If I'm right, a lot more than dirty laundry is going to come out," Jesse said. "There's been some deaths back in the city where she's been living."

His father's eyes widened. "You don't think she—"

"No. She isn't a killer." How did he know that? He

just did. Just like he knew she was Angela Dennison. "I'm afraid she's in trouble." Hell, he *knew* she was in trouble—that saddlebag full of money, the APB out on her. He just didn't know how much.

He looked over at his father, saving the worst for last. "Dad, I need to know where my mother is."

Lee reared back as if he'd been punched. "Why would you—"

"Do you know where she is?" Jesse watched his father's face. "You do." Jesse groaned. "You've been sending her money all these years." He couldn't believe it.

"You're wrong. But I would have if she'd asked. She's your mother."

"She was *never* a mother to Mitch and me, and you know it."

"She brought you into this world," Lee said. "For that, I owe her. And so do you."

Jesse gritted his teeth. "Where is she?"

"You're asking as a deputy now, aren't you?"

"Yes. She could be a material witness in the kidnapping. She was at the Dennison house just before Angela disappeared and she was never questioned because she skipped town that same day." Jesse narrowed his eyes at his father. "Don't tell me you haven't wondered if she had something to do with Daisy Dennison's baby disappearing."

He expected his father to argue that Ruth Anne Tanner would never steal the woman's baby to get back at her because of the affair. He didn't. Couldn't. Even if Ruth hadn't given a damn about her husband, she had tried to blackmail Daisy. When Daisy threw her out without a cent, Ruth might have decided to get even and they both knew it.

"I don't know where she is," Lee said, his voice sounding hoarse. "My only connection to her is through my attorney and hers."

"Your attorney still Matthew Brooks?"

His father nodded with obvious reluctance. "Jesse, please don't go see her. No good can come of it."

"I don't doubt that," Jesse said, hearing the fear in his father's voice. Like Jesse, he must fear his former wife had kidnapped Angela and involved Bud Farnsworth out of vengeance.

Or maybe for money. It seemed Maggie had ended up with wealthy adoptive parents. He could only guess how that had happened. "This has been a long time coming. I'm sure you know that."

Lee wagged his head. "I don't want to see you boys hurt."

"Then don't tell Mitch," Jesse said. "I'll protect my little brother for as long as I can. But if my mother took that baby…"

Lee looked away. "For Daisy's sake I pray Angela really is alive and that your mother had nothing to do with taking her."

Jesse studied his father, seeing something that he'd missed years ago. Lee's feelings for Daisy Dennison. How deep did they run? Jesse wasn't sure he wanted to know.

"You won't say anything to Mitch about this?" he asked his father.

Lee looked up in surprise. "And have Charity find out? It would be on the front page of her paper by tomorrow." He smiled as if admiring her tenacity, the same tenacity that had her now about to marry Mitch.

"No matter what you find out, son, we're a family. We'll weather this storm just like we have all the others."

Jesse nodded, wishing he could believe that. "Tell your lawyer I'll be contacting him."

Lee sighed and looked out into the darkness. "I hope you know what you're doing."

As Jesse walked back to his bike, a few white clouds cruised by over the tops of the trees obscuring the stars and moon, darkening the night to as black as his mood. Maggie was out there somewhere. He could feel it. Fate had made their paths cross. But maybe not for the reason he'd originally thought. Or desperately wanted.

Either way, she needed him. And he doubted she realized it. He just hoped he could find her before it was too late.

As he reached to start the bike, he felt the damned cell phone vibrate in his pocket.

"Jesse!" Daisy Dennison cried the moment he answered the phone. "Someone has broken into Dennison Ducks. The thief is still there. The new production manager is on the other line calling from her cell phone outside the plant watching it happening right now. Someone's in Wade's office with a flashlight going through the files!"

"I'm on my way." Jesse snapped off the phone and headed the bike toward Dennison Ducks, already pretty sure he knew who the thief was and what she was looking for.

Chapter Nine

Maggie had just dropped through the air vent into the second-story office section of Dennison Ducks when she heard it. The soft scuff of a shoe on the concrete first floor below her.

She froze, listening. Had she only imagined it? She waited, heard nothing then snapped on the small flashlight and shone it around the office.

Quickly and quietly she moved past the secretary's desk to Wade Dennison's office. Her light caught on an eye gleaming from the corner. Her heart leaped to her throat, choking off her scream. She settled the flashlight beam on the eye, ready to run.

A large duck, its plastic eye sparkling, looked back at her. She realized the room was full of ducks. Every size, shape and color stared down at her from a shelf that ran the entire circumference of the room.

Hurriedly, she scanned the file cabinets, not sure exactly what she was looking for until she spotted the locked file drawer directly behind his desk. She moved soundlessly to the desk, picked up the letter opener and approached the file drawer.

The lock was old, the cabinet handle dusty, as if it hadn't been opened for a while. She pried with the letter opener until the lock broke and, holding the same flashlight in her teeth, quietly slid open the drawer.

That's when she heard the sound again. Someone moving through the plant below her. A stair creaked. Then another. Someone was coming up the steps to the office.

Deputy Jesse Tanner? Had someone spotted the light in the office and called the cops?

There was only one file in the drawer. The rest of the space was covered in dust. She grabbed the file, stuffed it into her jacket, turned off the flashlight and, not bothering to close the drawer, retraced her steps quietly across the room.

She could hear someone coming up the steps now, see the faint glow of a penlight. She reached out in the dark, located the desk and climbed up onto it. Any moment the person would enter the office.

She froze, immobilized with fear, as she caught a whiff of the same odor she'd smelled on the pier right before Blackmore had tried to kill her.

He was almost to the top of the stairs. Maggie pulled herself up into the vent and moved fast, no longer afraid of making noise. She could hear the thunder of running footsteps across the office, the rattle of the vent grate as it was banged aside.

In an instant she was on the roof and racing across

to the pine tree she'd climbed for access. She scrambled down through the limbs, afraid someone would be waiting for her at the bottom.

But once on the ground, no one appeared out of the darkness.

She leaped onto her bike, started it quickly, taking off down the road at full speed. She hadn't gone far when she saw the headlight of the other bike. It came roaring up the hill, the headlight catching her broadside in its sights.

Jesse was almost to the decoy plant when he spotted the single light coming out. A biker. Moving fast.

In his headlight he saw the gleam of the biker's helmet, recognized both it and the bike as she turned to look in his direction. First the newspaper and now Dennison Ducks.

She saw him, turned hard to the right, throwing up gravel as she took a shortcut across the ditch and flew up onto the dirt road headed away from town.

He went after her, telling himself she couldn't outrun him on this narrow rutted dirt road that wound through the mountains. She didn't know the road as well as he did. Nor could she take the familiar curves the way he could—and had on many occasions in his youth.

But then he'd forgotten that he wasn't dealing with just any woman. Maggie had been racing bikes since she was a girl. She stayed ahead of him no matter how hard he tried to catch her, hugging the corners, riding high on the road and staying in the lead.

Damn. He feared she would kill herself trying to get away from him, and yet he had to catch her. He couldn't let her get away from him. Not again.

They roared through the darkness, the dense forest rushing by, the road a winding ribbon of rutted dirt track.

He realized that the dirt road would soon connect to the main highway. The way she was riding and given the capabilities of her bike she'd outrun him once she hit pavement again.

He stayed right with her but just as he'd known once she roared up onto the highway she was gone, leaving his Harley in the dust.

He stopped, tore off his helmet and swore as the last red glow of her taillight faded in the distance. That woman could ride, but he'd known that about her.

He wondered, as he stared after her down the highway into the darkness, what else he would learn about Maggie Randolph before this was over—and that's what had him worried.

He shifted the cycle into gear and headed back toward Dennison Ducks. He still had to deal with Daisy before the night was over. But somewhere out there in the forest was a biker with a personal interest in Angela Dennison's kidnapping. A biker with a bunch of money in a saddlebag and a West Seattle homicide detective after her.

And he had no way to help her. Even a woman as capable as Maggie Randolph might be in more trouble than she could handle. He wondered when he'd see her again.

Not soon enough to suit him.

Maggie took a series of back roads she'd memorized from the old logging road maps, putting as much distance as she could between her and the deputy. And the man who'd been in the decoy plant with her tonight.

Detective Blackmore wasn't just in Timber Falls. He'd been at Dennison Ducks. He'd been that close. Had he followed her to the decoy plant? Or had he just known that's where she would show up?

Her heart was still pounding. She'd smelled him. That same rank smell she'd caught on the pier just before he fired at her and she'd rolled off the pier with Norman's dead body and splashed down into the churning surf.

And right behind the killer had been Deputy Jesse Tanner. She'd known the moment she saw the single headlight who it was. She'd seen his bike in the garage, an old Harley. Had Detective Blackmore called him? Or had someone else?

She hadn't been sure she could outrun Jesse. It had been close until she reached the highway and opened her bike up.

Now she pulled over to the side of the logging road, shaken and weak from the fear. She shut off the engine to listen. The silence engulfed her like the darkness. She breathed in the night air and let it out slowly. She was safe. For the moment.

But now both Blackmore and the deputy knew she'd been at Dennison Ducks. Maybe even knew it had been her at the newspaper. Jesse Tanner was smart enough to put it together given her mode of entry into the buildings.

Detective Blackmore must have called the deputy to help him capture her under the pretense of taking her back to Seattle. And wouldn't Deputy Jesse Tanner have to give her over to Blackmore? Wasn't that the way the law worked?

Her heart rate began to slow. And she felt a stab of regret that Jesse hadn't caught her. That she hadn't *let* him catch her. By now she would know one way or the other if Blackmore had gotten to the deputy.

That kind of thinking could get her killed, she reminded herself.

So why did her instincts tell her Deputy Jesse Tanner could be trusted? And with more than her life. Or maybe she just wanted to believe that because she liked him. She smiled at that understatement.

Jesse found Daisy's new production manager waiting outside the back door at Dennison Ducks.

He parked his bike and walked toward the woman, surprised in more ways than one. He'd heard Daisy was taking over the running of the decoy factory now that Wade was in jail, but as far as he knew there'd been no announcement of a new production manager since Bud Farnsworth had been killed there in October.

Since Daisy had never shown any interest in Dennison Ducks—other than spending the income from it—Jesse, like the rest of the town, wasn't sure what to expect from her as far as management skills.

"You must be Deputy Tanner," the woman said, extending a hand. "Mrs. Dennison told me to wait for you here. I'm Frances Sanders, the new production manager."

Frances was tall and blond, in her late fifties with a kind face and a strong grip.

Jesse shook her hand, trying hard to hide his surprise

since he knew damned well that Wade would never have hired a woman for the position.

"You expected a man," Frances said with a smile. "Don't let my gender fool you. I know what I'm doing. My father was a decoy carver. I grew up in the business."

"Didn't mean to infer otherwise," he said and returned her smile. "You're just a lot different from the last production manager."

"I should hope so from what I've heard about him," she said smoothly, then looked toward the plant. "I came by to pick up some reports and saw a flashlight beam bobbing around inside the main plant and called Mrs. Dennison at once. A few minutes later, I saw the second flashlight."

"Second flashlight?" he asked in surprise.

She nodded. "There was definitely two of them. One on the lower floor, the second upstairs in Mrs. Dennison's office."

Mrs. Dennison's office? Formerly Wade's office.

"I got a glimpse of both of them as they were fleeing. The one who took off over the roof was small and slim, a woman, I think. The other was definitely a man, larger."

Could he be wrong about Maggie? "They were *together*?"

She shook her head. "I got the impression the man was chasing the woman. She took off on a motorcycle, but you know that since I heard you go after her."

He smiled, impressed. "And the man?"

"Just caught a glimpse of him going through the trees." She pointed in the opposite direction. "Then I heard the sound of an engine. Truck, I'd say. Can't be sure, it was too far away."

He nodded. "Nice job. Have you been inside yet?"

"I waited for you. I didn't want to destroy any evidence."

"Let's take a look." And he stood back while she opened the door.

It didn't take him long to find where someone had broken in through a window at the back. Maggie had come in through an air vent via the roof, same as she had at the newspaper office. He'd known she hadn't come to steal decoys so finding what she'd been after was a no-brainer.

"Looks like the lock on the top drawer of the file cabinet has been broken," Frances noted.

The drawer was open, as if Maggie had been interrupted again. The drawer was also empty but he could see where possibly one file folder had been. The rest of the drawer was covered in fine dust. It seemed odd that Wade would keep this drawer locked and yet it had held so little. "Any idea what was kept in here?"

She shook her head. "Only Mrs. Dennison could tell you that."

Mrs. Dennison. He glanced around. Nothing else seemed to have been disturbed. What had Maggie been looking for? He could only guess. More information on Angela Dennison.

And what had the second intruder been after?

Maggie Randolph.

"Thanks for your help," he told Frances as she locked up after him. She was like a breath of fresh air compared to the last production manager. "Good luck with your new job."

Jesse had hoped he wouldn't have to see Daisy Dennison again. Twice in one day was way too much. But he climbed on his bike, deciding to get it over with tonight.

The Dennison mansion was a couple of miles from the decoy factory. As he turned onto the road that led to the house, he saw that all the lights were on, including the porch lamp. Daisy had obviously been expecting him. She answered the door herself after only one ring.

"Did you catch the thief?" She had a drink in her hand and she looked as if it wasn't her first.

"You mind if I come in?"

She looked contrite, stepped back and waved him inside. "What can I have Zinnia bring you to drink?"

"Nothing for me."

She seemed disappointed and he wondered if she got lonely in this big house with Desiree usually off getting into trouble. He wondered how Daisy would take the news if he was right about Maggie.

"As far as I can tell the only thing taken might have been a file from a locked cabinet in Wade's office," he told her.

Daisy looked down at her glass, then held it to her lips and took a drink.

"What was in that file?" he asked, seeing that she knew something about that locked filing cabinet drawer.

Turning her back on him, she walked into the living room. "Wade's...*personal* papers," she said over her shoulder.

Anger drove him deeper into the house. The place smelled of scotch and some too-sweet scented candle. He felt nauseous. "Let's not play games, okay? The newspaper was also broken into tonight. The burglar took only one thing. A file containing stories about Angela's kidnapping."

Daisy froze.

He could almost feel the tension emanating from her. "So I'll ask you again, what was in that file?"

When she spoke all the steel had gone out of her. "Why can't people just leave my family alone?"

He could think of several answers to that question, starting with the family's bad behavior, but he had a feeling the question was rhetorical. And he'd already shared his feelings with her earlier today. He doubted she'd put up with another lecture.

"Please," she said, turning to look at him. "Sit down." As if on cue, the German housekeeper appeared with a tall glass of lemonade he hadn't asked for and another drink for her mistress.

Jesse took the chair Daisy offered him and the lemonade. It was better than his. "Great lemonade," he said to Zinnia's retreating back. She gave no sign that she'd heard him.

"She doesn't speak much English," Daisy said.

He nodded, figuring Zinnia probably spoke more than Daisy realized. He wondered what it took to live in the same house with these people, let alone serve them the way Zinnia did. He shuddered to think.

"I'm not sure what was in the file," she said after a moment. "I know that he kept the correspondence with private investigators during the many years we searched for Angela. False leads, dead ends. I guess Wade didn't want me to see it. He had the only key and the cabinet was always locked."

"Whatever secrets were in there, they're going to

come out," he warned. "If there is anything you want to tell me…"

Daisy put down her unfinished drink and didn't pick up the new one. Her eyes were shiny with booze and possibly regret as she looked up at him as if she'd been somewhere else. "The DNA tests were in there," she said, her voice barely a whisper.

"What DNA tests?"

"The one Wade took to prove that he was that woman's father. Hers was in there, too." Her voice was barely a whisper. The woman in question was the product of an affair Wade Dennison had had almost thirty years ago with the nanny.

So now Maggie had the DNA test results.

Daisy met his gaze. "You look more like your father than even Mitch does." She was crying as she started to reach for the intercom to buzz the housekeeper. "Zinnia will show you out."

"I can find my own way."

Once on the road into town, Jesse opened up the bike and let it run. The night air was cold and damp. He watched the ribbon of dark road disappear under his front tire and felt that old pull.

But it wasn't as strong as it had once been. Instead, his mind quickly shifted to Maggie Randolph as he reached the edge of town—and how to find her.

The Duck-In bar was closing as he cruised through town on his way home. He was tired and was hoping for a few hours of sleep before he went looking for Maggie.

But as he passed the bar, he saw Desiree opening the passenger side of her red sports car. The top was up but he'd gotten a glimpse of the man behind the wheel.

He swore and flipped a U-turn in the middle of the street and went back.

Desiree turned at the sound of the bike, then smiled when she saw who it was and waited, holding the door open, not getting in just yet. Her gaze met his as if in defiance and she glanced toward the guy behind the wheel, no doubt wanting to make sure Jesse had seen who her date was. Bruno, the guy who'd been hanging out with Betty.

Jesse pulled alongside the car where Desiree was standing with the passenger door open. She seemed pleased that she'd gotten a reaction out of him. His contempt for her antics must have shown. Did his guilt show, as well? He couldn't help but think she was as confused as he was about their relationship and that of their parents.

"I was just at your house," he said. "Someone broke into Dennison Ducks. Your mother isn't doing too well."

The smile flickered and died. "Is Mom—"

"She's fine. Upset, obviously. Scared."

Desiree had paled. He could see that even under the glow of the Duck-In neon. She closed the passenger door and started around the car to the driver's side. She opened the door and motioned without a word for Bruno to get out.

"Hey, I thought we were going to *party?*" Bruno said.

"Out," she said. "Now."

He looked from her to Jesse, then slowly slid from the seat with obvious disappointment.

Desiree climbed in and, slamming the door, started the car.

"Don't speed," Jesse yelled over the powerful engine, his words lost as Desiree threw the car into Reverse and, tires squealing, headed home.

Jesse stared after her, figuring he'd at least saved her from Bruno, for tonight, anyway. He turned his gaze on the man. Bruno was still standing in the bar parking lot, his eyes hard with anger and booze. He was big, with wide shoulders and a blockhead on a thick corded neck.

From the looks of things, his nose had been broken more than once. Jesse suspected he was a bar brawler, someone who liked to fight and throw his weight around. He also had a good ten years on Jesse.

As Bruno advanced on him, Jesse stepped off the bike and pulled out his badge, shaking his head as he held it up. Jesse had done a little fighting himself in the old days. But while the thought of kicking the crap out of Bruno had its appeal, he wasn't in the mood tonight.

"You don't want any of this," Jesse said.

Bruno stopped, seemed to give it some thought then turned and sauntered down the street toward the faint glow of neon at the opposite end of the street. Betty's Café.

Jesse pocketed his badge, swung his leg over the bike and started the engine. His body was wired, ready for a fight, and it took him a while to calm down.

He roared through town and out onto the open highway, letting the darkness engulf him, the air and the night soothing him a little. Still, part of him wanted to take the easy way out, just keep going and not look back. In the old days, Jesse would have been long gone. No goodbyes.

But that was the old Jesse. The Jesse who hadn't settled down, built his own cabin, met a woman who he couldn't quit thinking about, right or wrong.

He turned onto the jeep trail that led to his cabin and drove up through the trees and blackness. He parked his bike in the garage, closed the door and stood for a moment just looking at the cabin with a sense of pride—and awe. Home. He'd never needed it as much as he did tonight. He thought of Maggie standing here last night looking up at it.

Inside the cabin, he headed straight for his studio, shrugging out of his uniform and donning a pair of paint-covered cutoffs. He opened the windows to let in the night air, then turned toward his easel.

For a while, he just stared at the blank canvas, then picked up a brush and began to paint, trying not to think about anything. Especially his conversation with his father. Or the Dennisons. Or Bruno.

Mostly he wanted to forget just for a little while that he was now a cop. *The* cop in Timber Falls. Or that it was his job to find Maggie and arrest her.

After a moment, he lost himself in his work, in the feel of brush bristles in the paint, the paint on the canvas. The ability had been there for as long as he could remember, first drawing as a boy when he could make something appear on paper with just a pencil. Magic. That's how he thought of it. As if it came from somewhere else, certainly not from him.

A shape started to emerge on the canvas, almost startling him as he realized what he had painted. He stepped back and stared at the partial face and the expression he had captured. Maggie Randolph. Eyes the same rich brown as her hair. Smiling.

He tried to remember if he'd seen her smile like that in the short period of time he'd been around her. No. And yet he knew that when she really smiled she would look exactly like she did in the painting. The smile lighting her face from within. Radiant. Breathtaking.

He put down his brush. What the hell was he doing? This woman could be a murderer on top of everything else.

He glanced at his watch—almost 3:00 a.m. Too late or early for anything but sleep. Unless you were a man who couldn't sleep and you knew that somewhere close by there was a woman...

He quickly cleaned his brush, then went down to his bedroom. He put his uniform back on and strapped on the state-issued hip holster, before sliding the gun into place, not wanting to think about needing it. Worse, using it.

Then he headed for his truck. Maggie Randolph wasn't through with Timber Falls. He felt it in his gut. That meant she had to be hiding somewhere nearby. She'd had a tent and sleeping bag strapped on her bike. But neither had been there when he'd chased her earlier.

He considered the direction she'd taken when she'd hit the highway, just before he'd lost her. Away from where she was camped. He'd bet on that.

So he headed south, feeling as if he knew this woman. She hadn't been off his mind for twenty-four hours. He'd been tracking her, putting together tiny fact after tiny fact about her, discovering more and more that intrigued him. And worried him.

He knew how she would think because he would have thought the same way were he in trouble...and he'd certainly been there. He'd been face-to-face with the woman only a short time and yet he felt as if he had been waiting all his life for her.

Given who her father might be, that scared him more than he wanted to admit. Fate couldn't be that cruel.

The highway was empty, the night dark. This area of the country was littered with campgrounds, small intimate campgrounds that were completely deserted this time of year. Many of them closed. Because the forest was so dense, she would pick an empty campground to hide in.

The campsite would be as far from the road as possible. There were so many and with no one around, she would feel safe. No, not safe enough. She'd pick a campground that wasn't open thinking no one would look for her there.

Then she'd hide at the densest part of the rain forest. And like a nocturnal animal, she would sleep during the day and do whatever had brought her to Timber Falls under the cloak of darkness.

But after her exploits tonight, she would be holed up by now, trying to get some sleep. She would think she was still safe, that no one would come looking for her at this hour.

No one except a man who couldn't sleep. A man possessed.

Chapter Ten

It was just breaking day by the time Jesse found her. He spotted a single tire track in a muddy spot at the edge of the pavement a quarter mile past the locked gate of a closed campground.

He kept going down the road without slowing, then parked the truck and walked back, hoping for the element of surprise.

Following the track, he wove his way through the dark woods, the sky above him a palette of pastels. As the bike track drew him deeper into the dark woods, he could hear the sound of the MacKenzie River, smell the water mingling with the scent of cedar.

This was the first morning in months that it hadn't rained—at least not yet. A sure sign that spring was coming.

The sky lightened over the tops of the trees as he

walked. She'd hidden well. No one would look back in here for her. No one but Jesse Tanner who'd been raised here and knew all the good hiding places from back when he was running from the law instead of enforcing it.

As he moved cautiously through the empty campground, it dawned on him that she might not be alone. That maybe the production manager at the plant had been wrong and that Maggie *had* been with the man.

No, his gut instinct told him she was traveling solo. Whatever mission she was on, she was on it alone. She wouldn't have dragged anyone into this. The man Frances Sanders had seen had to have been chasing Maggie, just like it had seemed. Who, he wondered, was after her? And why?

Jesse was at the farthest point from the highway when he spotted the dark-colored tent through the trees. It blended in nicely with the terrain. He wondered if she'd planned it that way. He didn't see the bike anywhere around. Maybe she hadn't returned yet.

Cautiously he moved closer, the rush of the river next to the tent masking his footfalls.

Other than the river, the day seemed unusually quiet as if holding its breath—just as he was doing as he neared the tent.

It was a two-man tent. The flap on one end was open and he could see that the space inside was empty. That seemed odd. He felt a stab of worry cut through him. She wouldn't have left the closure unzipped unless—

He caught sight of her bike out of the corner of his eyes. It was partially hidden in the vegetation a half-dozen yards behind the tent near the river.

She was here. Somewhere. Had she seen him approach? Was she hiding? More like waiting to attack him when he got too close?

He moved cautiously toward the bike. If she was planning a quick escape, she wouldn't want to be far from her mode of transportation.

That's when he saw her. Just a flash of flesh through the trees. He swore under his breath as he saw that she was standing buck naked in a pool of river water, her back to him.

The water pooled around her waist as she sudsed her hair, working quickly in what had to be freezing cold water. Nothing could get him in the river this time of year, he thought with grudging admiration. She was tougher than he was.

He stepped closer, feeling the pull of her. She had taken over his life the past twenty-four hours. And now he had her in his sights.

Her back was lean and strong. Her shoulders in perfect proportion with her hips and height. Her skin seemed to glow in the first light of day, glistening from the droplets of water on her skin and soapsuds, only the hint of creamy white breasts at her sides, and he wished that he could paint her just like that. A water sprite at dawn.

He looked away, reminding himself that if he was right about this woman she was off-limits to him. He'd found her but she might always be as elusive to him as she'd been for the past twenty-four hours. The mere thought struck him like a blow.

That's when he spotted her clothing hanging from a tree limb at the edge of the river. He moved toward the clothing as she dipped below the surface of the water, coming up almost immediately.

Eyes closed, she flipped her long, dark hair back over her shoulder. It fell in a wet wave, plastering itself to her back. She let out a soft sound, shivered and hugged herself against the cold, one arm over her breasts as she turned, the other hand outstretched reaching for her clothes.

Her fingers touched the now empty limb, felt around then froze. Her eyes flew open.

Maggie sensed his presence just an instant before she realized her clothing was gone from the tree. She blinked water from her eyes and saw him standing on the rocky shore just inches from her and he had her clothes.

She stifled a cry of surprise and alarm and hugged herself from the cold, hoping he didn't see how scared she was.

He held the clothes out to her and she realized he was trying not to look at her nakedness. He'd probably already seen everything there was to see but she was still surprised and touched by his chivalrous behavior.

She wondered how long he'd been standing there watching her. He was wearing his sheriff's deputy uniform, his expression solemn. There was no doubt he was here in an official capacity. Where was Blackmore? Waiting up on the road?

"Hello, Deputy Tanner." Her words sounded much calmer than she felt. Her mind was racing. He'd found her? How?

She studied Jesse Tanner's face feeling emotions that surprised—and worried—her. He was a deputy of the law. He would turn her over to Detective Blackmore. He would have to.

"You must be cold," he said, still holding her clothes out to her, keeping his eyes averted.

She *was* cold. Freezing. Her body felt numb from the waist down. She took a step toward him and her clothes, afraid she would stumble and seem even more vulnerable. Like being naked in the middle of the river with a cop holding her clothing wasn't vulnerable enough.

Looking away, he held out his free hand to her.

For a moment, she considered ignoring his offer of help. But she knew that would be foolish. Her body ached from the cold water and she had no chance of escape without her clothing.

She took his hand and let him steady her as she climbed over the rocks, all the time working on a plan of escape. All the time praying he hadn't already made some deal with Blackmore that involved the Seattle cop taking her back to the city.

"Nice little town you have here," she said.

He nodded, seeming a little amused, and without looking at her, handed her the bra, the white lacy one she'd been wearing the night she went to meet Norman at the pier. She put it on. Jesse seemed to be staring downstream as if completely unaware of and unaffected by her nudity.

She knew better than that but she liked that he tried damned hard to hide it.

He handed her the shirt.

She couldn't help thinking about his art, about him. He wasn't like Blackmore. A man she would bet would have leered before he drowned her in the river.

"You a local?" she asked, buttoning her shirt and trying to get some warmth back into her body. She would need to move fast when she got the chance.

"Born just down the road," he said. "I left for a while."

He handed her the matching white lace panties, seeming almost a little embarrassed. She balanced on a rock on one foot to pull them on. He held out an arm to steady her, eyes still averted. She accepted his help again, then held out her hand for her jeans.

He handed them to her and she pulled them on over the panties, buttoned and zipped them.

"Spent some time in Mexico," she said.

He smiled. "My paintings. You seem to know more about me than I know about you."

"Somehow I doubt that," she said. "What made you come back to Timber Falls?"

He shrugged. "I got homesick for something familiar and I missed my family."

"Yes." She certainly knew that feeling. She dropped her gaze, not wanting him to see the tears that suddenly burned her eyes.

"How's the ankle?" he asked.

"Better."

He nodded, turning to face her now that she was dressed.

She pointed to her boots a little farther from the river on the bank. Her socks were sticking out of the top of each boot. He moved out of her way to let her go to them.

If she could have felt her feet, she might have made a run for it. But she had no chance barefoot and she doubted she could outrun those long legs of his even with her boots on.

She sat down on a rock along the bank, feeling the sun rising behind her back, the day growing brighter.

He looked good in his uniform. But she hadn't missed the gun strapped to his hip. At least he hadn't drawn it, wasn't now pointing it at her. But, then, he might think he had nothing to fear from her.

Didn't he realize she would do whatever she had to if he tried to turn her over to Blackmore? Maybe not.

She slipped on her biking boots, then stood, hands on her hips, feeling warmer. She was still scared but at least dressed she might stand a fighting chance.

"I thought we should have a little talk," he said. "You had breakfast yet?"

"Breakfast?" Was he serious?

"I know a place that serves great pancakes."

She looked down the river for a moment, then at him. "I'd rather not go back into Timber Falls."

He smiled. "Not in the daylight, huh? I had a feeling you'd say that. I was thinking we'd avoid town and go to my place."

She eyed him and looked around, expecting Detective Blackmore to show up any minute. "You come out here alone?"

He nodded.

She studied him. "Why pancakes? Why not just run me in? Or shoot me right here? Better yet, you could have drowned me in the river when you had the chance and no one would be the wiser."

He seemed to flinch, those dark eyes widening in surprise. "I know you're running from something but what would make you think I would want to kill you?"

She shook her head. "Maybe because the last cop I trusted tried to?"

His eyes darkened. "Don't worry. I'm not much of a deputy. I've never killed anyone and I'm hoping I don't have to before this uniform comes off in a couple of months."

"That's supposed to make me feel better?"

He laughed. It was a great sound, deep and rich. It made a humming in her chest like an echo.

"Look," he said, "I suspect you're the kind of woman who seldom needs help, probably doesn't know how to ask for it even when you do. But I think right now you could use some breakfast—and maybe a good listener." He held up both hands as if in surrender. "I've been in trouble a few times myself. I know how hard it is to trust anyone. Especially a stranger. Especially someone in a uniform."

Except he didn't seem like a stranger. She'd felt safe with him. Her heart told her that if she couldn't trust this man, she couldn't trust anyone ever. Suddenly her chest gave as if she'd been holding her breath for days. She fought the tears that stung her eyes. "Pancakes?"

Jesse smiled and nodded, seeing her relax a little. "An old family recipe."

"Your mother's?"

He shook his head. Not likely. "My dad's. He used to get up every weekend and make pancakes for my brother and me." He smiled at the memory. "I think it was the only thing he knew how to cook at the time."

She returned his smile but he could still see the tension in her body like a coiled spring. He'd have to keep an eye on her. But the tentative smile had made him desperately want to see a real smile. A smile like he'd painted, a smile like he knew she would smile. Eventually. If he could get her to trust him.

A little voice at the back of his mind warned him he could be all wrong about her. He ignored it. He'd learned a long time ago to live with his heart not his head. It had gotten him into some tight spots that was for damned sure. But it was the way he'd lived his life and he wasn't about to change that just because he'd put on some uniform.

"You have what you took from the newspaper and Dennison Ducks?" He was still Timber Falls' only deputy and Charity would have his hide if he didn't get her file back. Also, he was anxious to see what had been in the locked file cabinet in Wade Dennison's office.

She nodded and he walked with her to the tent. Everything he'd felt the first time he'd laid eyes on her was there and then some. The woman had some kind of hold on him. He hated to think what that hold might be—the one thing that would make her off-limits the rest of his life.

Whatever emotions she evoked in him, that one simple possibility wasn't something he was likely to forget.

"If you don't mind," he said, ducking into the tent with her. It was close quarters inside, but he had to make sure she didn't have a weapon stashed under the sleeping mat. "Sorry," he said after he'd checked and found nothing more lethal than a toothbrush.

She handed him two files both thick, one from the *Cascade Courier,* the other from Wade's personal file cabinet at Dennison Ducks. Wade's file had just what Daisy said would be in it. All the reports from the investigators they'd hired to find Angela and the biggest prize of all, the DNA test results on Wade and an illegitimate daughter he'd had by the family's former nanny.

"Charity will be glad to have these back," Jesse said of the newspaper clippings.

"You know Charity Jenkins?"

He nodded, meeting her gaze. "She's my soon-to-be sister-in-law. She's marrying my brother. The sheriff."

Maggie tensed. "Your brother's the *sheriff?*"

"Afraid so," he said with a smile that he hoped would reassure her. "I try not to hold it against him."

"Tell me why I should trust you?" she asked, sounding scared again.

"Because I make great pancakes and I'd bet you haven't had anything good to eat for a while," he said. "Also, you need my help."

"Do I?" She seemed amused by that. "I thought you just said you weren't much of a deputy."

He laughed. "You've got me there."

They stepped out of the tent. The sun peeked over the treetops, turning the forest to emerald.

"Mind if I ask what you're going to do with me after breakfast?"

Oh, he had all kinds of thoughts on that subject but none he could act on. "After breakfast you can tell me why you had to rob the newspaper and Dennison Ducks," he said.

She eyed him with obvious suspicion. "And then?"

"And then I do everything in my power to help you."

She met his gaze, then nodded slowly. "I believe you mean that."

"I do."

"I need you to promise me something," she said and bit down on her lower lip. She had to know he couldn't make her any promises. "Promise me you won't turn me over to Detective Blackmore," she said, her voice breaking.

She'd said the last cop she'd trusted had tried to kill her. Blackmore? Jesse was in no position to promise her that. Not only was he *the* law in Timber Falls, he could go to jail for aiding and abetting a criminal, if she turned out to be one.

He met her gaze and saw fear flashing like madness in her brown eyes. "I promise."

Her relief was so profound she seemed to sag under its weight.

He reached out and gripped her arm to steady her, shocked by the touch of his skin to hers. He let go as if he'd been burned.

"We'll break your camp and I'll come back and take care of your bike," he said, hoping she hadn't noticed his reaction to her. "I'm going to have to insist that you come with me in the truck. Not that I don't trust you."

"Right," she said, but smiled at him. He saw that flicker in her gaze. She wanted to like him. The thought warmed him more than it should have.

Back at his cabin, Jesse watched Maggie put away another stack of his pancakes. He'd taken back roads after hiding her bike and thought they would be safe. At least temporarily. He poured them both more orange juice.

"These are the best pancakes I've ever eaten," she said between bites.

"Either that or you just haven't eaten for a while," he said, smiling across the table at her.

She stabbed the last bite with her fork, soaked up the butter and syrup from her plate and popped it into her mouth. She looked up at him. Her eyes were several shades lighter than his own, hers rich with gold and ambers.

He stared into them realizing he hadn't quite captured her eyes in the painting he'd started of her.

"Thank you," she said.

"My pleasure. It gave me an excuse to make them."

"I'm not talking about the pancakes," she said quietly. "But the pancakes *are* amazing." Her smile brightened the entire room.

"Wait until you try my dad's," he said, basking in that smile and all the time hoping she'd be around long enough that she'd get the chance. "It's his recipe and he's had years of practice."

"Your mother didn't cook?"

He smiled at that. "She passed on when I was nine."
Passed on being a mother.

"Oh, I'm so sorry." Her eyes turned to warm honey. "I lost my mother five years ago. I can't imagine losing her when I was nine. That must have been very difficult for you. Your dad lives close by?"

"Just down the road."

"I envy you." She ducked her head in what he figured was an attempt to hide the depth of her pain. "I lost my father two months ago."

The plane accident. "I'm sorry. You were close."

She looked up again, nodded and seemed to be swallowing back tears.

"Maggie, let me help you."

She got to her feet, scooping up her plate and silverware and taking them over to the sink. "The last man who tried to help me got killed." She rinsed her dish, then shut off the water and turned to look at him, leaning back against the sink as she did.

He stared at her for a long moment, then got up and went to the couch and sat. "I've always found it's easier to start at the beginning," he said. "I haven't read you your rights so anything you say can't be used against you in a court of law."

"If I tell you, I will be jeopardizing *your* life," she said, sitting down to face him from the opposite end of the couch.

"I'll take my chances," he said, turning toward her so he could watch her face. "Also, the job came with a gun." He saw that she got his humor. What more could a man ask for?

"Detective Rupert Blackmore is trying to kill me. I know that sounds crazy...."

"I've heard crazier stories."

She cocked her head at him. "Well, try this one on for size then. The reason he's trying to kill me is because I'm Angela Dennison."

He nodded.

"You don't believe me."

He wished he didn't. "Why don't you tell me why *you* think you're Angela."

Maggie took a breath and told him everything, starting with the fact that her parents had always told her she was adopted. She told him about the plane crash that killed her father, the conversation Norman Drake overheard just before her father's attorney, Clark Iverson, was murdered, the phone call from Norman demanding ten thousand dollars in return for proof that her father's plane crash wasn't an accident, her call to Detective Rupert Blackmore and finally what had happened the night at the pier.

"Whoever was behind my kidnapping has successfully kept it a secret for twenty-seven years," she told him. "They thought they were safe. If my father hadn't found out and decided I needed to know the truth..."

"Why do you think he did that?" Jesse asked.

She shook her head. "He hadn't been well since my mother died." Her voice trailed off. "I think he was worried that if I didn't know…"

"That once he was gone, the kidnapper might show up."

"My family is fairly wealthy," she said, as if it were some dirty, dark secret she wished she could keep.

Fairly wealthy. He smiled at her obvious understatement. "And you're the only child."

She nodded and met Jesse's gaze. "You knew this already," she whispered, her eyes widening with fear.

Jesse quickly said, "I knew some of it, but not all of it. I ran your bike plate. There's an APB out on you. You're wanted for questioning in both Clark Iverson's and Norman Drake's murders."

She let out a cry and was on her feet. "I didn't kill anyone."

"I believe you."

She stopped moving, stared down at him. "Detective Blackmore was at Dennison Ducks last night. He almost caught me." She moved to the window to look out, as if she half expected him to be coming up the road right now. "It's just a matter of time before he shows up on the pretext of taking me back for questioning. If you hand me over to him, I'll never make it back to Seattle alive."

"You're positive the man on the pier was Blackmore? You'd seen him before?" Jesse asked.

She nodded as she turned to look back him. "His photo was in the paper." Her gaze pleaded that he believe her. "He'd been given some award for bravery in the line of the duty. I know now that's why Norman didn't go to the police. He said he didn't recognize the voice of the man who killed Clark Iverson. I didn't believe him. Now I know why he lied."

"You think he recognized Blackmore?"

She nodded and sat down again on the end of the couch. "When I told Norman that I'd called the detective on the case, he went ballistic. Just seconds later Norman was shot and killed and…" Her voice trailed off. "Just before I rolled off the pier using Norman's body as a shield, I saw the killer. It was Blackmore."

Jesse didn't bother to ask why she hadn't gone straight to the police. Or the FBI. For the same reason Norman hadn't. She feared she wouldn't be believed and with good reason. What did Blackmore have to gain by killing her and the lawyer and his assistant while Maggie had just inherited a fortune?

Her story would spark an investigation. If this cop really was a killer, he was too smart to leave a trail. Instead, the heir who'd just inherited would be the number one suspect.

The plane crash would suddenly be suspect. The facts in Clark Iverson's death and Norman Drake's could be twisted just enough to make Maggie Randolph look like a greedy adopted only child who couldn't wait for her last parent to die to get the money. She had to get rid of her father's attorney because he'd become suspicious and Norman Drake had heard her kill him and was blackmailing her. That would explain the money in her saddlebag and the fact that Norman went swimming with the fishes.

Any other woman and Jesse might have believed it himself. But not Maggie.

"There is something I need to tell you," he said and he saw her tense. "I ran your prints after the newspaper break-in. I suspected Blackmore had inquiries about you tagged so he would know about them immediately. That could be how he found out where you were."

She shook her head and reached over to touch his hand.

He jumped at her touch, both startled and uncomfortable by it, and jerked his hand back.

If she noticed, she didn't say anything as she was quickly on her feet and pacing again. "He knew I would come to Timber Falls once he realized I was alive. I'm sure he realized that when Norman's body washed up and mine didn't. He will contact you for help." She looked at Jesse for his agreement.

Jesse shook his head. "If he was going to, I would have heard from him by now."

She took a shaky breath. "You think he plans to take care of me himself without involving you?"

"It certainly looks that way."

She shook her head. "I just don't understand what it is that he's afraid I'll find out. That I'm Angela Dennison? In that case, it's too late. Or that I'll find proof that he was behind my kidnapping?"

Maggie saw Jesse's worried expression.

"The actual kidnapper is dead," he said, obviously hoping to put an end to any thought she might have of looking for the kidnapper. "He confessed."

"I read about that in the newspaper articles. The former Dennison Ducks production manager might have stolen me from my crib, but according to the paper he did it on someone else's orders."

Jesse smiled. "I wouldn't believe everything you read in the newspaper. Especially in Charity's."

"Then you think the kidnapper has been caught?"

He rubbed a hand over his stubbled jaw. He hadn't shaved in at least forty-eight hours. "I didn't say that."

She smiled, relieved he didn't lie to her.

"I'd agree that Bud Farnsworth wasn't the mastermind behind it," he continued. "I think the first step is to prove that you are Angela Dennison. You already have Wade's DNA test results. I've checked and they can be compared to your DNA to determine if you're his daughter, but then you will still need Daisy Dennison's DNA to prove you are Angela."

She stared at him, surprised by something she'd heard in his voice. "You really do believe I'm Angela."

He nodded slowly, as if he didn't want to believe it.

Maggie fought to hide her relief. Tears burned her eyes. Dammit, she would not cry. She'd let herself cry only that once in the tent; she wouldn't cry now.

But she hadn't realized how badly she wanted this man to believe her. Needed him to. It validated the risks she'd been taking and so much more. This man who'd helped her that first night on the highway…there was something about him that had kept him in her thoughts ever since.

And that worried her. Just as this feeling she had when she was around him that she was safe. He made it hard to remember that there was a formidable killer after her. She wasn't safe. Would never be safe until Blackmore was behind bars.

And now she'd put Jesse's life in danger, as well.

Jesse saw a determined look come into her brown eyes.

"I have to find the people responsible before they find me," she said.

"Now wait a minute—"

"You were born here, right? You know these people. I was kidnapped here." She was pacing again and talking fast. "How did Blackmore find me? Did he know this production manager who supposedly took me out of the house that night? And why kill me? It doesn't make any sense to kill to cover up a twenty-seven-year-old kidnapping. But I have to find out."

"Yeah, but hold on," he said, getting to his feet. "You start trying to get proof of who you are and asking a lot of questions and you'll bring the killer right down on you. You need to go somewhere safe and stay there until I find out who is behind this."

"No way." She was staring him down even though she had to look up to do it. He had her in height, girth and strength, and yet he could see that she would take him on in a heartbeat if that's what it took.

"If you're right, Blackmore has already killed three people and wounded you and he almost caught up to you last night," he said, trying to reason with her. "You can't take the chance that next time he won't miss."

"You're right," she said, throwing him off guard. "All I would be doing is waiting around for him to find me and kill me."

He told himself she'd given in too easily. There was a gleam in her brown eyes that he didn't like.

Before he could open his mouth, she said, "That's why I'm going to announce to the world that I'm Angela Dennison—and I know the perfect place to do it."

Chapter Eleven

"*Rozalyn Sawyer's party?*" Jesse exclaimed.

"I saw the ad in the newspaper. Everyone in town is invited. It's the perfect place to make my debut as Angela Dennison," Maggie said, leveling her gaze at him, daring him to try to stop her. "The Dennisons will be there, won't they?"

"The ones who aren't in jail."

"Let's start with them then," she said as if it were a done deal.

"You can't be serious. No way."

Her eyes were shiny and bright, her jaw set in stubborn determination. "I'm a target no matter what I do. But once I announce that I'm Angela Dennison at this party one of two things will happen. Blackmore will get out of Dodge, figuring it's over, there is nothing he can do now."

"Or he'll kill you because then he will know where you are and how to get to you."

She smiled and nodded. "Exactly."

"And you think this is a *good* plan?"

"Come on, you know I'm right."

"I know you're suicidal," he said.

"It will be like hiding in plain sight," she argued. "I will be a harder target to hit because everyone in town will be curious about me, right? They'll be watching me everywhere I go in a town this size. I'll be front-page news. Only someone really desperate will try to hurt me with all that heat on me." She smiled. "I'm right and you're starting to see it."

"Yep, it's definitely the fastest way to get yourself killed," he said, but he knew he didn't fool her. She had a good point and as much as he wished otherwise, he was starting to see some merit to her crazy scheme.

"Of course, I wouldn't want to spoil the party so I would do it at the end."

"How very thoughtful of you," Jesse said, hating that she was right. She was already in danger. Announcing who she was wouldn't add to that. Maybe it would even make her safer, although he wasn't counting on it.

"Under two conditions." He held up his hand before she could interrupt. "Keep in mind that I have every right to lock you up in jail if you don't agree."

She clamped her lips shut, eyes narrowed as he proceeded.

"First condition, you never leave my side the entire night," he said.

She rolled her eyes as if to say, "Don't push your luck."

"Second, do you know anything about firearms?"

"Let me see," she said, cocking her head to inspect the one he was wearing. "That would be a Glock nine-millimeter, ten-shot magazine, steel slide, double-action trigger, autoload."

"But can you shoot one with any accuracy?" he asked, only a little surprised at her knowledge of fire-arms.

She mugged a face at him. "I don't happen to have my marksmanship certificate with me but my father used to take me to the indoor firing range and I always hit what I aimed at." Her smiled faded. "I guess Dad thought it was a skill I might need one day."

So it would seem. "Shooting at a target is one thing, firing at a living, breathing person is a whole different ball game," Jesse said.

"You told me you never killed anyone," she reminded him.

He shook his head. "That doesn't mean I never *shot* anyone." He waved her next question off. "It was a long time ago. I was young and cocky and foolish."

She studied him openly as if she still found him to be at least two of those. But her look said she didn't find that to be a bad thing. "This will work," she said as if she thought he still needed convincing.

He smiled ruefully. "I wish I didn't agree with you but it sounds as if Blackmore is already in town. The best way to protect you is as Angela Dennison because you're right, everyone will be watching you. The news will spread like wildfire. And hopefully, it *will* make you a harder target to hit. That doesn't mean he won't try to kill you."

She nodded. "He's risking so much, I can't believe

he's acting alone. Unless I can find a connection between him and the Dennisons or Timber Falls...."

He groaned. "Which, of course, you're not going to be doing."

She shot him a look. "I have to find out why I was kidnapped, who was behind it and why they want me dead. You aren't going to try to stop me, are you?"

"I could put you in jail for breaking into two businesses," he pointed out.

She smiled and shook her head. "Then I would be easy pickings for Detective Blackmore. He would try to take me back to Seattle for questioning in Norman's and Clark's murder and I would never make it there alive."

Jesse quaked at the thought. "What makes you think he won't try that, anyway?"

"You'll stop him," she said and looked up at him.

At that moment, he would have wrestled Bigfoot for her. "You have a lot of confidence in me, more than is warranted, I fear."

"I know you're going to help me find whoever is after me." Before he could argue the point, she added, "And you need *my* help. I'm the only one who can identify Blackmore as the man on the pier who shot Norman and tried to kill me. But I need proof. Unless I can find the connection between Blackmore and my kidnapper..."

He cocked an eyebrow at her. "It's been twenty-seven years. What makes you think you'll find the real kidnapper after all this time? Even if he lived in Timber Falls back then, it doesn't mean he does now."

She smiled. "You don't believe that any more than I do. Blackmore wouldn't be trying to kill me if he thought I couldn't uncover something—and not just that I'm Angela Dennison. There has to be more."

"It's just crazy that anyone would try to cover up a kidnapping with multiple murders."

She nodded. "So the motivation isn't fear of prison for kidnapping charges. It's much more personal and complicated than that."

He stared at her. "What is worse than losing your freedom?"

She shook her head. "That's the way you and I think. Someone else might be just trying to save his skin."

"Like Blackmore."

She nodded. "Or keep their part in the kidnapping a secret because they regretted what they'd done so many years ago and now would lose their family, friends, social standing... I don't know. Different values for different folks, right?"

Yeah. But he had another theory. Some people cared only about themselves and did what made them feel good no matter how many people suffered because of it.

He realized he was thinking of his mother and when he looked up, Maggie was frowning at him.

"Did you get enough to eat?" he asked as he went back into the dining area to clear his dishes.

"Gobs," she said, following him. "I'm going to need something to wear to the party, a drop-dead dress—if you'll excuse the expression—one that won't show that I'm carrying a gun," she said, then seemed to realize that she'd never answered his question. "You asked me if I could pull the trigger if someone was intent on killing me. Someone who already killed my father, who for the record, was a very kind nice man. A killer who has already tried to kill me once?" She met his gaze. "In a heartbeat."

He saw that she believed it. He prayed if push came

to shove, that she could do it to save herself. Because everything about her told him, that like her adoptive father, she was a very kind nice person. And the more he knew about her, the more interested he became in this woman.

He set to work washing the dishes in the sink to quell those feelings. She moved in beside him, opening one drawer and then another until she found a clean dish towel, completely ignoring his. "I can do these, really."

"If I couldn't shoot the person after me," she said as if he hadn't spoken, "I wouldn't stay with you." She picked up one of the plates and began drying it carefully. "I know that I'm jeopardizing your life by being here." She put the plate in the cabinet and looked over at him. "You're risking your life because of me. I have to be able to do the same for you."

"That's the last thing I want."

"Too bad, because that's the way it is," she said, and stepped to him, standing on tiptoes. Her lips brushed across his cheek like a sweet whisper, sending sparks shooting along his nerve endings.

He flinched and stepped back.

"Sorry," she said, looking both surprised and confused.

"You shocked me, that's all. Static electricity, you know." He could see the lie reflected in her gaze.

She studied him. "You shock easily."

He laughed, feeling like a fool, and took the dishrag over to the table, putting distance between them, but still intensely aware of her. He could smell the scent of her on his skin, a faint tangerine fragrance that lingered like the memory of her touch.

No woman had ever affected him like this. He told

himself it was because he couldn't have her. Might never be able to have her. But he knew it was a hell of a lot more than that or his heart wouldn't ache the way it did at the thought.

"Okay, what's going on?" she asked behind him. "I appreciate everything you've done for me, Jesse. But I feel like there is something else going on between us and I know you feel it, too."

He turned to find her framed in the sunlight spilling in from the window, her hair burnished mahogany, her eyes fired with gold, her hands firmly planted on her shapely hips.

"What is it you aren't telling me?"

Maggie knew she couldn't be wrong about the energy that sparked red-hot between them. "I know you're attracted to me. So what is it? You trust me, don't you? You don't think I killed Norman or—"

"No! I trust you," he said.

"Well, I know you're not…"

"Gay?" He laughed. "No."

She frowned. "Then, I must be wrong about you being attracted to me?"

He smiled ruefully and shook his head. "That's not it, believe me."

"Then what? Jesse, every time I get near you, you shy away as if you're afraid for me to touch you."

He met her gaze, his expression pained. "My father had an affair with Daisy Dennison twenty-eight years ago."

She stared at him at first uncomprehending. "You think I might be…" She laughed.

"Sorry, but I don't see the humor," he said.

"It's just that when I realized I was Angela Dennison and that Wade was in jail for shooting the sheriff, among other things, I wished anyone else in the world was my biological father."

"Be careful what you wish for, huh?"

She nodded. "That's why you want the DNA tests." She groaned inwardly. "What if we are half sister and brother?" The thought hurt. She couldn't believe her disappointment; it felt soul deep. Not that she hadn't always wished for a sibling but not Jesse. Not this man she'd wanted since the first time she'd seen him. She trusted him with her life but she wanted more. She wanted to know what it felt like to lie in his arms and—

Suddenly she felt like crying. She hadn't realized until that moment how much she'd been hoping that Jesse would make love to her before she had to announce to the world that she was Angela Dennison and wait for a killer to come after her.

"How quickly can we get these DNA tests?" she asked.

Jesse felt the cell phone vibrate. "Hold that thought." Once and for all, they would find out who had fathered Angela. They couldn't find out soon enough to suit him. He reached in his pocket, pulled out the phone and saw who was calling. "I still have forty-five minutes before I have to check in," he said to Sissy.

"Trust me, I wouldn't be calling you, but Daisy Dennison is demanding to talk to you and I mean now. You think *I've* got attitude?"

"I get the picture." He shot Maggie a look. "Put Daisy through."

"Have you heard the news?" Daisy barked.

"What news is that?" he asked warily.

"Wade made bail!"

Wade made bail? He looked over at Maggie again. Damn, this only made things more dangerous for Maggie until he could find out who was behind her kidnapping. If they were both right and she was Angela Dennison. "When did this happen?"

"Yesterday afternoon. No one notified me. He was released first thing this morning. That means he could be on his way to the house at this very minute," Daisy cried.

"You have a restraining order on him," Jesse pointed out.

"The same one he broke last time when he tried to kill me."

Jesse wanted to point out that his brother wouldn't have been shot and would still be sheriff and handling this if Daisy hadn't provided Wade with the gun. Better yet, if they hadn't been struggling over it. "I guess I could talk to Wade—"

Before he could explain that his hands were tied until Wade did something illegal, he heard a noise outside his front door. The soft scuff of footfalls on the steps. He tensed and motioned to Maggie to go upstairs and stay hidden and silent.

The knock at the door startled him. He hadn't heard a car engine. Whoever was at the door had walked up the mountain. His first thought was Detective Rupert Blackmore.

As Maggie disappeared up the stairs, he headed for the door, saying into the phone, "Mrs. Dennison, I'm going to have to call you back—" He opened the door. "Daisy."

She smiled, obviously satisfied that she had surprised him. "I'm glad you've dropped that ridiculous Mrs. Dennison stuff," she said, stuffing her cell phone into her purse as she pushed her way into the cabin. "I need to talk to you."

She wore an off-white linen suit. Her purse and shoes were white-and-brown and matched. Her hair was brushed back from her face and she looked younger.

For a woman who'd been a recluse for years, she certainly had become social since her husband had gone to jail.

Jesse closed the door and leaned against it, arms folded over his chest, watching her as she stopped in the middle of the room and looked around.

"You share your father's talents, I see," she said, turning to look back at him. His father had built the house Jesse and Mitch had lived in as boys.

"If this is about Wade making bail—"

She waved a hand through the air. "I've decided to hire a bodyguard since my gun was taken as evidence."

Jesse lifted a brow. A bodyguard? He guessed he should be glad she hadn't decided to purchase another weapon. "Do you really think that's necessary?"

"That isn't the reason I'm here," she said, ignoring the question. "Is there any news on the break-in at the decoy plant?"

He shook his head. "Nothing to report yet." He hoped Maggie stayed hidden until tonight. Once she made her big announcement all hell was bound to break loose. He wanted to be ready for it. As ready as possible.

He watched Daisy look around the cabin and realized all of this could have been handled on the phone. So why had she walked all this way and in those shoes?

She seemed to see something and headed for the

stairs before he could push away from the door and stop her. "I heard you were painting again."

"Just a minute—"

She kept going up the wide wooden stairs toward the third-floor studio.

He went after her, glad to see his bedroom door was closed as he passed. "I don't really have anything you can see," he said as he took the stairs after her, unable to contain his anger. "It's all at the framer. But you're welcome to come to the show I'm having in June."

He stopped at the top of the stairs.

She stood in the middle of the room, her back to him. She didn't turn. Nor had she responded to his words. She seemed rooted to the spot, her body rigid.

As he moved toward her, he saw that she had one hand to her mouth. Her face was deathly pale and she was trembling.

He swore under his breath as he realized why she'd come up here. What she'd seen. The partially completed painting resting on his easel. He had captured only a likeness of Maggie, but enough that Daisy must have seen the resemblance to Desiree.

"Daisy—"

She turned. Her eyes welled with tears.

"Daisy?"

She bolted down the stairs. He heard the front door slam.

A minute later, Maggie appeared at the top of the stairs to the studio.

She looked past him at the painting of her, then moved toward it like a sleepwalker. She stared at it for a long moment, making him nervous.

He feared she didn't like it, didn't think it did her justice, that it might offend her.

"You have captured a part of me I've never seen before," she said quietly. She turned then to look at him. "She saw the painting, didn't she?"

He nodded.

And Maggie had seen *her,* he realized. "You think she knows it's me?"

"I think it spooked her."

Maggie nodded. "She was definitely upset."

He knew that, like him, Maggie was wondering if Daisy was upset because of the resemblance to Desiree or if she had recognized her other daughter, maybe had known where Maggie was this whole time, had followed her life because Daisy had been the one to get rid of her twenty-seven years ago—and was trying to again. Only this time permanently to protect herself. And she was using Detective Rupert Blackmore to do it.

"Are you all right?" he asked Maggie, fighting the urge to take her in his arms and comfort her.

"It's a shock to see her, in person. I thought I was ready to meet her, but I wasn't."

"You don't have to go through with this tonight."

She smiled at that. "We both know better than that. I can't spend the rest of my life looking over my shoulder. I heard you say Wade Dennison has been released on bail. He's still a suspect, too, isn't he?"

"My future sister-in-law thinks so," Jesse said.

"Charity? She must have good reason to believe that, being a journalist."

He smiled at that. "I think it's time you met her and my brother. We'll take along the DNA test results you got from Wade's office. We need to put as many pieces of the puzzle together as soon as we can."

"You know what the tests are going to tell us. That I'm Angela Dennison."

He nodded. "And who your father is. Or at least isn't."

Chapter Twelve

Mitch couldn't believe it. Florie arrived with the news just after daybreak—long before the *Cascade Courier* hit the streets.

Wade Dennison had made bail.

Anyone who hadn't been planning to go to Rozalyn Sawyer's gala party that evening quickly changed their minds, according to Florie. Clearly, no one wanted to miss the fireworks when Wade showed up at the party later tonight—restraining order or no restraining order.

Mitch had to agree there was little doubt that Wade would show up. Wade Dennison *was* Timber Falls and Roz's party was the highlight of the year so far. Plus, if a man was prone to making scenes what better arena than a party with everyone in town in attendance?

"I got scooped," Charity bemoaned as she brought Mitch his breakfast tray. The phone had been ringing off the hook all morning as the news spread. "It's all over the county by now."

Mitch sat up a little straighter in his recliner. "I think you're missing what is really important here, Charity. Wade Dennison has no business being out on bail. He's dangerous."

"You don't think he'll come gunning for *you* again, do you?"

He smiled at the concern in her voice. "No," he said with a laugh. "It isn't me I'm worried about. It's you. And Daisy."

Charity was already shaking her head. "Wade doesn't scare me and I don't believe for a minute that he tried to kill Daisy. If anything I think she might want *him* dead."

"Well, now that he's out on bail, she just might get her chance," Mitch said. He had a feeling this was going to be a long divorce.

And the worst part was, he was trapped in a cast. He'd never felt more useless in his life. He couldn't wait to get back to work. Jesse was capable enough but wasn't really trained for this type of trouble.

Mitch had thought about calling in a state officer, then rejected the idea. Jesse would see that as a lack of confidence in him and Mitch didn't want a rift between him and Jesse, not after all these years of being apart.

No, he just prayed that Wade didn't cause any trouble, but even as he thought it, he knew better. It was almost as if Wade had a black cloud hanging over his head, following him around.

If Wade had anything to do with baby Angela's disappearance twenty-seven years ago, then maybe this was his bad karma coming back to haunt him. Damn, Mitch realized he was starting to sound like Florie.

The phone rang. He reached over and answered it before Charity could do even that for him, then realized it would probably just be another call from gossip center.

"Little brother?" Jesse said.

Something in his tone warned Mitch. "What's wrong?"

"Is Charity there?" Jesse asked. "Can you get rid of her for a little while?"

Mitch could feel Charity watching him. He laughed and smiled. "You scared me." He shook his head at Charity to indicate nothing was wrong, just his brother Jesse being Jesse. "What you need to do is buy yourself a good miter saw. You can use it to cut your own frames after you finish this project."

"She's standing right there," Jesse said on the other end of the line.

"Exactly. Maybe you don't want to cut your own frames now but when you're famous—"

"Would you mind if I went out for a while?" Charity whispered. "Sorry, but I need to stop by the paper."

"Just a minute, Jesse." He cupped the receiver. "Take your time, Jesse is coming over. He's trying to build—"

"You two have fun," Charity said, grabbing her purse. "Build whatever you like while I'm gone." And she was out the door.

Charity had heard plenty about the building of Jesse's cabin while it was going up. Fortunately, her eyes glazed over whenever the two of them talked about anything to do with hammers and nails now.

"She's gone," Mitch said into the phone the moment he heard the door close.

"We'll be right over." Jesse hung up.

Mitch stared at the phone in his hand. *We'll* be right

over? And whatever it was, Jesse didn't want Charity to know about it. Another bad sign.

Charity couldn't believe her good luck. She'd been trying to come up with a good reason to leave the house all day. Mitch had been acting suspiciously, knowing she was on another story—and worried about her. She didn't want to worry him and she knew he would have a cow if he found out who she was going to meet.

Once in the car, she pulled out her cell phone and dialed the number from the email she'd received just that morning.

He answered on the first ring.

"It's Charity. I was hoping now is a good time—"

"You got the message? Good. Yes, come now. You do remember how to get here, I assume?" He hung up without waiting for an answer.

Charity took the back way, ditched her car in the woods and walked the last few blocks through the woods to the back of Madam Florie's. As she sneaked around the rear of the former motel, she hoped her psychic aunt was hard at work giving advice to some lovestruck woman in Algona, Iowa, or a gambler in Elko, Nevada, and not peering out her window at bungalow uno: Aries.

Aries was one of twelve separate bungalows that had been motor court units, but were now furnished apartments. Florie lived in the main office building and did her psychic business from there.

At Charity's tap, Wade Dennison opened the door and quickly ushered her inside. The furnishings were sparse. A sunken couch with worn cushions, a threadbare overstuffed chair and a cigarette-marred coffee table.

She could see through the doorway into both of the only other rooms. A small bath with a sink, toilet and shower stall. A bedroom with a bed and a beat-up chest of drawers. It could have been a rental in any town in the nation.

"It's not much," Wade said with obvious embarrassment. He'd fallen far from the mansion he'd built for Daisy. Charity knew it must irk him that he couldn't go near the place because of the restraining order Daisy had on him.

"Please sit down," he said.

She took the chair he offered. He perched on the arm of the couch. Jail seemed to have made him calmer. Or maybe he just wanted her to think that.

For just an instant, she considered what she'd done. Coming here. Worse, not telling anyone where she was. It hadn't been that long ago that Wade Dennison had threatened to kill her.

"You said you wanted to set the record straight," she said, pulling out her reporter's notebook and flipping it open to a clean page. She snapped her ballpoint pen and looked up expectantly.

If it was a trick to just get her here, she figured now was when he would make his move.

He didn't move. But he did hesitate, then he let out a long sigh and said, "I'm innocent. I didn't shoot the sheriff."

Another innocent man unjustly accused. "Your fingerprint was on the trigger," she pointed out, hoping this hadn't been a complete waste of time.

"But Daisy's finger was on top of mine," he said.

"Daisy is trying to set me up. She's taken my freedom, my home, my business. Daisy called me and said she wanted to see me that night. She planned to kill me. I see that now." His voice broke. "Worse, I think she might have had our daughter kidnapped." He buried his face in his hands.

She wasn't buying it. "Why tell me this, Wade? You've never talked to me about anything."

He raised his head slowly. "I'm desperate."

"As flattering as that is…"

"Haven't you ever considered that I might be innocent?"

She thought that over for a moment. She'd definitely considered it. But right now he looked guilty as sin.

"Why would Daisy have her own child kidnapped?"

"I threatened to throw her out if the baby wasn't mine and take Desiree from her. I knew she had been having an affair—"

"With whom?"

He shook his head. "I didn't want to know. But a man can tell when his wife has been with someone else. I think she was in love with him and I think the baby was his. But I would never have harmed a hair on that baby's head. Never. And I wouldn't have really thrown her out or taken Desiree like I threatened. I think that's why she got rid of the baby, you know, because she was afraid I'd find out the truth and go through with my threat."

This was a theory she'd actually considered. It certainly explained those years Daisy was a recluse. Getting rid of one child to save another.

"The last time we talked you told me you were convinced Angela was your baby," Charity pointed out.

He shook his head. "I hoped she was. She could have been. There was this one night when Daisy and I…"

She got the picture. "Was Daisy thinking of leaving you for this other man?"

His expression told her she'd hit the bull's-eye!

"She wouldn't have done that. The only reason we're apart now is that she's mad at me after my illegitimate daughter showed up."

"Or is she mad because you offered your illegitimate daughter one million dollars to keep it quiet?"

"That wasn't it," Wade said, getting to his feet. "I had an affair when Daisy was pregnant with Angela. That's what she's mad about."

Charity's brain was freewheeling. Was it possible Wade had engineered Angela's kidnapping because he thought it was the other man's baby and he knew Daisy wouldn't leave him with the baby gone?

It was a far-fetched theory, but it made as much sense as any of the others.

"Daisy seems happier now," she said. She left off, "Now that you aren't in her life."

Wade let out a laugh. "She has *everything* and if her lawyer has his way, she will leave me penniless if not in prison."

"You *shot* Mitch," she reminded him.

"It was an accident. That night was so crazy. I think that's when I realized what Daisy was up to. I know I was acting strangely."

"You almost *killed* Mitch."

He nodded, ducking his head. "I feel terrible about that. That's why I contacted you. I was hoping you'd do some of that snooping you do so well."

She took that as a compliment. "What am I snooping into? The shooting seems pretty cut-and-dried."

"Not that. Angela's kidnapping. Find out once and for all who took that baby and clear my name. I've had this hanging over my head for too many years. When the truth comes out…"

He believed he would be exonerated of everything and would be back in the mansion, back on top? Obviously so. Was it possible he really was innocent?

"You really think Daisy had something to do with it?" she asked.

"I think Daisy might be capable of anything, including getting rid of that baby so I would never find out it wasn't mine."

Charity closed her notebook. "Someone hired your production manager to take the baby out of the house. Did Daisy even know Bud Farnsworth?"

"Of course she knew Bud. But I think she told Bud to get rid of the baby and he gave it to someone else and really didn't know what happened to Angela after that," Wade said.

Charity remembered the night in the plant when Bud had tried to kill her over a blackmail letter that incriminated him in the kidnapping. Daisy had shown up, wounded Bud. What had she kept saying to him? "Where is Angela?" Could Wade be right about her?

"Bud couldn't have gotten into the house without some inside help," Wade said, his voice low. "Someone left the window in Angela's room unlocked."

Charity didn't have much to go on and Wade knew it. The case was ice-cold. Twenty-seven years. And it wasn't like she hadn't tried to solve it from the time she was a kid.

What intrigued her most was this mystery man Daisy had the affair with. Charity had heard rumors for years. But was this a man Daisy had actually fallen for? Someone she would have left Wade for? Now that was interesting.

The resemblance was unmistakable, Maggie thought as she and Jesse entered the back door of the house and she saw the man sitting in the recliner. The same deep dimples, dark hair and eyes, and easy smile.

"Meet my little brother, Sheriff Mitch Tanner," Jesse said. "Mitch? Say hello to Angela Dennison."

Mitch's mouth was agape as he stared up at her.

Maggie smiled tentatively.

"How… Where…" He shot a look at Jesse. *"Angela?"*

"Looks like a slam dunk but we still need the results from the DNA tests," Jesse said. "We just couriered a batch to the lab in Portland. Albert said he should be able to get us the results in twelve hours. Midnight tonight."

Mitch looked from his brother to Maggie again. "I'm sorry to stare but…"

"It's all right. I know I look a lot like Desiree." She saw a look pass between the brothers and groaned. "You aren't telling me that Desiree might also be your half sister?"

"It's possible," Jesse admitted.

"You told her?" Mitch asked his brother in surprise.

Jesse nodded and shrugged. "Kinda had to."

"Oh," Mitch said, studying him. "It's like that, is it?"

Jesse grinned bashfully.

Mitch shook his head. "Other than looks?"

"It all adds up—dates, background, recent events," Jesse said.

"I *am* Angela Dennison. I would stake my life on it. Actually, I am."

Mitch frowned.

"Someone's trying to kill her," Jesse said. "A Seattle cop."

Mitch groaned and leaned back, closing his eyes. "What the hell is it with this rainy season?"

"There's more," Jesse said.

Mitch opened his eyes and narrowed them at Jesse. "How did I know there would be?"

"The cop is in town. He's killed three other people and tried to kill her, as well."

"You haven't gone to the Feds?" Mitch demanded.

"It would be her word against his and he just happens to be an old cop with a lot of commendations, his most recent from the mayor."

Mitch swore under his breath. "A Seattle cop? How does he fit into all this?"

"That's what we're going to find out," Maggie said, making Jesse smile at her determination.

"We don't think he acted alone in the kidnapping. We need to find out how he ties in," Jesse said. He quickly filled his brother in on everything. When he finished, Mitch was looking at Maggie with open admiration. Jesse couldn't help but smile since he had to admit his choices in women in the past had left something to be desired.

"So," Maggie said when he'd finished, "we realized the best approach would be for me to announce who I am at the party tonight and see how it shakes down from there."

"Rozalyn Sawyer's party?" Mitch cried, echoing his brother's earlier surprise. "*We* decided? Are you nuts?"

Jesse shrugged. "I felt the same way when Maggie first came up with the idea."

"Maggie?" Mitch asked.

"I was raised as Maggie Randolph," she said. "I'm going to need a dress for tonight. Can your fiancée help me with that?"

"Charity?" Mitch looked to his brother. "You aren't suggesting—"

They heard Charity's car pull up out front.

"She's going to hear about it tonight, anyway," Jesse pointed out.

Mitch was holding his head as if it ached. "Do either of you have a clue what you're about to do?"

Jesse smiled. *"I* have an inkling. Maggie's in for a surprise."

Charity came through the door just then. Maggie hadn't been sure what to expect given the way the men were acting.

A beautiful woman about her own age with a long mass of reddish-blond curly hair swept in. She had bright blue eyes and instantly Maggie felt drawn to her.

"You must be Charity Jenkins," Maggie said, going to greet her. "I've read a great many of your newspaper articles. You write very well."

Charity looked both surprised and confused and decidedly curious. As Mitch had done, Charity stared at her as if she thought she should know her.

"I'm Angela Dennison and I need your help," Maggie said.

"Charity speechless. It's a wonder to behold," Jesse said as he took his future sister-in-law's hand and led her to the couch across from Mitch and started to fill her in, as well.

Charity, if anything, was a quick study. "You're the one who stole my file."

Maggie nodded. "Sorry. Jesse has it. I kept all the stories in proper order."

Charity smiled at that and looked to Jesse. "Is she really—"

"We'll have the DNA test results by tonight," Jesse said. "Maggie wants to make her announcement at the party."

Charity looked at Maggie. "You're using yourself as bait?" she asked, cutting right to the chase.

"Something like that. I'm going to need a dress," Maggie said. "One that I can hide a small handgun in. Can you help me?"

Charity had been watching Jesse and Maggie while they'd told their story. Now she looked at Mitch and smiled that sly matchmaking smile of hers.

Mitch groaned, knowing it was impossible to stop Charity without telling her that Maggie might be his half sister—and Jesse's. That was one can of worms that would be opened soon enough.

Charity stood. "Come on. You're about my size. Let's see what we can find in my closet. I live next door. So you and Jesse just met?"

As they went out the door, Mitch shook his head. "Dad know about this?"

"Yep. He already gave me his DNA test."

Mitch looked up at him in surprise. "Then it's possible…"

Jesse nodded solemnly. "I'm afraid so."

"This is a damned dangerous plan."

Jesse couldn't agree more. "That's why I want you there, carrying. I might need all the help I can get.

I don't expect the kidnapper to make a move at the party—"

"You're hoping for some reaction, though, aren't you?" Mitch said. "How are you planning to protect her after the party? Especially if this Seattle cop is determined to get to her?"

Jesse took a breath and let it out slowly. "For starters, not let her out of my sight."

Mitch just looked at him.

"What?"

"You've got it bad for this woman."

"Bro, I can't explain it. That's why I have to get those DNA test results and get my head around however they come out."

"Charity's going to flip when she finds out that I've been keeping this secret for all these years," Mitch said.

Jesse smiled at his brother. "I think she'll still marry you. Anyway, June is a long way off. She might not even still be mad at you by then."

"Where are we going?" Maggie asked as they left Mitch's and took back roads as they had earlier. She had pulled her hair up into a ponytail and was wearing a baseball cap that Charity had lent her.

"My dad's house. His name is Lee Tanner. He's a good guy. You'll like him."

Her look said she'd make up her own mind about that.

He liked that about her. He liked a lot of things about her. He just wished he knew for sure who her father was if she really was Angela Dennison. Until he did, he'd have to keep her at arm's length. And that was the last thing he wanted to do.

Chapter Thirteen

Rupert Blackmore had brought a tent but the rain changed his mind about camping. He checked into the only motel in town, the Ho Hum. He used cash, but he wasn't worried about being recognized—not with his old pickup, fishing hat and gear.

He liked to think that the only person who knew him in this town was Margaret Randolph and he was looking for her—not the other way around.

Of course, he couldn't be sure her kidnapper didn't also know him—just not in this disguise. Nor was the kidnapper expecting him to turn up in Timber Falls, right?

He was pleasantly surprised how small the town was. Finding her should be easy—if she was still around. He figured after him almost catching her last night at Dennison Ducks she would have split. Since she hadn't already gone to his superiors or the Feds, he figured she wouldn't. This could be the end of it. No one in this town would ever have to know of her existence.

He spent the day fishing, keeping his eye out for her, but deciding to take advantage of where he was. Hell, he might as well consider this a little vacation. Admittedly, he was relieved he wasn't going to have to kill her.

She was rich. She'd return to Seattle. She'd keep her mouth shut. He'd retire and move to Arizona. None of this would ever have to come out.

He'd convinced himself that everything was going to work out as he drove through town, stopping at the gas station. A teenager came out to pump his gas.

Rupert got out of the truck and walked back to the restroom on the side of the building. When he came back out after using the facilities, he saw that the kid was washing his windows so he wandered into the office.

It was one of those old gas stations with nothing more than a counter and a pop machine in the office, an attached single-bay garage and two pumps.

As he was leaving, he picked up a newspaper, leaving thirty-five cents on the counter.

He walked back out to his pickup, paid cash for the gas and sat for a moment as the kid went back inside, paying no attention to him.

His hands shook as he read the story about Daisy Dennison of the famed Dennison Ducks decoys. He remembered the bumper sticker he'd seen on the guy's pickup that night, the night a man he'd never seen before met him in a deserted warehouse parking lot and handed over a wriggling baby wrapped in a tiny quilt with little yellow ducks on it.

He'd put the bundle on the passenger seat, looking up as the pickup and driver took off into the night. That's when he'd seen the sticker and the muddy Oregon plates. He couldn't make out the plate number. Even then had he planned to find out where the baby was from? Probably. After all, he was being blackmailed and now he had a clue who his blackmailer was. A Dennison Ducks bumper sticker on the back of the retreating pickup. Timber Falls, Oregon. Home of the famous decoys.

He pulled away from the service station, reminding himself that he'd been a good cop. Before and even after that one fateful night.

He'd been young, a little too cocky, a little too convinced that he wasn't just going to save the world, he was going to be one of those cops who got commendations all the time on television and in the newspapers.

And he had, despite what happened that night thirty years ago. It was a convenience-store robbery and he and his partner were just around the block. They came screaming up in the patrol car just as the perpetrator took off down the dark alley.

Rupert had been the first one out of the car. He ran down the alley. It was so dark. He'd yelled for the perp to stop, heard him climbing a chain-link fence at the end of the alley and in what little light there was, fired.

The pressure had been on him to succeed. He'd found out that Teresa had another guy interested in her; he wanted to look good and prove to her she was marrying the right guy.

He had wanted the bust. Needed it.

But when he neared the fence and the downed body lying in the pool of blood, he saw that it wasn't the perp at all but a kid of not more than nine, shot once in the back of the head.

He'd been so upset, he'd dropped his gun. It had gone off and shot him in the leg. A freak accident. Unlike killing a nine-year-old boy in an alley. He must have been in shock after that, sick to his stomach, throwing up, barely conscious when his partner found him.

By that time, his weapon was missing. Later he would realize that someone had come in behind him and picked it up carefully from the ground. An opportunist who saw that the gun with his fingerprints on it could be valuable in the future.

His partner, a guy named Wayne Dixon, came upon the scene, saw Rupert on his knees, wounded, bloody and missing his gun and thought that the perp had overpowered him, taken his gun and shot him and the kid.

Rupert had been in no condition to tell him he was wrong. Later... Well, later, he'd let the lie stand. Telling the truth wouldn't bring the kid back and would only hurt his career and his chances with Teresa.

She'd come to see him at the hospital. He'd proposed on the spot and she'd accepted.

He put the rest behind him, thinking it was over.

Over until the night he got the call to meet the man in the warehouse parking lot. To get rid of a baby. And the blackmailer would get rid of the gun. He would never be contacted again, he'd been promised by the distorted voice on the phone.

So he'd met the man at the warehouse parking lot, taken the baby. But then the baby quilt had moved and a small cry emitted from deep inside. That had been his mistake, opening the quilt and looking down into that little face. It had taken his breath away.

If there had been any way, he would have taken her home to Teresa. But he and Teresa had only been married a few years and he hadn't known then that they would never have a child of their own. Plus how would he have explained the baby to her? He didn't want her to know about the mistake he'd already made in his life. He would have done anything to keep her from knowing. He still would.

He'd bundled the baby back up and driven away from that warehouse parking lot, heading for Puget Sound, thinking he would get rid of the baby and maybe the blackmailer would never contact him again. That was the deal, wasn't it? And everyone knew blackmailers kept their word.

Right.

But that didn't mean he didn't abhor being blackmailed. He guessed that was partly why he balked at the order and instead of getting rid of the baby in Puget Sound, he sold her to the Randolphs' attorney, Clark Iverson. The other reason was the money. He bought Teresa a house. He made some rich couple parents. For twenty-seven years everyone had been happy with the outcome.

And then the adoptive father got sick, stumbled on the truth and decided his daughter needed to know so she could be united with her biological parents.

And Rupert Blackmore, once a good cop, became a killer again.

Not that he ever forgot about the bumper sticker on that pickup. Or the blackmailer. He'd done a little investigative work and found out who the baby was and that she'd been kidnapped. And then he'd let it go, thinking he had a place to start looking for the blackmailer if he ever heard from him again.

A few months ago he'd read about Bud Farnsworth being killed and that he had been the alleged kidnapper. Rupert had recognized the guy in the newspaper article. He was the man who'd brought him the baby. But it had been clear that night that this Farnsworth guy was working for someone else—someone he feared.

Now Rupert Blackmore wondered if Margaret Randolph had seen this story. Would she be so stupid as to knock on the Dennison family door and tell them who she thought she was? Tell them about what had happened at the pier?

No one would be that stupid, especially given the mess the Dennison family was in right now.

He tossed the newspaper on the floor and drove down Main Street toward his motel. Maybe he'd stay around another day. Just to make sure Margaret wasn't still around.

He drove past the sheriff's department. It was little more than a narrow building that shared half the space with city hall. From what he'd heard, the town sheriff had been shot and his brother was acting deputy. The brother had little to no experience, so he wasn't too worried about either of them.

At the edge of town, he pulled into the only café. If Margaret had been stupid enough to go to the Dennisons' this morning then it would be all over town by now and he'd been in enough dinky towns to know where to find the gossip in this one.

Still wearing his sunglasses, he parked and went inside Betty's, making a point of sitting by the window in the sunlight.

A fiftysomething bottle blonde came out from behind the counter with a menu and a glass of ice water. She set both down in front of him.

"Still got cherry, butterscotch and chocolate pie," she said. "Homemade."

Rupert looked up at her after a cursory glance at the menu. "I'll take a cheeseburger loaded, fries, a chocolate milkshake and a piece of the cherry pie," he said.

She smiled. She wasn't bad-looking, but hey, he was no Prince Charming. And her name tag read Betty.

"Bigfoot hunting or fishing?" she asked, clearly taking him for a nonlocal.

"I've never heard of Bigfoot fishing," he said flirting with her a little. What the hell? He figured it couldn't hurt. "How exactly is that done?"

She brightened to his smile. "Everythin' bites if you got's the right bait," she said, murdering the expression.

He laughed. "I don't care if they bite. I just like fishing."

"That's good because this isn't the best time of year for fishing around here," she said, eyeing him.

"But it's quiet and the river isn't crowded."

"Can't argue that," she said, and went to place his order.

She came back to the counter where she had a cup of coffee she'd been drinking before he came in.

"I've never been up here before," he said to her and turned to look out at the deserted street. "Is it always this quiet?"

She shook her head. "Everyone's getting ready for the party tonight."

"Party?"

"Sawyers. The daughter, Rozalyn, returned to town

and she's throwing a party. Just redid this old Victorian on the edge of the town. You might have seen it on your way in?"

He shook his head.

"It's kinda back off the road. Great old house." She sipped her coffee. "You staying at the Ho Hum?"

He nodded.

"You'll probably hear the party, then," she said with a laugh. "I hope you aren't a light sleeper."

He shook his head. "I sleep like the dead."

A bell dinged and she went to get his meal. As she slid the food across the table to him, several more customers came in. They looked like regulars. They glanced at him, took him for what he appeared to be, and sat down.

Outside, low dark clouds scudded past. It looked as if it was going to rain any minute.

He ate, listening to Betty talking to the other customers. A no-big-news day. Good. Except for this party tonight. Sounded like the entire town would be there.

He ate his burger and fries and watched the street. No fancy motorcycle went past. No word circulating of a young woman in town looking for her past.

Yep, she'd fled town. He finished off his milkshake, cleaned his plate and started on the pie.

But, he wondered, what would she do next? What could she do? She had no proof. It would be his word against hers. If she couldn't go to the cops and she couldn't run, wouldn't she have to return to Seattle? The woman was rich. Her father had left her dozens of businesses around the world. She would have to return to Seattle eventually.

Sure he'd put an APB out on her, but that was just

for questioning in the murders. It was possible he could reach some sort of deal with her. Once she understood that she was only alive because he'd spared her.

Maybe he wouldn't have to kill her. He liked the idea more than he wanted to admit.

And then he would just fade away into the background. Arizona. It was far enough away that she'd feel safe.

He was feeling good by the time he left a big tip for Betty and headed for his motel room. Maybe he'd take a nap and come back later for the dinner special: pork chops and dressing, applesauce, green beans, mashed potatoes and pork gravy.

The kidnapper would never know that he hadn't held up his end of the bargain.

Lee Tanner came out onto the deck as Jesse drove the pickup into the yard and shut off the motor. Lee's gaze went to the young woman who climbed out. He looked as if he'd been cold-cocked with a sledgehammer.

She had that effect on people. Maybe especially on Lee Tanner given how much the woman looked like Desiree.

"Maggie, meet my father, Lee Tanner," Jesse said as they climbed the steps to the house.

Lee extended a hand. Maggie took it. "You're Angela," he said. It wasn't a question but she nodded, anyway. "I just finished lunch but I could—"

"We've eaten," Jesse said, cutting his father off. Charity had cooked up lunch, all the time talking fifty miles an hour with Maggie. Hadn't he known they would hit it off?

"Were you planning on going to Roz Sawyer's party tonight?" Jesse asked him.

Lee shook his head. "Why?"

"I thought maybe I could change your mind," he said. "Maggie's going to announce who she really is tonight at midnight."

Lee lifted a brow.

Jesse grinned wryly. "Yeah, by then we'll actually know who her father is. We'll still need Daisy's DNA test results to prove without a doubt that she's Angela but I don't expect any surprises there."

"What can I do?" his father asked.

"You still have a gun?" His father nodded. "I'd like you to come to the party and have it, just in case."

"This have to do with those murders back in Seattle?" Lee asked.

"Yeah. There's a cop after her. He's already killed three others." Jesse pulled out the faxed copy of the photo of Detective Rupert Blackmore and the mayor. "He's the one on the right. It isn't a great photo."

"I'd recognize him if I saw him but you're not expecting him at the party, are you?" his father asked.

Jesse shook his head.

"We don't think Blackmore is behind the kidnapping," Maggie said, speaking up. "We think it was someone local."

Jesse met his dad's gaze. "Someone inside the house left the baby's window unlocked."

"It wasn't Daisy," Lee said. "It wasn't her."

Jesse nodded, although not sure of that and wondering why his father was so adamant. "Well, there were other people in the house that day." His mother for one. He hadn't told Maggie about that yet.

"I'll be at the party," his dad said. "Just let me know if there is anything else I can do."

"Thanks." Jesse grinned at his old man. "I knew I could count on you." He turned to Maggie. "She's also quite capable of taking care of herself."

Maggie smiled at that.

Jesse shook his dad's hand and watched while Maggie hugged him. He could see the conflicting emotions in his dad's face. Clearly, Lee Tanner wouldn't have minded if Maggie turned out to be his daughter.

Jesse hoped his dad would have to settle for daughter-in-law, but then again, that was way down the road and he wasn't sure it was the road Maggie wanted to take. There were fireworks between them and some bond neither of them understood. Until the possibility of shared blood was established or eliminated...

He wouldn't let himself think about it. There were too many hurdles yet to leap. Keeping Maggie alive. Finding out the truth about her biological father. Finding the kidnapper.

Maggie was right about that. She wouldn't be safe until they did.

He watched her walk over to a wall filled with photographs his father had taken of him and Mitch from the time they were babies. She ran her finger over a black-and-white of him.

Jesse felt his father's gaze on him, a look of worry in his expression. His dad knew him too well, knew how much this woman meant to him...how much was at stake tonight.

Chapter Fourteen

Jesse heard a sound, looked up and saw Maggie at the top of the stairs. His heart leaped to his throat. He had never seen anything so breathtaking. So beautiful.

Maggie wore a bright red dress that accentuated every one of her assets. Her dark hair was down and floating over her bare, lightly freckled shoulders.

"You are amazing," he said, his voice breaking.

Her dark eyes glowed as she started down the steps, the dress a whisper against her skin.

"You're just saying that because you know I'm carrying a weapon under this dress," she said, obviously trying to lighten the mood and maybe feeling a little embarrassed by the fact that he couldn't take his eyes off her.

She had a weapon hidden under that dress all right and it wasn't a gun. It was enough to knock him to his knees just thinking about it.

"You can't tell where, right?" she asked, looking worried.

He shook his head. "I would never know you were armed."

She smiled, pleased.

She wouldn't be using the weapon unless he had failed and the target was closing in. He had no intention of letting that happen. His hope was that Maggie wasn't going to have a need for the gun. Not tonight. Not ever.

She moved toward him like a dream.

He stood transfixed. "You look stunning," he whispered.

She smiled as she took the last few steps down the stairs to him.

He caught a hint of perfume, something exotic that fit her perfectly. Charity's doing.

She touched a hand to his cheek, her brown eyes dark as she looked up at him. Her lush lips were painted a pale inviting pink. They parted in a sigh and he felt his heart do a flip inside his chest, all the air rushed from his lungs and it was all he could do not to take her in his arms and kiss her.

Maggie felt tongue-tied as she looked at Jesse in the tuxedo. Had a man ever been so handsome? And yet it was his dark eyes that captivated her as she moved toward him as if her body had a mind of its own.

She ached to touch him, to feel his arms wrapped around her, to lose herself in his embrace.

Just one kiss. She would have given anything for just one kiss. Tonight she would know if her feelings for him would always be forbidden or if she could have her heart's desire. Just the thought made her forget that there was at least one killer after her, and maybe more after her announcement tonight.

She stepped to him, so close she caught his male scent mixing with the soapy clean smell of him. No aftershave. Just a maleness that made her knees weak. If she even thought of Jesse's lips on hers, Jesse's arms wrapped around her...

"You are extraordinary in that tux," she said, her voice breaking. Everything about him made her blood fire and her skin warm.

When he looked at her with his dark eyes, her heart hammered with a need like none she'd ever known.

"You know how I feel about you—"

He touched his finger to her lips and shook his head. "I know."

She swallowed back the tears that threatened. She wanted him, needed him. She'd known few men intimately. Most had not interested her enough that she wanted to go beyond a few dates.

Jesse had captivated her that first night. His art alone had seduced her. But it was when she'd watched him from the screened-in room, watched him run his hand over her bike that she'd realized she yearned to feel the warmth of his palm on her bare skin, his gentle fingers, the whisper of his skin pressed against hers.

He removed his finger from her lips, his gaze like a caress.

"Jesse," she said on a breath, as if that one word swelled with the emotions she felt for him.

He seemed to tense as if he knew what she wanted, what she needed, and he felt the heat of this banked fire between them and knew that if they fanned even the slightest ember it would flare and burn blindingly bright, sweeping them up in a maelstrom of passion that neither could nor would resist.

He didn't move. Didn't reach for her. But she could see it was as hard on him as it was her.

"Ready?" he asked, his voice low.

She nodded, unable to speak. She had to be strong tonight, whatever happened with the DNA test results. Whatever happened after her announcement.

"A hug for luck?" she asked softly.

He'd been afraid to touch her, afraid he would be lost. But he opened his arms, knowing that tonight could change everything between them, and she stepped into them and rested her head against his chest, her arms looping around his waist. He closed his arms around her, hugging her tightly as he closed his eyes at the wondrous feel of her. They stayed that way for a long moment, holding each other.

Then she stepped back and he reluctantly let go of her. She smiled up at him. "Showtime?"

He nodded and glanced at the clock. Almost eleven-thirty. She would make her announcement at the stroke of midnight—the same time Albert had promised to call with the DNA test results. Another thirty minutes.

The cell phone vibrated in the pocket of his tux. He pulled it out.

"How you holding up?" Mitch asked.

"Okay. What's the news there?"

"Roz just announced her engagement to Ford Lancaster," he said. "Charity's crying tears of happiness. Roz also did as you requested, announced that she had a special surprise at the stroke of midnight."

"Good. We're on our way."

"Be careful."

"Always." He disconnected and looked at Maggie. "Ready to rock and roll? The stage is set. You're the star performer come midnight."

She nodded. "I have my fingers crossed."

He nodded, knowing she was referring to the DNA test results. "Me, too."

The party was in full swing as they sneaked in the back way. Charity opened the door for them. "Everyone is here," she reported. "Daisy showed up with a body-guard and you'll never guess who—Bruno. Betty's here, too. Talk about a strange trio."

"What about Wade?" Jesse asked.

"Haven't seen him yet. Roz has a couple of guys out-side watching for him. If he shows up, they will detain him until midnight." She glanced at Maggie. "Wow, that dress looks sensational on you." Then she looked back at Jesse and grinned.

"Go on back to the party," he told Charity, not appre-ciating her matchmaking right now. "We'll be upstairs."

She took off and Jesse watched after her for a mo-ment, hoping the fact that she hadn't spotted any unfa-miliar faces was good news.

They took the back stairs, climbing up to the third floor. Music and a cacophony of voices rose from the lower floor of the large old Victorian.

Jesse glanced at his watch. "Five minutes and count-ing."

Maggie nodded. She didn't look nervous or worried now. He watched her check her gun, then shoot him a grin. He couldn't help but admire her determination. He would give anything to have this night over.

Sneaking out to the stairs, he peeked over the railing and spotted Mitch in a corner in his wheelchair.

Daisy Dennison was indeed in attendance with Bruno and Betty close by. Desiree was flirting with several local guys who hung out at the Duck-In.

Lydia was in a more modern wheelchair than Mitch's, sitting demurely in a corner with Angus looming over her, seeing to her every need.

Roz and her fiancé, Ford Lancaster, were at the center of the room accepting congratulations. Roz's father, Liam, was talking to some woman—

With a start, Jesse saw that it was Charity's aunt Florie. She looked so different. Her hair was a warm brown color instead of fire-engine red and it was cut into a cap of short curls rather than being wrapped around her head like a turban. And her eyes didn't have that thick turquoise eye shadow over them, either. Nor was she wearing some blindingly bright caftan. She wore a simple blue dress and she had obviously totally captivated Liam Sawyer. He seemed to be hanging on her every word.

As Jesse's gaze scanned the rest of the crowd, he spotted his father. Daisy looked beautiful. He saw that reflected in his father's gaze and felt a sharp jab at heart level. Oh God, his father still felt something for the woman. Th,e realization shocked him.

He turned to look at Daisy. Her eyes were locked with Lee Tanner's across the room. Was this the first time they'd seen each other in all these years?

It was clear that whatever had been between them hadn't completely died.

Just then, the large old grandfather clock began to chime the midnight hour.

"It's time," Maggie said next to him.

He glanced at his watch and nodded. They took the back stairs down to the second floor, then Jesse moved out to the top of the stairs.

The music was louder down here, the chattering crowd a dull roar. Jesse caught Charity's eye. She said something to the leader of the band and the music stopped instantly.

As the grandfather clock finished chiming midnight, Roz called for everyone's attention. The crowd quieted and followed Roz's gaze upward to the stairs.

A hush fell over the huge room below as Jesse held up his hands for quiet.

"There is someone here tonight—" Jesse was interrupted by a disturbance at the front door. Wade Dennison came bursting in, his face flushed. "You're just in time," Jesse said, and Maggie joined him at the railing.

A murmur rippled through the crowd.

Maggie smiled down on everyone. "I apologize for interrupting the party. Rozalyn was kind enough to let me make my announcement here tonight with all of you together."

She glanced toward Daisy, who was looking up at her in shock. Wade just looked confused.

"My name is Angela Dennison," she announced.

The murmur rose to a roar. And at the middle of it, Daisy let out a cry. Jesse saw her expression. Shock. Then horror. Just before she fainted.

Jesse motioned for silence as the crowd moved back to give Daisy air and Desiree rushed to her mother. Lee had gone to her, as well, and was demanding someone get him a cold washcloth.

"What the hell kind of stunt are you trying to pull,

Tanner?" Wade demanded. "That woman is not..." His voice broke. He stared at Maggie, then seemed to shrink back from her as if no longer sure of anything.

"I'm here tonight because whoever is responsible for my kidnapping is now trying to kill me," Maggie said.

Lydia was fanning herself, Angus leaning over her.

Another roar from the crowd. Jesse touched Maggie's arm. He wanted to get her out of here. She'd done what she came to do. Now he just wanted her far away from here and safe.

"I intend to get to the truth. To find out who kidnapped me, who wants me dead now."

The crowd was in an uproar. "Is it really her?" Betty was asking no one in particular. It was as if Angela's ghost had appeared and everyone seemed shaken and excited.

Jesse glanced at his watch. Albert still hadn't called with the DNA test results. But it was time to clear everyone out and get Maggie out of here. He motioned to Charity and she touched Roz's arm.

"Party's over!" Roz announced and she and Ford began ushering the guests out. "Thank you all for coming."

Betty offered to keep the café open late for anyone who wanted coffee.

Daisy had come around. Lee and Bruno helped her up into a chair. She sat looking up at Maggie as if she'd just seen an angel. Jesse knew the feeling.

Desiree stared up at her sister for a moment, then turned on her heel and left, no doubt headed for the bar. Jesse hoped she would be all right. He knew this had to be a shock for her and Desiree had had too many surprises in her life lately.

Lydia was still fanning herself in the corner. Angus was frowning in Jesse's direction, obviously upset that Lydia was distraught. Wade had slumped into a chair on the opposite side of the room from Daisy, his head in his hands.

Liam had offered to take Florie home and as Roz and Ford closed the door on the last of the other guests, Jesse's cell phone vibrated.

"We'll be in the kitchen helping the staff clean up," Roz said as she and Ford left them alone.

"Yes, Albert," Jesse said into the phone as he ushered Maggie into the first room off the stairs. "We're ready for the test results." He met Maggie's gaze, his heart in his throat.

"Okay, here's what we've got. Two matches each, but the two groups don't match."

"In English," Jesse snapped.

"Quite simply, your test and your father's match. Miss Randolph's test and Mr. Dennison's match." Wade was Maggie's father!

"Albert, I could kiss you." Jesse let out a long breath. Maggie's eyes were on him. He let out a howl and, dropping the cell phone, picked her up and spun her around. As he brought her down, he dropped his mouth to hers and kissed her.

Her arms came around his neck and she pulled him closer, her lips parting, her breath mingling with his. Her mouth was pure sugar, her body soft and rounded and pressed to his. He never wanted to let her go.

Jesse slowly raised his lips from Maggie's, grinned down at her, their eyes meeting, a silent understanding passing between them.

"I guess it's time to make our second announcement," he said.

Maggie's eyes were shiny bright. She smiled ruefully, as if like him, she couldn't wait to get away from here and finally be alone with each other.

They descended the stairs finding everyone pretty much where they'd left them. Daisy got to her feet and walked toward Maggie. Jesse tensed.

"You're the woman in the painting," she whispered.

Maggie nodded.

"How long have you known she was alive?" Daisy asked Jesse.

"Until a few minutes ago, I couldn't be absolutely sure she was Angela Dennison," he said. "The DNA sample Wade supplied in the death of his illegitimate daughter matches hers."

Wade had come over to them, as well. He stood looking poleaxed. He didn't notice Lee Tanner slump down onto the couch, his face filled with anguish and relief as he buried his face in his hands.

"I—" Tears welled in Wade's eyes. He stepped to Maggie and gave her an awkward hug. "We'll find out who's trying to hurt you, who kidnapped you. We'll find him."

"We have to go now," Jesse said, looking over at his brother. Mitch nodded.

"I'll talk to you soon," Wade said, touching his daughter's hair, dropping his hand to hers. Jesse saw her squeeze his hand.

"We'll talk," she said and looked to her mother as Wade left.

"I don't know what to say to you," Daisy said, still looking stunned. "It's just such a shock."

Maggie nodded.

Lydia wheeled up. "Come see me, child," she said, taking Maggie's hand. "I'm your aunt Lydia. I own the Busy Bee antique shop in town. Promise you'll come see me?"

Maggie nodded and smiled down at her aunt as Lydia and Angus left. "I promise. As soon as I can."

"We have to go," Jesse repeated, and took Maggie's hand. He was worried that the longer they stayed, the more chance of an ambush as they left.

Mitch was already wheeling himself toward the back door, Charity at his side when she motioned that she needed to talk to Jesse a minute.

"You might want to keep an eye on Bruno," Charity said confidentially. "I did a little checking on him for a friend. His real name is Jerome Lovelace and he has quite a rap sheet."

"For a friend?"

Charity groaned. "For Lydia, all right? She got this idea that Bruno might be thinking of robbing the antique store."

Both Jesse and Mitch rolled their eyes at that, just as Charity no doubt figured they would.

"Don't make me sorry I told you," Charity warned.

Jesse laughed. "I appreciate the heads-up, Charity." The news didn't really surprise him. He watched his brother and Charity leave. When he glanced back, Bruno was by the front door, eyes hooded. Jesse hadn't heard him say a word all night. But Jesse could feel his eyes on them as they left. Mean eyes.

Rupert Blackmore tried to calm down. He'd been sitting in Betty's Café, having a cup of decaf when the door burst open and the café suddenly filled to overflowing with people—and the news.

Angela Dennison had announced she was alive at the party tonight.

Rupert could barely hear the clamor of voices over the rush of his pulse. Blindly, he dropped money on the counter and, sliding off the stool, stumbled out the door. He doubted anyone noticed him or the way he clutched his chest as he leaned against the side of his pickup.

If he was right, if the kidnapper still lived here in this town, then he knew that Rupert hadn't lived up to his end of the bargain.

What would he do? Turn in the service revolver with Rupert's fingerprints on it? Rupert could see the headlines now. His reputation would be destroyed, he might lose his pension and Teresa. Tears blurred his vision.

He'd have to tell Teresa himself. He didn't want her reading about it in the paper. What choice did he have? None.

It was too late to kill Margaret Randolph. The cat was out of the bag, so to speak. But she'd announced at the party that she was looking for the kidnapper and wouldn't rest until she found him. Worse, she'd taken up with the deputy sheriff.

Rupert was sure he'd covered his tracks well on the recent murders. It was time to go back to Seattle. Retire. Move to Arizona. Maybe if he changed his name...

He managed to get the pickup door open and pulled himself onto the seat, closing the door behind him. He'd left the key in the ignition, not worried about anyone in this town stealing his old pickup.

He started to reach for the key, leaning over the steering wheel as he did. That's when he saw the note. It was taped to the radio. It had his name on it.

He gripped the steering wheel. His heart was pounding so hard he thought it would burst from his chest as he looked out to see if anyone was watching him. No one he could see in the darkness.

Hands shaking, he pulled the note from the front of the radio. The tape gave. It was one small sheet of white paper folded in half, his name neatly printed on the front. Detective Rupert Blackmore.

He opened it and let out a cry as he read the words. *I have your wife. Finish the job. No loose ends.* The paper fluttered from his fingers and he grabbed his cell phone from his jacket pocket, his fingers shaking so hard it took him three tries to key in his mother-in-law's number. It was late. Teresa would be in bed asleep. So would his mother-in-law, Marlene. He'd wake them both and feel foolish.

The phone rang and rang.

He felt his heart drop to the soles of his flat feet.

Chapter Fifteen

Maggie watched the dark forest blur by the cab of the pickup, so many emotions racing through her she felt numb. Jesse hadn't said anything since they'd left Roz Sawyer's house.

She watched him look in the rearview mirror for the hundredth time and realized he was worried that Blackmore or the kidnapper might be following them.

She hadn't realized how much had been riding on tonight. The announcement and her biological parents' reaction hadn't surprised her. Her sister Desiree's had. It must have been such a shock to them all. At least her aunt Lydia had welcomed her and that warmed Maggie.

She glanced in her side mirror as Jesse turned onto the road to his cabin. As far as she could tell no one was following them.

Leaning back into the seat, she closed her eyes, remembering the look on Jesse's face when they'd gotten the DNA test results. She smiled to herself, opened her eyes and looked over at him.

He hadn't touched her since they'd climbed into the pickup. Nor had he said a word. His big hands gripped the wheel as he drove, his eyes on the road or the rearview mirror.

Now that there was nothing keeping them apart had he changed his mind?

He pulled up the pickup in front of the cabin, cut the engine and sat for a moment just staring out at the darkness.

She ached to touch him, to feel his mouth on hers, to lose herself in his arms. Silence and darkness settled over them. He seemed to be waiting for something.

A faint light blinked once, then twice from out in the darkness beyond the cabin.

Jesse seemed to relax and she remembered overhearing Lee Tanner's promise to check out the cabin before they returned. Obviously the flashing light signaled everything was okay and that state troopers were in position. Without looking at her, he opened his door and trotted around to hers, taking her hand but not looking at her as he quickly drew her up the steps all the time watching behind them.

Jesse remembered Charity's words just before they left Roz Sawyer's house. Charity had been waiting outside and pulled him aside.

"Do you have any idea who she is?" she'd asked, following his gaze to Maggie as she got into his old pickup.

"She's Angela Dennison."

"She's Margaret Randolph and Margaret Randolph is

now head of a huge business conglomerate. She's been running it for months, ever since her father's health began to fail."

How did Charity find out the things she did? He hadn't asked Maggie about any of that. It hadn't mattered. But now he realized what she was saying. Maggie had a company to run in Seattle. What were the chances she would ever want to stay in Timber Falls?

Charity had leaned in to whisper, "She's not just amazingly smart, she's incredibly rich."

What could a woman like Maggie see in a man like him? Especially long-term.

Now, as he led Maggie up the steps to his cabin, he feared Charity was right. As long as they'd thought they might be blood-related, they had kept their distance. Now that there was nothing to keep them apart, Maggie might be having second thoughts.

The moment the door closed, Jesse let out a sigh and turned to look at her. What had Charity said to him as they were leaving the Sawyers? Something that had upset him.

"Jesse, if you've changed your mind—"

He grabbed a handful of her dress and dragged her to him, his big hands cupping her face as he brought his lips down to hers.

"Oh, God, I've wanted to do that from the moment we left the party," he said against her mouth.

Her eyes filled as she looked up at him, her lips curving into a relieved smile. "I thought you might be having second thoughts."

He met her gaze and shook his head. "You?"

She smiled up at him and, circling his neck with her arms, pulled him down for a kiss.

When she drew back to look at him, he hugged her tightly to him, his breath against her hair. "Maggie." He said her name as if he couldn't believe this was real.

Then he covered her mouth again, his tongue teasing hers, exploring her mouth, her lips as he swept her up in his arms and carried her up the stairs.

A cry of pure joy welled in her chest. She could feel his heart pounding, in perfect sync with hers.

As the kiss ended, she touched his face, cupping his jaw, and looked up into his eyes. They'd reached his bedroom. He stood her on her feet, his gaze never leaving hers. His eyes were dark with desire and she felt a shaft of heat shoot through her. "Oh, Jesse."

Jesse just stood looking at her in that bright red dress. He'd never seen anything more beautiful. He'd never wanted a woman more in his life. What had he done to get this lucky?

He tried not to think about the future. Thought of nothing but Maggie and this moment he'd prayed for, the moment he could hold her, kiss her, make love to her.

Love.

He slipped one bright red strap from her freckled shoulder. She didn't move, her gaze locked with his as he slipped the other strap down. Her breasts swelled beneath the silken fabric as she took a ragged breath.

"I have wanted to make love to you since the first night I saw you," he said, his voice sounding hoarse.

She smiled. "I watched you from the window with my bike. Do you have any idea what you do to me?"

He shook his head. He only knew that this woman

had come into his life and it hadn't been the same since. He'd been restless that night, the first time he'd seen her, but that feeling was gone with her here. He couldn't bear to think what it would be like without her though.

He pushed the thought from his mind. Hadn't he always lived life minute to minute? This wasn't a time to be thinking about forever. Not now. Maybe not ever.

"All you have to do is look at me, Jesse, and I melt inside," she whispered, and brushed her lips over his, sending a quiver of desire spiking through him. "I have never felt more safe, more secure, than in your arms."

He started to tell her that she wasn't safe. Not by a long shot, but she hushed him with a finger to his lips.

"You make me feel things I have never felt before," she said, looking deep into his eyes. She slowly began to unbutton his shirt, her fingers brushing lightly over his bare skin as she shoved aside the material and flattened her palms to his chest. A fire swept through him, his blood ablaze for her.

Reaching with both arms around her, he unzipped the dress. It fell to the floor in a whisper. She wore a tiny pair of lace panties, black and in stark contrast to her pale freckled skin. The bra was also black, and her nipples were hard as pebbles against the lace inserts. He groaned at the mere sight. Between her breasts rested a small-caliber pistol.

He removed the weapon, putting it down gingerly on the dresser. He brushed his thumb over one nipple as he did. He heard her soft moan. It fueled the fire in him.

He swept her up and carried her to the bed where he laid her gently down, sliding her panties over her slim hips as he did. He tossed them aside and crawled up

onto the bed next to her, slipping the bra straps down
and unfastening the front hook.

The bra fell away to expose her full rounded breasts.
His mouth dropped greedily to each distended tip, the
nipple hard against his tongue. He felt her hands working at the tuxedo pants. The real world dissolved in
the distance as in minutes they were naked, wrapped
in each other's arms, their bodies one. Alone, safe, together. Nothing else mattered.

Rupert Blackmore realized he was getting too old for
this. The climb up the side of the hill had left him weak
and breathless. He leaned against the trunk of a large
cedar and tried to catch his breath.

He stood listening to the pounding of his heart and the
night. A breeze moaned softly in the dense pine boughs
overhead and he thought he could hear a stream nearby.

He tried not to think about Teresa, what she'd been
told, where she was, what had happened to her. He tried
not to let the fear or the anger make him stupid, force
him to make a mistake.

He'd already run across one state trooper. The blow
hadn't killed the man. Just bought Rupert time. He wondered how many more were in the woods around Jesse
Tanner's cabin. How many more he'd have to take down
before he finally reached Margaret Randolph.

This felt wrong. All wrong.

He told himself it was because he didn't want to kill
the young woman. But he would. He had to if he hoped
to see his beloved Teresa again.

He fought back the grief and regret that threatened to
completely overwhelm him and concentrated on the terrain in front of him. His eyes had adjusted to the dark-

ness. He moved quietly through the woods, figuring he should be coming up on another state cop pretty soon.

He hadn't gone far when he stopped to listen. A chill rattled up his spine. He'd survived this long as a cop on instinct and right now his instincts were telling him to get the hell off this mountain, to get the hell out of this state. To run.

But he knew he couldn't run far enough. And if he ever wanted to see Teresa again...

He heard the crack of a twig behind him. That's when he knew why this had felt all wrong. He'd been set up.

Maggie lay staring up at the wooden plank ceiling smiling to herself, her body warm, sated. She'd known he would be a wonderful lover. Just the thought made her quiver inside. No man had ever made her heart beat with such fierceness or her body respond with such joy.

But it had been more than physical. She had known that if they were allowed to come together it would be amazing. She still felt awestruck by the feelings he had evoked in her. She loved him. She felt like she had from that first night when he'd come to help her on the highway.

She listened to Jesse's rhythmic breathing next to her, his thigh against hers, his body still hot from their lovemaking, the scent of him still filling her senses.

Sleep beckoned but she fought it. Being here with Jesse felt so right but she knew it could be taken away from both of them in an instant. For a while she had forgotten about Blackmore. About her kidnapping.

She couldn't give in to this feeling of happiness. Not knowing that the killer hadn't given up. Blackmore would be coming for her. And he might not be coming alone.

Blackmore. There had to be a Timber Falls–Seattle connection. One that she'd missed in the research she'd done. Jesse had picked up the sheriff's department file on her kidnapping earlier and they'd pored over it before the party, but they hadn't found any link.

Where did Blackmore fit in? There had to be some connection.

She slipped from the bed.

"Are you all right?" Jesse said, instantly feeling the loss of her.

She smiled back at him. "I'm just going to check something. I'll be back."

She padded barefoot out of the room, grabbing his robe as she headed down the stairs to where he'd put all the information he'd collected. Printouts of stories about Blackmore, the official file on the kidnapping, everything gathered about the original suspects.

She looked through the sheriff's department file again first. Wade's and Daisy's accounts contradicted one another's. Was there something there?

She opened the file Jesse had put together for her on Blackmore. Within a few minutes, she felt Jesse come up behind her.

"Blackmore?" he said, reading over her shoulder. He dragged up a chair next to her.

"Look at this," she said, pointing to a photograph taken at one of Blackmore's many award ceremonies where he had been honored for his bravery, his heroism, his excellence as a police officer.

In this particular photograph, Rupert Blackmore was only in his late twenties. He was surprisingly handsome and almost bashful as he took the commendation from the then mayor of Seattle.

"Do you see it?" she asked.

Jesse leaned down to kiss her neck. He took a deep breath, breathing in her scent. Putting his arms around her, he buried his face in her hair. He wished she would come back to bed.

"Look at this," she said.

He pulled back and looked down at the photograph she was pointing at. It was a copy, black-and-white, and the resolution was bad. But he saw that she was pointing at the cutline under the photo, not the men in the snapshot.

He read the cutline hurrying over the list of names. Then reread them, leaning in a little. One name jolted him from any thought of sleep.

Blackmore, Hathway, Curtis, Johnson, Abernathy, Cox, Frank, Peterson. "Abernathy?" H.T. Abernathy. One of the cops receiving a commendation for assisting in some case.

"There must be a million Abernathys, right?" she asked. "What are the chances he could be related to Lydia?"

Jesse got up and went to find the cell phone. He dialed his brother's number. "I need to talk to Charity," he said when Mitch answered.

"Jesse? Do you have any idea what time it is?"

"Two-twenty-nine in the morning," he said. He could hear his brother call to Charity in the next bedroom.

"Do you ever sleep?" Mitch grumbled.

"Not much."

"It's Jesse," Mitch said. "He wants to talk to you."

"Yes?" Charity said, sounding sleepy as she picked up the extension.

"What was Lydia's husband's name?" Jesse asked her.

"What are you doing playing Timber Falls Trivial Pursuit?" Mitch asked.

"Yeah, strip Timber Falls Trivial Pursuit," Jesse said. "I'm losing so help me out, okay."

Charity groaned. "Don't talk about strip anything, okay? I want a white wedding."

"I admire that about you," he said.

"Yeah," she said. "Henry."

Henry. H.T. "Henry Abernathy?" Jesse repeated, hoping she didn't hear his excitement. "You know what his middle name was?"

"Are you kidding?"

"Okay, what did he do for a living? He owned an antique shop or something, right?"

"Jesse, are you drunk?" Mitch asked on the extension.

"No antiques," Charity said drowsily, as if she'd lain back down. "He didn't have anything to do with antiques that I know of. I think that was just something Lydia came up with after he was killed. He was a cop."

Jesse met Maggie's gaze. All the breath had rushed out of him. "Where was that?" he managed to say, afraid Charity had fallen back to sleep she was so slow to answer.

"Bellingham, Washington. Good night, Jesse." She hung up.

"Is everything all right up there?" Mitch asked, sounding concerned.

"Fine. Thanks." He hung up.

"What?" Maggie said on a breath as he put the cell phone on the table by the door.

"Henry Abernathy was a cop in Bellingham, Washington."

"That's not far from Seattle," she said. "It says here

they were working on a mutual case. That means they could have known each other."

He nodded, frowning. "But Lydia's husband died before you were born. Even if he knew Blackmore, it doesn't make any sense where you come into this."

"Unless Aunt Lydia also knows Blackmore." She was shaking her head, not wanting to believe it. That little old white-haired lady? She couldn't see her with a man like Blackmore.

"Did anyone mention how she ended up in a wheelchair?" he asked Maggie. When she shook her head, he told her how Wade had been driving the car. The night of the accident that killed Lydia's husband and put her in a wheelchair.

Maggie closed her eyes. "You think she would try to get back at him by stealing one of his children?"

"It sounds crazy to me but some people…"

She opened her eyes and looked at him. "If her husband knew Blackmore, it's the only link we have so far. She must know him. It's too much of a coincidence."

He nodded in agreement, obviously not wanting to believe it any more than she did. "I think we'd better pay Aunt Lydia a visit come morning."

Maggie rose from the table and went to him, putting her arms around him, just wanting to curl up next to him in the big bed for the rest of the night.

He stroked his hand over her hair and looked into her eyes, clearly thinking something along those lines.

That's when they heard the first gunshot.

Chapter Sixteen

Jesse rushed up the stairs with Maggie at his heels. He dressed quickly and grabbed his gun.

"Stay here." And he was gone out the door. She heard him lock it behind him.

Maggie dressed in jeans, a sweater and boots. She retrieved the small handgun Jesse had given her.

Where was Jesse?

She went to the screened-in deck and stood in the darkness looking down into the jungle of trees and ferns and vines. She couldn't see him. Beyond the screens, a breeze whispered in the pine boughs. Dawn softened the darkness to the east over the treetops. But it was still pitch black in the woods surrounding the cabin.

The moment she heard the two quick soft pops, she recognized them from the night at the pier. Someone shooting with a silencer. Jesse's gun didn't have one so he hadn't fired.

She turned and ran down the stairs, slowing down only long enough to open the front door and ease herself out onto the steps. She waited for her eyes to adjust to the darkness, then with the weapon in both hands, headed toward the place where she'd heard the shots.

She hadn't gone far when she saw the body. Jesse? Oh, God, not Jesse.

Breath left her as she started to rush forward.

"Maggie." She swung around, ready to fire. She pulled up short when she saw that it was Jesse.

She fell into his arms, surprising herself by crying. "Oh, thank God, I thought…"

"It's okay, baby," he whispered against her hair as he held her to him.

"Who is it?" she asked, glancing at the body on the ground.

"Bruno. His real name is Jerome Lovelace." Charity had investigated him for some story she was doing.

"The guy who was Daisy's bodyguard at the party," she said. "Is he…?"

Jesse nodded. "Dead, yes. Shot twice, both bull's-eyes."

She glanced up at him. "Blackmore."

"Whoever shot Bruno shot to kill."

She looked into the trees. Still hours before dawn. "What about that earlier shot?"

"Looks like it came from Bruno's gun."

She glanced at the weapon lying on the ground next to Bruno.

"It's been fired once."

She heard a noise and turned, bringing her weapon up.

"Easy," Jesse said. "It's just the state cops. They were

protecting the perimeter hoping to catch whoever fell into the net."

The state officer looked chagrined since the killer had slipped the net. "All our officers are fine. We had one down. Hit from behind. Possible concussion. One of the men caught a glimpse of the shooter as he escaped off the mountain. Big man. Older. Possibly wounded. Limping. He got away."

Blackmore.

Back at the cabin, Jesse checked to make sure they were alone while the state boys took care of Bruno.

"Why would Blackmore kill Daisy's bodyguard?" Maggie asked.

Jesse shook his head. Nothing made any sense. He picked up the cell phone and called Mitch.

"This better not be trivia again," his little brother warned him. "It isn't even light out yet."

Jesse heard a soft click on the line as Charity picked up the extension. "Bruno, aka Jerome Lovelace, is dead. Two slugs. Killer used a silencer. Bruno might have wounded the shooter, but he got away."

Mitch swore.

"Either Bruno came up there to kill Maggie and someone whacked him before he could," Mitch said. "Or—"

"Or he was here to kill someone else and got himself whacked," Jesse said.

"Did I mention where Bruno was originally from?" Charity asked, making it known she was on the line. "His last known address was a post office box in Seattle, but I found an old car registration in his glove box—"

Jesse heard Mitch swearing in the background.

"And he used to live in Plentygrove not far from where Daisy was originally from," Charity finished.

"Thanks, Charity. Talk to you later, bro." Jesse hung up and looked at Maggie. Plentygrove? "We need to take a little trip."

"Are we going to talk to Lydia?" she asked.

"There's something else I need to do first." He'd only put it off because he became involved with Maggie. "We're going to pay my mother a visit."

Maggie frowned. "But I thought your mother was dead?"

"She left my dad when Mitch was six and I was nine. She's been dead to me ever since."

Maggie raised a brow. "And you suddenly have an urge to go see her?"

"She was at the Dennison house on the day of the kidnapping," he said. "And it seems my mother lives in the same town that Bruno hailed from. Maybe it's a coincidence but I have to wonder what brought him to Timber Falls. Certainly not the weather."

All the way off the mountain, Rupert Blackmore could think of only one thing. Murdering the person who'd set him up. The person who had his wife. The person who'd been responsible for Angela Dennison's kidnapping. The person who'd blackmailed him.

He'd listened to enough gossip at the café to know who the obvious players were. But he'd found in his career that sometimes a man had to look behind the obvious.

He drove back into town, went to his motel room and took a shower, bandaging the flesh wound to his leg. He knew better than to run where Bruno had shot him. The state cops would have the roads out of here blocked. And he wasn't ready to leave, anyway.

He called one of his snitches.

"Do you have any idea what time it is, man?"

"Just listen." He opened the wallet he'd taken off the man who'd been sent to kill him. An amateur. "Find out everything you can for me about a man named Jerome Lovelace, and I need it yesterday." He gave him his cell phone number, hung up and began to go through Jerome's wallet.

Ruth Anne Tanner had remarried a guy named Art Fellers and lived in an older part of Plentygrove. That had been all the information his father's lawyer had been able to get on her but it was enough to provide Jesse with an address.

It turned out to be a one-story ranch built in the 1950s, but well kept up. It was late morning when he and Maggie walked up the sidewalk to the front door. The lawn had been cut recently and someone had planted geraniums in matching pots on each side of the door.

He rang the bell and waited. Inside the house he could hear music. He was trying to place the song rather than think about his mother when the door opened.

Jesse had thought she'd look older, be gray, maybe even fat. He definitely didn't expect her to be pretty anymore. But the woman who answered the door had a cap of dark hair that was only flecked with gray and she was slim, athletic-looking. She wore a cap-sleeved T-shirt that matched her Capri pants and white sandals. Her face was unlined; the only wrinkles were around her eyes as she squinted into the sun peeking through the clouds to see them.

"Yes?"

This woman didn't look almost sixty. She was pretty and, he realized, she looked happy.

Bitterness tore at his insides. "Hello, Mother."

Her eyes widened and she gripped the door, leaning into it as if she needed the support. She blinked either because of the glare or because she was trying to place him and didn't know which son he was.

"Jesse, but I can understand how you might have forgotten."

Her gaze shifted to Maggie and she seemed to regain her earlier composure. "Please, come in." She moved back and as much as he didn't want to, he stepped into her house after Maggie.

The house was clean and cool inside, the furnishings nice but not expensive.

"Jesse." Her eyes welled and she looked away as she wiped the tears at her cheeks. "Would you like something to drink?"

"Nothing—"

"I'd take something cold if you have it," Maggie said and followed Ruth Anne into the kitchen. "I'm… Maggie."

Jesse followed, just wanting to get this over with.

The kitchen was clean and cute. There was a photo on the fridge of a bald man with his arm around Ruth Anne at some party.

Obviously she'd left Timber Falls and made a new life for herself. He'd always imagined her alone, bitter, hateful, spending his father's money on booze or drugs.

Maggie touched his arm and he took the glass of iced tea she offered him.

"Please, sit down," his mother said, motioning to the breakfast nook.

"This isn't a social call," Jesse said more sharply than he'd meant to. He took a sip of the drink, his throat dry, his nerves raw.

"Do you mind if I take a look at your garden?" Maggie asked and didn't wait for an answer as she opened the patio door and stepped out, closing the door behind her.

Jesse waited for his mother to say something. Like she was sorry. Right. Could he ever forgive her? No. How was Mitch? What did she care? He thought she'd at least ask about his life.

She didn't. She sat down at the table, folded her hands in front of her and seemed to be waiting.

He wanted to yell at her. To tell her how badly she'd hurt him, his brother, his father. To ask why. To make her feel guilty.

But instead, he heard himself ask, "Did you have anything to do with Angela Dennison's kidnapping?"

She leaned back in her chair, her eyes clouding over as if the name forced her to return to a place she'd left far behind, something seeing him obviously hadn't done. "She was never found?" She sounded surprised by that.

He realized he had her eyes and felt an ache in his chest.

Tears welled again in her eyes and her lower lip trembled. "I can't explain the woman I was when I—" She made a swipe at her tears, as one coursed down her cheek, and shook her head. "I didn't take the baby. I never even saw her. As I was leaving I passed the nanny.

She had come down the stairs. She had a cold," his mother said, as if just remembering that detail.

All that had been in the sheriff's report. "Did you see anyone else in the house other than Daisy and the nanny?"

She shook her head. "Wade came home. I passed him on the road. His sister was with him in the car."

"Lydia?" he asked in surprise. That hadn't been in the file.

"Why are you asking these questions now after all these years?"

He looked past her to Maggie standing by a row of huge sunflowers. "That woman out there is Angela Dennison. Whoever kidnapped her is determined to kill her."

Ruth Anne winced and looked through the patio doors at Maggie. "She is beautiful. She looks like Daisy." She slowly shifted her gaze to Jesse. "And her father?"

"Wade," he said.

She nodded. "Good. I'm sure you're relieved since you're obviously in love with her."

Jesse got to his feet, angry that she could know anything about him. "Do you know a man named Jerome Lovelace? He goes by Bruno."

She shook her head, seeming distracted. "Your father... I always hoped he and Daisy would get together," she said as she stood.

He stared at her. Was she serious?

Maggie came back in and he ushered her toward the front door.

His mother didn't try to keep him any longer. Didn't ask about his life or Mitch's or their father's.

"Goodbye, Jesse," Ruth Anne said at the door. She smiled and nodded as if pleased by him.

He didn't say goodbye, just stepped out the door, but he couldn't help himself. He turned to look back at the last moment before the door closed. That's when he saw it behind his mother. One of his paintings on the wall in her living room.

The door closed and she was gone again.

"Are you all right?" Maggie asked, and took his hand.

He nodded, surprised that he was. "She seems happy. She was so miserable with us."

"People change. She wasn't even yet your age when she left, right?"

He nodded, surprised that he could no longer feel hate for the woman he'd just seen. "She made a lasting impression on Mitch and me. I didn't think Mitch would ever ask Charity to marry him he was so scared of marriage. I'm thirty-five and I've never been serious about anyone before."

She looked away. "I used to wonder what normal families were like."

He laughed. "Me, too. Think there are any?"

"She had your painting on the wall," Maggie said, and looked over at him. "She hasn't forgotten you or your brother. She just couldn't handle things at that time of her own life."

He nodded. "I guess I wanted her to say she was sorry."

"Would the words really have made that much difference?"

He shook his head. "She did tell me something about the afternoon of the kidnapping. She said she passed Wade coming home when she left. Lydia was with him."

"Her name keeps coming up," Maggie said.

"It's just strange that it never came up in the sheriff's report that Lydia had been out there that night," Jesse noted. "How did she get home? Did Wade drive her or did Angus pick her up?"

"You think Lydia might know something?"

"It's worth asking her." Jesse realized Lydia could provide an alibi for his mother. If Ruth was telling the truth, then Lydia had seen her leave *before* the baby disappeared.

And what if Lydia had looked in on Angela that evening? She might have been the last person to see Angela before she was kidnapped.

"Let's not forget the possible connection between her now deceased husband and Blackmore," Maggie said.

Jesse shook his head. He hadn't forgotten. So far, it was the only tie-in they had between Blackmore and Timber Falls.

Chapter Seventeen

Rupert Blackmore found only one thing of interest in Jerome "Bruno" Lovelace's wallet.

A business card. It was worn and soiled as if it had been pulled out a lot and there was writing on the back, hard to read notes.

He looked at the front of the card. The Busy Bee, Antiques and Collectibles. Proprietor Lydia Dennison Abernathy.

His cell rang. Teresa. But it wasn't Teresa, just as he knew it wouldn't be. His source had come up with information on Jerome Lovelace, a small-time offender from Seattle via Plentygrove.

There was only one offense that Rupert found interesting. The fencing of stolen property. The property in question had been antiques.

He'd learned a long time ago that cases had threads, threads that directed you where to go.

He studied the card, following the thread, following his gut instincts.

Abernathy? He rooted around in the drawer of the motel's bedside table for the phonebook. It was so small and thin he'd missed it at first.

Abernathy. Why did that name sound so familiar?

It was dark by the time they returned to Timber Falls. Jesse called Mitch as soon as he was close enough to town to get a signal on the cell phone.

He told Mitch what Maggie had discovered about Henry Abernathy and a possible connection to Blackmore.

He didn't mention that he'd seen their mother. "I also stumbled across a note that revealed Wade brought his sister home the night Angela was kidnapped. Maggie and I are headed there. We're almost to Timber Falls."

"Lydia was at the house that night?" Mitch said. "Why didn't she say anything years ago?"

Good question.

"Jesse, be careful."

Jesse had just clicked off the phone when he heard a loud pop an instant before the front tire blew.

"Get down!" he yelled at Maggie as he wrestled the steering wheel, fighting to keep the pickup on the road.

He shoved Maggie down as the windshield shattered with the impact of a second shot. The other front tire blew an instant later.

The pickup careened down into the ditch, still moving too fast. Jesse saw the tree coming up and tried to brace himself in that instant before the pickup crashed into it and the lights went out.

"Jesse!" Maggie cried, sitting up.

He was slumped over the steering wheel. She could see blood on his forehead.

"Jesse!" Still stunned from the impact, Maggie touched his shoulder, shook him gently. He didn't respond. She fought to get her seat belt unhooked. Jesse needed her. Her mind raced. She had to get him help. Get help. Someone had shot at them. Someone—

Her door burst open. Rough hands grabbed her and dragged her out of the pickup. She screamed and fought. A strong hand clamped a cloth down over her mouth. Something nasty-smelling on the cloth. She tried not to breathe, wriggling and fighting to free herself from the unyielding arms that held her.

She took a breath. It was the last thing she remembered.

Jesse woke to the smell of smoke. His first thought was Maggie. The house was on fire. Get Maggie out.

Only he wasn't in the house. He sat up, blinked at the wetness in his right eye. He lifted his hand to his forehead. It came away wet and sticky. Blood?

He glanced around, confused. He was bleeding and his head was killing him. He was in the pickup, behind the wheel and yet he could smell smoke, feel the heat of the blaze.

"Maggie?" The pickup was empty, the passenger-side door closed. Maggie was gone. Gone for help? Where—

He heard the clank of a door sliding closed and looked out through the thickening smoke, through the spiderweb around the bullet hole in the windshield and saw the blue van, glimpsed the familiar logo on the side.

Panic and pain rocketed him forward. It all came back in a flash. The sound of a shot seconds after the front tire blew. The windshield shattering. Another shot, another tire. Then the ditch. The tree coming up fast. Then blackness.

He seemed to be moving in slow motion. He unbuckled his seat belt and tried to open his door. Jammed.

He scrambled across the seat to the passenger-side door and tried to open it, then saw that someone had jammed a tree limb against it. Had jammed both doors, he realized, trapping him inside.

Flames crackled, smoke roiling upward, making it hard to see. *Maggie.* Whoever was driving that van had Maggie. He felt it at gut level, heart level.

He managed to get his gun out of the holster, steady it with both hands as he saw a figure shrouded in smoke come around the back of the van toward him.

He raised a foot, kicked out the already shattered windshield and fired. The figure veered back behind the van, disappearing.

A whoosh and flames flared in front of him.

Jesse began to wriggle through the hole where the windshield had been. He heard an engine rev. The van tires squealed on the pavement.

Sprawled on the hood of the pickup, he raised the gun again but knew he couldn't fire for fear that he might hit Maggie.

Flames leaped all around him, the smoke so thick the van seemed to dissolve in it as the vehicle roared away.

Get out of the pickup. Now!

He slid off the hood, hitting the ground at a run.

Blood ran down into his eyes. His head felt as if it would burst.

Behind him he heard another whoosh. The explosion, as the gas tank blew on the pickup, knocked him to the ground, knocked the air out of him.

He rolled over to look back at the pickup. It was a ball of flames. Past it, he saw the gas can at the edge of the woods, saw where the gasoline had been poured around the pickup and set on fire. The killer had planned for him to die in the pickup, burn to death.

What did the killer have planned for Maggie?

The thought terrified him. He had to get to her first.

He had the cell phone out of his pocket. He wiped a sleeve across his eyes and punched Redial. Mitch answered on the first ring.

Rupert Blackmore left his pickup at the motel and walked downtown. He took the dark side streets, staying to the shadows.

He was a block and a half away from the Busy Bee when he heard the sound of an engine. He stepped into a doorway, flattening himself to the dark entry.

As the vehicle passed, he saw that it was a van, dark in color with something printed on the side. All he caught was the word *antiques*.

The van slowed a good block before the shop, pulled in front of an underground garage. The driver got out and disappeared inside the building.

Rupert waited only a moment, then moved toward the van.

Maggie woke to darkness and the smell of old wood. She tried to move. Couldn't. Not even a finger. She was lying on her back on something hard and she could tell that there was something around her, close, something solid, as if she were in a box.

The thought filled her with terror. She fought not to breathe too fast for fear she would use up all the oxygen inside the space, but she knew she was failing.

She couldn't move her head, but cut her eyes to each side, saw little fissures of light leaking in at the edges of her vision.

She realized she could hear. She opened her mouth and tried to call for help. No sound came out.

Was she paralyzed? The pickup. She remembered crashing into the tree. Jesse?

Her pinky finger brushed against something rough. Wood. She heard a sound. Footsteps. A metal door rolled slowly open next to her. Light. Through the crack at each side of her vision, she caught the flicker of a flashlight beam.

Her body was lead. Only her little finger moved. She tried to scratch the side of her prison but it made only a faint noise.

She heard the groan of springs, felt herself tilt a little as someone stepped next to her. She was in a vehicle of some sort. The realization surprised her. Also scared her. Was she going to be transported somewhere?

She heard the soft scrape of something being moved next to the box she was in, felt the vehicle rock again, then smelled it.

Her heart stopped in her chest and if she could have, she would have cried out. Stale cigar smoke.

Charity waited to put down the phone after Mitch so he wouldn't know she'd been on the line and heard everything. She'd been working in the spare bedroom on this week's edition but now she went into the living room where Mitch was on the phone to his father.

"Honey, I'm going to take a shower," she whispered, pretending she had no idea what was going on.

He smiled and waved to her in acknowledgment. She headed for the large bathroom he'd added at the back of the house. The one right next to the back door.

It was crazy. But then she'd done worse for a story. She turned on the shower, then slipped out the back door. She couldn't very well take her VW. Mitch would hear her start the engine.

So she walked the three blocks to the Busy Bee. The light was on in the back. She knocked and waited, her hands in her pocket. One gripping her loaded Derringer. The other clutching the small can of pepper spray.

She hoped Jesse was wrong and that Lydia could explain—

The door opened. Charity hadn't even seen Lydia come out of the elevator at the back. Maybe she'd been in the shop. Sitting in the dark?

A chill rippled over her as Lydia opened the door.

"Charity! I was just thinking about you," Lydia said. "Come in. Come in."

Charity stepped inside the darkened shop, thinking this was probably the worst idea she'd ever had.

Rupert shone his penlight into the back of the van. It held a half-dozen pieces of furniture, an armoire, a cedar chest, a vanity, a chest of drawers and the most unusual piece of all, an old Chinese coffin by the door.

He thought he heard a scratching sound like mice. He froze. God, he hated mice. When he was a boy a mouse had run up his pant leg. The memory even after all these years made him break out in a sweat.

He started to back out, slowly, staying low, keeping the penlight on the floor, just in case one of the mice came after him.

He was just about to step off onto the loading ramp next to the side door of the van when he heard it.

Breathing. It was coming from the coffin.

Maggie waited for him to open the box and kill her. Instead, she heard him let out a curse, heard the rustle of fabric, then heard him standing over her.

The lid groaned and something metallic rattled. A padlock. The box was padlocked shut. Her heart raced as she listened to him try to open it. Didn't he have the key?

The padlock rattled again. Then silence.

Her left hand began to tingle as feeling came back into it. She could move her little finger of that hand now and several more fingers on her right hand but she couldn't lift her arm.

He must have given her a drug of some sort that paralyzed her body but not her mind.

Oh, God, what had he done to Jesse?

Feeling was coming back into her body. She just had to remain calm. Time. She would be able to move if he gave her a little more time.

He was still standing over her. She could hear him breathing.

Then she heard another sound. This one in the distance. Footsteps. Someone was coming! Jesse?

Closer, a metal door slid quietly shut, then movement near her, the sound of furniture being moved, then stillness.

The footsteps beyond her prison were coming closer. A car door opening. The vehicle rocked and seat springs groaned. A door slammed closed. An instant later, the engine started and she was moving again.

"Where's Angus?" Charity asked as she stepped inside the Busy Bee and the door closed behind her. "I didn't see the van."

"It's his day off," Lydia said. "He went to a movie in Eugene, but he didn't take the van. It should be parked in the garage. Why don't you keep me company until he returns. I just put on a pot of tea and I have cookies. I thought you might be stopping by."

Charity followed Lydia to the elevator, telling herself that Jesse had been mistaken about the van he'd seen. Or someone had stolen it. Or—or it wasn't really in the garage and Lydia was lying.

The elevator opened on the second floor directly into Lydia's beautifully furnished apartment.

Like a sleepwalker, Charity followed the older woman as she zipped in the wheelchair through the living room to the kitchen and large dining room.

The teapot was whistling as they entered the warm kitchen. A plate of cookies had been put out. Lydia proceeded to pour them both a cup of tea.

Charity watched her closely, afraid she might put something in her tea. But Lydia made the tea just as she always had and smiled as she handed Charity a cup.

Charity took the seat at the table Lydia indicated and set down her tea.

"Here dear, have a cookie. I know you can't resist my cookies."

* * *

Jesse saw lights coming up the highway, recognized his father's pickup and rushed up the road to meet him.

"My God, son," Lee said, as Jesse climbed in.

"The Busy Bee," Jesse said. "Take me to the Busy Bee. Hurry."

His father spun the pickup around in the highway and took off toward town. Jesse filled him in.

"Mitch said Lydia should be alone at the apartment. It's Angus's day off. He always goes into Eugene on his day off," Lee told him.

"In the van?"

Lee shook his head. "Usually that BMW Lydia bought him."

"Then who has the van?"

Lee shook his head. "They probably leave the keys in it. You know how people are in Timber Falls."

He knew.

"What do you want me to do?" Lee asked.

"Drop me off. I'll take the back. You watch the front. Don't come in unless you hear gunfire."

Lee nodded as he neared Timber Falls. "I love you, son," he said as he slowed and Jesse jumped out, running down the street to the back of the Busy Bee.

Jesse was almost there when he saw the van up the street. The taillights flashed. It was leaving!

The van started to back up. But then as if the driver had spotted Jesse, the van pulled forward.

Jesse started to grab for the cell phone in his pocket to call his dad when he saw where the van was going.

Rupert couldn't see the driver. He'd hidden behind a large piece of the furniture that blocked him from the driver's view, as well.

He thought the driver would leave town. Maybe take Margaret Randolph somewhere out in the woods to kill her. But he heard a large garage door clank open and when the van moved, it didn't move far. The garage door clanked down and Rupert realized the driver had pulled into the underground garage. That was odd.

The engine shut off.

Rupert held his breath as he slipped the gun from his pocket to his palm. He was wedged behind the armoire. While he hadn't been able to see the driver, he could see the antique coffin and he could hear breathing still coming from inside. Just like the scratching noise he'd heard.

He waited.

The side door of the van slid open. He felt the van rock as someone stepped in. A man. Large from the way he rocked the vehicle.

He felt rather than saw the man bend over the coffin and work a key into the padlock.

Rupert waited for the *click* of the padlock opening. Waited for the man to slip the padlock from the hasp.

Click. Click.

Silence. He heard the man rise slowly, warily, and knew he'd either been spotted or sensed. Either way, he had to move. And quickly.

Maggie listened as someone bent over the box she was in. The padlock rattled. She could hear him breathing. Jesse!

No, not Jesse, she realized with a sinking heart as she heard the person insert a key into the padlock. It was whoever had put her in here.

She prepared herself for when the lid opened, willing

her arms to work enough that she could fight him off. But first she would lie perfectly still. Let him think the drug was still working. That she was no danger to him.

The lock clicked open. Her heart leaped to her throat. Light. Air. Out of this horrible box.

That's when she heard the first gunshot. A boom that echoed like a cannon blast in the small space almost deafening her.

With all her might, she shoved at the lid of the box, flinging it open.

Another gunshot. Something large fell, rocking the vehicle. She heard a curse and a groan. Then the lid of the box was slammed shut again as something heavy fell against it.

Rupert had stepped out from behind the armoire and seen the man turn. Something metallic flickered in the man's hand.

Rupert had been struck by the fact that he'd never seen the man before. Somehow he'd expected his blackmailer to be someone he knew.

That instant of surprise was his first mistake. Not pulling the trigger more quickly was his second.

The knife blade glimmered in the dull light. Long and slim. As it shot through the air and buried itself to the hilt in his chest.

Rupert had gotten off two shots.

And then as he fell forward, he saw Teresa in his mind coming toward him, toward the aquamarine pool next to their RV. She had a cocktail in both hands and she was smiling.

"Everything is going to be all right now that you've retired," he heard her say. "Didn't I tell you you would love Arizona?"

* * *

The building was an old warehouse with a loading dock and underground garage. Jesse thought it was empty, abandoned. All the windows were covered with weathered sheets of plywood crudely painted with No Trespassing.

But as Jesse pried a piece of plywood from one of the windows, he saw that someone had been using the place and for some time.

The first floor was filled with antiques. Good stuff. Tons of it. He slipped in, dropping to the floor and moving as quietly as possible through the pieces to the stairs that led to the parking garage.

That's when he heard the shots.

Charity took one of the cookies, but didn't take a bite. "Lydia, I know you were at the house the night Angela was kidnapped."

Lydia looked up in surprise. "Who told you that?"

"It doesn't matter. It's true. A while back you told me the nanny overheard Wade and Daisy arguing. But it was you. What about the baby? Did you go up to her room?"

Lydia looked down into her cup. "It was a horrible row just like I told you. Wade and Daisy thought I'd left, thought Angus had already picked me up. I knew Daisy had been having an affair. I didn't want my real niece growing up with some bastard's child." She met Charity's gaze.

"What did you do, Lydia?" Charity whispered, her hand dropping to the pepper spray in her pocket.

"You haven't eaten your cookie, dear. Angus made them especially for you." Lydia's hands had been on her lap. Now she produced a gun from under the knitted throw draped over her lap. "I've always told people how you can't resist my cookies. You wouldn't want to make a liar out of me, would you?"

At the sound of the gunshots, Jesse rushed down the stairs into the underground garage. The blue van was parked just inside, the side door open.

At first all he saw inside were more antiques. There had to be a small fortune in antiques in this warehouse. What the hell?

Then he saw Blackmore lying at the back of the van, his chest a red bloom of blood, his eyes wide and dead.

An armoire had been knocked over. Jesse straightened it to get to Blackmore, pushing it off the coffin. To his amazement and horror, the lid of an antique Chinese coffin began to rise and there was Maggie.

"Jesse," she whispered, the word barely audible.

He shoved back the lid of the coffin. Her movements were jerky and she couldn't seem to use her legs. Oh, God. He swept her up out of the coffin and carried her around to open the door and placed her in the front seat of the van.

"Baby, are you all right?" he cried.

Maggie nodded, her head jerky, her body awkward, at odds with itself. "Drugged. Wearing off," she whispered. Her voice was hoarse, her throat hurt. She managed a smile and she thought he would break down and cry as he rocked her in his arms. She looked over his shoulder, suddenly afraid. "Where—"

"Blackmore's dead in the back of the van." He pulled away to look at her. "How did you—"

She was shaking her head. Or at least she thought she was. "Not Blackmore. Someone else."

He tensed. "Who?"

She shook her head and then her eyes widened in alarm as she caught the glitter of steel. "Knife!"

Jesse spun around, using the van door as a shield. The knife hit the door and clattered to the concrete floor.

He had his weapon drawn again but he could see nothing in the dark corners of the garage. He glanced up, saw the large overhead light. If he could get to the switch.

"Can you lock your door?" he asked Maggie without turning around. He heard the soft snick of the lock as his answer.

He reached over and slid the van door closed and locked it.

He used his boot toe to move the knife closer, but he didn't dare bend down to pick it up. He kicked it back under the van and, locking and slamming the van door he'd used as a shield, moved fast toward the garage door.

In the blind darkness, he raked a hand down one side of the wall. No switch. Rushing to the other side, he did the same.

He heard the noise behind him. Shoe soles on concrete, then cloth on concrete. The killer was under the van, going for the knife.

Jesse found the light switch. Jerked it down, knowing as he did that he would provide the killer with the perfect target. As the overhead light flooded the garage with a dingy gold glow, he leaped to the side, crouching at the end of a tool bench.

Where was the killer?

Maggie could feel life coming back into her body, but she was still so weak.

She watched, feeling helpless, a horrible feeling for a woman who'd never needed help before. She thought of her mother. In a wheelchair all of those years and yet not helpless. Strong. Courageous.

Tears wet her eyes. She watched Jesse disappear into the darkness at the edge of the lit garage.

Where was the man with the knife? The man who had killed Blackmore?

She glanced over and saw the keys dangling from the ignition. Moving awkwardly, she slid over behind the wheel. She started the van.

Suddenly a face appeared at her side window, startling her. She let out a shriek. Angus tried the door, swore when he found it locked.

She threw the van into Reverse, swinging it around. Angus leaped out of the way. She saw Jesse come out of the dark, the gun in his hand. But Angus was facing her. She caught his expression.

She shifted the van into First and gunned the engine as she let her foot up off the clutch.

Angus had the knife in his hand and was turning when she hit him. He went down, disappearing under the hood of the van. But the knife was already in the air. It whizzed past Jesse's head missing him only by a breath.

Then Jesse was at her door. She opened it and he took her in his arms and he rocked her, his breath damp against her neck.

"Eat your cookie," Lydia said calmly. "Angus put a special ingredient in it, just for you."

Charity stared down at the cookie in her hand, then at the gun Lydia had pointed at her.

"I wouldn't eat that cookie if I were you," said a voice behind Charity.

Relief washed over her at the sound of Lee Tanner's voice. He moved into her view. He held a gun in his hand and it was pointed at Lydia.

"I'll shoot Charity," Lydia said, not seeming all that surprised to see him.

"It's over, Lydia. Angus is dead."

Her gaze shifted to him, tears suddenly welling in her eyes. "Angus?"

In that instant, he stepped to her and jerked the gun from her hand. She didn't fight him.

Charity dropped the cookie in her hand, swearing off sugar cookies for the rest of her life.

"Not Angus. I can't lose another man I love," Lydia said. "He's such a good man. Just like my Henry. You know Henry was a cop."

"Yes, Lydia, I know," Lee said.

"It's all Wade's fault," Lydia said. "Angus never forgave him for putting me in this chair and killing our Henry. Then when Wade married that tramp and we thought she'd had another man's baby…."

"Daisy isn't a tramp," he said.

She looked up at him. "It was you, wasn't it?"

Charity looked at her soon-to-be father-in-law.

"You were the one Daisy was in love with," Lydia said and let out a soft laugh. "Why didn't I see it before?"

Epilogue

Jesse stood in the art gallery, the bright sun shining in through the windows.

Spring had finally come to Timber Falls. Mitch had mended and taken over as sheriff again. Jesse had turned in his uniform and his gun and had gone back to painting.

But he didn't kid himself. Everything had changed. Maggie had come into his life. He'd almost lost her. And then, she'd left again.

He hadn't seen her in several months now. She'd had to return to Seattle. Her father's businesses needed tending, she had a house to see to and was needed to testify in the murders of her father, Clark Iverson and Norman Drake.

"Don't worry," Charity had told him. "She'll be back for my wedding. Maggie wouldn't miss my wedding."

Jesse wasn't so sure about that. He hadn't been able to reach her for the past few weeks. Her assistant at company headquarters said she was out of the country and wasn't sure when she'd be back.

The last time they'd talked he'd felt frustrated. He needed to hold her, to talk to her in person, so he hadn't had much to say. Now he regretted it, wished he'd told her how he felt. Even long distance.

"Son," Lee Tanner said, coming up to rest a hand on his shoulder. "Your art show is a tremendous success. You should be proud."

His first big show. He couldn't believe that most of the paintings were already marked Sold. "Thanks."

Lee studied his son. "Have you heard from Maggie?"

He shook his head. "She has a lot on her plate right now." The truth was, there really wasn't any reason for her to return to Timber Falls and Jesse knew it.

Timber Falls had quieted down. There hadn't been a Bigfoot sighting in months. Nor a murder. Angus Smythe was dead. Lydia Abernathy behind bars awaiting trial for kidnapping, blackmail and multiple murders.

Before his death, Detective Rupert Blackmore had left a detailed account in his motel room at the Ho Hum of what had happened thirty years ago in a dark alley and the blackmail that had resulted in it.

It seemed Maggie owed her life to him. Not once, but twice.

Blackmore had saved her that night in the garage. His wife, Teresa, and her mother were found unharmed. They'd been detained by a policeman back in Iowa where Blackmore's mother-in-law lived, and held overnight in a jail cell. It wasn't until the next morning that the policeman had realized he'd been sent a false arrest warrant for the two.

Charity had been so sure that Bud Farnsworth was trying to tell Wade who'd hired him to kidnap Angela just before Bud died. If that was the case, then Bud had been trying to tell Wade that it had been Lydia, Wade's own sister.

Over the weeks since, the story had been hashed out at Betty's Café for hours on end. Rumors had been running rampant, as was Timber Falls' style.

Most everyone in town believed that Lydia had become embittered after the accident and was set on getting even with her brother and that's why she'd kidnapped Angela. Others believed Lydia did it to spare her brother the embarrassment when it came out that the baby wasn't his.

Whatever had motivated Lydia, Wade had hired her the best lawyer his money could buy. But, then, he didn't have much money. Daisy was going through with the divorce. It was rumored there was a new man in her life. In fact, several people had seen her with Lee Tanner.

The general consensus was that it was nice that the two had found each other, especially after what they'd both been through.

The antiques Angus had stored in the warehouse turned out to all be stolen. It seemed Angus had been working with a man named Jerome "Bruno" Lovelace for years. Lydia was right about one thing, Angus was quite wealthy in his own right. And he'd left it all to his favorite step-niece, Desiree. She had gone away to college but she'd called Jesse before she left.

"You are the one person in town who will appreciate

this," she said. "I took a DNA test. I guess I've always known but I wanted to be sure, you know, after everything that happened. You and I…"

"You're my sister," he said.

She laughed lightly. "You knew, too."

"I figured. You were too wild, too much like me," Jesse said.

"I guess we'll all have to get together one of these days, you, me and Maggie," Desiree said.

Jesse knew Maggie would like that. "Let's do that."

"I guess you know about our parents," she'd said before she'd hung up. "I'm okay with it. Wade, well, he's talking about leaving town. I think it's the best thing. Mom's taken over the decoy plant. Who knew she had it in her?"

Lee Tanner turned now as Daisy came into the art gallery. Jesse couldn't believe the change in his father. His step was lighter. He was definitely happier.

It was good to see Liam Sawyer with Florie, too. Roz and her fiancé, Ford Lancaster, had also stopped by and bought one of the paintings.

As Jesse looked around the gallery, he was glad to see how many of the locals had turned out. Timber Falls was an okay town. He would hate to have to leave it. That, he realized, would be up to Maggie. If she still wanted him.

He noticed that only one of his paintings hadn't sold. It was one he'd done of a Mexican cantina. In it a young woman was dancing and the men at the bar were watching her. He noticed that someone had put a Hold sticker on it.

And then he turned. How had he known it was her? Maybe the way the air seemed to contract. Or his heart kicked up a beat. But there she was standing in the doorway. Maggie. And he knew then who'd had the painting put on hold.

She moved to him, hesitant at first. She must have seen his expression because she broke into a smile and ran the last few steps, throwing herself into his arms.

"I thought I would never get home," she said.

"Home?" he echoed, holding her close.

She pulled back and looked up at him. "I'm never leaving you again, Jesse Tanner. Never."

He heard his brother's voice behind him. "Ask her to marry you, fool."

Jesse laughed and looked down into Maggie's brown eyes, losing himself in them. He'd wanted her from that first night, had been waiting for years for her to come into his life. He couldn't believe how kind fate had been to him. Florie said it was written in the stars.

He figured heaven did have something to do with it.

"I'd planned on something a little more romantic..." he said, then cleared his throat. "Will you marry me, Maggie Randolph?"

"Tell her you love her, fool," Mitch whispered behind him.

"We could have a double wedding," Charity said.

"Shush," Lee Tanner told them both. "He's doing just fine."

Maggie laughed, glanced around the room at all the people waiting to hear her answer, then she smiled up at Jesse. "I love you, too, Jesse Tanner. Marry you? Absolutely."

* * * * *

We hope you enjoyed reading

AGAINST THE STORM

by *New York Times* bestselling author

KAT MARTIN

and

WANTED WOMAN

by *New York Times* bestselling author

B.J. DANIELS

Both were originally MIRA® and
Harlequin® Intrigue stories!

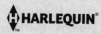 **HARLEQUIN**®

I N T R I G U E

Edge-of-your-seat intrigue, fearless romance

From passionate, suspenseful and dramatic
love stories to inspirational or historical,
Harlequin offers different lines to
satisfy every romance reader.
Up to eight new books in each line
are available every month.

 HARLEQUIN®

www.Harlequin.com

NYTHRS0318

Get 2 Free Books,
<u>Plus</u> 2 Free Gifts –
just for trying the *Reader Service!*

STRS17R2

Rachel slipped her arms around his neck and kissed him back.
Not shy or reluctant, it was a bold, hungry kiss that set him on fire.
He swayed against her, drunk on the thrill of her lips on his, their
tongues tangling, their breaths mingling.

Seconds later, she pulled away and placed an open hand against
his chest, gently pushing him away. He was crazy with wanting her
and was certain she could feel the pounding of his heart.

"See you tomorrow," she whispered as she opened the door and
slipped back inside the house.

Tomorrow couldn't come too soon.

Dawn was lighting the sky before Rachel gave up on the tossing
and turning and any chance of sound sleep. Her life was spinning
out of control at a dizzying pace.

Two days ago, she'd had a career. She'd known what she would
be doing from day to day. Admittedly, she'd still been struggling to
move past the torture Roy Sales had put her through, but she was
making progress.

Two days ago, she wasn't making headlines, another major
detriment to defending Hayden. The terrors she was trying so hard
to escape would be front and center.

People would stare. People would ask questions. Gossip magazines would feed on her trauma again.

Two days ago she hadn't met Luke Dawkins. Her stomach hadn't fluttered at his incidental touch. There had been no heated zings of attraction when a rugged, hard-bodied stranger spoke her name or met her gaze.

A kiss hadn't rocked her with desire and left her aching for more. She put her fingertips to her lips, and a craving for his mouth on hers burned inside her.

This was absolutely crazy.

She kicked off the covers, crawled out of bed, padded to the window and opened the blinds. The crescent moon floated behind a gray cloud. The universe held steady, day following night, season following season, the earth remaining on its axis century after century.

She didn't expect that kind of order in her life, but neither could she continue to let the demonic Roy Sales pull the strings and control her reactions.

She had to fight to get what she wanted—once she decided what that was. She'd spend the next two or maybe three days here in Winding Creek trying to figure it all out. Then she'd drive back to Houston and face Eric Fitch Sr. straight on.

There were no decisions to make about Luke Dawkins. Once he learned of her past, he'd see her through different eyes. And he'd definitely learn about her past, since she was making news again. He'd pity her, and then he'd move on.

Who could blame him? Her emotional baggage was killing her.

Don't miss
DROPPING THE HAMMER by Joanna Wayne,
available April 2018 wherever
Harlequin Intrigue[E] *books and ebooks are sold.*

www.Harlequin.com

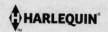

INTRIGUE

EDGE-OF-YOUR-SEAT INTRIGUE, FEARLESS ROMANCE.

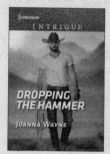

Save $1.00

on the purchase of ANY Harlequin® Intrigue book.

Available wherever books are sold, including most bookstores, supermarkets, drugstores and discount stores.

--- ✂ ---

Save $1.00

on the purchase of any Harlequin® Intrigue book.

Coupon valid until June 30, 2018.
Redeemable at participating outlets in the U.S. and Canada only.
Not redeemable at Barnes & Noble stores. Limit one coupon per customer.

52615649

5 65373 00076 2   (8100)0 12354

NYTCOUP0318